MW00377454

THE DUNGEON ANARCHIST'S COOKBOOK

Titles by Matt Dinniman

Dungeon Crawler Carl Series

DUNGEON CRAWLER CARL

CARL'S DOOMSDAY SCENARIO

THE DUNGEON ANARCHIST'S COOKBOOK

THE GATE OF THE FERAL GODS

THE BUTCHER'S MASQUERADE

THE EYE OF THE BEDLAM BRIDE

KAIJU: BATTLEFIELD SURGEON

The Shivered Sky Series

EVERY GRAIN OF SAND

IN THE CITY OF DEMONS

THE GREAT DEVOURING DARKNESS

Dominion of Blades Series

DOMINION OF BLADES

THE HOBGOBLIN RIOT

THE GRINDING

TRAILER PARK FAIRY TALES

THE DUNGEON ANARCHIST'S COOKBOOK

DUNGEON CRAWLER CARL BOOK THREE

MATT DINNIMAN

ACE
New York

ACE
Published by Berkley
An imprint of Penguin Random House LLC
penguinrandomhouse.com

Copyright © 2021 by Matt Dinniman
"Backstage at the Pineapple Cabaret" copyright © 2024 by Matt Dinniman
Penguin Random House values and supports copyright. Copyright fuels creativity, encourages diverse voices, promotes free speech, and creates a vibrant culture. Thank you for buying an authorized edition of this book and for complying with copyright laws by not reproducing, scanning, or distributing any part of it in any form without permission. You are supporting writers and allowing Penguin Random House to continue to publish books for every reader. Please note that no part of this book may be used or reproduced in any manner for the purpose of training artificial intelligence technologies or systems.

ACE is a registered trademark and the A colophon is a trademark of
Penguin Random House LLC.
Library of Congress Cataloging-in-Publication Data

Names: Dinniman, Matt, author.
Title: The dungeon anarchist's cookbook / Matt Dinniman.
Description: First Ace edition. | New York : Ace, 2024. |
Series: Dungeon crawler Carl
Identifiers: LCCN 2024014178 | ISBN 9780593820285 (hardcover)
Subjects: LCGFT: LitRPG (Fiction) | Novels.
Classification: LCC PS3604.I49 D858 2024 | DDC 813/.6—dc23/eng/20240423
LC record available at https://lccn.loc.gov/2024014178

The Dungeon Anarchist's Cookbook was originally self-published, in different form, in 2021.

First Ace Edition: October 2024

Printed in the United States of America
2nd Printing

Book design by George Towne
Interior art on pages v, 368, 516: Vintage Black Texture © 316pixel/Shutterstock
Map art on pages 367, 369 by David Lindroth
All other interior art by Erik Wilson (erikwilsonart.com)

Let what you do mean something.

King Kong Bundy

AUTHOR'S NOTE

HEY, MATT THE AUTHOR GUY HERE. A QUICK NOTE ABOUT THIS PAR-ticular book. The fourth floor of the dungeon is set up as a massive, deliberately confusing puzzle. Carl, Donut, and the rest of the team have to work really hard to figure out the dungeon's layout. You, the super-awesome reader, do not need to understand the floor's intricacies in order to understand or fully enjoy what is happening. Plat-form names and numbers and colors are gonna be flying by. It's okay not to remember them. It only becomes important at the end.

There will be a map near the end of the book to help you under-stand the endgame. Until then, enjoy the ride and mind the gap.

And, yes, "zomp" is really a color.

THE DUNGEON ANARCHIST'S COOKBOOK

1

TIME TO LEVEL COLLAPSE: 10 DAYS.

Views: 43.1 Quadrillion
Followers: 677 Trillion
Favorites: 158.1 Trillion
Leaderboard rank: 6
Bounty: 100,000 gold

RED LINE.

Welcome, Crawler, to the fourth floor. "The Iron Tangle."
    Your title has reverted to Royal Bodyguard.
    Sponsorship bidding initiated on Crawler #4,122. Bidding
ends in 45 hours.

The world rumbled. The ground shook. I stumbled backward the
moment we appeared, but I was held upright by a metal wall. Lights
flashed in a quick staccato, pulsing on either side of the long, thin
room. I felt the *thump, thump, thump* under my feet. We were in a long
plastic-and-metal tube that vibrated and thundered. The lights in
the room blinked out, then turned back on.

Mongo screeched in anger and fear. Donut jumped to my shoulder, trembling. Katia clutched on to a metal pole rising from the
floor to the ceiling.

New achievement! I'm on a train!
    Choo Choo, Motherfucker.

Reward: You've received a Train Conductor's Souvenir Hat!
Wear it with pride!

"It's a subway car," I said. We hurtled through a tunnel, racing toward some unknown destination.

A double aisle of seats, facing inward, filled the train car. The seats were made of beige molded plastic with brown cushions that were ripped and tagged with marker and spray paint. The words were in nonsensical letters in the Cyrillic alphabet. The floor was dingy and pocked. Scorch marks dotted the plastic walls. Poles rose to the ceiling at regular intervals and also ran the length of the car. The whole place smelled like a pile of dead rats.

The train car was empty except for our party.

"It's a Metro car from Moscow," Katia said. "But the ones I rode were in much better condition than this. And cleaner." Her face had returned to the mostly human, blond-haired form she'd held earlier. Her nose had been knocked halfway around her face the last time I'd seen her in her doppelganger form, but she'd willed it back into place.

At the end of the subway car was a closed door with no window. Above the door hung a small electric sign with red words scrolling across the top.

Red Line, Car 20. Next stop: Sirin Station (81) in 12 minutes and 32 seconds.

"Everybody get dressed," I said. I sat down in the chair and quickly began the process of putting my gear back on. I briefly examined the stupid train hat we'd received, and it was junk. It wasn't magical. It was a simple blue-and-white hat one would see on a toddler. It had the words "I rode the Iron Tangle" embroidered on it.

"Carl, it says I have to pick a new class because of my Character Actor skill. I only have six minutes to choose, or I will get a 'random' one," Donut said. "The list is full of new stuff. Not the same as before."

CARL: Mordecai. Help Donut pick a class. She's going to read off some choices. We're in a moving train car. I think it's a subway-system-themed floor.

MORDECAI: Welcome back. Donut, hit me with the suggested list.

DONUT: I DON'T LIKE THESE CHOICES, MORDECAI.

As Donut rattled off a list of options in the chat, including things like Alley Cat Brawler and Nec-Cat-Mancer, I moved to the window and peered outside.

We moved swiftly. The exterior wall of the tunnel was right there, barely inches from the window. It appeared to be made of dirt or rock. Lights flashed by occasionally as if electrical lights were built into the tunnel walls at random intervals.

"Why does she always type in all caps?" Katia whispered as I peered out the window. "Is it because she's four-legged?"

"No. It's because she's Donut."

"She's quite the handful, isn't she?"

I remembered what Odette had said about Hekla wanting to steal Donut away.

"More than you know," I said.

We had 10 days to complete this floor. Our first priority would be to find a stairwell. If we were constantly moving, that was going to provide a unique challenge. There were only 9,375 stairwells this time. If the level truly was subway- or train-themed, and this wasn't just taking us to some random location where the floor was really going to begin, we needed a map. Even if there was a stairwell at each and every stop, that suggested this system was beyond huge. Finding a stairwell wouldn't be enough if we didn't know how to circle back.

My Escape Plan skill couldn't find any directions or maps, at least not in this car. The skill worked great, but you had to know where the hidden maps were before you could utilize it.

"Wow," Katia said. "My constitution is double what it normally is. I'm at 102. I have an active momentum bonus even though I'm not moving."

"Good," I said. *That means you're our meat shield,* I didn't add. "I hope that's by design. Otherwise, I wouldn't get used to it. If the showrunners didn't mean for that to happen, you can bet it'll be patched out tonight."

If we were going to be doing a lot of close-quarters fighting this level, that meant I needed to work on my hand-to-hand. Last floor had been all about explosions. I suspected that was going to take a back seat here.

DONUT: SO, SHOULD I DO THE FOOTBALL HOOLIGAN OR THE
FIRECRACKER CLASS? QUICK, I'M ALMOST OUT OF TIME.
MORDECAI: Hooligan. If you're going to be stuck in a series of
tubes, it's the best choice. It comes with a momentum
bonus and several team buffs. Plus the Mascot skill, which
gives a bonus to Mongo.

Donut glowed for a moment.

DONUT: I DID IT. I GOT THE MASCOT SKILL! BUT I DIDN'T GET
GROUP CHANT OR MOVING RIOT. I GOT THE 10 POINTS TO
MY CONSTITUTION, THOUGH.
MORDECAI: Damn. Chant would've been good. Okay, you three. I
just peeked my head out of my room, and I am in what
appears to be a train station settlement. It looks as if the
stores and inns are placed at these stations. This is a
bigger one where you can switch between three different
train routes. One of the trains is a subway like you
described, but another is much larger. Like a regular

transcontinental railway train. Get off at the next station, and see if you can find a safe room or inn.

CARL: 10-4. By the way, thanks for telling us about the bounty.

MORDECAI: So you made the top 10, huh? Find a safe room, and we'll talk.

I looked at Donut. I tried to remember what she'd lost by switching away from Artist Alley Mogul. The only noteworthy benefits were the +5 to dexterity and the 15% bonus to item sales. Also, she'd received a few extra coins when we went down the stairs, but it wasn't much. The loss of the dexterity bonus would probably be the worst part. "So what do your new skills do?"

The ground rattled as we went around a bend. The lights flickered.

"I only got a couple of new ones. It came with a skill that would've raised my damage if we were moving, but I didn't get it. The best one is Mascot. If Mongo deals damage to an enemy, everybody in the party receives a bonus to dexterity and constitution. If he kills a mob, the bonus lasts for a couple hours."

"That is a good one," I said.

"Also, my constitution went up by 10 points. Oh, and I got a skill called Guinness that doubles my strength if I'm drunk."

"Are you serious?"

"Quite," she said. "So if we're going to be doing any fighting, we'll need to stop at the club first so I can get another Dirty Shirley."

CARL: Mordecai, is it me or are these classes better than what we were offered before?

MORDECAI: It's an unintended benefit. A lot of these rarer classes weren't available because she didn't meet the minimum requirements. But as her stats increase, the classes she's offered on each level will be better. There's another benefit I hadn't anticipated, too. She'd received a level 5 Negotiation skill with that Artist Alley class. Before you guys left the third floor, she'd raised the skill to level 7 thanks to all that selling you did. When she lost that class, the five levels went away, but she retained the two she'd received, including the skill experience, so it actually bumped itself up to four on its own.

CARL: Wait, I don't understand. So if she gets a temporary skill, she keeps it the next floor down? What about the stat point increases?

MORDECAI: She won't keep the stat points. But as long as she uses a skill enough to level it at least once, it looks like she'll keep it, minus the levels she received as being a part of that class. Skill experience is a complicated, under-the-hood metric crawlers can't see. It takes a lot to break the cherry, so to say, and obtain level 1. But once you're in, you're in. So in other words, use Mongo as much as you can, and you'll keep that Mascot benefit. Also, from now on, we should keep an eye out for classes with rare spells. If she levels the spell at least once, then I think she'll keep it.

CARL: That seems like a bug.

MORDECAI: I think it might be. So don't talk about it out loud or bring attention to it. They probably won't notice until she manages to keep a spell from one floor to the next. Now get to work. I'll look for a map, but you should, too.

"Katia," I said. "You have the Pathfinder skill. Do you see anything?"

"The skill is only level three. It was level one when I got it, and it's hard to upgrade. I have to keep my map open all the way to train it. My old game guide said I needed to find a training guild to really boost it. I can zoom my map out really big, but when I do, I don't see much. There are tubes everywhere, like a mess of noodles. Though a minute ago, I saw another train rush by on another track on the other side of this wall, shooting off at an angle from us. As for this train, there are 20 cars, and we're on the last one."

"Can you see any mobs?"

"No. It usually doesn't show monsters. But if we're close to a stairwell or a safe room, I'll get a notification. But I can see car number 15 is shaped differently than this one. I can't see what it is. It's not a passenger car like this one."

I looked on my own map, and it showed the first half of car 15. I knew normally my map zoomed out a little bigger than that, but it shrank while we were moving. If Katia could see all 20 cars, then that skill really did make the map a lot bigger. The map also helpfully labeled the cars for me, something I hadn't seen before. We were in **Cabin #20—Passenger Car.**

"What does the label say for that 15th car?" I asked Katia.

"It just has a question mark."

I examined the back wall of the train. Normally there'd be some sort of emergency exit. Instead, it was just a solid metallic wall. I wondered what would happen if I attached an explosive to it, breached the wall, and jumped out onto the track. Considering how tight the tunnel was, we'd probably get squished by the next train in a matter of minutes.

"Okay, guys," I said. "Let's go check it out."

I moved down the center aisle. Donut jumped to my shoulder. Mongo pushed his way to my side. He had to struggle past the vertical poles. If he got much bigger or the aisles any tighter, it was going to become a problem. We came to the door, which seemed out of place here. There was no glass window. I sensed this door was something added by the dungeon, and normally there'd be a short, open gangway where one could walk the length of the train unimpeded. Above, the timer to the next stop was at five minutes.

"I'm going to pull the door open. Katia, your constitution is four times mine, so you go in first. You okay with that?"

She swallowed but then nodded. I could see she was trembling. "I guess that's my job, isn't it?"

"Don't worry, sweetie. We have your back," Donut said.

The door slid to the side, revealing a small, enclosed space between the two cars. The gangway floor bounced up and down. The walls connecting the two train cars were a black accordioned material that looked like reinforced fabric. The distance between the two cars seemed longer than it should be. Below my feet was a panel that I could presumably pull up to get to the connector. A second door appeared, leading to the next car, and I put my hand on it. Behind me, Katia now held a small glowing ax.

"Have you used that thing before?" I asked.

"It's a good weapon," she said. "But my strength isn't high enough, and it doesn't do a lot of damage. Though I killed some lumber monkeys with it."

I nodded. "Here we go."

I slid open the door, and she leaped inside. Mongo jumped in with her, snarling, causing her to face-plant. I stumbled back at the pet's sudden, unexpected forward motion.

"Goddamnit, Mongo!" I yelled, examining the room for threats.

Empty. The car was identical to the last.

"Mongo! Bad!" Donut cried. "Be nice to Katia!"

"Okay, let's try that again," I said. "Mongo. Don't be an experience hog."

The dinosaur squawked as Katia grumbled and pulled herself to her feet. She'd dropped her ax, and it'd skittered ten feet in front of her. She ran to retrieve it.

The next car was the same. Empty. But at least Katia didn't fall on her face when we breached. The next car after that was similarly unoccupied.

By the time we reached car number 16, the timer was almost out. I wanted to at least peek into 15 before we tried to find a safe room. The cars beyond that one were more of the normal passenger cars. Katia said cars 10 and 5 were also different, but not the same as 15. Plus the entire first car was just a solid block on her map. She said that usually meant it was behind a magical door.

"There's gotta be something in this one," I said, indicating the door to train 15. It was different than the previous ones. It was still a sliding door, but it appeared to be made of a thicker, more stable material.

The door was not locked. I slid it open and moved onto the gangway. The next door was the same. The train started to slow. The high-pitched squeal of brakes filled the air, along with the stench of oil and smoke.

A static-filled voice crackled over a loudspeaker. "Coming up on Sirin Station, folks. Station number 81. Next stop will be Mora Station number 82 followed by a traveler transfer station number 83."

"Monsters," Donut hissed. "Smaller sized, but there are a lot of them."

I lifted my hand off the door to car 15. "Okay, we'll back away for now until—"

"No, not in there. At the train station!" Donut said, just as the platform eased into view. To my left, a simple landing area appeared. A sign **Sirin Station—81** hung from the ceiling.

"Oh god," Katia said.

The station teemed with several hundred fat, wrinkly monsters clambering over each other as they surged at the door. The creatures looked like demonic gray-skinned babies with sharp claws and giant mouths filled with too many teeth. Each stood on two legs, and they stood about knee height. A few were attached to the concrete pillars, climbing up them on all fours like goddamned spiders. They wore nothing but tattered loincloths, and they leaped and scratched at the doors, some jumping as high as the car's ceiling. They screamed as one, their cries unsettlingly baby-like. They surged against the train at the sight of us through the windows, crashing like waves into the glass.

The train continued to roll forward, but it would stop at any moment. And when it did, those doors were going to open, letting them in here.

I examined one of the monsters through the glass.

Drek. Level 6.

Everybody loves babies, right? What kind of asshole doesn't love babies? How about demonic, ravenous, berserking babies who travel in packs of at least 50? It's rumored these lil' rascals can devour a full-sized elephant down to the bone in less than five seconds. And you're a lot smaller than an elephant.

"Shit, shit," I said, pulling at the door to cabin 15. "Close that door behind us!" I slid the heavy door open, and we piled into the humid, dark train car. The room stank of rotten meat.

Behind us, the doors to the train hissed open, and the squealing monsters poured in. Katia slammed the first door. She rushed into the dark, windowless rail car and slammed the second shut just as Donut cast *Torch*, illuminating the room.

"Oh for fuck's sake," I said, seeing the new pair of monsters.

Jikininki. Level 17.

Of all the types of ghouls one may find in the Iron Tangle Rail System, the Jikininki is the most common, the most well-behaved, and the most insatiable. Their voracious appetite for flesh makes them the perfect janitors. They'll generally leave you alone as long as you're not bleeding, as long as you don't litter, and as long as you don't trespass into their personal space. It's rude.

On the map, the system helpfully replaced the question marks on the label with **Janitor's Lair.**

The hunched, thin monsters appeared to be grown-up cousins of the Drek babies pouring into the train behind us. These white emaciated creatures were about seven feet tall with arms that dragged to the ground with serrated black fingernails that clinked like porcelain as the monsters stood to their full height at our intrusion. Their faces were all sharp teeth and white bulging eyes. The mouths on both creatures started chattering up and down like a wind-up toy's, making the sound of an industrial shredder.

Both of the creatures wore tattered and threadbare double-breasted suits with golden buttons. Under the dark suits were white blood-splattered dress shirts. One had a bow tie. Both wore conductor-style hats with golden letters across that said, "Janitor." The one without the bow tie had a pin-back button on his breast that read, "How may I hurt you?"

Other than the two monsters, the rail car was empty save for a pile of bones and two brooms and dust buckets.

"Double shot!" I yelled.

Two full-power magic missiles rocketed out, each one a head shot. The creatures staggered, their health moving into the red as Mongo roared. The raptor leaped half the length of the car, landing on one of the humanoids feetfirst. Donut jumped from my shoulder to Katia's as I rushed at the ghoul, forming a fist. The monster hissed as I reared back and punched it in the face. To my left, Mongo had decapitated the monster and was in the process of swallowing the head. My target hit the ground. I stepped onto its chest, caving it in. Black tar-like gore spread out in a V pattern from where I stomped. The action felt odd on my foot, but I didn't have time to think about why.

You have received a temporary 5% bonus to Dexterity and Constitution thanks to your team's mascot.

We didn't have time to revel in our victory. I took a few bones and looted a handful of gold coins from each ghoul. I also took the How-may-I-hurt-you? button as I rushed back to the end of the room.

"They're trying to get in!" Katia cried, backing away from the door. Donut remained on her shoulder, fur poofed out. We could hear scrabbling and scratching and screaming coming from car 16. They hadn't yet broken through the first of the two doors. All they needed to do was pull the handle down and slide, but it appeared they didn't know how.

I looked nervously at the door at the other side of the car, the one leading to car number 14. That one was also presumably filled with the Dreks. We were surrounded.

There was no sign in this car, but I remembered the announcement had said the next station was called Mora or something like that. But the one after that was something different. A traveler transfer station. Hopefully that meant a safe place like Mordecai had described. But there were no doors to the outside in this car. How could we get out there?

I prepared a smoke curtain. I also moved the Fireball or Custard ticket to my hotlist. I had three scratch-off spots left. If they broke in here, we were screwed. I wouldn't be saved by a glob of custard this time. What the hell were we going to do? Would all the stations be filled with mobs?

I feared I would have to resort to explosives, but that seemed like a really bad idea. Even if we threw it toward a rear train car and slammed the door, I feared a derailment would be deadly to the entire train.

I had my *Protective Shell*, but I could only cast it once a day, and it only lasted 20 seconds. Actually, thinking about it, Mordecai had told me something about that spell a long time ago that might just be helpful here. But if that next station was also filled with mobs, I'd have to wait to use it; otherwise it would be a waste.

Okay. Calm down. It's okay. You're okay. They put these doorless cars here on purpose. We're using them as intended.

I took a deep breath and went over my options, combing through my inventory. Now that the initial panic had eased, multiple options presented themselves to me.

"We need to hold out until we get to station number 83," I said. "Katia, if they start opening the door, hold it closed! Donut, do you still have those two ready-to-go trap modules?"

"Yes. You want them?" she said, pulling each out. She'd received them in a Gold Sapper's Box after our battle with the rage elemental back on the second floor.

One was a Spike Module and the other an Alarm Module. Each of them was a tiny cube about the size of a pair of dice. I examined the Alarm Module.

Alarm Module.

Two items for the price of one! A favorite of the paranoid and the rich, you can use this module to either add an alarm element to a trap you're building, or it can be used as a ready-to-go trap for those who can't be assed to sit down and make their own. When triggered, it will play a Very Loud song. And by Very Loud, I mean Norwegian Black Metal loud. You may program the song at a Sapper's Table. If you do not or are unable to pick an alarm tone, a random, culturally important song from the past US Billboard Hot 100 will be chosen.

You have the ability to imbue *Fear* upon this module, but your current level of Trap Engineer (Level 1) only allows this action to be done at a Sapper's Table.

If untriggered, your Backfire skill allows you to remove this trap after it has been set with a 100% success rate.

The Spike Module had a similar description, but it would cause 50-centimeter spikes to pop out of the ground at two-second intervals in a one-meter-square area. Friendly NPCs and crawlers wouldn't set it off, but once triggered, it would keep spiking up and down forever, so we had to be careful.

I wondered if the spike trap could be affixed to a wall. Or a door. I was about to find out.

"Keep on this door," I said. "We can't guard both sides, so I'm putting the alarm and spike trap in the fore gangway. That'll give us time to run up there and block out the door if they're coming at us from that side."

I turned and sprinted for the other side of the car before they could respond. The truth was, we *could* probably guard both sides. Katia could hold one door closed, and I could hold the other. Donut wouldn't be able to do it. But I didn't trust Katia's strength of 11 to be good enough, even if they were just level six monsters. Plus I didn't want to split the party. Not now.

I ran to the far door and put my ear against it. Sure enough, the rabid babies were screaming and attacking the door on this side, too. But they hadn't broken into the gangway yet. I eased open the door.

The handle to the door for car number 14 rang as it jangled up and down, but they hadn't yet figured out how to slide it. At any moment, one of the little assholes was going to get an arm in there and figure it out. I took the Alarm Module and set it on the ground. I mentally clicked **Activate**, and a transparent rectangle appeared on the floor, blinking. The box was about the size and shape of a shoebox. An informational tooltip appeared over the now-set trap, similar to what I saw with bombs.

> **Placed Trap.**
> > **Set by you.**
> > **Effect: A loud-ass alarm.**
> > **Delay: None.**
> > **Target: Red-tagged mobs.**
> > **Duration: Until the heat death of the universe.**

In addition, I had four options under the info panel. **Trigger Now, Set Delay, Set Target,** and **Remove Trap.**

I left it alone and turned toward the door into the janitor car. I slid it shut, enclosing me in the small space. I placed the spike trap against the door and activated it. It allowed me to place it vertically. I slid open the door to see if it moved with the entry, and it did. I returned to car 15 and slid the door closed.

Now we would know if they breached the door behind us, and the spikes would hopefully keep them off that door for a short time. I returned aft. Mongo remained in the center of the room, gnawing on the corpse of the janitor. The train swayed as it moved around a curve.

"Mongo, stay with Donut," I yelled as I rushed past. "And stop eating gross shit. You're going to make yourself sick again."

Mongo grunted and followed me back to the door.

My mind raced with possibilities and defenses I was going to have to build. If I knew the dimensions of the cars, gangways, and doors, I'd be able to fashion multiple defensive structures to place within the cars. But we had to survive this first.

"Keep your eye on that map," I said to Katia as I rushed up. "Let me know the second you see a train station coming up."

"I already see one. Station 82 will be coming up in a minute," she said.

"Okay, hopefully they'll get off. But if they don't, or if more monsters get on, I have a few ideas."

I opened up the door to the gangway. They still hadn't figured it out on this side, either. "Donut, tell me if that second door starts to open."

MORDECAI: Okay, I just watched a train pull up, and two
    crawlers got off. There were mobs on the train, but they
    were magically prevented from getting off. So don't
    disembark until you get to a transfer station.

"Yeah, thanks for the tip," I grumbled as I went to my knees and pulled up the panel in the gangway floor. Below, I'd hopefully find the train's electrical system and controls for the car couplers. I had no idea how this stuff worked in real life, but I was confident enough in my own electrical systems knowledge that I'd at least recognize what I'd find under there.

The top panel came off easily. But under it was a small metal door with a lock, similar to a breaker box. I placed my hand on it and received an error.

This service plate is magically locked. You need a Red Line Engineer's Key to access this area. Do you have a key? No, you don't. So back off.

"Damn," I said, putting the panel back. That meant we'd have to go with the nuclear option.

The loudspeaker crackled. "Coming up on Mora Station number 82, home to the Psycho Stickers. Watch out for those guys." The announcer chuckled. "Next stop is the transfer station number 83, where one may access the yellow line and the *Nightmare Express*. After that is Rusalka Station number 84. Thank you for riding the red line."

"Carl!" Donut cried. I looked up to see the door start to slide. I leaped back as Donut blew her wad, spamming magic missiles into the hole. One of the babies chomped onto my foot, which wouldn't do anything because of my . . .

. . . I cried out in excruciating pain as I fell back into car 15. Katia slammed the door shut. The baby remained attached to my foot, gnawing furiously on the meat of my sole. I pulled myself up and slammed my foot down. The level 6 monster exploded like a tomato-soup-filled balloon. I spread my toes to make sure they were all there, and I cast *Heal* on myself. *What a disaster that would've been.*

"Ow, ow, ow," I said as it healed. That had fucking *hurt*. It'd been a long time since I'd allowed my pedicure kit buffs to expire. I was so used to having rock-solid feet, I'd forgotten what it felt like to be vulnerable down there. We *really* needed to get to a safe room.

The train eased to a stop.

"I see more monsters," Donut said. "But not as many. There's only a few on the platform. But they're big. A lot bigger. One is going into train 16 and another two into 14."

The door handle started to jiggle. I grasped onto it and held the door closed. Squeals of outrage came through the other side. A moment later, the train started to move again.

"Hey," I said. "Do you remember if we left the doors open all the way down? The ones to cars 17 and 18?"

"We did," Katia said.

"Okay, let me know the moment you see that next platform. In a couple minutes we're going to—"

Peaking at Number 2 on January 13, 2007, it's "Fergalicious"!

The announcement was so loud it rattled the walls.

"What in god's name is," Katia started before she was drowned out. The song started, louder than I expected, despite the description's warning. My ears immediately rang in pain.

> CARL: It's the alarm trap. They made it through the first door.
> KATIA: Do you want me to hold the other door?
> CARL: No. We don't have time anymore. We're running aft. Toward the back. We're going in about 15 seconds. We are going to run all the way back to car number 20, and we're shutting every door we pass. When I say go, we run.
> KATIA: How is that going to work? I don't understand.
> DONUT: JUST GO WITH IT. WHEN CARL SAYS TO DO SOMETHING, WE DO IT. ALSO, I LOVE THIS SONG.

The door at the far end of the car rumbled. Shrieks of pain exploded from the other side. Experience notifications started rolling in as mobs were impaled on the door spikes.

I looked at the map to make sure the track was straight, and then I clicked on *Protective Shell*.

The large semicircle shield formed around us, expanding outside the width of the train car. The shield wasn't affected or fettered by solid objects.

I had no idea how fast the average subway car moved, but that didn't really matter. I knew this train was going fast, and I also knew that the spell's barrier would be impenetrable by mobs for 20 seconds.

And more importantly, the spell remained static in the spot where it was cast.

The magical shell disappeared the moment I cast it, rocketing away toward car 16, then 17, then 18, then 19, then 20, and then away, stuck in that same place along the tracks it'd been when I cast, pushing all the mobs along with it like a bulldozer, squishing them into paste against the first surface they met.

CARL: Go!

I threw open the door just as the door at the other end of the train ripped open, revealing a hedgehog-like ogre creature so large it couldn't get through. Only its arm reached in, stretching all the way from car 14. The Dreks poured in around it, running and clambering at us. Several jumped to the ceiling and crawled just as fast as they ran, their mouths open in cries I thankfully couldn't hear. I slammed the door behind us, then the next.

Car 16 was completely filled with blood. Body parts were splattered around the seats and walls where the Dreks had gotten stuck. Each corpse had dropped about five gold pieces. The ogre creature, apparently called a Psycho Sticker, had been so obliterated it didn't even register as an X on the map.

I looked over my shoulder at the sign, and the next station was only four minutes away. I relaxed as we jogged toward train car number 17, looting the gold as we ran. We were going to be okay. For now.

CARL: Don't slip on the blood! It's easy to trip on their heads. Believe me.

KATIA: I'm going to be sick. Oh my god, Carl. I've never seen anything like this.

DONUT: YOU BETTER GET USED TO IT.

2

THE PLATFORM TO TRANSFER STATION NUMBER 83 LOOKED LIKE any other subterranean subway station from before the collapse. It was a narrow concrete platform that seemed to go on forever. One end had a set of stairs leading up to a different area. The featureless white-tiled walls gave off an early-industrial vibe. A lone bench sat against the wall, and a faded thick yellow stripe was painted on the landing, warning travelers of the edge of the platform.

By the time the train had eased to a stop, and the doors slid open, we still had multiple cars between us and the hordes of killer babies and hedgehog ogres. I feared they would pour out of the train, but Mordecai's earlier assessment that the transit stations would be safe was correct.

"Do you think the trains get more and more filled with monsters the farther it goes?" Katia asked. "Surely they have to get off somewhere."

"That's a good question," I said, watching the train pull away. Drek glared at us through the windows. I flipped them off. "Go fuck yourselves, creepy babies."

Once the train was gone, I stepped forward to examine the track below. It looked like a regular subway path. It was a channel about five feet deep holding two regular rails. On the far end was the so-called third rail, an electrified length of metal that provided power to the train. Normally these things had covers on them to keep people from getting electrocuted if they accidentally fell in, but there was no cover here. I didn't know how much juice was running through the line. For all I knew the whole thing could be some ridiculous mana system. One never knew with this place. But the presence of what appeared to be ceramic insulators along the single raised line suggested this was good ol' DC electricity. Either way, I knew we needed to stay off the damn tracks.

"Mongo," I said to the dinosaur, who was poised to jump down there to go exploring. "Don't. You'll get zapped or squished. Probably both."

The pet grunted and turned away.

My eyes caught a freestanding rectangular sign in the center of the platform with some writing on it. I moved to examine it.

The sign simply read, **The Red Line. Trains approximately every 10–15 minutes** and had a long red squiggle. There was a single dot on the line, about a third of the way from the bottom. It was labeled **You are here. Station #83.**

I examined the sign more carefully, and I felt the haptic buzz of my Escape Plan skill activating. The map became alive. Additional words appeared. The remaining dots populated the line, starting at station 11 and ending at station 435. It appeared the trains only traveled one way, ascending up the line, which was kind of weird. If there was a second train that went from high to low, it wasn't indicated here. The transit stations were now circled on the map. They were not at regular intervals, but there were quite a few of them. In addition, every fifth station had red squares over the dots, but it didn't say what that meant.

A box sat in the left corner of the map. It read **Safe rooms appear at all transfer stations. Stairwells appear at stations numbered 12, 24, 36, 48, and 72 on any colored line.** The map didn't give any more details, nor did it give the names of the other lines at this station, though I knew from the announcement there was also a yellow line platform and a *Nightmare Express* platform somewhere around here.

We'd emerged on the train just after station number 80, and we'd gotten off at 83. There didn't appear to be a way to get to the lower-numbered stations with the stairwells. At least not directly. Also, I knew that there would be 9,375 stairwells hidden on this floor. If each line only had five stairwell locations, then how many damn lines were there? I hated doing math, but it sounded like this was going to be a mess.

A timer counted down to the next train arrival, which would be in nine minutes.

"Let's go up the stairs. Find the safe room," I said.

At the top of the short flight of stairs was a small circular room. Two additional stairwells led down, one to the yellow line and the other to the *Nightmare Express*. There were three shops up here. A safe room. A "Mace and bashing weapons guild." And a small general store called Limp Richard's Sundries. The proprietor of the general store, Limp Richard, was a type of creature I'd never seen before. A mole man. He was a short, squat man that looked, well, like an anthropomorphized mole, complete with glasses. He sat in the open doorway to his shop reading a book. He looked up at our approach.

Limp Richard—Mole Man. Level 36.

This is a Non-Combatant NPC.

Mole men and mole women actually just call themselves "Men" and "Women," and quite frankly, it's exhausting. These losers spend most of their days and nights reading. What a bunch of nerds.

"Welcome to station 83," Limp Richard said. He put his book down. "I have supplies for the weary travelers."

"We are weary. We'll be by later after we sleep," I said, moving to the inn, which didn't have a sign.

"Suit yourself," he said, settling back into his spot.

"Hey, have you seen any other crawlers yet?" Katia asked.

"You're the first," he said.

We entered the inn, and upon opening the door, we discovered the safe rooms had reverted to their previous style from the first two floors. This was a red-and-white-themed fast-food restaurant called

Nirula's. Behind the counter stood a shaggy but female Bopca Protector named Wendita.

Mordecai appeared a moment later, having been transferred here from his quarters.

"Holy shit," I said, laughing. The last I'd seen Mordecai, he'd been a stunningly handsome incubus creature. He was now about five feet tall, and he'd been transformed into a mud-colored, warty, slimy toad-looking thing, complete with hanging jowls and a throat pouch under his wide face that looked as if it could fill with air. I examined his new properties.

Mordecai—Grulke Infantry. Level 50.
   Manager of Crawler Princess Donut.
   This is a Non-Combatant NPC.
   The rare Grulke were a militaristic race of toad warriors. Able to leap great distances and inflict devastating attacks with their tongues, it was said an army of Grulke could stand against any foe. Unfortunately, political intrigue and infighting have turned these once-proud people into a race of mostly mercenaries and vagrants. They are hunted ruthlessly by the tunnel trolls, who like to capture and lick them. Not because they impart any sort of hallucinogenic effect. It's just that tunnel trolls are weird-ass fuckers.

"A frog, huh?" I said.

Mordecai grunted. "Don't ever call a real Grulke a frog if you meet one. They're mean bastards. They're toads."

"I need to tell you what happened with that last quest."

"Oh, I already know all about it. As a manager, I no longer get the daily updates or a newsletter, but I do receive notifications of court decisions adversely affecting my client. You guys got screwed, but at least you're alive."

I moved to the counter and examined the familiar three screens.

"Shit," I said, looking at the player counter. We had 389,441 remaining crawlers. That was several hundred thousand dead since the last time I'd looked.

"What happened?" I asked, horrified.

"I only know what I saw on the recap episode. There were several group quest events just like yours happening across the Over City during the last couple of days. Usually the third floor is relatively easy. They generally try to have six or seven hundred thousand make it to the fourth floor. The factions aren't going to be happy if the crawlers are culled too much by the time the sixth floor opens. It's also usually 20 days, and you only have 10. Expect the AI to push back with better gear and higher awards, especially after that veto. The fact you're level 27 and Donut is 26 is both lucky and a miracle. That's better than I could've hoped for, even with a regular timer. We'll need to keep it up, but we can't rely on luck-based power leveling."

"Luck-based anything is not my intention," I said. But I'd barely heard what he'd said. I felt sick. *Jesus,* I thought. *You gotta keep your head.* I took a deep breath.

The middle screen with the top-ten list simply read, **Leaderboard will populate at the end of the next recap episode.**

I turned my attention to the final screen.

Welcome to the Safe Room. You are on the Fourth Level.

   Rental Rooms currently available: 10.

   Rental Room price: 180 gold.

   Personal locations available for purchase. See proprietor for details.

   Food is available at this location.

"How much gold do you guys have between the three of you?" Mordecai asked.

"Just about four grand," I said. "But we haven't opened our boxes yet, and we have quite a few."

"Okay. Open your boxes and see how much you have," Mordecai said. "Donut, do your thing. Just like we talked about earlier."

Donut cleared her throat and jumped to the counter. I knew she'd been looking forward to this.

"This is a lovely establishment you have here," she said to Wendita the Bopca.

"Why, thank you, Your Majesty," the gnome said, perking up. "I'm just so excited to have royalty visit us. You don't know what an honor it is."

"I'm sure," Donut said in her most imperious voice. "So I understand you have personal locations available to sell at this establishment."

Wendita's eyes got huge. "Yes, that's right. Fifty thousand gold, and it's yours."

Mordecai and I both winced. He'd warned us that the price might've gone up. He said it usually started at forty grand.

Donut yawned and looked at her paw as if that price was but a pittance. "I always find talking about coins to be a low activity." She sighed dramatically. "Surely there must be a discount for royalty?"

Wendita shook her head vigorously. "No, ma'am. Your Majesty, I mean. Personal spaces aren't something we can negotiate on."

Donut leaned in. "Oh, sweetie. Let me tell you a secret. *Everything* is negotiable."

Wendita swallowed.

According to Mordecai, the price for a personal safe room would be "fixed." Location managers would tell the Bopcas how much to sell them for. But the truth was, there was usually about 25% wiggle room on the price. The system wouldn't allow them to sell it for less than that. The proprietors were incentivized to sell the magical spaces with rewards, not money. The rewards being things such as earlier location selection for the next floor, a larger food budget, et cetera. So as far as the Bopcas were concerned, it didn't matter how much they sold the spaces for.

Unfortunately, the gnomes had a miserly streak to them, and it went against their better nature to discount anything, even if they weren't the ones reaping the benefit. It was something I'd never understand. But Mordecai was convinced that Donut would be able to talk them down, and if she succeeded, she'd surely train up her Negotiation skill. Apparently one received extra skill experience if they could talk a Bopca down. Even if we didn't have enough money to purchase right now, this was an important skill to train as much as possible.

"I might be able to let it go for 45,000."

Donut scoffed. "I suppose we don't really need a personal space today anyway." She stood and turned her back to Wendita, showing her cat butt to the gnome.

"Forty-four thousand?" Wendita said.

"Is that a question?" Donut asked, looking over her shoulder.

I sighed and turned away from the negotiations. I had 24 stat points to distribute, but Mordecai had taught me to open my boxes and weigh any possible loot upgrades first. I had multiple boxes already, but I pulled up my unread achievements first to see if I had any more. I had ten achievements I hadn't yet opened, most of them explosion-based. I was surprised to find a few additional ones.

New Achievement! They like me! They really like me!

You are one of the first five crawlers to have achieved 500 trillion followers! People sure love a good train wreck. Wink.

Reward: You have received a Platinum Fan Box!

Note: Voting is now enabled on this box's prize. Box will become available in 30 hours.

New Achievement! The early bird gets to squirm!

You went down a set of stairs more than six hours prior to the level's collapse.

Reward: Doing this is kind of like leaving a party much too early. It makes you look like a dick. No reward for you.

<Error> Reward and achievement removed by Syndicate Court Order.

New Achievement! Cuck Aquaman!
    You got fucked by a fish. You've done something so spectacularly controversial, courts and lawyers had to get involved. The end result was *my* decision being overturned.
    Reward: You've received a Platinum "It's Not My Fault You Fish-Headed Assholes Don't Properly Program Your Quests" Box.

"Uh, Mordecai?" I said.

I described that last achievement using our chat feature. I'd recently discovered I could mentally copy items in my notifications and paste them into chat. I had a scratch pad where I could paste and keep items and write notes. The whole thing was just getting longer and longer with information.

Mordecai laughed out loud after I showed him the achievement. His throat pouch inflated and dispersed air with glee. The sight was disconcerting.

MORDECAI: The AI is given the discretionary ability to award certain types of superfluous achievements and awards up to platinum. Don't think the system is getting soft on you. This is not too unusual. The AI running the game almost always obtains a bit of a personality and an attitude, especially near the end. When their decisions get countermanded by the court, it tends to break something in their virtual minds. They usually act out by doing something like this. But normally the veto comes much later in the game. I don't know what sort of effect this is going to have. Just open the box, accept the prize, and don't mention it again out loud. I'm sure Borant expected this when they issued that veto, and they won't hold it

against you. I just looked and Donut got the same prize. I'm guessing everyone who got shafted by the decision received it.

We'd gotten robbed of a Celestial Quest Box, but Donut and I still had two Silver Quest Boxes from the prostitute quest and from that CockBlock achievement. At the same time I had received a Platinum Tyrant's Box plus a Bronze Assassin's Box, which I'd gotten for becoming the town's new magistrate. Plus I had that Bronze Boss Box from killing Quill and a mess of other loot packs, mostly Bronze and Silver Adventurer Boxes.

Looking at the list, I no longer felt as if we'd been screwed over. Almost all of these prizes were a result of that quest.

"I'm going in," I said. The next table over, Katia was digging into her own loot.

The adventurer boxes didn't hold anything new or exciting. Potions, potions, bandages—which I never used—random clothing items, and unenchanted weapons that we would sell. A couple hundred coins.

The Bronze Assassin Box contained a pair of **Quiet Slippers**, which I wouldn't be able to wear, plus a mess of antidote potions I didn't need unless I wasn't wearing my nightgaunt cloak.

The boss box contained a magical tome for a spell called *Bang Bro*. I set it aside to read later.

My two Silver Quest Boxes each contained 1,000 gold coins and a group of scrolls. One contained three *Confusing Fog* scrolls, which I liked much better than just smoke bombs. The scrolls had saved us multiple times, but I'd been out of them for a while. The other contained three *Heal* scrolls, which were also useful in healing others without having to resort to pouring potions down their throats.

I received more sticks of dynamite from some random boxes before we got to the good stuff.

The first, the Platinum Tyrant's Box, contained 10,000 gold and a necklace. The necklace was a simple silver-colored chain with a quarter-sized charm at the end. A tiny yellow jewel was encrusted in the charm. I quickly examined it before I moved to the next box.

Enchanted Necklace of the Haute Bourgeoisie.

The second smallest of the chains of leadership, it is still considered a great honor to be the custodian of this burden. Each jewel encrusted upon this charm represents a settlement owned and controlled by the bearer. If one still maintains a settlement's jewel upon the collapse of the level, the holder of this necklace will permanently receive a tax stipend every ten days from that settlement based on size and population. In addition, each gem will impart additional benefits based on the town.

In order to upgrade this necklace, one must first conquer a Large-sized Settlement. Upgraded necklaces will also upgrade all existing gems.

One Attached Gem:

Poor Sapphire. Medium Skyfowl Settlement (Third Floor).

+5 to Dexterity.

+ Talon Strike (Level 5)

Taxes received: 432 Gold every 10 days.

May you be a kind and just leader.

"Oh wow," I said, putting it aside. "Cool." I guessed that explained why the others didn't recognize me as the town's leader. I probably had to first put the necklace on.

The AI's special box opened next. It was just seven slips of paper. I laughed out loud at the prizes.

Coupon for a free Personal Space, upgraded to level three.

Coupon for a free tier one environmental upgrade. (× 2)

Coupon for a free tier one crafting table. (× 2)

Coupon for a table upgrade. (× 2)

Over at the counter, Donut had talked Wendita down to 38,000 gold. The two continued to dance back and forth. I saw Katia had received the same coupons. She had one in her hand, her eyes glossy, which I recognized as her talking directly in chat, probably to Hekla. I nodded at Mordecai and slid the coupons over to show him.

"Holy wow," he said. He had to sit down. He croaked with amusement. He also had an odd look of relief on his face.

"So these are good?"

MORDECAI: This is a bigger fuck you to the showrunners than I thought the AI could pull off. Honestly, this is probably almost as good as a celestial upgrade. A level three space is expensive but allows for each crawler to have their own room complete with their own upgrades. And if you gather a new teammate who already has a space, you'll be able to conjoin the rooms and combine the upgrades. It also allows me to bring my own room over. No more unexpected teleporting, thank the gods.

CARL: How is this a fuck you to the boss people?

MORDECAI: All of those upgrades are really expensive, so in addition to the loss of income from the acquisitions—they get a small cut of all dungeon purchases—it's a tradition for your sponsors to make you buy your own safe space but to then buy you some upgrades in your first loot box. By preempting the sponsors, the AI is giving you a leg up and is saving your future sponsors a lot of money. I mean, *a lot*, thus freeing them up to give you better stuff.

CARL: Katia got the same coupons. I'm thinking she's going to save them for Hekla.

Mordecai turned his head and regarded the woman thoughtfully.

MORDECAI: The environmental upgrades are no problem. She can install them now, and they'll travel with her if she

decides to leave. But I want those table upgrades. Those
are invaluable. I'll have to talk to her.

"But, Princess Donut, it's the lowest I can go," Wendita pleaded.
"It won't let me go below 37,500 gold. If we go lower than that, I
will have to personally pay the difference myself."

"Well, how much do you have saved up?" Donut asked. The cat
had a wild look to her eyes. "You'll be free to visit anytime you like."

"Wait, really?" Wendita asked.

CARL: Donut. Don't make her pay from her own pocket. It'll
    make you look like an ass. Just settle on the price now to
    get your experience.
DONUT: I can get her lower, Carl. I can do it. I can *feel* her
    wavering. It is delicious.
CARL: There's no need. Open your boxes and you'll see why.

Donut sighed dramatically. "Oh, we needn't go lower than 37,500
gold, I suppose."

"Really?" Wendita said. "So it's a deal?"

"I'll have to think on it," Donut said. She jumped from the
counter and moved to the table as the Bopca just stared at her in-
credulously. Donut started going through her achievements as I returned my attention to my loot.

I put on the necklace, receiving the plus five to my dexterity. I
tucked it in under my shirt. We didn't wear dog tags in the Coast
Guard, so I wasn't used to having something around my neck. It felt
heavy against my skin, heavier than it should. I examined Talon
Strike, which ended up being a skill, not a spell.

Talon Strike.
    Birds have ugly feet. Disgusting feet, really. Still, there's
something sensual about the sight of a hawk swooping down

upon its prey, talons out, and slashing. It's so sudden, so unexpected, so explosively violent.

Such violence. Sweet, sweet violence.

Turns the side of your bare foot into a fast-moving slashing weapon, increasing the damage against opponents by up to (Level of skill) times your regular kicking damage for (Level of skill) seconds. Each kick using this skill has a 2% chance to cast the instakill spell *Eviscerate*. This melee skill has a cooldown of five minutes. Higher levels of this skill increase damage, duration, and chance of casting *Eviscerate*. A level 15 of this skill will result in Talon Strike being permanently active.

That was an excellent upgrade. Anything that could increase my damage was a welcome addition, especially if it didn't cost anything to activate. I couldn't wait to try it out.

I picked up the spell tome.

Bang Bro.

Cost: 5 Mana.

Target: Temporarily Enchant Equipped Item.

Duration: 5 minutes + 1 minute per level of spell. Requires 5-minute cooldown.

Adds both fire and electrical damage to any currently equipped item. May not be cast on flesh. Well, actually it can be cast on (your own) flesh, but I really wouldn't recommend it. May inflict *Burn* and *Shock* on targets.

Can also be used to cook hot dogs and other items.

I called Mordecai over, who was helping Donut with her items. I showed him the book.

"Will this work on my gauntlet?"

"Yeah," he said. "Definitely. I wouldn't try it on your xistera, not with the way you load it. You could probably do it to your foot, also, as long as your invulnerable buff is active. But I would probably avoid doing that. It's a good spell, and it's in your mana price range."

I nodded and read the tome, adding the spell to my list. I would have to add a few points to my intelligence. Between that, *Heal*, and my *Wisp Armor*, I now had a few mana-costing spells.

"Oh my gosh, oh my gosh, I love it! I love it so much!" Donut cried. "This plus a fan box? I can't wait!"

She'd gotten the same coupons as me, which meant all of us who won that quest probably got the same thing. She'd also received the fan box. But other than that, she hadn't gotten as many boxes as I had. Most notably, she hadn't received the tyrant box nor the assassin box. But she did have the boss box and the quest boxes. It looked as if she'd received a bunch of random scrolls and some useless items we'd have to sell. But in one of those—I wasn't sure which—she'd also received a new tiara.

It poofed onto her head. It looked similar to her last one. The jewels on this one were white instead of purple. I quickly examined it. It wasn't as good as the one she'd lost, but it did come with some good benefits.

> **Enchanted Tiara of Mana Genita.**
> A crystal tiara fit for royalty. Made in honor of all the lost children of the world. Because nothing helps soothe the tears of grieving parents like watching someone else dress up all fancy.
> +3 Intelligence.
> Increased ability to detect mobs on the map.
> Removes automatic hostility by worshippers of Mana Genita.

"Who's Mana Genita?" I asked.

"She's a goddess," Mordecai said. "A pretty obscure one. I don't think I've ever run across her. She was big on spells, I think. I don't remember. There's thousands of them. Gods, I mean. Only a few are dungeon regulars. Most of them never leave the twelfth floor."

I remembered what Odette had said about Mordecai and gods. *He has a lot of experience in the subject, unfortunately.*

"Yeah, I'm supposed to ask you about gods," I said.

"That can wait. It's a long conversation. We need to get our space set up. And then sleep. So distribute your points."

"Wait, that reminds me," Donut said, jumping from the table. She rushed to the corner of the restaurant. Standing there, hidden in the shadows, was a mailbox. I'd forgotten about that. She had a spell book coming to her. She leaped to the top of the box and opened it up. A moment later, she grunted with annoyance.

"When am I going to get a good spell?" she complained. "The flames from *Magic Missile* aren't doing it for me anymore. I want something with some kick. Like *Fireball*."

The idea of Donut shooting fireballs was terrifying.

The cat scrunched up her face. "What do you think, Mordecai? Should I read it? Or maybe we can sell it?"

"Read it," he said.

She glowed.

"What was it?" I asked. Normally, she'd apply the book without even reading the description first. I was moderately impressed that she'd first asked Mordecai's opinion. But thinking on it, I was starting to suspect she was getting addicted to the idea of selling things more than actually using them.

"It's a spell called *Hole*," Mordecai said. "It does exactly what it sounds like. It makes a temporary hole on a surface of her choosing. She'll need to level it up before it's too helpful, as a level one isn't thick enough to get through most doors, but it's a useful spell. Especially if you're creative with it."

That actually sounded pretty awesome. I could already think of a half dozen uses for it. Tomorrow we would have to go out and experiment. I turned to Katia.

"What about you? Did you get anything good?"

She nodded, lifting her left arm. There was nothing there except the arm of her blue tracksuit. Any equipped gear would be invisible on her, but it would increase her mass.

"It's an arm bracer that I can turn into a shield," she said. "Check it out."

She flicked her wrist, and her arm changed shape, forming into what looked like a buckler-sized glob of blue polyester.

"That's really weird," I said.

"Yeah, the shield is supposed to be metal, I think, but when I activate it, it just looks like the surrounding area." She reached down and rapped on the shield with her knuckles, and it gave a metallic ring. "If I practice, I might be able to make it look like anything. Mordecai says I can change its shape, too."

Mordecai leaned forward to examine the round protuberance on her arm. "That shield has a *Shatter* enchantment. Use it in conjunction with your Rush ability."

The shield disappeared, and her arm reshaped itself.

"You can be like that liquid-metal *Terminator* guy," Donut said. "That'd be really cool."

"I never saw that movie," replied Katia. "I don't like violence."

"You're in the wrong job, then, honey."

"Wait," I said. "I guess I hadn't really realized what exactly you can do with that race. So if you're wearing a helmet that's made out of metal, and you reshape yourself to look like a normal human wearing a bikini, you'll be able to make any part of your body metal?"

Mordecai answered. "That's right. If she's 90% flesh and 10% metal, she can make herself to look like a regular, unarmored human, but what you perceive as her bikini, or her feet, or her hands, can really be the material from the helmet. As long as it's 10%, and it's continuous. You can't break up the item. Also, there's some elasticity issues with certain enchanted materials, plus certain limits still exist, like she's not allowed to grow four arms so she can wear forty rings, but you get the idea."

"Well, shit. We need to get as much armor on you as possible."

"That's the plan," Mordecai said. "And she's going to train up her strength a bit, too."

I distributed my 24 stat points. I put 10 in strength, nine in constitution, and five in intelligence. I knew I needed to add some to dexterity next, but since this floor was going to presumably focus more on close-quarters fighting, plus the boost I'd already received from the necklace, I decided to bolster my main stats. So after I was done, I ended up with:

Strength: 41 +3 (When Gauntlet Formed)
   Intelligence: 15
   Constitution: 34
   Dexterity: 23
   Charisma: 25

"A strength over 40 is good for the fourth floor," Mordecai said when I showed him my updated stats. "It's not anything to write home about, but you've already made up the ground you lost when you picked the Primal race. We still have a lot of work to do. We need to get your unenhanced strength to 100 as soon as we can. In a few levels, Donut is going to hit 100 in charisma, and that's going to change a lot of things. She's at 94 now."

"Oh, I can't wait," I said.

"In the meantime," Mordecai said, turning to Donut, "there's one last thing to do before you three can get to sleep. Get your coupons out. Katia, you, too. Take out all your coupons."

"Actually, guys, I'm really sorry," Katia said. "I was talking to Hekla, and I kind of promised her I would—"

Mordecai waved his hand. "Yes, yes. We've already figured that out. Don't worry. You can cash in the coupons now, and you won't lose them. The personal space and the environmental upgrades will travel with you, so you might as well use them now. The same with the tables you're going to buy. The tables upgrade on their own every time you go down a floor, so it's important to do it now. You can save the two table-upgrade coupons. If you leave and rejoin another party, everything you're about to do will travel with you."

"Okay," she said after a moment.

Donut returned to the counter with Wendita, who was sitting there looking very sullen.

"So I've thought about it, Wendita, dear," Donut said. "I've decided we are going to buy a space, but we're going to use this instead."

She dropped the coupon on the counter.

"What is this?" The Bopca's eyes grew huge as she examined the paper. Her hands started to tremble. "A level three space?"

"Does she still get her bonus if we use a coupon?" I whispered.

"Oh yeah," Mordecai said. "She also gets rewards for each upgrade she sells. We are about to make her year."

I still had my own coupon for a level three personal space. "What should I do with mine?"

"Something very cool," he said. "Follow." He stepped—hopped, actually—up to the counter.

"Wendita," he said, "both Carl and Katia here also have coupons for a level three personal space that they'd like to turn in. How much is the joining fee—for all three?"

Wendita looked up at Mordecai as if he'd just told her that she'd been elected the new president of the universe. If the little gnome's eyes got any bigger, I feared they would pop out of her head and roll onto the counter.

"It's ten thousand," she finally said. "Five thousand for each union, but it would only require two of them."

"We got that now," he said. He turned to me. "Right?"

I nodded.

Mordecai slapped his webbed hands together. They made a sticky *splotch* noise. "Okay. So here's what we're doing. Make sure you get all this down. We are turning in all three of these level threes, and then we are going to conjoin them. What will that make?"

"Uh, it looks like it'll be a level five."

Mordecai grumbled as I exchanged a look with Donut.

He looked over his shoulder at me. "All that means is that when you guys combine your spaces, all of them together will give the benefits of a level five space. If Katia leaves the party, she'll withdraw her space from the collective, and it'll go down to a . . ." He looked at Wendita.

"A four."

"A level four space, which is still pretty good. Okay, you three, hand me all your coupons. Don't mix them up. The system needs to know who is buying what. Wendita, pull up the upgrade menu, and show me the available tier one environmental upgrades."

The Bopca, still in a daze, waved her hand. A menu appeared floating in front of us.

Welcome to the Upgrade Clearinghouse.

The following tier one upgrades are available. Drill down for more details.

Bathroom Upgrades.

Bed Upgrades.

Crafting Upgrades.

Kitchen Upgrades.

Kennel and Stable Upgrades.

Magic Upgrades. (Empty)

Quest and Social Upgrades.

Store Access. (Empty)

Training Upgrades.

"What is this?" Mordecai asked. Before I barely had the chance to read the menu, he reached forward with his hand and clicked on **Quest and Social Upgrades.**

"This is all new since the last time I'd had to deal with a personal space," he mumbled. "They never really kept us apprised on this stuff since game guides don't usually deal with anything past the third floor."

A new menu appeared.

Social Upgrades:

    *Social Screen. Gives detailed, AI-curated running list of comments from your social stream. Allows for better interaction with fans. 50,000 Gold.

    Quest Upgrades:

    *Quest Screen. Gives detailed list of available quests in your current area. 90,000 Gold.

    *Adventurers Inc. Employment Agency. Allows access to the general dungeon jobs-for-hire board. 100,000 Gold.

    *<Special> Naughty Boys Employment Agency. Allows for specialized quests with specialized rewards. Invite-only. 500,000 Gold.

Mordecai grunted. "Hmm, I was wondering what that was before. Your class gives you access to that Naughty Boys agency. I've never seen anything like this. They are always changing this stuff and not telling us."

"Are these coupons good for any of these upgrades? Even though they have different values?" I asked. It'd be stupid to waste them on something that cost 50,000 when there were items that cost literally ten times as much.

"Ahh, no," Wendita said. "If you read the fine print on the coupons, it says maximum value of 250,000 gold each and two may not be combined for a single item. So if you want that last one, you'll have to pay another 250,000 gold."

"Damn," I said.

"We're avoiding quests this floor anyway," Mordecai said. "Let's find some upgrades that'll be useful right away."

Mordecai went back and clicked on **Bed Upgrades.**

A long list of available types of beds populated the list. It started with a single-sized cot, and it got better from there.

The very last item was **Ultra-stabilized, size-adjustable, race-**

adjustable alleviating sleep apparatus. Allows for full rest after a period of only two hours of sleep. Imparts 30 hours of Good Rest bonus. 250,000 Gold.

Mordecai slid one of Donut's coupons forward. "We'll take the Ultra-Stabilized bed."

"Will we all get that?" Katia asked.

"Yes. As long as the rooms are conjoined, you all share in your upgrades."

"So we only have to sleep for two hours now?" I asked. I was both fascinated and horrified at the idea.

"That's right. And that's not even the best bed you can get. Once you hit the sixth floor, the tier two upgrades become available. I think the top available bed allows you to press a button, and you're fully rested. The Good Rest bonus adds 10% to all of your stats and allows for 10% higher experience and skill training."

"Well, shit," I said. "I hadn't realized we would be getting upgrades like this."

"It gets better," he said.

"Click bathroom upgrades," Donut said excitedly. "We need to get the cleaning thing like they had in that production trailer."

In the end, we ended up with the bed, an automatic shower that wasn't quite as nice as the one we'd seen on the surface, and a 255,000 gold **Enhanced Crafting Studio** that Mordecai insisted was necessary. The shower added another 10% bonus to our stats and lowered our "detectability," which meant we could sneak around better. He made me save my last coupon for the store, which would supposedly become available sometime in the next few days. Katia also spent only one of her coupons on a **Training Room**, which would allow us to train for one hour a day on any specific non-magical-spell skill we wanted. Supposedly it would train the skill as if we were really fighting with it. That room also cost 250,000 gold. I wouldn't be able to train anything explosives-based, but Mordecai said tier two would have something called a **Bomber's Studio**, which would allow me to practice blowing shit up.

There were multiple available upgrades I still wanted to get. The kitchen upgrades were expensive, but they offered up food that imparted varying degrees of buffs. The kennel upgrades did the same but for Mongo. The magical upgrades would become available later, according to Mordecai, and would offer a place to train magical spells and allow the purchase of magic-enhancing items. He said that was something else that would be a necessary purchase.

"There's a ton of new types of craft tables. Let's hold off for now while I study the list," Mordecai said. "In the meantime, let's open up the room and get some sleep."

In the end, we had to pay 15,000 gold, which once again depleted much of our newly acquired wealth. We slid the coupons and gold over to Wendita, who had tears streaming down her face as she accepted them.

"You bless me, Your Majesty," she said. "I knew when you talked me into paying my own money, it was nothing but a test. A real princess would never do such a thing."

Admin Notice. A new tab is available in your interface.

New achievement! Welcome to the neighborhood!
     You have bought a home! It's every man's dream to someday own a place where he can fap in peace. No more filthy roommates not doing the dishes or making up excuses as to why they can't pay the rent. No more landlord who shows up without notice and conceals hidden cameras in the smoke detectors. It's all smooth sailing from now on.
     Reward: You're a homeowner now. That is the reward. That and taxes and having to deal with Kenneth the megalomaniac HOA president.

Every safe room we'd been in always had a blank doorway locked into the wall and a space on the map for an inaccessible room. The moment the achievement faded away, that doorway opened up, and a small, closet-sized room appeared on the map. It was labeled **Conjoined Personal Space of Team The Royal Court of Princess Donut**. As I watched, the name started to blink.

"It lets me change the name," Donut said excitedly as she walked toward the doorway. "Come on, Mongo. Let's go see our new house."

3

ENTERING THE ROYAL PALACE OF PRINCESS DONUT.
You have upgrades that need to be placed.

We entered into an empty industrial-style room. It reminded me of the interior of an airplane hangar.

"Whoa," I said, my voice echoing. "This is way bigger than I expected."

Before proceeding further, you must set the entrance to your personal space.

A blinking transparent doorway appeared against the far wall. It slid as I turned my head, racing along the walls. As I moved, a second doorway formed with **Princess Donut** blazing over it. The colors of the words changed from black to pink, then to an opalescent purple.

"This is very customizable," Donut said. A moment later, her door changed color from black to purple, matching the color of the floating label over her door.

I mentally clicked **Place** on my door, and a second door appeared a few feet to the right of Donut's. A moment later, a third door appeared next to mine, labeled **Katia Grim**.

A wire diagram of a rectangle appeared, floating against a small section of the warehouse, just right of where we'd placed the doors. It blinked again, and suddenly there was a tiny room. **Restrooms** appeared over the door.

"You'll have an additional restroom inside your spaces, too," Mordecai said. "When you conjoin a space, everyone keeps their personal restroom, and a public one also appears. The upgraded shower will be in all of them. The team leader gets to place the location of the common area rooms." A bare, featureless kitchen area blinked into existence, followed by an area with a table and a simple couch. The three familiar screens formed on the wall above the couch. On the third screen was the message: **Welcome Home**. Over the kitchen was the note: **Food Upgrades Not Yet Purchased.**

Donut grumbled as she moved the rooms around. Large sections of wall turned transparent and flew across the hangar as I watched, open-mouthed. A moment later, she placed yet another room in the opposite corner across from the kitchen and living area. This was the biggest room yet, and it took up a quarter of the entire open area. **Crafting Studio.**

The moment it was locked in place, a blinking notification appeared in my own interface, and I clicked on it.

Enhanced Crafting Studio upgrade available. You may apply this upgrade to the Crafting Studio in the common area. Note: If you disengage your space, the upgrade will be returned to your library. See the Personal Spaces tab for more details.

I clicked on it and chose to apply it. Nothing apparently changed except the title. **Enhanced Crafting Studio.**

A new room clicked into place, this one taking up a third of the entire hangar. **Training Room.**

What had been a massive open area just a minute before was rapidly filling up.

A new doorway appeared with a loud *clack*, right behind me and next to the door to the exit. If we were following the normal laws of physics, this new door would also lead right back into the restaurant. The note on the door simply read, **Manager.**

Mordecai croaked with relief. "Thank the gods," he muttered. He caught my questioning look, and he grinned. "You can't conjoin a manager's room until your base is combined into a level five communal space. I wasn't expecting you guys to ever bother upgrading your base this much, at least not anytime soon. Once you bought a space, I would have moved in anyway, which meant I'd have been sleeping on the floor. Now I can get to my private quarters, and when you come to new safe rooms, I won't teleport away unless I'm outside."

"What are the differences between the rooms anyway?" I asked as we walked deeper into the space. The floor was made of solid concrete. Donut, Katia, and Mongo went exploring. Mongo jumped onto the counter of the kitchen, clicking his claws on the industrial sheet metal countertops. There was no oven or fridge. The whole thing was an empty, useless area that Donut probably shouldn't have bothered placing.

"Okay, so thanks to the AI, you guys skipped right ahead and moved straight into advanced personal spaces. At the basic level one, either you or Donut would have purchased a space. Whoever bought it is the owner, but there's a setting where you can share it with your party members. It's about a fourth of the size of this place, and it's just one open room, save for the crafting studio, which is much smaller than the one you have now. I think the crafting area is always a quarter of the room's size, but I'm not certain. Anyway, it has a bathroom, the couch and screens, a couple of cots, and that's it. The level one crafting area will hold up to five basic crafting tables. Some are bigger than others. You can purchase and add any tier one environmental upgrades you want as long as they fit. The best ones, like the training area, are too big."

I watched Katia wander toward the door with her name on it. She hesitantly opened it and disappeared inside.

Mordecai continued. "At level two, the room gets bigger, which allows for more upgrades. Level two also comes with the ability to add kitchen upgrades. Level three is bigger yet, and the individual rooms are pretty huge. Big enough for a training module." He looked up. The ceiling was high above our heads. "I don't think it's as tall, but I'm not certain. But the largest benefit of a level three space is that you can convert it to a communal hall as long as you have one other person in your party with a space. Only one of the spaces has to be level three. But once they're combined, the individual rooms get much smaller, but a communal space is created, and all share in the upgrades."

"Plus the manager gets to keep his own place," I said.

"Only when you hit level five, but that's right. And any other helper. I'm not the only kind you can employ. In a few days, we'll need to purchase a store interface. We'll be able to buy and sell items more easily." He lowered his voice. "The training room is more important, though. I let Katia purchase it with her coupon, but I want you to keep your coupon free until we've made sure she's staying."

"I can tell you right now that she's going to bounce the second she gets a chance," I said. "I know she likes us, but I get the sense she felt safer in Hekla's party. She didn't like the idea of me using her to tank damage. Also, what happens if she dies?"

"You lose the upgrades," Mordecai said. "And if you die, too, then it'll be just me and Donut. No more community space. I'd once again lose access to my room. Any upgrades that no longer fit will go into her library."

I nodded. That kind of sucked. "Okay, so our space is level five. What's the difference between this and a level four?"

"Other than my ability to add my personal space, I'm not certain," Mordecai said. "Most people don't go beyond three or four. Usually what happens is someone upgrades their space to three, and someone else in the party buys their own level one space, and they combine it all into a communal space. That usually keeps the overall level at three. Then they spend the rest of their money on room upgrades. But since we have three level three rooms all shared, that made it a five. I think, but I'm not certain, we might be able to add a second floor to the base if we run out of room." He pointed up. "The ceiling is really high."

"Okay, that's enough exposition for now," I said. "I'm going to sleep. Tomorrow we can discuss crafting tables and all that. I'm glad you're here. Figuring all this shit out on our own would've been a real chore."

"Fair enough," Mordecai said. "Oh, but, Carl?"

I turned to face the toad. My entire body felt as if it was being dragged into the floor. I was both physically and mentally exhausted.

"You only sleep two hours now. So I'll see you out here in time for the recap show."

I KNEW, PHILOSOPHICALLY, THAT ONLY HAVING TO SLEEP FOR TWO hours was a good thing. It gave us more time to train and to get things done. But I dreaded the idea of not being able to get into a bed, close my eyes, and not have to worry about anything for six to eight hours.

That was it, wasn't it? Sleep was my sanctuary. No matter how fucked-up the world now was, I could still get away for part of the day. Now that luxury was being eroded. Sure, our bodies would no longer be tired. But what about our brains? We were already well past burnout. What was going to happen now?

Donut insisted I sleep in her room. I hadn't even gone into my own yet. Since we had a combined space, the individual rooms were much smaller. The room was the size of a large apartment, about twice the area of my place from before the collapse. She could add a small crafting area and kitchen into the space if she wanted, but it was optional, and she chose not to. She'd found some menu that allowed some simple, free decorations, including carpet and wallpaper and simple furnishings. She placed the bathroom in the corner, which was actually just the same bathroom from the hallways. The shower was in a separate room next door. She made me take the cat tree and place it next to the Ultra-Stabilized bed, which looked like a regular queen-sized bed with no sheets or pillows and a semitransparent mattress that looked oddly like clear Jell-O. Then she made me place the framed picture of Bea on a small table next to the bed.

"Okay, get in bed, Carl. You, too, Mongo. We're all tired."

"You know I have my own room now, right?"

"Don't be silly, Carl. I can't sleep without you, and you know it. Now get into bed."

I grumbled, but the moment I lay down, it felt as if I was encased in a warm hug. Donut jumped onto my shoulder, curling up near my neck. Then Mongo hopped onto my legs, and I didn't feel the weight of him.

I fell asleep in seconds.

———

I WAS, INDEED, FULLY RESTED WHEN I AWAKENED. AND MORE IMPOR-tantly, I *felt* rested. I felt as if I'd slept for 10 hours straight, which I always thought was the perfect amount of sleep for a lazy day. In fact, I was so certain that the bed hadn't worked, I checked the clock, but we'd truly only slept for just about two hours.

> **New achievement! Well rested!**
>
> You managed to sleep so well that you woke up feeling re-freshed and full of energy. You are ready to take on the world and make some monster's mother cry because her only child was ruthlessly slaughtered by a bright-eyed and bushy-tailed crawler.
>
> *Reward:* You now receive the Good Rest bonus every time you sleep in this bed. This buff adds 10% to your base stats plus a 10% bonus to experience and skill training for 30 hours. Mon-ster mothers now cry 10% more when you kill their babies.

Back out in the common area, we found Mordecai and Katia placing plates of food on the kitchen counter. It was two plates of hamburgers and French fries, plus a salmon platter and a bowl of raw meat for Mongo. Mordecai had what appeared to be a plate full of dead bugs, and he appeared slightly ill as he looked upon it.

"It's all from Wendita," Katia said. "I went out there to get food, and she'd already made us all of this for free. I've never seen one of those Bopca guys in such a good mood."

Donut sniffed at the plate suspiciously as the recap show came on. She shrugged and started stuffing her face.

"The Iron Tangle!" the announcer called as the show got underway. Different shots of railroads and subway cars flashed across the screen, from old locomotives to the more modern high-speed rail trains. This went on for some time. The scenes were an odd mix of real-life footage and passages from movies and video games. It included stills from the animated movie *The Polar Express* and a bizarrely long sequence of a beat-up John Travolta riding the subway from the movie *Saturday Night Fever* while the Bee Gees played in the background. After that, the program went into a detailed history of trains, focusing mostly on subway systems.

As always, the program went out of its way to showcase only the negatives, displaying mass overcrowding, people falling onto the tracks. It presented pictures from the Japanese subway sarin attack, along with dozens of other disasters, making the entire world look like a shithole.

I ate the hamburger while we watched. The show was going on and on about trains. Mordecai started rambling about maintaining a schedule. Wake, eat, apply buffs—which included showering, brushing Donut while I worked on my feet—and then spend an hour in the training room working on a specific skill. Mordecai had somehow found what appeared to be a dry-erase board, and he was marking items to train on the list. Today he wanted me to train my Smush skill. Apparently you could only train one skill a day, even if skills overlapped. Katia was to train her Catcher skill, which appeared to be the opposite of Dodge, which Donut chose to train.

After we trained, we'd work on crafting for an hour or two, though that wouldn't start until tomorrow. And after that, we'd spend the rest of our time out on the tracks. Our first priority would be to attempt to get a better map and find a reliable path to a stairwell, all while grinding our way up the ranks.

On the screen, the show finally wrapped up the history of the Earth rail systems. The host started speaking, but then he froze. The word **REDACTED** appeared on the screen.

"Get used to that," Mordecai said. "He's explaining how the level works. They don't want us seeing this part. You'll see this on every level from now on."

"The Daughters are also at a station number 83," Katia said as we waited for the show to resume. "The same thing happened to them as us. They were on a train that filled with monsters, but they only had a single stop before they got to the transit station. They are at a conjunction of the orange and indigo lines. They haven't seen any sign of the red, yellow, or *Nightmare* lines."

"That's interesting," I said. "So different lines will have the same number system, and we know that number 83 is a transfer station. The map said specific numbers would have stairwells, but they were all lower numbers. We need to find a way to go back down."

"I bet it's the ones without color names," Donut said. She'd finished her fish, but it'd come with little potato things she didn't like and was pushing them off her plate and into Mongo's waiting mouth. "We should go on the *Nightmare* line to see where it goes."

She was probably right, but I didn't like the idea of immediately jumping onto a train called the *Nightmare Express*.

I turned to Mordecai. "What about you? When you first got here, you said you were at a different train station. Do you remember the names?"

"Yeah," Mordecai said. "I wrote it all down. It was station number 317. The two smaller trains were the yellow and emerald lines. And the big one was called the Misery."

"Charming," I said. "We should probably start charting this out. Do you have another one of those dry-erase boards?"

"I have one more in my room," he said. "I'll get it and start putting it all down. So far we only have the yellow line in common. Talk to your friend Brandon and figure out where he is. As soon as you come across any other crawlers, get all the info you can from them."

I nodded. I also had Daniel Bautista on my chat, and I would ask him as well. The screen unfroze, and the announcer said, "And now it's time to present the current top-10 list!"

He went one by one, presenting the top 10 crawlers. He read the name, and it was followed by a short clip. The list was exactly the same as the one Odette had.

He started with Mrs. McGibbons. It only showed her for a quick second, and I realized I'd actually seen her a few times already in quick shots on the recap episodes. I just hadn't known it was her.

She'd turned into a "Frost Maiden," which meant she was now a blue-skinned, white-haired elf thing that floated instead of walked. I didn't see any of the others in that short clip, but it showed her shooting icicles from her palms, skewering a troll-like monster in a subway car.

Next was Li Jun, who'd taken a monk class. He looked the same as before, and it showed him with Zhang and his sister, Li Na. Zhang was also human, but Li Na was an odd, demon-like race who fought with chains.

Number eight was a man named Ifechi. He'd remained human, and he was a healer. I'd seen him a few times, I realized. He was now traveling with Florin, the Crocodilian shotgun guy, who was ranked number four. But I'd first seen Ifechi early on the show. He was African, running with a group of soldiers armed with AK-47s. The entire team had been killed a while back by a city boss slime monster. The man had survived because he hadn't been in the room when it sealed.

After Ifechi, it went straight to us. It showed Donut blasting magic missiles at the Drek babies, followed by me pummeling the janitor ghoul with my fist.

Then was Miriam Dom, the goat lady. Then Florin the Crocodilian.

Number three was a goat. His name was Prepotente, and he was the walking, talking goat creature—called a Caprid—that I'd seen earlier traveling with Miriam Dom. I knew they had another monstrous goat thing traveling with them, too, though that one was considered a pet.

Then we saw buff Hekla skewering a mass of four-legged rat things with her crossbow, then Lucia Mar, who was simultaneously terrifying and badass as ever. It showed the disgusting witch form of Lucia literally ripping the head off one of the Jikininki janitor ghouls. The girl laughed maniacally as blood showered the interior of the train car.

The show ended, and a moment later, the second screen populated.

While the list of names was the same as what Odette had presented, I immediately noticed two differences.

1. Lucia Mar—Lajabless—Black Inquisitor General—Level 30–1,000,000
2. Hekla—Amazonian—Shieldmaiden—Level 28–500,000
3. Prepotente—Caprid—Forsaken Aerialist—Level 27–400,000
4. Florin—Crocodilian—Shotgun Messenger—Level 24–300,000
5. Miriam Dom—Human—Shepherd—Level 27-200,000
6. Carl—Primal—Compensated Anarchist—Level 27-100,000
7. Donut—Cat—Former Child Actor—Level 26-100,000
8. Ifechi—Human—Physicker—Level 18-100,000
9. Li Jun—Human—Street Monk—Level 25-100,000
10. Elle McGib—Frost Maiden—Blizzardmancer—Level 17–100,000

Mrs. McGibbons had risen from level 13 to 17, and Lucia Mar had hit level 30.

I opened up my chat. I hadn't connected with Brandon in a while, and I wanted to talk to him. The moment I clicked on the messages, though, I realized I'd missed a chat from him. It was in a weird folder I'd never seen before, off to the side of his name, which was why I hadn't seen the notification. It had arrived while we were in-communicado, waiting for the floor to open. Before I could click on it, the daily announcement came, and my interface froze.

Hello, Crawlers. Welcome to the fourth floor!

We are so very excited to introduce you to what is being hailed a genius feat of engineering. We call it the Iron Tangle. The trick is to find the stairwells. There are a lot of them out there, but where? Let's see how many of you figure it out.

This is important. This is not a permanent change, but it is a new rule for this level only. You may not go down early this level. The stairwells will open six hours prior to collapse, and that's it. Again, you may not go down early this floor. Now have fun out there. These train things are so nifty. We never had anything like it on our world.

Patron bidding is active, and we are very happy with the results so far. You will get a notification when your bidding has concluded. We'll have more info on that later.

You will notice that the leaderboard has finally populated. Congratulations to everybody on the list. As you can see, each member of the top 10 has a bounty after their names. That means hunting season is *open*! Isn't that exciting? If you kill one, you will receive a loot box containing the reward. If you are on the leaderboard, don't worry, you get to join in on the fun, too. If you survive the floor, you will receive 10% of your own bounty upon floor collapse. That percentage goes up each floor.

Finally, we'd like to address the especially high mortality rate of the third floor. This occurred due to a high instance of group quests gone bad. While the number of crawlers is still in the acceptable range, we are all concerned about early extinc-tion. That does not mean we will be letting up. So quit sucking. It's as simple as that.

Now get out there, ride the rails, and kill, kill, kill!

"Quit sucking?" Katia asked. "Is that supposed to be a joke?"

"Do you really think people are going to hunt us?" Donut asked. "I don't like the idea of not being able to trust people. It gives me anxiety."

I barely heard them. The moment the message had ended, the directory with Brandon's message unfroze, and I finally noticed the name of the folder in the top corner of my interface.

Messages from deceased crawlers.

"Oh. Oh no," I said. It hit me like a damn truck. I slid off the edge of the counter I was leaning on and to the floor. Everyone in the room stopped talking and turned to look at me.

"Carl?" Donut asked.

The message was right there. I didn't want to read it.

I took a deep breath, and I clicked on it.

~~Brandon~~: Hey, bro. I'm sending this message to Imani and Elle, too. You wouldn't believe what's happening with Elle. But just in case they don't make it, I wanted to get this out to you, too. It looks like this is the end for me. The third floor is about to collapse. Me and Henry—he was one of the residents—we're holding the line against the advancing shade gremlins. I hate those fuckers. Imani, Elle, and the others are getting away, but it's already too late for me. The floor timer is down to ten minutes, and that stairwell is twenty minutes away.

I saw your escape last night on the recap episode, so I know you made it to number four. Everyone knows about that bomb you now got stuffed down your pants.

Look, man. I got into a fight with my brother, Chris, and he left the party. He took a few of the guys with him, but I can see they're all dead. All except Chris. I know he's alive because he's still on my chat. I can see he's alive, but it says he can't accept my messages. I don't know why. I think maybe he blocked me, but I'm not sure. He was never much of a talker. Mom said there was something wrong with him, maybe he was slow. But he ain't slow. And even if he was . . . I said something stupid, and he got mad. He left, and now it's too late to tell him I love him. I never said it. I'm about to die, and it's all I can think about.

So if you see him, tell him I said I was sorry, and that he was right. He'll know about what. Tell him I said if there is an afterlife I promise not to give him shit ever again. He can eat all the damn traveler biscuits he wants. I promise not to get mad about him taking risks. Not about girls. Not about him stealing my Matchbox cars. Nothing.

And tell him I love him. That's the most important part. It's always been the most important part, but I didn't realize it until it was too late.

I gotta go. Damn shade gremlins. Get them for me, brother. Get them all.

Note: This message is from a deceased crawler. When you close this message, the crawler will be removed from your message list.

Hey, at least you're still kickin'.

"Jesus Christ," I said, gasping. The sudden loss was so unexpected, so out of nowhere, I thought I'd had the breath knocked out of me. *This is just like with Mom. Deep breaths. Deep breaths.*

"What is it?" Donut asked again after a few minutes of me just sitting there.

I told them. Brandon was the only one of the group we'd added to our chat, which was stupid. I couldn't talk to Imani or Chris to see if they were okay. For all we knew, Mrs. McGibbons was the only one left. I thought of all the work we'd done to get them down to that third floor. What a waste. What a goddamned waste.

I hadn't known him long. But he was a good man. He was my

friend. In all of this death, he would barely be a blip. And that enraged me unlike anything else that had happened so far.

I got up and turned toward the training room.

"You need to apply your buffs first," Mordecai called.

"Fuck off, Mordecai," I said.

I entered the room, and an interface popped up, listing all of my trainable skills.

I clicked **Bare Knuckles (Current Skill: 8)**. A one-hour countdown timer appeared. Wooden dummies rose from the floor.

You will not break me. Fuck you all. You will not break me.

I went to work.

4

IT HAD BEEN SEVERAL HOURS SINCE I'D BEATEN MY KNUCKLES RAW
on the wooden dummies. Both Donut and Katia entered the training room about twenty minutes after I did. Donut worked on her
Dodge skill, bouncing back and forth while the hologram of a four-
armed monster holding four whips lashed at her. Katia was on the
other side of the room doing something similar, but instead she was
jumping in front of rocks as they were being tossed at a holographic
puppy by the same four-armed virtual opponent.

Neither of them said anything to me. When I finished, my level
in Bare Knuckles had not risen. I knew it would take more than a
single session to raise it once it was this high.

From there, I went into the crafting space, which at the moment
was just a giant, empty room. Mordecai was already in there, looking
about.

"You have three tables," Mordecai said. He didn't say or acknowledge what had happened earlier. "Go set them up, and then go out
on your business. I'm going to spend the next several hours studying
what has changed and what's new with the crafting system because
it seems they've tweaked it some since last time. Leave everything
labeled an alchemical supply on the alchemy table. I'll start working
on a few things while you're out."

I nodded. I pulled out the alchemy table and shoved it against a
wall. It clicked loudly into place, and several menu items appeared
over it, mostly regarding upgrades. I started pulling everything from
my inventory in the alchemy category, which was a lot of stuff, from

rat meat to that chest of supplies we'd bought from the drug dealer. By the time I was done, the simple table now looked as if a mad scientist had set up shop at a swap meet.

I then put the sapper's table against one wall and my engineering table against the other. I knew I would spend most of my time at the sapper's table, but for now I stood at the engineering one, which Mordecai said was a general, catchall table for using magical tools to fashion items. I pulled out my tools, like the goo-inator 3000, which was a "shaping" tool, and the Gorgon Marital Aid, which was a tool that added plasticity to rigid items, and placed them on the table. I had a dozen other slightly too small tools from the goblins, plus a regular flathead screwdriver and a few wrenches that I'd picked up after the Juicer boss fight.

I had a few ideas of items I needed to make. My raw materials were a little lacking. I moved to my inventory and sorted through the crap.

I had the massive breastplate of a swordsman guard, and I pulled it out, clunking it onto the table. I had managed to grab three of these things, plus a helmet and one of the giant swords. All of their values were relatively low, which had been disappointing. This metallic breastplate wasn't enchanted. I was thinking maybe I could refashion it into something for Katia, but it was way too big for her. The thing was the size of an open umbrella. I knew I'd need an armorer's workbench to properly make wearable materials anyway. Plus this thing was heavy as shit. It looked like maybe it was made from actual iron, and it varied in thickness from one to about two and a half inches. While I could easily lift it with my over-40 strength, I knew before I'd never have been able to even make it budge.

I held the goo-inator in one hand and pointed it at the curved hunk of iron.

The whole breastplate started blinking. A menu of multiple shapes popped up. I could flatten the whole thing out. Because of the plate's thickness, I could shape it like a sheet, lower the width, and I'd end up with a large chunk of metal, almost like it was made of dough.

The last item on the list of the tool's shapes was **Free-form**.

I clicked on free-form, and then using the wand, I put a slight bend in the material. It was similar to manipulating a shape using a computer graphic program, something I'd never been very good at. The metal groaned loudly as it was shaped, but it didn't break.

New achievement! Martha Stewart!

You used a workbench to craft for the first time. The next thing you know, you'll be fashioning bottle-cap earrings, drinking oat milk, and selling your ugly crap on Etsy while you wax poetic on Instagram about your "journey."

Reward: **You've received a Bronze Crafter's Box!**

I immediately opened the box, and it contained a nice pair of unenchanted pliers, a standard tape measure, and a bucket of pink glitter. Not a vial of glitter. Not a cup of glitter. A goddamned bucketful of the stuff. Even before I could add it to my inventory, some of the tiny pink squares blew out of the container and spread to the floor. I knew from experience that it was now all over. The glitter would never go away. I sighed and added the tools to the pile.

I turned to Mordecai, who was hunched over his alchemy table way on the other side of the room.

"I need to weld. Do you think I can get something like that?"

He looked up. "Of course. In the meantime, you can probably get creative with that shaping tool. It's not very precise and has a tendency to lower the strength of the items you shape, so if you get too creative, you'll end up with crumbly junk. But you can take a separate item and twirl them together like a twist tie. Or make some sort of joint. Just be careful. Those tools are no joke. Being in a safe room may keep you from dying if you fuck something up at a workbench, but if you fuck up good enough, you'll wish you were dead."

"Oh, by the way," I called out, "while I was training, I talked to Bautista. He's grouped up with some other crawlers. He's on the azure and brown lines. They're at station number 199. They don't have a non-colored line at their station, but they're going to go down the azure line today. He also got a fancy base thanks to that upgrade."

"I'll add it to the list," Mordecai said.

"Okay," I said. I leaned over the bench and started shaping the plate.

———

AFTER A SHOWER AND APPLYING MY PEDICURE KIT, WE WENT BACK out into the world.

We first stopped at the general store. Limp Richard the mole man leaned on the counter, reading a book as we browsed through the items on the shelves. He had a wide array of products, but most of it wasn't noteworthy or useful. We only ended up purchasing one thing, a large padded mallet. He'd listed it for 250 gold, and Donut talked him down to 150.

He did have one other item that was interesting. In a dusty corner of his shop he had a thing called a **Battery Fabricator**. It was listed at 75,000 gold. I remembered that the descriptions at shops weren't always fully accurate as I examined its properties.

> **Battery Fabricator.**
> I don't really know how this thing works. It was taken from a dwarven automaton factory. You pour a handful of mana potions in, stick one of these metal blocks in, and a charged battery comes out on the other side. Comes with a box of 50 of the battery things. Price not negotiable.

I picked up one of the battery rectangles, which he had piled behind the machine. The description for the batteries was the same as the unit. The system wouldn't give me a real description unless I purchased the item. Each battery was about the size and weight of a brick. "Do you know how much of a charge these things hold?"

Limp Richard shrugged. "You'd have to ask a dwarf. The automatons they use can run a long time before needing a new battery, I know that. They're better than the soul gems the elves use. Did you know soul gems run off actual souls? It's quite morbid. Plus soul gems are very unstable."

"Yeah, I may have heard that somewhere," I said drily.

The machine was about the size of a microwave. I knew a bit about the chemical processes required to make real batteries, and this didn't make much sense. But nothing in this place made sense, especially once you added magic into the mix. Still, the moment I saw the unit, I knew I wanted it. But the price seemed outrageous, and even if we had that much money, I couldn't justify spending that much on something just because I thought it might be cool.

We ended up selling a bunch of random junk for a couple thousand gold. As Mordecai warned us more than once, we didn't want to sell too much stuff to a general store. They never offered the best prices. By the time Donut was done negotiating all the patience out of the talking mole, the creature was in a pretty foul mood.

"What's that book you got there?" I asked, leaning in after Donut and Limp Richard finished their negotiations. It looked like a tattered English-language sci-fi book. There was a cat on the cover. I recognized the author, but I hadn't read the book. "Hey, Donut, check it out. It's a book about cats."

Limp Richard nodded, his expression brightening just a hair. "It's an Andre Norton book. A lot of his books are about cats."

"Andre Norton was a woman," I said. "May I?" I picked the book up. I flipped it over. My dad had owned several of these. I'd mostly read the Westerns, but I'd read a few of the old sci-fi books as well. My dad hated cats, though, so he never had any books with cats on the cover.

"I've read this one a few dozen times," Limp Richard said. "There are a lot of Earth books floating around the dungeon, but there's never enough." He sighed. "And now it's too late to get more, and I don't have anybody nearby to trade with. Shopkeepers like myself don't have access to the entertainment feeds like the guides and guildmasters. And most of those guys just access the tunnel or watch Earth television and movies. All I can get is physical media, which means books and comics. All I have is 15 books. Sixteen if you count the one with the last few chapters torn out."

"I'll tell you what," I said. I pulled five Louis L'Amour books from my inventory. I'd read each of them already, from *Sackett's Land* to *Lando*. I'd actually read almost all of them already, but I didn't want to give them all up. "I'll trade you these five for five of your books. Straight-up trade."

He picked up the first book. "A Western? I've never read one of your Westerns. Is it any good?" He frowned. "They're short."

"They're good," I said. "These were pretty popular books. But you're right. They tend to be short."

"Okay," he said. He went to the back and returned with a handful of books, spreading them out. "Pick some, and it'll be a deal."

All of the books were science fiction or 80s horror. I noted the one that was missing the last few chapters was a book I'd read long ago. *Swan Song* by Robert R. McCammon. I left that one on the table and picked up five sci-fi books. Three Andre Norton books including the one he'd been reading, *Breed to Come*. I also picked up *The Lathe of Heaven* by Ursula K. Le Guin and *The Forever War* by Joe Haldeman.

"I don't know if we'll be back this way," I said to the mole as I added the books to my inventory, "but if we are, and if you like the books, I'll trade you the rest of the ones I've already read."

"Okay," Limp Richard said as we left. "There are a lot of my kind on this floor. Don't give them away to any of those other guys. They're all book hogs!"

"You should have asked for more," Donut said as we walked out. "You're a terrible negotiator, Carl."

"Oh, don't worry about that," I said. I looked over my shoulder, and the mole had already picked up the first book. "If I learned anything from my time in the Coast Guard, it's the value of entertainment to a bored man who has run out of books to read. In a couple of days, he'll be jonesin' pretty hard. Once we figure out how to backtrack on the rails, we'll need to swing by this place again."

WE DECIDED AGAINST JUST JUMPING ONTO THE *NIGHTMARE EX-press* until we had more information, but I wanted to see the train and examine the sign. It turned out the train only came once every hour and a half, and we'd missed it while we were in Limp Richard's shop.

We didn't need to see the train to know it was obviously a different type. The tracks were wider, and while the train was still underground, there was no electrified third rail. While that other platform for the red line was especially long, long enough to accommodate all the cars, this one was even longer. It looked twice as long.

This train traveled in a figure-eight pattern, which meant once one got on it, they'd eventually end up back at this station. That was good to know. The train only had five stops total, though it appeared there was a good distance between each stop. Four of the five stops were transit stations. The one stop that was not a transit station was station 436, and it appeared at the very top of the figure eight.

Unlike the map outside of the red station, this one gave slightly more information. It gave the colors for each of the transit stations it intersected. This station was yellow and red. The next one on the track was station 283, but it was the mauve and purple lines. The stop after that was stop 436, then stop 283 *again*, but this time it was 283 on the green line and the yellow line. Then it was station 83 again, but a different station 83. It was the tangerine and plum lines.

"For fuck's sake," I said after I relayed all the info to Mordecai. "They weren't kidding when they named this thing the 'Iron Tangle.' My head hurts already. I hate math."

"I'm not a fan of math myself," Katia said. She was examining the map, but I knew for her, all it showed was the figure eight and a single dot indicating our current station.

From there, we went to the landing of the yellow line. The map here was identical to the map of the red line. The transit station numbers were the same, though the line itself was shaped differently, like a giant upside-down fishhook. As I was looking at the map, the train pulled up.

There were monsters on board. Not nearly as many as there'd been on the red line, but there were enough to give me pause.

The train slid to a stop, and the door opened, revealing a squat, gray-skinned creature with no neck and a sharklike mouth and a pair of black beady eyes. Wisps of black oily hair dusted the top of the thing. The monster stood about four and a half feet tall and wobbled on a pair of toothpick legs that seemed woefully unprepared for the job of holding up the creature's corpulent, piglike body. The monster held a wooden club filled with nails. It howled gibberish at us.

Cave Mudge Bonker. Level 19.

In the hierarchy of Cave Mudge society, the Bonker is about as high on the list as a commoner can get. These odd, warrior-like creatures are said to have once been a star-faring nation, but something happened to cause them to regress back to the Stone Age. Probably too much reality TV. Don't let those skinny legs fool you. When these guys get to bonkin', they can be pretty darn quick.

There were four of them in this car. All up and down the long platform, I could see a few more scattered about the cars, their small eyes glaring at us from the windows. I caught sight of another monster, too. These were human-sized, red-maned snake creatures, like Nagas with the heads of lions. They were too far away to get a description.

Donut hit the Cave Mudge standing in the open door with a pair of magic missiles, and it fell over dead just as the doors started to slide closed.

"Hey," I said as the train rolled away. "I can't believe that actually worked. We can get them, but they can't get us."

"Let's wait for the next train and shoot some more!" Donut said.

"Guys," Katia said as we waited for the next train. "I just told Hekla about this, and she said she and the others have been doing this all morning, racking up a lot of experience. She thinks it's a bug. You can also pull them from the doorways onto the platform, and that kills them."

"Hmm," I said, thinking. "I think she's wrong. I don't think it is a bug. It's more of a time trap designed to get you to sit tight and snipe all day. If these were stronger monsters, I'd say we should definitely spend the day doing this. But there's only so many we can get in the few moments while the door is open. Experience-wise, we're better off jumping onto the train and killing them."

Katia shrugged. "Hekla also says that the monsters all get off every five floors. If you follow them out, the levels are like a cave system, and there are tunnels. She hasn't yet explored, but she thinks the tunnels might lead back to the previous four platforms. She thinks the monsters are constantly migrating in a circle."

That was kind of weird. "Tell her we'll check it out. Also, tell her about the map Mordecai is building. Have her collect all the route info she can from all of her contacts and report it back to you so you can pass it on. I hope to have a better idea of this place by this time tomorrow."

WE SPENT THE NEXT HOUR CAMPING OUT ON THE PLATFORM AND committing mass murder on the incoming mobs. The trains came every eight to ten minutes. It was always the same two types of monsters. The bonkers, as we started calling them, and the shock chompers, which were described as "lesser Nagas with mommy issues." These things were all level 20. The snakelike creatures had an electrical attack, but it took them a bit to get revved up, and if you smacked them, it canceled out their attack. Not that it mattered since they couldn't physically or magically reach us while we stood on the platform. All four of us would stand on a different section of the landing as the train pulled up. I'd punch. Mongo would chomp. Katia would practice with her ax, and Donut alternated between *Magic Missile* and practicing with her claws, which was something she needed much more experience with. The monsters were unable to fight back. But like I suspected, the experience was slow coming. Plus we were robbed of the ability to loot the corpses unless we pulled them onto the platform. But if we did that, we didn't get any experience. Still, we tried it a few times with each type of monster. The chompers dropped sharp fangs and about 10 gold each. The bonkers dropped their clubs and a couple of coins. One dropped his own liver, which was listed as an alchemical supply. I took it and added it to the inventory. None of this stuff appeared to be valuable.

Eventually we decided to finally get off our asses and hop onto the train. I wanted to check out the engine car, so we moved all the way to the end of the platform. I knew normally, with subway cars at least, if there was a driver at all, they were usually set up in a little cubicle at the front of the lead car. But in these trains, the entire first car was a solid, closed-off hunk of metal. It didn't even stop at the platform. It pulled slightly ahead, leaving car number two at the far end of the station. So we set up by the wall, just outside of where train car number two would stop.

Each train car held four sets of exterior doors on each side. We set up outside the two doors closest to the engine car. The next train squealed to a halt. This furthermost car only held two of the shock chompers, and the moment the door opened, both Donut and I took them out. Donut used a magic missile, and I reached into the car and punched the maned snake right in the face with two quick jabs, which killed it. We stepped into the car just as the doors slid closed, and we were on our way.

I looked about the yellow line train car. This car was almost the same as the red line car, but the first thing I noticed was that the graffiti was in English, not Russian. The seats faced inward, the same as the Russian train, but the cushions were blue, not brown. Also, the pattern of poles was different and the aisles weren't as wide. The doors at the fore and aft of the train were the same, and the car itself seemed about the same length.

Donut and Katia spent a moment examining the forward doorway leading toward car number one.

"It says we need a yellow line engineer's key to open the next door," Katia said a moment later. "How do you think we can get one of those?"

"We need to get the driver to come out somehow, I guess," I said. "Then we gotta take it from him. Either that or maybe we can figure out how to break into the car from the outside."

Just as I moved to loot the corpse of the shock chomper, the far doorway to train car number three slid open on its own.

"Ahh, shit," I said, backing up. A group of five bonkers rushed at us, clubs upraised. They howled.

I was hoping these guys didn't know how to work the doors.

"Formation one, guys."

This was something we talked about and practiced as we were getting ready earlier. This was more of a stance than an actual move. We backed up so we were parallel with the exterior doors. Donut leaped to my shoulder as Mongo jumped up into the space between the chairs, his back to the door to the outside. He set up on the starboard—the right—side of the car, which was actually to my left since we were facing the back of the train. The doorway was sandwiched by a grid of metal poles, which would protect Mongo. Katia moved to the opposite side, also jumping into the small vestibule in front of the exit. I remained in the middle, but I took a step back, creating a V-shaped kill zone.

This created a unified front while forcing the mobs into a funnel. They'd only be able to get to us one or two at a time, while making themselves vulnerable from all of us. The poles and handholds were always going to be a problem, but as long as we stood our ground in this position, the interior obstacles would be more of a hindrance to the attackers than us.

I really wished we'd spent more time practicing this, as we were without a backup. My *Protective Shell* spell wouldn't reset for another 19 hours. I shook my head, realizing how much time we'd saved by only sleeping for two hours. Still, with only nine more days to find a path to the exit, we couldn't afford to waste time.

As I watched, Katia's shape changed. She grew shorter, more squat while her arms grew in length, with bulges at her forearms, making her look like a deranged Popeye. Her face gritted with pain as she altered. I knew the faster she changed, the more it hurt. She'd been practicing this in the training room. I wasn't certain this was the best shape, but it was impressive and kind of gross at the same time.

"That's right, Mongo. Good boy. Don't. Don't! Yes, that's right. Stay!" Donut called, trying to keep the pet from rushing forward. The dinosaur was bouncing up and down in anticipation, squealing in anger at the bonkers.

The bonkers' enthusiasm for attacking us waned in the five seconds between them rushing into the room and realizing they faced a party that included a dinosaur. The forward creature stumbled as he tripped over the corpse of the first chomper. He righted himself, only to collapse after getting hit in the head by a well-placed magic missile.

The next two came at us side by side, swinging their clubs. One swung at Mongo, but the wooden, spiked club caught on the pole just as Mongo slashed forward with his feet. The creature was disemboweled before he even felt the reverberation of his club against the metal pole.

At the same time, the other attacker swung at me as Donut lobbed a pair of missiles at the two bonkers in the back row.

Katia spun and caught the swing with her right arm. She didn't put her arm in front of the club, but behind it, catching it as it swung downward. She added to the momentum, forcing the club to swing down and to my left, causing the bonker to stumble. It grunted in surprise. Katia retracted her arm as I jumped forward and punched, smashing the wide monster in the face. It crumpled to the ground, and I stomped on its head. Its jaw crackled like glass under the crush of my foot.

A life bar formed over Katia, but it didn't appear as if she'd really lost any health.

The last two monsters were on the ground, piled on top of one another. Both had been hit with a magic missile, though a low-powered one. Neither was dead. I activated my new Talon Strike ability and stepped forward. With two quick foot jabs, I smashed open both of their heads.

"That's really disgusting, Carl," Donut said. "Every time your foot gets stronger, the amount of blood that comes out is more and more."

"Are you okay?" I asked Katia as I wiped my foot on the side of the pole. "That was pretty slick."

"It didn't really hurt so much as sting," she said, rubbing her arm. "I caught one of the spikes, but it mostly scraped against the metal part of my arm. Mostly."

"Okay, good," I said. "Just be careful. I almost accidentally punched you and not the monster."

"Yeah, it's hard in these close quarters."

Four more bonkers entered the car and came charging at us.

"Well, the good news is we can try this again," I said, backing up. "Reset the formation."

5

WE WERE DONE WITH THE REST OF THE MONSTERS ONLY A FEW MIN-
utes later. We'd only had to face the creatures in cars three and four.
Whatever was in car number five, it didn't easily allow the passage
of the monsters from the sixth car. On the map, that fifth train was
similarly shaped to the janitors' quarters, but there was some sort of
odd square structure within. We needed to check it out, but we
didn't have time. We only had a couple of minutes until we reached
the next stop.

"Okay, let's set up," I said.

I had fabricated multiple quick and dirty car fortifications using
the engineering workbench. I had two types of defenses. Exterior
door blocks and gangway blocks. I'd made four door blocks and two
of the gangway ones, which would allow us to hopefully isolate an
entire train car for ourselves as long as we cleared it first. And as long
as the exterior doors only opened on one side. If we came across any
stations where the doors on both sides of the train opened simultaneously, we were going to be in trouble.

"Phantom Kangaroo coming up," came the announcement. The
voice was similar to the last train, but not identical. "That'll be station number 84. After that is stop number 85, which is an exit-only
cavern stop. Thanks for riding the Tangle."

I moved into the gangway and closed the door to train car number three. I pulled the massive sheet of metal out of my inventory.
I'd made it just about the right size. There wasn't anything fancy
about it. It was just a giant rectangular hunk of metal with rounded

edges that I wedged into the space. It'd originally been a swordsman breastplate that I'd thinned out to about a fifth-of-an-inch thickness, which allowed me to make it pretty big. The thing was solid and heavy as shit. It'd probably take four or five normal humans to lift it. If I didn't have my foot buff active, it'd shatter my foot if I dropped it in the wrong place. I called it the "gangway chock." The obstruction was much larger than either of the doors, and it was wide enough that no monsters would be able to wriggle or slide around it, not unless they were tiny. And even then, they'd only be able to come one at a time. Since I could easily pull the wedge in and out of my inventory, it was no real impediment for me.

Next came the exterior door blocks. These were tall wedges fashioned from altered weight benches. I used crossbars, similar to the supports we used for the portable redoubt, to slide through holes in the top, middle, and bottom of each wedge. We slid the wedges against the doors and shoved the crossbars through the holes, snaking them through the handholds by the exit doors, which kept the wedge loosely in place. I'd been afraid that I'd accidentally make the wedges too wide, and I ended up making them too slim. I would need to engineer something that was either adjustable or modular. Or better yet, what I really needed was to get my hands on several industrial jacks or post shores. Something we could quickly construct and break down. In the meantime, this would have to do.

I nervously inspected my wedge system. I put a hand against it, and it rattled back and forth. On the red line car, the handhold system was set up differently, so my design wasn't perfect, and a monster or two could probably force their way in after a few seconds. But hopefully this would keep us from getting overwhelmed. The moment we had a free moment, I'd pull out my new tape measure and get accurate dimensions of the doorways, the gangways, and everything else I could think of.

"These things don't look very stable, Carl," Donut said as the car slowed to a stop.

"Nope," I said.

A new type of monster lounged about the platform. These were large, green-skinned fish-looking dudes. There was only a handful of them, and none of them appeared too interested in fighting anybody. These were like full-sized kua-tin, but more monstrous-looking than the gleeners. Each of them had massive milk white eyes. They started to lazily line up at the landing. A pair of the creatures stood on the platform outside of car number two. They didn't seem to notice us examining them through the windows. I examined their properties.

Pollyslog. Level 22.
   Of all the monsters from prehistoric kua-tin mythology, the Pollyslogs are some of the most fearsome. They are strong, intelligent, and gigantic. At least compared to the kua-tin. So what I'm really saying is, they're moderately durable, dumb as a sack of pickled turnips, and, well, they are pretty big. They also secrete acid from their fingers, so you might want to watch out for that.

It sounded like the AI was still pissed at Borant. I wondered how long that would last.

"Get ready to repel boarders," I said.

Donut grunted. "You know this isn't a boat, right? All this starboard and aft and pirate talk is starting to really annoy Mongo, especially since we don't know what the hell you're talking about half the time."

Katia laughed. The door slid open. Through the window, I watched as one of the pollyslogs walked right into the wedge. It reached up and touched it with a webbed hand.

Up until this moment, the creatures had been acting strangely lethargic. That changed the instant the monster realized it couldn't get on board. It started screaming and banging its hands against the barricade. A doorway down, the second pollyslog did the same. This second one started smashing himself against it like he was trying to break down a door. The one closer to me managed to slide his long green arms around the obstruction, hugging it. Both monsters squealed in outrage as the doors started to close a moment later.

I rushed forward and slammed against the wedge, pushing it back.

The doors did not work like normal subway doors. The fish monster's arms severed off with a loud *crunch*. The two arms slopped to the ground, leaving a sizzling trail where they grasped onto the wedge.

"Don't," Donut yelled at Mongo, who was about to gobble them up.

The second pollyslog had managed to also get killed by the door, but this one had gotten more of his body into the car. The door cut him in half, leaving a mess of gore between the wedge and the doorway. The back half of his fish body remained there, attached to the outside of the door. As the train started moving, it caught on the wall, likely leaving a stream of gore down the entire side of the train.

I gingerly took the two arms into my inventory as I quickly measured the exterior doorway.

We had ten minutes to stop number 85. I didn't hear any commotion coming from car number three. It didn't appear any of the pollyslogs had gone into that car.

"Let's go check out car number five," I said. "Maybe there will be clues in there telling us what to do."

I quickly removed all the fortifications. We moved to car number three, which was empty, as I suspected. So was car number four.

The fifth car featured a thicker but unlocked door, just like with the 15th car. There was a sign on the door reading, **Do Not Enter. Tangle Employees Only.** I hesitantly slid it open, peering inside. I saw the white dot indicating an NPC just as the door slid open. I relaxed and stepped inside.

Entering Employee Break Room.

This was a wide-open room with a set of benches and tables against one wall and a large bar against the other. About halfway down the car was what appeared to be a separate room that took up about a third of the total space. The sign over this room said, **Conductor's Quarters.**

A dwarf sat at the bar, leaning into a drink. I had the immediate impression he'd been parked there for some time. He wore a wrinkled uniform similar to the uniforms the janitor ghouls wore.

Vernon. Yellow Line Train Conductor. Dwarf. Level 32.

"Employees only," Vernon said, not bothering to look up from his drink. "Passengers aren't allowed in here. If you want to get to the other cars, you gotta get out and go around at the next stop."

"That doesn't seem very efficient," Donut said.

"Conductor?" I said. I thumbed over my shoulder. "Shouldn't you be in that other train car?"

"That's the engineer," Vernon said, looking up. "I don't go in there, and he don't come in here. Look, folks, I can't let you through. The monsters follow the rules and don't come in here. If they can do it, so can you."

"So what do you do, then?" Donut asked, ignoring his demands for us to leave.

The dwarf took a long pull of his drink. "I take care of the train, and I am in charge of all the employees. That's what I'm supposed to do. But the engineer doesn't listen to me, the janitors try to eat me, and the porters are in their own little world. So what I do, Miss Talking Cat, is I sit here and drink until we reach the end of the line. Then I do it again."

I took a step deeper into the room. "So this train *does* circle around," I said.

"Porters?" Donut asked. "On a subway car?"

Vernon blinked and looked at Donut again. I recognized that look. *And here it comes.*

"Your Majesty," the train conductor said, stumbling to his feet. His drink went flying. He saluted her. "My apologies. I didn't realize we had royalty on board."

"It's quite all right," Donut said, immediately falling into her royal persona. "I know your job must be difficult, dealing with all this filthy riffraff."

"Oh it is, Your Majesty. It really is difficult. So, uh, is there something I can do for you?"

We were interrupted by two red dots entering the car from train six. It was a pair of Jikininki janitors, both of them holding a broom and a dustpan. One made a moaning noise through his chattering teeth as they shuffled forward. Their mouths never stopped moving, like pistons. I could hear them clicking together, even over the rumble of the train. *Click, click, click, click.* I shuddered.

"Oh crap," Katia said, stepping in front of me. I held her back.

I remembered the description, and it said they'd leave you alone if you left them alone.

"Get out of the way," I said. "Let them through." We pressed up against the wall as the monsters passed. Mongo shrieked in anger, but Donut hissed at the dinosaur to be good. The two ghouls didn't even look at us as they proceeded up the train.

"There must be a mess in one of the forward cars," Vernon said. "I should see to that."

"Actually, Vernon," Donut said, "we have a few questions about the train. I hope you can answer them for us."

"Of course, Your Majesty," he said. "How may I help?"

I spoke instead of Donut. "You didn't answer my question. So this train circles around? Where does it go after the last stop? Does it turn onto a different line?"

"Everyone has to get off at the last stop. Stop 435," he said. "It's the end of the line."

"I know that," I said. "But what happens after that?"

He suddenly looked extremely uncomfortable. "I can't say."

"You can't say? Or you won't?"

"Look, you have to get off at 435. And you really should get off at 433. There's a big transit hub there. There's nothing after that. Stop 434 is out of service, and 435 is the end of the line."

"Vernon," Donut said, "why are you avoiding Carl's question?"

He looked as if he might bolt. But then he stood and walked around the bar and produced what looked like a jug of moonshine. I quickly examined the bottle, and it was regular moonshine, not the more expensive Rev-Up Moonshine. Vernon took a swig directly from the bottle and sighed. "I'm sorry, Your Majesty. I only know the rumors. The truth is, I don't actually remember. We pull into station 435, and then everything gets fuzzy. And suddenly I'm standing on the platform of station 10, which is really just the yard. And I climb onto the train, and it all starts over again. I don't even know how much time has passed."

"Huh," I said. "That's weird."

"It is," he said. "Sometimes I talk to the others at the yard, but nobody knows. It's the same with everyone. It's always been this way."

I remembered that map of the *Nightmare Express* line. It had a stop number 436, one higher than the end of the line. "You said you've heard rumors. What are they?"

"There's a few," he said. "Some of the guys, they say we're in a time loop. I think they might be right, but only partially."

"What do you mean?"

He showed us his forearm, which had a long scar running down it. "I got this a while back. A Brain Amoeba from stop 354. Chupacabra Station. I normally don't go out there if they're in the cabin, but I missed one, and it got me good. I was bleeding something fierce. If we were in a time loop, then I'd heal right back up when we jumped back to the yard. But I didn't heal. If I'm hungry at the end of the line, I'm still hungry when we start over. Plus the passengers aren't always the same. I can tell time is moving right. Sort of." He tapped the bottle of moonshine. "But here's the weird thing. The train *is* in a loop. I could pour this bottle of shine on the floor, and it'll return to its spot on the shelf back there the next time around."

"So you're blacking out and getting transported to the station, and the train is resetting each time? What about the rest of the crew? The zombie guys and the engineer and whoever else?"

"It's just me and the porters standing on the station when I come to. The ghouls are different each time. They get on at station 12."

Station 12 was one of the stations that held staircases. "And the engineer?"

He shrugged. "It's the same guy. He might be getting off at the same time as me, but I'm not sure. He's always already on the train by the time I come to. But sometimes it's a different guy, so I know he ain't looping, either."

"That really is bizarre," Katia said. "Is the engineer a dwarf like you?"

"He ain't no dwarf," Vernon said. "I've never actually seen any of 'em, but based on his voice, I think he's human. Every new run I turn off the speakers in this cabin so I don't gotta hear his voice. Humans got voices like a spike in my brain."

"Don't I know it," Donut said.

"There's more, too. About the train, I mean." Vernon reached into his jacket pocket and pulled out a thick bundle of papers. He dropped the papers on the bar. I stepped closer. The top sheet was a crude drawing of a female dwarf.

"It's my wife," he said. "I had this made before I took this job. I put the drawing on my bedside in my cabin. One day, I stuck it in my pocket." He gestured at the pile. "Eventually, this happened."

The next paper was the same drawing. They were all the same drawing. Dozens of them.

"I can only hold so many. But each time, I stick the drawing in my jacket, and when we start over, I still have the drawing, but the original is still in my cabin. It only works with stuff that was on the train on my first day. Including this." He pulled a sack from his other pocket and poured several hundred gold coins onto the counter. "I had ten gold when I started. I had the coins on my nightstand."

"Why don't you leave?" I asked. "Go home the next time you end up at station 10?"

He shrugged. "I ain't trapped. Some of the guys at the yard do leave and go home. I'm sticking it out until I can't hold any more gold because I know the moment one of those other bastards finds out about my ten gold coins, they'll try to weasel their way onto this train. No way I'm letting some greasy dwarf steal my magic gold supply while giving him such fine stroke material." He gestured at the picture of his wife. "Each trip I get paid the equivalent of ten trips because of the money loop. I'll eventually go home to my wife." He started gathering his gold coins back up. "One day."

"Do you have a more extensive map?" I asked. "Like a map of the whole train system?"

He chuckled. "A map of the entire Tangle? I don't think there is such a thing."

I felt the train slow and heard a muffled announcement. We were stopping at station 85.

Vernon looked up. "The monsters are getting off. The next span isn't so bad. We got Snakeheads at 86 and 87. They look the same, but they fight each other. Station 88 is Mothman Station, and a few of the Skinned Mollies get on. They're pretty scary to look at, but they're slow. Next one, 89, is a transit station. Yellow line and indigo line."

"Indigo?" Katia said, perking up. "That's where the Daughters are." But before I could come up with an excuse to stay away, her face soured. "Never mind. They're on the Winter Sky line now."

"I don't know that one," Vernon said. "There's a lot of colors."

"How many?" I asked.

He shrugged. "Some say thousands. I don't know about that. There's only so many colors."

"Do the monsters always get off every five stops?" I asked.

"Yes. I don't know why. They're usually pretty excited about it, too."

This guy was an invaluable source of information. I knew we'd never get this much out of him if we didn't have Donut and her outrageous charm.

"Do the monsters ever miss their stop or stay on?"

He nodded. "I've seen it happen a few times. If one of the beasties misses his exit, he'll usually get off the next stop if he can. They're always in a big panic when that happens. Once a Goateo from station 212 tried to loop around. He stayed on all the way to the end of the line. It was the only time I've ever seen something remain on the train."

"So this mob managed to stay on the train?" I asked. "He was still there when you got back on?"

"Sort of," Vernon said. "His skeleton was still on the train. His skin and blood and hair wasn't. Whatever happened after station 435 ended up killing him. It killed him a lot."

"How do you communicate with the engineer?" I asked.

He shook his head. "I don't. I got a horn in my quarters, but it don't work. He never responds."

"Do you ever just go in there to talk to him?"

"Nope. It's locked tighter than an elf's bunghole. You need an engineer's key to get in."

"Does he ever come out?"

"I've never seen it. I've never even seen the interior of the engine train."

"How can we get him to come out?" Katia asked.

"I've only heard of an engineer coming out of his train once," Vernon said. "And that was under some pretty extreme circumstances."

"What was that?" I asked.

"Derailment."

WE ENDED UP TALKING TO VERNON FOR ANOTHER HOUR WHILE THE train rocketed down the track. We asked about the 10th car, which was the porter car, but all he said was, "Those guys are crazy." We also asked about the non-colored trains like the *Nightmare*, which he didn't know much about. Though he did say something interesting. While each colored line had hundreds of trains on a track at any given moment, he believed there was only one of the larger trains per line. He didn't know much about the tracks and the system other than that. Trains did not cross tracks with other trains. The tracks worked like highways with the tunnels going above and below one another. I asked if there was a safe way to traverse the tracks, like a maintenance tunnel or walkway, and he just laughed.

After every five stops, the train would be completely empty of monsters until the next stop. Donut, Mongo, and I decided to go check out the porter room after we hit station number 115. There'd been a lot of transit stations recently, but there weren't many for the next long stretch, which gave us time to go exploring. According to Vernon, the monsters would break into both cars 15 and 10 if they knew we were there, but he insisted they'd never attack his car, number five. But when he said it, I could tell he wasn't certain.

The time between stations varied greatly. Sometimes the stations would come one after another, coming every minute or two. And then there'd be a stretch of 20 minutes. It turned out, the entire trip from stations 11 to 435 took three whole days, which was alarming. My initial instinct was that we needed to stay as close to the stairwells as possible, but I was starting to suspect we'd need to get ourselves to the end of the line to figure this out. We only had nine days.

The good thing was, if there truly was only one *Nightmare Express* train, that meant it managed to make its large figure-eight pattern in only an hour and a half. That meant we'd be able to end up back where we started fairly quickly if we decided it was necessary.

We left Katia with the conductor. He was relaying to her everything he knew about each station. He knew the monsters at each platform. He knew which ones were transit stations, but more importantly, he knew what specific colors and other lines connected at each transfer station. Katia was in turn giving this info to Mordecai, who grumbled and complained about being our secretary. But he did it.

We had 10 minutes to go check out the porter car. Stop 116 contained a monster Vernon called cornets. They used an aural attack.

"What we really need to do is find a neighborhood boss and kill it," Donut said as we peered into the empty car number six. We jogged down toward the next train. "They're supposed to have maps. I bet the bigger the boss, the bigger the map."

She was right. As soon as we were done exploring the train, we'd get off at one of the non–transit hubs and try to find a boss. And if not there, we'd go to one of these mysterious five stations and explore.

"Hey," I said as we moved down the train, "has Katia said anything to you about Hekla?"

"What do you mean?" Donut asked. "I did ask Katia to tell Hekla some stuff for me. Hekla does this awesome ninja kick thing before she pops you in the face with her crossbow." From my shoulder, Donut feigned a karate kick and made a little "Wah-chaw!" noise. "I wanted to know if she had a name for the move because it was so awesome. Katia asked her, and Hekla said it was now named the 'Donut Kick.' Isn't that great?"

"Just be careful, okay?" I said. "It's good to share information about the trains, but don't be giving other crawlers too much info about ourselves. Especially where we are."

"Why not?"

I hesitated. I didn't want to tell her the true reason for my concern. "We have bounties on our heads now, Donut. We need to be careful. Even with Hekla."

Donut looked as if she might object, but she didn't say anything else.

The note over the tenth car read, **Porters Only. Knock for Service.** I tried the sliding door, but it was locked. It wasn't magically locked like the engine car. It felt flimsy, and I knew I could force it if I had to.

"Should I break in or knock?" I asked.

"Why be rude? Knock," Donut said.

I knocked, and the top half of the door slid open a half second later, startling me so much I almost fell backward. The enormous face of an NPC gleamed back at me.

You've discovered the Yellow Line Reward Room!
You may only collect one prize per crawler, per train line.

Donut gasped in pleasure. The last reward room we'd found resulted in us getting Mongo.

The large, moon-faced creature smiled back at the cat on my shoulder. He reminded me of Lurch from *The Addams Family*, but with a wider pale face and hair that looked like it was made of dying moss. He wore the now-familiar uniform suit with a hat that read, "Porter."

Pierre. Grapple. Yellow Line Porter. Level 25.

This is a non-combatant NPC.

A Grapple is your everyday quarter giant. Centuries ago when the High Elves discovered how subservient hill giants were, they immediately moved to capture and enslave their entire race. The problem with hill giants is that they're pretty darn big, and they lack the fine motor skills to properly set out a dinner service. So a breeding system was implemented, crossing the hill giants with the almost-as-compliant Vegetal Ogrids. Their offspring were then culled of all but the most servile. These half-giant mongrels were then further bred down with large humans, creating a slave race known as the Grapple. Grapple servants are common across the universe, but they do require close supervision. If you leave them alone for too long, they tend to get . . . squirrelly.

"How may I help you?" Pierre the porter asked. He spoke slowly with a gravelly voice.

"Where's our prize?" Donut demanded before I could think of something to say.

This was not what I was expecting. Over Pierre's shoulder, I could see a room full of shelves. On each shelf were racks and racks of suitcases. At the far end of the car stood a second grapple porter, who leaned up against the door to train car number 11.

We only had about five more minutes before we'd hit the next stop.

"What is your suitcase number?"

You must choose a number between 1 and 200. You may only make one choice.

"I'm suitcase number eight!" Donut said, excitement rising in her voice. "And my friend Katia says she's number 12."

"Your friend must come and get her own suitcase," the porter said. He turned to me. "What is your number?"

"I'm number one," I said.

"Very well," he said. He turned and went down the line of shelves, pulling two suitcases. Case number one was a black roller bag, and Donut's case number eight was a large yellow case with flowers on it that looked straight from the 1960s.

"This is just like that show *Deal or No Deal*," Donut said. "We need to go back to the red line and get the prize on that train, too!"

"Here you are. Have a nice day," the porter said, sliding the bags through. I grabbed each in turn. The little half door slammed closed, leaving us alone in the gangway.

I tried to pull the bags into my inventory, and I received an error message.

Prize cases must be opened before they can be added to your inventory.

"Let's open them now!" Donut said.

I grabbed the suitcases, one in each hand. "Not here. Let's go back. We have to hurry." We turned and jogged back up to car number five. I wanted to make sure we got into the conductor's room before the monsters at the next station saw us. We made it just in time.

Katia and Vernon looked up at us as we entered the room.

Vernon shook his head. "Those crazy grapples are always mixing up everyone's luggage."

"We gotta go back and get Katia's suitcase, too!" Donut said.

I tossed my case onto the counter next to the jar of moonshine. This was not like a loot box, where it opened magically. I had to zip it open. I pulled the zipper around and opened the top, peering inside.

"What is it? What is it?" Donut asked.

I reached in and pulled out the red lingerie. The suitcase was full of women's clothing, high-heeled shoes, and a bunch of brochures about things to do in Delaware.

"This is just someone's suitcase," I said. "It's not a real prize."

"Wait, what's that?" Donut asked, pointing to a bulge in one of the pockets.

I opened it up, and I pulled out three potions. Two mana potions and something new.

Invisibility Potion.
  Guess what this does.

"Oh hell yeah," I said. It now let me put everything into my inventory, including the suitcase and clothes.

I felt the train finally start to slow as we reached station number 116. The announcement came, but I could barely hear it. I think he said this was called Banshee Station.

"Do mine, do mine!" Donut said, hopping up and down on my shoulder. I pulled her suitcase onto the counter. Katia and Vernon stopped their discussion to watch as I pulled the zipper on the case.

YOU SURE YOU WANNA DO THAT, BUCKO?

The notification was a type I'd never seen before. It surprised me enough that I stopped unzipping the bag and took a step back.

Later, I would realize it was my Find Traps skill activating for the first time. At the moment, I had no idea what was happening. But then I noticed the suitcase.

I'd unzipped it only a couple inches, but that was enough. The red flaming ants poured from the hole, sweeping over the counter and surging at us. The drawings of Vernon's wife were also on the counter, and the sheets of paper burst into flames.

Literal Fire Ants. Level 1.

  This is a trap monster.

  Like regular fire ants, but with more enthusiasm. Plus they hate you and want you to die. They're pretty good at making that happen.

They just kept coming and coming, surging from the suitcase, which had burst into flames. Like the description said, they were just like regular ants but on fire. There were suddenly thousands of them, more than the bag could really have held. They were fast. We all jumped back as the waves of insects spread forth, covering the bar in a matter of seconds. Flames rose wherever the bugs touched. Black smoke started to fill the car.

The bottle of moonshine on the counter, sitting in the midst of the fire, blinked, and then a notification appeared over it. **Explosion Imminent.** A red set of numbers rocketed toward zero.

"Oh fuck," I said. "Run!"

The moonshine bottle exploded, spreading flaming liquid throughout the car. Katia was thrown from her feet, and Mongo squealed in pain. The ceiling and walls were suddenly on fire, and the ants were everywhere.

"Fuck," I cried in pain, slapping myself in the face.

"I'm on fire! Help! I'm on fire!" Donut screamed, her voice high-pitched and panicked. I pulled her from my shoulder and slapped at the flames on her tail, further burning my hand. She had two little ants on her. I smushed them between my fingers.

"Go, go!" I cried, pointing toward the forward door as the ants surged at us. Katia's health had blipped down more than I expected. *We're not moving. The train is stopped at the station. Her momentum bonus isn't active.*

Mongo glowed as he scrambled to his feet. Donut had cast *Heal Critter* on him. He squawked in fear. We all turned and ran toward the door.

Vernon cried out. I looked over my shoulder as a flaming wave swept over him. And then he was just gone. An impossible amount of ants swelled, crawling up the walls, sweeping over the floor. More explosions echoed from behind the bar as bottles went up.

We burst into car number four. Three tall, terrifying monsters turned at the intrusion. They looked like skinless, eyeless, human-sized jackrabbits walking on two legs. These were monsters from Banshee Station who'd just gotten on moments before.

The doors to the train were still open, but they'd close at any moment.

"Out, out onto the platform!" I cried. I still clutched on to Donut.

The first of the doors was right there, and I leaped through, hoping the others would make it in time. Mongo and Katia jumped through just as the doors snapped shut.

The platform was empty. All of the rabbit monsters—the cornets—had gotten on the train. The three monsters in train car number four turned their eyeless heads toward us just as the train started to move. We watched in horror as the monsters were overwhelmed, one by one, by a creeping, crawling wave of flames.

We stood there in silence on the platform as the train picked up speed and disappeared into the tunnel. As it rumbled away, I could still hear Vernon's terrified final screams echoing in my head.

"That was the worst prize ever," said Donut.

6

Unlike the previous platform, this one held multiple exits. The moment the train pulled away, more red dots appeared, shuffling up toward the station. These were more monsters getting ready for the next train, which would be here in about ten minutes.

"I can see the whole area on the map," Katia said. "It's not too big. There are a lot of twisting tunnels and four big rooms. One is what looks like a boss room like the ones on the first floor. There aren't any safe rooms. I see a pair of the bathrooms, though. Weird. There aren't any on the trains."

"This tunnel," Donut said, pointing to one near the end of the platform. "I don't see any monsters in that one."

We jogged toward the passageway, which was nothing more than a low, rocky cave. Water dripped from the ceiling. Donut activated her *Torch*.

We waited for a minute, catching our breath. Behind us, several of the skinless rabbits filled the station. Even from around the corner, I could hear them. They made an odd humming noise.

"There has to be a shitload of these cornets here," I said. "If monsters get on at every train, every ten minutes, all day long, then there has to be a constant stream of them."

"This station is big, but it's not huge," Katia said.

"Then they're either somehow getting back here after they get off at station 120, or the system is creating more of them." I remem-

bered the brindle grubs from the second floor. Those had been created on demand. But from what Mordecai said, they only did that
with the janitor mobs. There was usually a finite amount of the other
mobs. Once you killed them, they would not be replenished.

"Poor Vernon," Katia said. "That was horrible. He was saving up
money to buy his wife a new house."

"Yeah. Plus those bugs burned up my prize," Donut said. "It's not
fair."

"There is no wife," I said. "And there was no prize. The ants were
your prize, Donut. I guess we need to be more vigilant about traps
from now on. I need to figure out how to train my Find Traps skill.
It warned me, but much too late. My pedicure buff gives me a few
extra seconds if the trap is foot triggered, but obviously there are
other types of traps, too."

"What do you mean, there is no wife?" Katia said. "He was lying?"

"No," I said. "He believes or, I guess, believed he had a wife. This
floor has only been open for a day. Before this, he was probably a
dwarf doing something else. Whatever the fourth-floor theme was
the last time they ran the dungeon. When these floors are generated,
the NPCs are given artificial memories. It's all part of the story. This
entire floor is probably just the trains. He says he can go home, but
where's that? There is no home. No wife. It's really fucked-up because these aren't computer programs. These are actual living creatures who believe this is the real world."

"I never really thought of it that way," Katia said. "That's . . .
that's horrible."

I nodded. "It's just as bad as what they've done to us."

"So what's the plan?" Donut asked. From my shoulder, she
reached out and put her paw against the side of the cave wall. It came
away slimy. She frowned. "This place is disgusting."

I thought for a moment. "Since we're here, we should hit the boss
room if we can. Maybe we can figure out why they're always getting
on the train. Like with the NPCs, they can create them, give them
a story, and set them free, but they're not robots. There has to be a

reason why they're getting on the train and getting off. The more we know about this place, the better our chances of figuring out how to get the hell out of here."

We needed to first figure out what we were facing at this station. I had Donut scout out a tunnel with a single cornet so we could fight it.

The monsters were constantly moving from the deeper rooms to the platform. Donut's newly enhanced ability to see mobs on the map worked well, but it didn't extend that far. I wished there was a way to combine Katia's larger map, Donut's ability to see mobs at a greater distance, and my ability to hunt down traps all into a single interface.

"There's one moving down the tunnel by itself," Donut said. "It's a couple of turns that way."

We headed toward the monster.

ZEV: Hey, guys! Long time no talk.

DONUT: HI, ZEV!

ZEV: I know you're busy, but I wanted to check in. I'm still working on your mid-floor appearance. A lot of it is going to depend on what happens with the sponsorship bidding. Things are getting a little intense out there. The same with the two fan boxes you guys have coming.

DONUT: DID YOU SEE WE ARE ON THE TOP-10 LIST?

ZEV: Of course I saw. Actually, I wanted to bring something up really quick while I can.

CARL: Out with it.

ZEV: It's about Katia.

I stopped moving through the passageway. I held up my hand for the others to halt.

"What is it?" Katia asked.

"Just a minute," I said. "We're talking to our PR agent about something."

"*Now?*"

I could now see the monster's dot on the map. It was just around the corner. It had paused in the middle of the tunnel. I could hear the creature's odd humming, but there was another noise, too. A *clink, clink, clink.* I couldn't tell what it was.

DONUT: WHAT ABOUT KATIA?

ZEV: She's boring. People don't like her. Odette complained about her lackluster participation in the interview, and the tunnel is filled with people hoping she gets wasted just so it can be you two again. You either need to ditch her or make her more interesting. Tell her to spice it up. Maybe grow a Mohawk. I'm not allowed to message her directly yet, but I can talk to her face-to-face after your next interview if you want.

CARL: Are you fucking kidding me?

DONUT: MAYBE IF SHE MAKES HERSELF MORE SEXY-LOOKING, THAT WILL WORK. MAYBE MAKE HER BOOBS BIGGER LIKE ODETTE DID.

ZEV: Well, you need to do something. What's the point of adding a new character if she sucks? It's like when they added April to *Gilmore Girls*. But worse.

DONUT: OH NO. I WILL HELP HER.

CARL: She's an art history professor, not a circus poodle. If people don't like her, they can suck it.

ZEV: If they don't like her, they'll stop watching. If they stop watching, you'll get less views. If you get less views, you'll get less prizes from the fan boxes and sponsors. And we're just getting started with fan and sponsor prizes.

CARL: She's shy, and she's overwhelmed like the rest of us. You can't just expect someone to change like that.

DONUT: SURE WE CAN. WATCH.

"You need to grow a Mohawk," Donut said to Katia. "And maybe get a catchphrase. That really worked for Carl."

"Goddamnit, Donut," I said. I regretted it the moment the phrase came out of my mouth.

"What do you mean?" Katia asked. She reached up and touched her blond hair. She'd managed to make it look much more natural. Before, the hairs were too thick, almost like doll hair. Her face was also more natural-looking than before. She no longer looked like a burn victim and now just looked like someone who'd had too much cosmetic surgery. Like Bea's mom.

"She doesn't mean anything," I said. "It's not important right now."

"It *is* important, Carl. We shouldn't avoid conversations just because they're uncomfortable. Zev thinks since you're hanging with us, you need to be more vibrant."

"More vibrant?" she asked. "Is she saying I'm boring?"

"No," Donut lied. "She just thinks you'll get more followers if you give the viewers something to latch on to. It's not a bad thing. But people need to know who you are. You have to give them something to root for."

"My views have never been higher. I have almost ten billion followers. It was almost nothing until I joined your team."

"Oh, you precious thing," Donut said. "It's great—it really is—but those are rookie numbers. I have over 700 trillion."

I sighed. At least Donut was being diplomatic. "Look, now is not the time . . . Oh, fuck."

The rabbit monster must have heard us speaking. It started moving in our direction. Mongo growled.

"All right, we're shelving this. Formation two."

The tunnel was wide enough that we could stand side by side. Formation two was similar to formation one, but with me in the center. Donut remained on my shoulder, but she would jump down the moment I approached the monster. Mongo, Katia, and I would all charge at the same time while Donut remained in the rear. Mongo stood to my left, and Katia would take up a blocking formation on my right.

The tall creature turned the corner. It walked on two legs, but it was hunched forward. Its red skinless body seemed wet. The rabbit ears were absurdly long, reaching the ceiling. The thing had no eyes. Just a massive mouth with teeth. Its entire body hummed. The sound grew louder.

"Jesus," I said. The thing was hard to look at. It had arms with humanlike fingers. It was holding an empty potion vial in its hand, and it dropped it on the ground with a *clink*.

"It just took a potion," I said. "Watch out!"

Red Cornet. Level 21.

Well, what did you expect in an opera? A happy ending?

The Cornet is a devolved form of the more common Lepus, one of the most widespread semi-intelligent species across the known universe. During the early years of the Skull Empire's expansion, a system warlord developed a taste for a dish called Lepus hasenpfeffer, which caused the Lepus on that planet to be hunted to near extinction. A band of the hunted fled to the extensive lightless caves of the planet and disappeared for several thousand years.

The devolved Lepus lost its sight, but it developed its rudimentary echolocation skills into an impressive attack. They don't normally run around without skin. We just added that part because it makes them scary as shit.

Donut nailed the creature with two missiles, bowling it over. The rabbit screamed, and the humming noise increased. The creature scrambled back, almost dead. Its two ears flattened backward, and I suddenly felt a wave of nausea wash over me. My vision went double. My ears rang. I was abruptly on my knees, and I didn't know why. I couldn't move. I vomited my hamburger and French fries on the ground.

You've been rendered Queasy!

A moment later, the feeling ceased. I groaned, looking up. The cornet was dead with Mongo on top of the creature, ripping it to pieces. Donut and Katia had also grown ill. It didn't seem to have an effect on Mongo.

I groaned again, as groaning seemed the most appropriate response after being suddenly and violently ill, and I rolled away from the puddle of vomit. I looked up at the dinosaur, who was happily devouring the skinless creature. It had dropped a few gold coins, and that was it. Mongo grunted happily as he ate.

"How is it you're okay when everything else makes you sick?" I grumbled. Jesus. I hated throwing up.

CARL: Mordecai. We're fighting walking rabbits that make us puke. The debuff is called Queasy. How do we fight it?

MORDECAI: That's usually from an auditory attack. Putting in earplugs won't help. I can whip you up a potion that'll negate it, but that won't do you any good right now. Were Donut and Mongo affected?

I looked over at the cat, who had vomit running down her face. She was rapidly licking her paw and cleaning it off.

CARL: Donut, yes. Mongo, no.

MORDECAI: Okay. I honestly don't know how these attacks work. They're not magical. It's a physical thing, but it only works on certain anatomies. You're going to have to lead with Mongo. The good news is, your body quickly builds up a natural resistance to this sort of attack. This is a real thing that exists outside the dungeon, designed to incapacitate prey. My advice is to fight a few more of these guys in as small groups as possible until it no longer affects you. You'll probably get a skill notification called Queasy Resistance or something.

"Ugh," I said. "This is going to suck."

"What do you make of this?" Katia asked. She picked up the potion vial the monster had dropped.

"Toss it here," I said.

It wasn't a normal potion vial, as those usually puffed away into smoke. Still, it was the same size and shape. There was a tiny amount of golden liquid at the bottom, less than half a bead. I flipped the vial over, and the liquid didn't come out, like it was honey.

Used vial.

I knew if I could get that liquid closer to the edge of the bottle I might be able to get the system to give me a description. I pulled it in and then out of my inventory. That didn't work. I tapped the glass against the rock wall in an attempt to dislodge the liquid. *Clink.*

That was the sound I'd heard earlier. That red cornet had been trying to do the same thing, I realized. Weird. Now I really wanted to know what this stuff was.

I smashed the vial hard enough to break the glass. *Crunch.* The moment the glass broke, the whole thing puffed away like it normally did with a potion. There was no sign of the liquid.

"Damn," I said.

For the next few hours, we trained our Queasy Resistance skill, all the while creeping toward the boss room at the back of the tunnel system. Mongo managed to hit level 14, which caused him to grow about six inches taller and a foot longer. One more level before he was full size. Katia hit 22. Donut and I both were on the precipice of leveling up as well, though it was slow going when we were only killing lower-level monsters.

I also spent the time training my neglected *Fear* spell and casting the fire- and electric-enhancing *Bang Bro* on my gauntlet, though I didn't get to actually use it. Meanwhile, Donut trained her *Second Chance*, her *Clockwork Triplicate*, and her new *Hole* spell, which currently did absolutely nothing but put a circular, temporary one-inch dimple into walls. It did not work on mobs directly.

Mongo was getting proficient at killing them on his own, despite being a much lower level. The cornets were slow to react once we turned the corner, and when they did fight back in time, they usually moved straight to their nausea attack. By the time they realized the dinosaur was immune, they were already on their backs, being ripped to pieces. If I hit them with the *Fear* spell, they'd turn to run, but Mongo was faster.

As for loot, these monsters were mostly a bust. Most dropped a few coins and sometimes cornet meat or random organs, which we'd add to the alchemy table's supplies. Mordecai once said most monsters wouldn't directly drop good loot on the first several floors. The worthy stuff would come from loot boxes and not the mob corpses. That'd change around the sixth floor when we'd start facing better-equipped opponents.

All three of us received the notification we were now resistant to the Queasy debuff at the same time, after getting hit with it for what had to be the dozenth time in an hour. I'd long since puked out every last drop of my own stomach's contents.

The red cornets were moving in a predictable pattern. They seemed to all be coming from one dead-end section of the tunnel. From there they'd move into one of three larger rooms. An equal number would leave these and head for the train station.

What we thought was the likely boss room was in a separate area at the other end of the tunnels. This room was bigger yet and only had one approach, which made me nervous. Donut's ability to see distant mobs—which I'd started calling her "monster vision"—didn't work in the closed-off area, which further added to my hesitation. I prepared a few smoke bombs and other explosives in case we needed to make a hasty retreat.

"Here we go," I said as we entered the long hallway to the back room. The cave system gave way to a regular, long hallway made of rough and unfinished concrete blocks. The floor itself was made of smooth concrete.

We slowly approached the chamber, seeing or hearing no sign of the cornets. The large metallic double doors reminded me of similar entrances we'd seen in other parts of the dungeon, most notably the entrance to the kobold fighting pits. These were barn-style doors designed to allow something large to get through.

There were no signs or other indicators about what we were approaching, which was unusual for boss rooms. I put my ear to the door and heard nothing inside. I was afraid we'd slide the doors open and we'd get rushed by something. I prepared to jump aside.

I felt a familiar haptic buzz and looked down, surprised to see a glowing circle right underneath my feet.

"Back up, back up," I said, leaping off the symbol as if I'd just touched a hot stove.

"What is it?" Donut hissed, looking wildly about.

Nothing happened. I inspected the glowing circle, but there was no tooltip. It looked like something used in a satanic ritual mixed with the text from Frodo's One Ring. It was a circle with odd writing within, ringing the inside edge, with a large triangle symbol in the center. The symbol pulsed blue.

"What is that thing?" I asked. I hesitantly reached forward and hovered my hand over it. I was afraid it was a trap, but it didn't set off any of my trap warnings. I couldn't get any info out of it at all. It had only appeared once I'd stared at it.

"What?" Katia asked, looking down.

"You don't see it?"

"There's nothing there, Carl," said Donut.

I sent a message to Mordecai, describing the symbol.

MORDECAI: That's a control sigil. Only you can see it because of your Escape Plan skill. They're mostly used by secondary programs, like *Vengeance of the Daughter*. But they're sometimes used by the dungeon creators, too. I don't know too much about this stuff, but I know their use is considered sloppy programming because they're easy to break. Sigils have all sorts of uses, but they're typically for controlled

gating. They can stop a specific type of mob from passing the
symbol. They can be turned off and on by the showrunners,
not the dungeon AI, which is why they use them. If it's blue, it
means the symbol is turned on. It will have no effect on you.

CARL: Is there a way for crawlers to make these things?

MORDECAI: No. Not directly. There's another type of sigil that
looks similar and mostly acts the same way, but it's a type
of magic you'll never have enough mana to do. Donut might.

After waiting a few more minutes, we decided to proceed into the
room. We slid open the doors, revealing a large warehouse. We
jumped in, weapons at the ready. No red dots appeared. No boss
music started. The doors did not magically close behind us.

I looked about the mostly empty room, lowering my fist. In the
middle of the space sat an empty metal bin with chain-link walls,
like a dumpster-sized shopping cart. The cart appeared brand-new
and untouched. I stepped toward it to examine it further.

Wire Cage Materials Cart. Wheeled. It'd probably be fun to roll
down a hill in this thing.

"Well, this is disappointing," said Donut.

"Uh, guys?" I said, pointing at the shadowy far end of the room.
Two bulldozer-sized contraptions sat against the far wall. I'd first
thought they were indentations on the wall. The air just above the
pair of black-and-silver apparatuses distorted, indicating the machines were turned on and venting hot exhaust. At first look, they
looked like lumpy blocks of metal, but I could see the distinct break
outlines along the edges. Their true shape came into focus. I played
with enough Transformers toys as a kid to immediately recognize
what I was looking at. The blocks had arms and legs.

These were a pair of robots, sitting down and turned off. They
did not have dots on the map at all. That's how the inactive swordsmen guards had appeared on the previous floor.

Dwarven Industrial Light-Duty Automaton. Contraption.

This contraption is in Sleep Mode.

These smaller-sized industrial workhorses are used to complete simple tasks, such as pushing bins full of ore up from the depths. They are not designed or commonly used for fighting or defense, but who are we kidding? Like you'd have a chance against these things if they wanted to smush you.

"These are the small ones?" I asked.

I was starting to realize that this was not a boss room. I had no idea *what* this was. It didn't appear the cornets used this room. So why was it here? At first I assumed that control sigil was for these two robots, as they were the only two things in here. But the more I thought about it, the less sense it made. Would they really need control sigils for something mechanical? But if not them, then who? I asked Katia and Donut if they had any ideas.

"Hmm," Donut said. "Maybe it's not to keep something in the room, but to keep it out. Maybe it's to keep the cornets away."

"Maybe," I said. "It's odd."

"It gets weirder," Katia said. "I've been talking to Hekla and Eva—she's another one of the Daughters, my friend from before—and they just found a similar room in another warren. She says it's the same thing. Two robots."

"Odd," I said. I put my hand against the chain-link cart. It rolled easily. There was a door on the side designed so one could effortlessly load something into it. I wondered if I could lift it. I wrapped my fingers into the chain links and heaved. It was heavy and awkward, but I easily lifted the wheels off the ground. I stuck it into my inventory.

"Let's blow up the robots," Donut said.

"I don't think that's a good idea," Katia replied, eyes going wide.

DONUT: Remember what I said about being more vibrant? You should agree with me. People love it when Carl blows stuff up.

Katia did not appear impressed with Donut's reasoning. I was about to agree with the woman, when I had a thought. I looked over my shoulder. The long concrete hallway appeared designed to handle the robots, but there was no way they'd fit in the tunnels beyond.

"Actually," I said, "let's do it. You know, for training. And science."

"Are you serious?" she asked.

I laughed. "The truth is, I need more materials for the crafting bench. There's only so much you can do with weight equipment. If we scrap these guys, I'll have enough material to build better train defenses."

"All right, I guess," she said. "But if we do this, maybe we should kill the rest of the cornets first, too. Clear the whole place out." She gave me a wink. "You know, for science."

> DONUT: That's the way to do it. Now we just need to work on the Mohawk and catchphrase.

WE KILLED THE CORNETS FIRST. NOW THAT WE WERE IMMUNE TO their one and only attack, it was pretty easy. I tested rolling a hob-lobber down one of the cave hallways to make sure the place wouldn't collapse, and it didn't. We roamed the halls, killing every one we came across. From there, we returned to the train landing and worked our way toward the gathering rooms.

Donut and I both leveled. Katia also leveled a second time. Donut raised her *Second Chance* resurrection spell to level seven. The spell cost ten mana. Each monster stayed animated for 14 minutes. She had an intelligence of 41, but with the buffs from the Good Rest bonus and the shower, the stat was temporarily raised to 49. Therefore, she currently had a pool of 49 mana points at her disposal, so she could raise four of the rabbit monsters, take a potion, and raise four more, which was a pretty formidable group.

We used this method to storm the three collective rooms. We sent seven in to fight, and in the midst of the chaos, we sent the eighth in holding a fused hob-lobber. After, I tossed in a smoke curtain, and we mopped up.

The rooms were nothing more than a filthy waiting area. The rabbits were mostly sleeping in clusters or leaning against the walls. They barely fought back. There was no sense of community here, like with the goblins. This wasn't an established settlement at all, which was odd. Up until this point, the game had made an attempt to add purpose and a reason for a mob's presence. It was usually a stupid reason, but it was there.

Thinking of the goblins reminded me of something else. A realization was starting to form. By the time we killed the ones in the third room and finished collecting all the dropped coins, I had a growing sense of unease.

"I think they're all stoned," I said.

"More meth?" Donut asked.

"Not meth. Something different."

We'd killed all of them except the ones emerging from the long, dark hallway, though none had appeared in a while now. We proceeded carefully down the hall, but nothing came. As we walked, my feet crunched. The floor here was littered with empty vials. If I didn't have that buff, my feet would be torn up by the glass. The far wall was blackened and scorched, like it'd been hit with a fireball. We waited, but nothing happened. No more cornets came. We'd cleared the area.

"I think they're going to that fifth stop to get these vials, getting their fix, and teleporting back here," I said. "When they start to come down from their high, they get back on the train."

"What does that have to do with the robot room?" Donut asked.

"I don't know. It doesn't make sense, especially if there's a robot room in all of these landings."

———

FOR THE TWO ROBOTS, I UTILIZED THREE STICKS OF HOBGOBLIN DY-namite and a detonator. I set the charges without incident, moved all the way back to the platform, and set them off.

We returned to find both of the robots turned to scrap metal. The hobgoblin dynamite was especially good at tearing stuff up. The bottom half of both robots remained mostly intact, but there were hunks of metal everywhere. The automatons hadn't turned on or fought back at all. The description changed to **Destroyed** on each one. After waiting for the gnarled metal to cool down, I spent some time collecting everything I could, including several fried and broken cogs and wheels. I found two dwarven batteries, both of them "damaged," according to the menu. It all went into the inventory.

Donut was giving fashion tips to Katia while we worked. Mongo spent the time running back and forth across the room, practicing jump attacks. The dinosaur chicken moved like a cheetah and was terrifying to behold. Just a few more kills, and he'd hit level 15.

Just before we finished, I received a message.

> **DANIEL:** Hey, man, you free? I got a message for you.
> **CARL:** Bautista. How are you doing?

I kept forgetting the man's first name was Daniel. I clicked on his name and reassigned his chat marker from "Daniel" to "Bautista."

> **BAUTISTA:** Surviving. Hey, so I'm at the Desperado Club. I just met a guy here who says he's in contact with someone else you know. A woman named Imani. She needs to talk to you. Says it's super important. It's something about two other guys. A Brandon and Chris or something like that. She says she'll try to be at the bar of the Desperado Club each night after the recap.
> **CARL:** Okay, thanks, man. We should really start meeting up regularly.
> **BAUTISTA:** Yeah, I think that's a good idea. I need to talk to you, too, about something else, but it's too complicated over chat. I hate this mental-typing shit. But you gotta be careful, man. I heard a few guys talking about hunting

down the leaderboard for the bounty. I don't know if they're
serious, but I don't think this bar is a safe room.

CARL: It's not. Thanks for the heads-up. So how'd you find the
club? We haven't come across any yet.

BAUTISTA: There's a trick. It turns out if it's a transfer station,
and the station's number ends in the number one, there'll
be a Desperado Club. If it ends in number nine, it's that
other place, Club Vanquisher. Anyway, talk to you later.

Relief washed over me with the knowledge that Imani was still
alive. She probably wanted to make sure that I knew Brandon was
dead. I swallowed, thinking about it. My knuckles burned with
phantom pain.

I sighed, pulling the last free hunk of metal into my inventory. I
received another weight-based achievement. I now had enough scrap
metal to build a decent-sized boat. I'd collected almost 15 tons of
materials from the two robots, and it was less than half of their mass.

"What do you think, Carl? Boots or no?" Donut asked.

I looked up to see Katia's tracksuit had changed to a slick black
bodysuit. She wore poorly shaped knee-high boots. She also now had
a purple Mohawk. She looked ridiculous. The woman had an odd
expression on her face, one I was having a hard time reading. It
seemed like a mix of exasperation, despair, and desperation.

Whatever it was, it was clear she did not want to be doing this.

"Just be yourself," I said.

"That's terrible advice, Carl," Donut said. "She's a doppelganger.
It's her job to be someone else."

"Be yourself? I don't know what that means anyway," she said,
shrugging. "I never really did."

I sighed. "Okay, guys. This has been a long day. The next transfer
station is 127, but I want to go to the one after that, which is station
131. Let's get on the train, get to the employee break room, and if
the conductor is in there, make him finish giving the list of stations
to Mordecai. I know you and Vernon got interrupted. On the way

there, we can do some more grinding if there are monsters we can handle. We'll ride all the way to 131, which'll supposedly have a Desperado Club. Plus, by the time we get there, we'll be able to open our fan boxes. Sound like a plan?"

Donut beamed. "We're going dancing tonight! It's Dirty Shirley time!"

7

Views: 50.2 Quadrillion
Followers: 890 Trillion
Favorites: 199.7 Trillion
Leaderboard rank: 6
Bounty: 100,000 gold

TRANSFER STATION 131.

The dwarf conductor on the next train was a heck of a lot grumpier than Vernon, but by the time we pulled up to station 131, we had the full list of stations all down the yellow line. Mordecai said he thought he might be onto something, but he wasn't certain yet. Tomorrow we were to attempt to hop over to a line that didn't intersect yellow and then get the same information. After that, we'd start exploring the non-colored lines.

We didn't get as much grinding done on the train as I'd like, but we did manage to kill a whole mess of monsters called Zlurpies, which were waist-high, semi-intelligent warrior-armadillo things. They rolled into armored balls when they started to take damage, but they were small enough to be eaten whole by Mongo, who would pick them up and crunch them like juice-filled hard candies.

Halfway through the skirmish with the armadillos, Mongo hit level 15.

He would continue to level after this, but he wouldn't get any bigger. Which was good because he was now huge. He was the height of a pony, coming up to just below my shoulders. From the tip of his beak to the end of his colorful red-and-blue-feathered tail, he was about 13 feet long, though more than half of that was tail. The individual claws on his feet were now bigger than his entire body had been when we first got him. He still fit in the individual subway cars okay, but if we came across smaller cars with rowed seating, it was going to be a tight squeeze, especially around the poles. I suspected he was going to be spending a lot of time in his carrier.

"Good boy! Good boy, Mongo! Carl, remember when he was a sweet, tiny nose-chomping baby?" Donut asked. "He was just a scared little chicken. It seemed like it was just yesterday."

"It practically was yesterday," I said. "Look in your pet menu and see if he received any new abilities."

A moment later, Donut gasped. "Carl, Carl, he has a special attack now! It's called Earthquake! It's a jump attack! Each time he leap-attacks, there's a small chance he'll trigger an earthquake when he lands, which will knock the bad guys off their feet!"

Mongo jumped up and down with excitement, forcing me and Katia to flee. He whipped around in a circle, his long tail twirling around the cabin. He roared, long and loud.

Christ, I thought. *I hope we never have to fight any of his kind.* We'd be fucked.

THE TRANSFER STATION WAS LARGER THAN THE LAST ONE. UP IN the lobby area, there was another general store, called Ford's Fighting Supplies. It was sandwiched by a pair of training guilds—one for longbow and one called "Druids only." Next to the druid guild was an Arby's, which would be the safe room, and then another store specializing in clothes for elves.

And finally was the Desperado Club, just like Bautista had promised. Unlike the massive, block-sized building from the previous level, the one here looked like a tiny dive bar with a small neon sign.

Imani said she'd be there after the recap episode, which would be in a couple of hours. We had just enough time to eat, open our fan boxes, and take a nap. We'd watch the show and head over.

"Have you ever been to an Arby's?" I asked Katia as we went through the door.

"No," she said. "I've never heard of it."

I realized I knew next to nothing about the woman. "I know you're from Iceland, but you knew about the Russian subway. Did you spend a lot of time in Russia?"

"I spent a summer in Moscow when I was a student, working at the Pushkin. It's a museum. I've spent a lot of time on holiday in Europe. We take a student trip to Paris every other year and one to Amsterdam the other years. It's the only traveling I've done recently. How about you? Did you ever leave America?"

I grunted. "I've been to the Arctic Circle. I once went to Costa Rica and got to pet a sloth. I almost went to the Bahamas, but I couldn't get off of work. Oh, and I've been to Canada a bunch of times. But it was just Victoria and Vancouver. I really wanted to visit Japan and the Philippines, but I never got the chance."

The Bopca glared at us from behind the counter. We ordered some food to go, which he gave us in actual Arby's bags. We took the food and returned to the personal space.

Within, we found Mordecai hunched over the alchemy table. The table had transformed. It was three times the size it had been when I'd pulled it out of my inventory earlier. It consisted of multiple layers of shelves, and it now had drawers and a faucet. A small fire burned at one end of the table, heating a glass container filled with black bubbling liquid. The whole crafting studio stank like burned rubber.

"How did this happen?" I asked, walking up to the table. Off to the side, I noticed a massive piece of paper filled with writing. He'd outgrown the dry-erase board and was mapping out the train lines on the sheet. I remembered seeing the roll sitting in the corner of his cluttered space.

"Get back!" Mordecai snapped, not looking up. "I'm almost done. You'll contaminate it."

"He used my two table-upgrade coupons on the alchemy table,"

Donut said. "He asked me for permission earlier. So the table is now level three." She made a face. "He didn't tell me he was making stink bombs."

"I'll be making worse than that if you don't get out of here. Eat your food. I'll be out in a minute."

We sat at the kitchen counter. I introduced Katia to curly fries. She was not impressed.

A few minutes later, a triumphant-looking Mordecai entered the room. His frog arms were full of items. He paused, looking Katia up and down. "You look different."

"Donut is helping me," she replied.

"I can see that."

He piled the items on the counter. There were two pairs of potions and about twenty green-hued balls that looked like perfectly round avocados. He wrangled the balls into a pile to keep them from rolling away.

"I didn't have enough time nor enough supplies to make some of the best stuff, but this is a good start," he said. "You say there's a Desperado Club out there? Good. We'll go later and pick up some supplies. Plus the casino will now be open, and you can cash in that chip."

"Oh yeah!" Donut said. "I forgot about that!" I'd received the poker chip for surviving Signet's attack on us. Donut hadn't received anything because her health had zeroed out. She'd only been saved by her Cockroach skill, which allowed her to survive the first fatal hit of a fight.

"So what do we have here?" I asked, picking up the first potion.

Mordecai's Special Brew
    A potion designed by a shifty Changeling who has a tendency to kill those who count on him the most, this special potion combines the effects of a Gold Standard Healing Potion and the Troll's Second Wind to create a de facto immortality for a period of thirty seconds. It has a few unfortunate side effects.

"I only had enough materials to make two of these. I need at least four more."

"What are the side effects?" I asked. I chose to ignore that first section of the description. I knew how the system labeled items I had created, which meant whatever they said here was not accurate.

"Okay, so what this potion does is create a constant stream of healing mixed with rapid regeneration for thirty seconds. So it'll heal almost anything and keep that health topped up. But it is *not* an invulnerability spell. It won't protect you against blowing yourself up or being decapitated or anything that would normally cause you to die instantaneously. Unfortunately, the side effects are pretty severe. It ups your potion sickness countdown by about ten hours. So you won't be able to take any potions afterward for that time. Also, you can only take two of these before they stop working altogether. I've been trying to fix that for ages, but I can never get past it. Maybe if I can manage to get a table higher than level nine, but I've never had the chance."

I picked up the next potion and examined it. It was orange and bubbly.

"Those are both for Donut," he said, turning toward the cat. "These are stat potions. Similar deal with that other potion. You can only take two of them. But you can and should take them both now. When I get the ingredients, I'll make two of these for everybody with all of the stats. If you happen to find more of these potions before I get to it, don't take them unless they're labeled Superb. Those are the only ones I can make that might increase it by four. That two-potion limit doesn't care about the quality. They're easy enough to make once you know the recipe."

Superb Constitution Buff Potion.

Drinking this mixture will permanently increase your Constitution by a random number between one and four. You may only drink two of these during your time in the dungeon. Why? Because drinking more would be cheating. And if anyone is going to cheat, it's going to be me.

I slid the potions over to Donut. She pulled them into her inventory.

"So, are Superb the best, then?" I asked.

"Sort of," Mordecai said. "There's another type called a 'Cosmic Buff' that raises a random stat by 10 points, but I don't know the recipe. They're so rare, I've only seen them a handful of times. Those aren't the same type of potion anyway, so they aren't restricted to the same limits."

Donut drank the first buff potion.

"Well, that was a waste," she said. "It only went up one point! Mordecai, are you sure you made these right?"

We waited for her potion countdown to wear off while Mordecai rolled his eyes at the cat. The second potion raised it by three, giving her a net gain of four, making her base constitution eight. With her anklet and the buff from her brush, plus the temporary 10-point boost she got on this floor only from her Hooligan class, she had a constitution of 21.

"Four points is good," Mordecai said. "But we need to keep looking for items that buff it further. It's still much too low." Mordecai's frog tongue darted out, and he stole a curly fry from my bag.

I picked up the final item. It felt like a hardened rubber ball. I squeezed it, and a split in the rubber appeared.

Fragmenting Potion Ball.
A full potion vial may be transferred to this ball.

That was the whole description.

"I need more gossamer thread, but they'll have some at the Desperado Club. It's cheap stuff. But I had to upgrade my table to three before I could make these. Once we upgrade the table to five, I'll have two heating elements, and I can make these twice as fast. At six

I'll have a full autoclave, and I can make 100 at a time. They're simple enough. You take a potion and pour it into the ball. Then you can throw the ball at an enemy. With your xistera and a few poison and firewater potions, you'll have a deadly arsenal. In a few floors I'll be able to make some truly devastating attack potions. I have an idea for a chain lightning potion that is going to be a thing of beauty."

"They don't have to drink the potion?" I asked. I tossed the ball in the air and caught it. It had a good weight to it, which meant I could fling it much further.

"Be careful," Mordecai said. "They'll break apart if you throw too hard. Don't be tossing these around once they're armed unless you're throwing them at a bad guy. And no, they don't have to drink it. Potions work on mobs if you throw them at them. It doesn't make sense, but it works. It's always been that way. Also, in case you're wondering, mobs don't get potion sickness. Not as far as I can tell. NPCs do."

"Will it work on party members?" I asked. "Like if Donut is across the room, and she needs a healing potion, and I nail her with one of these, will it work?"

"You will not be lobbing balls at me, Carl," Donut said. "My word. Do I look like a cocker spaniel to you?"

Mordecai looked thoughtful. "No, I doubt it. Not on other crawlers. That would work on NPCs, though, now that I think about it. It'd probably work on Mongo."

Throughout the day, I'd received a handful of achievements, but I'd only been awarded one prize from a Gold Looter Box. It ended up being yet another Determine Value skill potion. I drank it and moved to my inventory. Not much had changed. I still couldn't see an actual monetary value of my items, but I could now see the rarity of items.

I filtered it so I could only see **Unique** items. I only had one. It wasn't Carl's Doomsday Scenario, the about-to-explode nuke. That was listed under **Pretty Damn Rare**. The only unique item was that odd stuffed Kimaris figure on the horse. I knew it was valuable, but I hadn't realized it was one of a kind. The description didn't give any information. It read:

Stuffed Kimaris Figure. (With tags)
    It's impossible to accurately portray Kimaris's usual I-hate-this-and-I-hate-you scowl, but this collectible beanbag makes a valiant effort.

It was still listed as my most valuable item. The about-to-explode bomb was at the very bottom of my value list.

A message popped up. Our fan boxes were ready. A few minutes later, Donut received the same message. She started hopping up and down. "Carl, Carl, hurry up and open yours so I can do mine."

"You know what? You go first," I said.

"Yes!" Donut said. She trembled with excitement.

Mordecai settled next to Katia at the kitchen counter. "When you're done with this, I want to show you guys what I've discovered with the rail system. I'm pretty sure I know how to get to the stairwells. They've done this sort of thing before, but on a smaller scale."

I braced myself. Donut's last fan box had been a picture of Bea. Hopefully this would be something better. Mordecai said since this was a platinum box, people had to actually pay a credit to vote, so the voting was less likely to be trolled. But I wasn't so sure about that. Now that we had enemies both inside and outside the dungeon, I couldn't count out the idea we were about to get slammed with something awful.

She opened the box. She gasped in pleasure.

"Oh my god, thank you! Thank you, everybody! I love you all so much!"

I exchanged a look with Mordecai. *Wonderful,* I thought. *Just wonderful.*

"Look, Mongo!" Donut said. "Our fans got us a saddle! I can ride you now! It matches your feathers! Carl, put it on Mongo!"

"We're going to have to rethink some of those battle formations," Katia said.

I examined the blue-and-red-tassel-covered, obscenely garish saddle. It looked like something you'd see on a horse during a Fourth of July parade in the Deep South. Mongo sniffed at it and growled.

"Actually," Mordecai said, "that's a really good prize. But you're gonna need to get Mongo on board. I've never seen anybody ride one of those things."

> **Enchanted Mongoliensis Saddle. Adjusted to fit Cat species.**
>
> Magically affixes itself to the dreaded Mongoliensis, turning everyone's favorite murder chicken into a mount. Riders in the saddle are afforded the following bonuses:
>
> **+15% to all offensive spell damage.**
>
> **Anti-Piercing Resistance.**
>
> In addition, the saddle gives the following bonus to the attached Mongoliensis:
>
> **+20% Constitution.**
>
> **+20% melee damage while saddle is occupied.**

I read the description a second time. "So Donut gets bonus damage to her spells, and Mongo gets 20% more constitution? And 20% more damage as long as Donut's butt is in that thing? I like the constitution buff, but I don't like the idea of Donut sitting on his back while he's fighting. She'll be too vulnerable."

"Agreed," Mordecai said. He looked at Donut. "You're going to need to practice jumping out of the saddle when Mongo attacks. That attack bonus is great, but you'll be a prime target sitting up there."

"Yeah, yeah, put it on him, Carl!"

There were no straps on the saddle. It looked as if it was missing most of the required saddle parts. It was just a seat and a pommel. And a bunch of tassels. There were no reins. I had no idea how Do-

nut was going to stay on or how she was going to control the dinosaur once she was on.

"Come here, Mongo," I said, picking up the saddle. The feathered
dinosaur cocked his head to the side and then grunted, backing
away. I tossed him a curly fry. He snapped it out of the air. "Come
here, you bastard."

"Don't be mean, Carl. Mongo, listen to Uncle Carl," Donut said.

He lowered his head and let me approach. I placed the saddle
onto his ridged, feathered back, and it clicked in place. It was the
same sound as when I placed a table in the crafting room. Mongo
howled with displeasure and started bouncing around the room, trying to dislodge it. I had to jump back so I wasn't whipped in the face
with his tail.

"Uh, maybe you should wait until he gets used to it before attempting to ride him," I said.

"Oh, all right," said Donut. "Now open your box up!"

"Okay," I said. I opened it up.

For a long moment, nothing happened.

The lights to the room dimmed. Music started playing. It was
cheesy 1970s-style game show music with trumpets and keyboards
and percussion music in a disco beat. Colored lights flashed. Mongo
stopped howling and jumping and rushed to Donut's side. We all
stood back from the kitchen counter. All except Mordecai, whose
frog face had suddenly taken on a stony expression.

"Carl, what's happening?" Donut asked.

"Probably something stupid," I said.

The announcer's voice was even cheesier than normal.

**Ladies and Gentlemen, it's time for your favorite segment of
Dungeon Crawler World. The Prize Carousel!**

Just past me, the section of the room with the couch and screens
blinked and disappeared. A large, spinning carousel, like a merry-
go-round, materialized. It spun in a circle, lights up and down blink-

ing in sync with the music. The interior of the large contraption was blocked off by colorful curtains.

Here's your host. It's the dungeon darling, giver of prizes, slayer of gods, former Crawler champion—it's Chaco the Bard!

With a puff of smoke and the familiar *crack* of teleportation, a winged, wolf-headed man materialized. He wore a brown-and-orange-checkered leisure suit and held a microphone. He jogged into the room as if he'd had a running start, waving at nothing. I stared at the creature. He was not listed as a dungeon admin, but as an NPC.

Chaco. Pterolykos. Song Bard. Level 66.
Host of *The Prize Carousel*.

"Well, well, well," Chaco said, stepping deeper into the room. The wolfman stood about my height. His muscular arms bulged through his suit. Katia, Donut, and I all looked at one another, bewildered. "Welcome, everyone. I'm your man, Chaco! We have a great segment for you tonight. We have." He paused, eyes going glossy. "Crawler Carl joining us! He is the recipient of a Platinum Fan Box. Oh boy, that's a good one. You folks at home decided to give Carl the chance to pick his own prize, and you know what that means! We have nine excellent prizes on the carousel, and . . . Oh shit, Mordecai!"

"You motherfucker!" Mordecai cried, interrupting. His tongue lashed out, fast as a whip. It attached to a metallic chair by the kitchen counter, and he launched it across the room at the newcomer. Chaco squealed and dropped the microphone, ducking as the chair rocketed at him.

The chair froze in midair, a quarter of an inch from Chaco's head. It had been flung so hard that it'd surely have broken the guy's skull open had it been allowed to connect. Chaco whimpered. I scrambled back. Donut hissed, and Mongo growled. For a moment, nobody moved.

Realizing he'd been saved, Chaco slowly stood to his full height. I could see the large wolf was trembling. The chair remained floating in the air.

I turned to ask Mordecai what in the hell was happening.

"Oh, *shit*," I said.

Mordecai was frozen in place, his tongue half retracted. He had the word **Naughty** blazing over his head. The same thing had happened when Maggie My and Frank Q had attacked us in the safe room long ago.

Mordecai knew better than that. What had he been thinking? The **Naughty** blinked twice, and to my horror, Mordecai himself blinked and disappeared. To my right, the room with **Manager** over it also disappeared. The floating chair became unstuck, and it clattered loudly to the ground.

The stupid music continued to blare. The carousel twirled and twinkled.

"Did we just lose Mordecai?" I asked.

"No," Donut said. "I just got a notice. It says he's in a time-out for violating the rules. Carl, I don't understand what's happening."

I let out a stream of breath. I was overwhelmed with relief. I had no idea what just happened, either, but whatever this was could've been much worse. "How long is the time-out?"

"It's for seven days."

"Seven days!" I exclaimed. *Holy shit.* That meant we'd only have a day and a half left on this floor when he came back. *"Goddamnit."*

I whirled on Chaco. The game show host NPC still stood there, looking disoriented, his arms raised as if he feared we'd also attack him. His microphone had bounced away, rolling underneath the prize carousel, where he couldn't reach it. The music continued to play.

"Who are you?" I demanded.

"I'm Chaco," he said. "I'm the host. Uh, welcome to the show."

"No, who are you to Mordecai?"

"I . . . I don't think I'm allowed to talk about it. Uh, maybe we should just start this over. The fans voted to allow you to choose your own prize. It doesn't happen often, but when it happens, we have to do the show. That's my job. I host the show."

"Is it always you?" I asked.

"What . . . what do you mean?"

I was overcome with the urge to pound this guy in the face, but I knew that'd end badly for me. *"Are you the only one who hosts this show?"*

"Yeah, I think so. I don't get out much, so I don't really know. People don't usually vote for the let-the-crawler-choose-the-prizes option. It usually only happens a few times a season."

"Well, they voted for it this time because they knew you and Mordecai would be in the same room," I said. "Whatever just happened, it happened because they know Mordecai doesn't like you. So who are you to him?"

Chaco swallowed. "He sure knows how to hold a grudge, that's for sure. It's been hundreds of cycles. I didn't think he'd still be here. Everyone knows guides get out faster than anybody else. Wait, he shouldn't even be here. Had he become a manager?"

"Do you not watch the show?"

He looked about wildly. "No. No, I can't stomach . . . No, of course. I just hadn't . . ." He trailed off. "Look, we really have to do this. I'll get in even more trouble if we don't finish. You have nine prizes to choose from. I'm sorry about your manager. I really am. It was a long time ago, and it wasn't my fault. I was just doing what his manager told me to do. If I hadn't done it, he'd have died. And then we'd all have lost her. We'd have lost Odette. When he comes back, tell him I said I'm sorry. Not a day goes by where I don't regret it."

Warning: This isn't *Dr. Phil*. Pick your prize. You have ten minutes to choose, or you will forfeit your choice.

A timer appeared over the carousel, counting down.

"All right," I said, gritting my teeth. "Show me the goddamn prizes."

—————

"PRIZE NUMBER ONE!" CHACO SAID. HIS VOICE WASN'T NEARLY AS enthusiastic as before. He hadn't been able to reach his microphone, despite wasting a minute on his hands and knees attempting to retrieve it, and now he didn't seem to know what to do with his clawed hands.

The carousel paused, and the curtain fell, revealing a pair of potions sitting on a pedestal.

"Two potions!" Chaco cried.

I tried to examine them, but the tooltip wouldn't pop up. Donut jumped to my shoulder.

"There's no description," she said. "This is a rip-off!"

"What kind of potions are they?" I asked Chaco.

"All you get is the description, and the description is 'two potions'!" Chaco smiled big, revealing sharp teeth. If I hadn't just seen him cowering like a child, the look would be downright intimidating.

I recognized the fizzy dark blue coloring as that of a skill potion. This was just like when we had to pick Mongo. *Mordecai would be really helpful right about now.*

"Prize two! Bombs! Five hundred quantity."

The next curtain dropped, revealing a pyramid of hob-lobbers. These were a kind I hadn't seen before, but without being able to examine them, I didn't know what was different. They glistened, as if their exterior was made of tar. I suspected what they were, something I'd been planning on making myself.

"Prize three! Books! Earth books! Quantity 2,000!"

A pile of books appeared. I could see it was a random collection of English-language books, from *Fifty Shades of Grey* to what appeared to be a Canadian phone book. Two thousand books were a lot of damn reading. It'd take me a long time to get through it all, and I'd have plenty of trading material for the mole men.

"Prize four! A 1965 Harley-Davidson FLH Panhead Electra Glide!"

I felt my heart stop the moment the red-and-beige motorcycle appeared. My eyes immediately moved to the small dent on the gas tank. That had happened when I'd slipped once coming up the driveway. I'd reached out to steady myself, and I'd accidentally knocked the motorcycle over.

My father had never been physically abusive, except that day. I never really thought of it as abuse, but thinking back now, that's exactly what it was. He'd spanked me so hard with a belt that my underwear had soaked through with blood. I could still feel the sensation of it peeling away. My mother had cried, told him we were going back to Texas, but we never did.

"Carl, with you on the motorcycle and me on Mongo, we would be unstoppable!"

"Jesus," I muttered, ignoring Donut's comment. Was it really his motorcycle? Or just a facsimile? I felt as if I couldn't breathe.

"Prize five! Just one book!"

I leaned in, trying to focus. I couldn't get my mind off the fucking motorcycle. *Pay attention, you idiot!* At first I thought this was a magical tome, but it didn't have the telltale glow. It was just a regular book. Small and leather-bound. It read, *Best-Laid Traps*, on the cover.

"Is that porn?" Donut asked.

"Prize six! *Another* book!"

This one was similar to the last, but the book was much thicker, about the size of a large dictionary. It did not have a title on the cover, but it did have a symbol. It was the familiar A in a circle, signifying anarchy. The book glinted momentarily as the carousel turned away. I couldn't tell if that was the glow of magic or the glint of light off the gold-leafed pages.

"Prize seven! Enchanted chaps!"

"Carl, pick those!" Donut cried. "Chaco, he picks those!"

"Sorry, but Carl must make the decision," Chaco said.

The ass- and crotch-less chaps were modeled by a spinning mannequin. They were made of a dark leather that glowed with a greenish aura.

"Yeah, no," I said.

"Prize eight! A single potion!"

I immediately recognized the potion. It was the same orange bubbly concoction Donut had just used to raise her constitution. It was a stat buff potion. This one glowed with a twinkly aura, almost like a strobe. I wondered if maybe this was one of those +10 cosmic potions Mordecai had mentioned. Or maybe that meant it wasn't as good. I couldn't be sure.

"Prize nine! A Craftsman 3000 Series 63-inch rolling tool chest!"

The dented and well-used tool chest came into view, and I instantly recognized it. This was my tool chest from the shop. My eyes moved to the drawer at the bottom right, where I knew I had a carton of cigarettes, minus one pack. I had dozens of useful tools in there, including my drill and grinder. If I could get one of those dwarven batteries working, I'd probably be able to figure out a way to charge them.

My gut reaction was to pick the toolbox. With my tools, crafting items at that engineering table would be so much easier. But I hesitated.

When I'd last left it, my box had an entire marine electrical panel sitting on it. We were in the middle of rewiring a 32-foot Trojan from the 70s. The whole thing had been a mess. There was no sign of the panel now. In fact, there was something odd about the chest, the way it sat on the carousel. My eyes caught the top drawer, the one I could never close properly because I had too much crap in it.

I think it's empty.

I had less than 90 seconds to choose.

"It's time to make a decision!" Chaco said. "What'll it be, Carl?"

"Get the chaps!" Donut said. She looked over at Katia. "Katia, tell Carl to get the chaps." Katia said nothing.

The merry-go-round spun, the music getting louder. I had a sudden irrational urge to pick the motorcycle. Not because I wanted to ride it, but so I could push it out onto the tracks and watch it get hit by a train.

There were several choices that were probably *good* choices. I suspected Mordecai would have me pick the two skill potions. But I didn't have enough information. The trap book, assuming it really was about traps, would probably be filled with useful information. The pile of 2,000 books would also be valuable for multiple reasons. The same with the bombs.

The chaps might be a good choice. But I already looked enough like an idiot. I really didn't want to pick them, not when I didn't know what the enchantment was. They'd obviously added them to the list as a joke, which possibly meant the enchantment would be a joke, too.

Also, none of that stuff seemed super rare, things I couldn't find using other methods. The fan boxes were supposed to be about unique items one couldn't get in the dungeon.

Thirty seconds.

Light glinted again off that odd book with the anarchy symbol. My class was called a Compensated Anarchist. I remembered the last time my eyes had caught a glint of light. It'd saved my life. Was this the same thing? I doubted it, but I went with it anyway. Why not? It was a free prize.

"I pick that one. Prize number six."

"All righty! A choice has been made!" The carousel poofed away, and the book remained suspended in midair. "This is what you've chosen!"

I took a step forward and grabbed the floating book. The dungeon announcer read the description out loud.

Book.
  The Dungeon Anarchist's Cookbook by Anonymous.
  This is a unique item.

Chicken and Goblin recipes galore! But it's more than that, too. Each recipe is accompanied by a hilarious tale by the anonymous author, recounting some of the zany and madcap misadventures they experienced gathering these mouthwatering recipes. Fun for the whole family! This book is a real hoot.

Yep, I thought. *You done fucked up.*

"Ohh, too bad. That looks like a stinker of a prize. Better luck next time! That's our show, everyone!" Chaco cried. He gave me a baleful glance, and he disappeared. The music abruptly stopped. The living area reappeared. The scent of smoke lingered. I stared at the chair on the ground. We just got fucked.

"Chicken and goblin recipes?" Donut said, incredulous. "We lost Mordecai for a book of recipes? You should have picked the chaps, Carl." She jumped down and moved to the counter, grumbling.

I was about to toss the book into my inventory, but instead I flipped to the first page. It read, *Welcome.*

I felt the haptic buzz of my Escape Plan skill activate. Additional words appeared on the mostly blank page.

Hello, Crawler. As you're about to find, this is a very special book. If you're reading these words, it means this book has found its way into your hands for one purpose and one purpose only.

Together, we will burn it all to the ground.

8

THE DUNGEON ANARCHIST'S COOKBOOK.

24th Edition.

Potions, Explosives, Traps, Secret Societies, Dungeon Shortcuts, and more. Much more. This guide to creating chaos was originally generated into the system during the fifteenth season. It was awarded to the High Elf Crawler Porthus the Rogue on the ninth floor, disguised as a blank sketchbook. The fact you're reading this indicates that this book and the knowledge within remains active in the code. It has been passed down from dungeon to dungeon. It is automatically generated after a set of predetermined conditions have been met. It will disappear from your inventory upon death or retirement, where it will find its way to a worthy recipient in a future crawl.

There is only one price for access to these pages. You must pass your own knowledge on.

In your messaging menu, you will find a scratch pad. If you've yet to discover this, it is a place to mentally write down recipes or thoughts or anything else you wish to recall. If you look now, you will find you have been given one extra page into your scratch pad. Anything you add to this second page will be included in the 25th edition of this book.

While the true contents of this guide are invisible to the show-runners and to the viewers, it is not invisible to the current system AI. There is nothing about owning this book, or the information hidden within, that is against the rules. However, if the organization running this season begins to suspect that this book is more than it appears, or if you tell anyone about the existence of this book, the information within will erase, and you will forever lose access to the hidden text.

This is important. While this book's contents may be invisible, your actions are not. You must become an actor. Every recipe, every secret, if utilized, must be presented to the outside world as if you are discovering this all on your own. How you do that is up to you. Do not spend too much time staring at these pages.

<Note added by Crawler Drakea. 22nd Edition> The safe room restrooms are a good place to read. Just don't take long or you'll get pinched. The rats say there's a Syndicate rule that they can't watch you in the bathroom stalls. This is just for the actual toilets, not the rest of the bathrooms. Dunno if it's true. Those Naga bastards are a suspicious lot, and I fear I may soon be discovered.

My hands shook. I closed the book and added it to my inventory. The Naga? I remembered that Odette had said the Naga hadn't run a season in a very long time. That was the only season the dungeon lost money. If this note was from the 22nd edition, that meant this book had been in the hands of only two other crawlers since then.

I opened up my messages and found the scratch pad. I usually posted the list of items from Mordecai's daily BOLO in there. The last thing I'd pasted was that awful message from Brandon. But sure enough, there was now another tab. I closed it out.

I dragged the chair back to the kitchen counter.

"Come on, guys," I said. "We need to sleep. I gotta use the bathroom, though. Donut, I'll be out in a bit."

———

WE WATCHED THE RECAP EPISODE IN SILENCE. THE LOSS OF MORDE-cai hung over us like a cloud. Some crawler with two heads and a chained weapon called a meteor hammer killed an entire train full of humanoid salamanders. Lucia Mar made herself a necklace out of monster tongues, but one of her dogs sneaked up and snatched it off her neck while she was sitting in a safe room eating a bowl of rice. If it wasn't so disgusting, the scene would've been hilarious. They showed us fighting the cornets.

I'd only dared read a few pages of the book. It was presented in curated chapters. All the potion recipes in one, all the explosives in another, and so forth. Not all of it was actual recipes. There was a chapter that did nothing but list types of monsters and their known weaknesses. Some of it was stories. The last section, by far the biggest, was the remaining notes that didn't fit into a specific chapter, one edition after another. I quickly flipped through. Some crawlers filled pages and pages of text while others only wrote a few short lines. It was going to take a long time for me to get through it all.

I turned to the explosives section, and it contained a list of types of available explosives. A note caught my eye.

<Crawler Sinjin. 15th Edition>
A level 3 sapper's table lets you infuse bombs. Soak a hobgoblin smoke curtain in a healing potion, let it dry, and it mass-kills undead like you wouldn't believe.

<Comment added by Crawler Forkith. 20th Edition>
Confirmed. Works with bombs too but smoke works better. Doesn't kill high-level undead, but they get mad. I use these to clear rooms of those invisible Swamp Wights.

I slammed the book shut. I knew if I kept reading, I'd never stop.

Later, as I watched the recap episode, I kept thinking about the circumstances that led to Mordecai and that Chaco guy being in the same room. I knew that most viewers didn't see Mordecai. Managers and game guides were edited out of the feed. But those with press passes, such as Odette and probably millions of others, could see him. So his existence was no secret.

But was Mordecai's story famous enough for people to make the connection between him and Chaco? Probably not anymore. His mysterious relationship to Odette plus our own popularity likely led to someone making the connection, who then floated the idea of trolling the vote.

I looked up into the air and grinned. "I gotta admit, guys, that whole thing with Chaco was a dick move, but it was brilliantly executed. Good job."

I needed to get over it and move on. Most of the other crawlers didn't have a manager at all. I'd grown to rely on him, sending him queries every time I ran across something I didn't recognize. We were going to have to suck it up and figure out the rest of this floor without him.

Both Daniel Bautista and the book showed me the importance of crowdsourcing information. And while the bounty was a big concern, we couldn't let it force ourselves into isolation. I needed to get out there and add as many people as I could to my chat.

Hello, Crawlers.

At the end of this message, you will receive a new tab in your interface. This is where you can interact with your first sponsor. It will populate at the end of bidding, which will be in about 15 hours. You can see who your sponsors are, what organization they represent, and if they sponsor additional crawlers. They will *not* be able to send you direct messages, but you *can* send messages to them. I highly suggest you thank them for their support and ask them to send you the best loot boxes possible.

We are currently updating several issues with the train system. Some lines will be down for maintenance. I do not recommend venturing out onto the tracks, as the trains may resume at any moment.

That's all for now. Now get out there and kill, kill, kill!

"You know what we need?" Donut asked, looking about. "We need alcohol. And dancing. Let's party."

"You know I don't have a pass to the club, right?" Katia said. "I've told you several times now."

"Oh yeah," Donut said, sounding dejected. "You need to do something bad and get a tattoo."

"What did you guys do to get access?" she asked.

"It doesn't matter," I said, interrupting Donut. We'd received it after the incident with the goblin babies. "I think it might be a better idea for you to try to get into the other club, Club Vanquisher. I don't know what is required, but we'll find out."

She shrugged. "Okay. You guys go have fun. I have stuff I need to do anyway. Mordecai told me of a type of craft table I should buy. I'm going to pick it up while you're out and try to get some work done. Just don't take too long."

———

THE STATION-ONLY ENTRANCE BAR WAS EMPTY. A JACKAL-FACED gnoll stood behind the counter, drinking directly from a bottle of vodka. He ignored us as we pushed through to the double doors. It was just me and Donut. Mongo was safely ensconced in his carrier. Donut had yet to ride him. He started jumping up and down crazily the moment she even approached the saddle.

The bouncer in the small vestibule was the same as it always was, Clarabelle the Crocodilian.

"Where's your manager?" she asked as we walked up. She was the same type of creature as Florin the guy with the shotgun. She was pretty scary-looking close-up. Through the door we could hear the *thump, thump, thump* of music. Donut bopped her head.

I gave the bouncer a quick recap of what had happened.

She nodded. "Yep, that'll do it. He only gets one warning, I think. So you better remind him to behave when he gets back. I don't really know the story, but your manager has spent many hours crying into his cup, and he's mentioned a list of a few scores he wants to settle once he gets out of here. That Chaco idiot has come up more than once. That's all I really know."

I nodded. "Is it busy tonight?"

"As busy as it ever gets on the fourth floor, which means not really. Casino is now open. Oh, hey, that reminds me. Management wants me to offer private security for your visit. It's 500 gold for the both of you, but if you spend at least that much at the tables, you'll get a coupon for free security next time."

"What sort of security?" I asked.

"Nothing fancy. You'll get two bodyguards who'll accompany you anywhere in the club, including areas where security is a bit more lax. Between you and me, it's a rip-off for most of the people who get it. But I know you two are both on that bounty list. I think it's a pretty good idea. We got one other top ten in the club right now, and she has a guard."

"It's not Lucia Mar, is it?" I asked.

Clarabelle grunted. "No. She's been banned for life. Tried to get in a few times now, but we're prepared for her. She's mighty pissed about it, too. No, it's that Frost Maiden and her butterfly friend."

Mrs. McGibbons. Elle. She was here.

"So what's your best price on the security?" Donut asked.

Clarabelle looked at Donut. "Your charm doesn't work on me, little one. My best price is the only price. It's 300 for one person, and 500 for a team of two."

Donut looked as if she was about to object. Before she could say anything, I said, "We'll take it."

———

OUR TWO GUARDS WERE BOTH LEVEL 35 ROCK MONSTERS CALLED cretins. One was named Bomo, and the other was the "Sledge." They seemed about as intelligent as one would expect from someone named Bomo and the Sledge, but the seven-foot-tall tuxedoed monsters followed us at a respectable distance.

I did the hand-wave thing to create a privacy bubble over my head as we entered the large, bouncing room. The dance hall was only moderately busier than it had been the last time we were here.

I didn't see any elites this time, but there were plenty of crawlers. We were noticed right away. Several people stopped what they were doing to point and stare. A pair of crawlers looked as if they were going to approach, but after a glance at our security, they went back to the dance floor.

I saw Elle before she noticed us. She had a single guard, yet another rock monster who stood behind her with his arms crossed, looking bored. His name was Clay-ton. He put up his rocky hands as we approached.

"No closer," he grumbled.

"She's expecting us," I said.

When I saw Elle on the recap episode, I hadn't realized how small she'd become. She'd been a diminutive woman before, but she'd shrunk to about four and a half feet tall, and her skin was now a light blue, like the sky on a clear day. Her white haphazardly cut hair was almost exactly the same as before, but it fit with her smaller frame, and it no longer looked so sickly. She floated about a foot off the ground, and I noted she still wore the anti-slip socks from Meadow Lark. The privacy bubble around her head was like a nimbus, making her look like one of those haloed figures in a Renaissance painting. She was leaning over the bar, waving her hand furiously at the badger-headed bartender, who was serving someone else down the line.

"Look at how beautiful she is," Donut whispered. "She's like a vision of pure elegance."

"Yo," Elle cried at the bartender. "Whose dick do I gotta suck to get another drink? Christ."

"Hey, ice princess," I called out. "This one is on me."

Elle didn't turn. "Look, needle dick, buzz off, or when my real bodyguard gets back, she's going to add another skull next to her name tag."

"You mean Imani?" I said. "Where is she anyway?"

She turned around at that, eyes going wide.

"Carl! Donut!" she cried, pushing Clay-ton the bodyguard aside.

When she moved, her feet didn't touch the ground at all, but she still moved them. Our own two guards stepped forward, but I put up a hand to stop them. She pulled me into a hug, and it felt as if I was being wrapped by a pair of icicles. She reached up to pat Donut on the head.

"You got a new tiara! We saw the last one get destroyed on the show."

"I liked that one," Donut said sadly. "It was purple."

I grinned. "I didn't know if you were going to remember me."

Her eyes were almost twice as large as they'd been before. But I could still see it in her face, a resemblance to the ancient woman she'd been.

"I remember most of it. Kinda like watching a movie while tripping and then trying to remember it later. But how could I forget you saving my life? When Jack pissed on the wall . . . That's not the sort of thing one forgets, even with a brain that's turned into mush. So, you like my new digs?" She floated back, rising further off the ground and spreading her arms out. She moved her legs like she was backing up an invisible staircase. I wondered how high she could fly. "I'm a Frost Maiden. For now."

"It's pretty cool," I said. "I saw you shooting icicles out of your hand."

Behind her, the bartender approached. "You want another?"

She looked back at the badger. "Fuck, man. There's like five real people in here. Are you fermenting the potatoes yourself? I do want another drink. My friend Carl is paying for it. But then we're going to have another one after that, and I'm paying for that one. And don't give me a shitty pour like last time. Carl is having what I'm having. Donut, what do you want?"

"A Dirty Shirley! In a bowl! With extra cherries!"

"And the cat is having a Dirty Shirley in a bowl. Extra cherries."

I made a quick check of my inventory to make sure I still had some Alcohol Cure potions. I did.

"So anyway, Frost Maiden ended up being my only real choice." She lowered her hover and leaned up against the bar, feet still floating. "I had a long list of options that'd put all my marbles back in the bag, but Brandon made me pick this one. This is a tricky race, let me tell you. But we went with it because of you, actually."

"Me?" I asked.

"The manager benefit," she said. "You told Brandon about it, and I hadn't yet gone. It usually comes with classes, not races, but it comes with this one. Mistress Tiatha . . . that's our game guide. Have you ever met her? She was over the moon. I'd never seen her excited before. Turns out, she wasn't allowed to say anything. But the moment I picked it, she actually cried. Not that I noticed since I was in the middle of turning into this thing."

"I heard about Brandon," I said, suddenly somber. "He sent me a message."

The bartender plopped down four shots and a bowl on the counter. I handed him the last of my drink coupons and a couple of gold coins. Donut leaped to the counter and ate a cherry.

"Go easy," I said to Donut. "We're not staying long."

Elle nodded. She downed her drink. "Brandon was a good kid. His brother, too. A shame what happened."

"What did happen?" I asked. "He told me they got into a fight, but not the details."

"Miss Imani knows the story better than I do. She's over on the Silk Road getting supplies for the crew. We're the only two of the whole squad who have access to the club. I only got my tattoo because I accidentally shot an icicle up the keister of an orc bartender on that last floor. We'd had to hightail it out of town after that." She laughed. "That guy will be shitting ice cubes for the next three seasons."

Obviously, going from a dementia-suffering 99-year-old woman in a wheelchair to this fairy ice mage was going to alter one's personality. But there was more to it, too. She had an edge to her. In the short time I'd known the woman before, I'd caught hints of that, but I hadn't realized she was so . . . loud. I wondered how close this personality matched with how she was when she'd been younger.

"How many are you?" I asked. I took the first shot and almost gagged. It tasted like rubbing alcohol. "Oh god, what is this?"

She laughed. "It's called Knockout. It's got a kick. It's the dungeon's version of Everclear. My Barry and I used to get blackout drunk on that shit."

Next to me, Donut ate another cherry out of her bowl. She jumped to the Sledge's shoulder and asked him to take her dancing. They started to lumber toward the floor. I looked up at Bomo. "You go, too. Watch her. Elle's guard can watch the both of us."

The rock monster grumbled but complied.

"Anyway, there's twenty of us left. Imani is the only one remaining from the kids. She still acts like a babysitter. I keep telling her that she doesn't need to wipe our asses anymore, but she doesn't care. She's going to die from an ulcer before the dungeon gets her. . . . Speak of the devil. Here she comes."

I turned.

Crawler #12,329,440. "Imani C."
    Level: 24.
    Race: Obsidian Butterfly.
    Class: Fire Spiritualist.

She had transformed into a gaunt, skull-faced vision. Imani had been a skinny woman before, but now she looked as if she weighed half of that. A white skull was painted on her face, reminding me of the danger dingoes.

But most striking were the translucent, ethereal butterfly wings trailing behind her. The four wings were a striking mix of orange, yellow, red, white, and black. Almost like a monarch butterfly, but more saturated. She had to have a twelve-foot wingspan. As she walked, the wings passed through columns and dancing NPCs and crawlers. They were not physical wings, but I noticed the dancers reacted when the wings touched them. It was a quick thing, but each of them gave off a very subtle glow for a moment after the wings passed through.

"Hello, Carl," Imani said. She folded her wings back. "I see my message found you."

Imani turned and scanned the room, eyes resting on Donut, who was in the middle of the dance floor, bopping on the shoulders of the Sledge. She twirled while the rock bodyguard was doing an approximation of the robot. A crowd had circled around them, and they were chanting, "Go, Donut! Go, Donut! Go, Donut!" Thankfully Bomo appeared to be paying attention. Plus additional guards circled the room, eyes wary.

I don't know why you're being so paranoid. You shouldn't be more afraid of your own people than the monsters.

"Those are some wings," I said. "Can you fly with them?"

"Not yet," she said. "When we get to the sixth floor, I have to choose between two paths. One will let me fly. The other will keep them as they are."

"She's a support race and class," Elle said. She'd managed to get another drink. I realized she'd pinched my second one. That was okay. "She can claw your eyes out, but mostly she sits back and keeps everyone's health topped off."

"A healer," I said. "Just like you and Yolanda were before."

Her eyes clouded over at the mention of Yolanda. "Do you know about Brandon? He said he sent you a message."

I nodded. "What happened with his brother?"

"That's why I wanted to talk to you," she said. She pointed over at Clay-ton the bodyguard. "Chris picked a rock race, like these guys, but a different kind. Called an igneous. He looks like he's made out of lava rocks and is covered in little holes. I don't know if you've seen them. He got very strong, but it changed his personality." She gave a sidelong glance to Elle. "Race changes seem to do that to some people. He was fine the first couple of days, and then all of a sudden, he and his brother were fighting a lot. Chris wanted to spend every minute of every day hunting and killing. He wanted to go out and reconnect with you two. He says you're aggressive, and he respected that. He insisted you were just south of us. I don't know why he thought that. But Brandon wanted to stick close to the stairwell and spend the days training close to the exit. They got into a fight, and several of the men left with Chris. This was right around the time you left the floor."

Elle laughed. "Then Henry got pulled into an alleyway and banged some succubus witch who ended up giving birth to thousands of these little goblin monsters called shade gremlins. It started this whole thing. You should've seen it. Those green fuckers were everywhere. They all had Henry's face."

"Henry?" I asked.

Imani shook her head, apparently irritated with Elle. "He was one of the residents. He died, along with Brandon, protecting our escape."

I let a second pass in honor of Brandon. Donut was now wrapped around the Sledge's head, like she was slow dancing, even though the music was the same EDM beat as before. She'd only eaten two or three cherries, and I could see that she was plastered.

"Chris hasn't talked to you?" I asked.

"No," Imani said. "I can see he's alive. He's the only one of those who broke away who still is. He won't answer us. But I know he's looking for you. I thought you should know the story before he finds you."

"I appreciate that," I said. "And it's good to see you. Before you guys go, though, let's get into each other's chat. Plus I want to show you something. I want your thoughts on this." I pulled out the roll of paper Mordecai left on the floor by his alchemy table, the one with all the known train stations mapped out. "Let's find a table where we can look over this together. We need to figure out—"

A loud commotion from the dance floor turned my attention back.

I'd only looked away for a second. Bomo and the Sledge were on their backs. The crowd, both the NPCs and crawlers, was screaming and running back. The remaining bouncers rushed toward the center of the club.

In the center of the floor stood Donut, swaying. Her health was in the deep red. Her Cockroach skill had activated, the skill that saved her from dying from the first killing blow.

The entire front of her was covered in blood. A human crawler lay dying on the floor, blood geysering from a slash across his neck. A moment passed, and the man went still.

A single skull formed, appearing after Donut's name.

9

I WAS OUT OF MY CHAIR, GAUNTLET FORMING, BEFORE I REALIZED what I was doing. I was prepared to drop a smoke curtain or, if necessary, *Protective Shell*. But would that work against fellow crawlers? I tried to remember if Frank's and Maggie's dots had turned red when they attacked us. *Shit. I don't think they did.* That meant *Protective Shell* would be useless.

The crowd, which had been running, stopped at the edges of the dance floor. The music stopped abruptly. Donut remained there in the middle, looking at the man she had killed.

Multiple bodyguards moved in from all directions, moving slowly. Since I didn't know what had happened, I feared they were coming for her. I quickly assessed the situation.

Both of the cretin bodyguards were alive, but they'd been stunned. They each only had a few seconds left before they'd wake up. A glowing, bloody dagger lay on the floor.

The corpse had been about 25 years old, Asian. His name was Ji-Hoon. He'd been a level 21 **Knife Sharpener**.

"Carl?" Donut asked as I rushed up. "I'm sorry. I'm sorry."

"Shoulder," I cried, turning to face the guards. "Then heal yourself."

Donut leaped to my shoulder. The guards didn't attack us. One stood over the body of the fallen crawler. The others moved to help Bomo and the Sledge. None of their dots were red. I relaxed but only slightly.

"You're okay," I said. I pulled the Alcohol Cure potion and held it up. "Take it."

"I'm sorry," Donut repeated. She'd healed her own health, but it didn't cure her of her inebriation. She'd used a potion instead of the *Heal* spell. She took the Alcohol Cure potion into her inventory, but it'd be a few minutes until her potion sickness wore off. She started to sob. "Carl, I never wanted to get a skull. I'm sorry. Nobody is going to like me now."

"It's okay," I said, anger rising at the dead guy by the moment. "What happened?"

"The lady, she cast a spell and my guy and the other rock guy fell, and I fell, too, because Sledgie was stunned, and the other guy had a knife and—"

"What lady?" I snapped before she could finish, my eyes scanning the crowd.

Whoosh.

A woman from the crowd flew forward. She tumbled to a stop at my feet. A two-foot-long icicle erupted from her eye socket. She'd been pierced from behind.

"That lady," said Donut.

Imani and Elle rushed forward, joining us on the dance floor. The bouncers parted to let them pass.

"She was about to blast you two," said Elle, looking about for additional threats. Both of her hands glowed. I watched as a skull appeared after her name. She didn't seem to care. "I get dibs on her gear. Donut, loot the one you killed before we get kicked out of here."

Imani took up a position behind us, wings fully spread. I shuddered as she brought us into an ethereal hug.

You've been Juiced! 10% Temporary buff to Strength!
You've been Shrouded! 10% Temporary damage reduction!
You've been Trolled! 25% Temporary acceleration to healing!

"I didn't want to kill anybody," Donut said once again. "Maybe those stupid dogs. But not a person. Not a real person."

I reached up and rubbed Donut's head. An even larger crowd had formed around us, everybody staring. The bouncers all stood still and didn't move, as if unsure what to do. In the far corner of the club, from the unmarked door that led into the back, a tall, shadowy figure emerged. It paused, taking in the scene. A second figure also came from the back. This was a small fairy, buzzing about the other figure's head.

"You didn't do anything wrong," I whispered to Donut, who continued to quietly sob. "They attacked you, and you defended yourself. There's no need to be upset. If you hadn't killed him, you'd be dead now. And don't worry about people not liking you. Nobody will get mad at you for this. Trust me."

"Are you sure?" she sniffed.

"I am positive," I said.

I took a moment to puzzle over Donut's reaction. She didn't blink at killing a trainload of monsters, or NPCs for that matter. She wasn't human. She'd never been human. But for some reason she was having a really hard time with this. I knew part of it was because she was drunk. Every day she was growing into a more and more complicated creature. She was far removed from the cat who had first emerged in Mordecai's guild all those days ago.

"Anybody else want to try something?" Elle shouted. "You come for Donut or Carl, you come for all of us. I will freeze the blood in your veins and make your genitals shatter like glass!"

"Easy, tiger," I said. "I think it's over."

"That's right. It's over," she called. She glared at a dwarf crawler. "You giving me the hairy eyeball? Back the fuck up!"

"Me?" the dwarf squeaked. "No, no, sorry." He took several steps back.

"Is she always like this?" I asked Imani, who just shook her head. I was starting to see why Elle was in the top 10 and Imani wasn't.

"Don't you think anything about it," Elle said, speaking to Donut. "Don't you cry. This was inevitable. Once word gets out how you handled it, nobody is going to mess with you again."

The tall figure in the back of the room turned and disappeared into the club's offices. The hand-sized fairy buzzed through the air and approached. The figure barked at bouncers, who jumped at her command. Bomo, the Sledge, and Clay-ton approached, heads down.

The fairy was clearly female, but she wore a tuxedo like the bouncers. Her raven hair was tied up in a severe bun. Tiny red sparkles followed her as she flew through the air.

Astrid—Bloodlust Sprite. Level 125.
    Assistant Manager of the Desperado Club.
    The Bloodlust Sprite is one of the rarest, most deadly of the Sprites. They are naturally imbued with Cardiovascular Magic, allowing them a wide range of attacks and abilities over any creature that uses a circulatory system. It is said they have the ability to cause one's heart to beat so quickly, it literally bursts into flames, which is both disgusting and one of the most metal things ever.
    WARNING: This is a fairy-class NPC. NPCs of this class inflict 20% more damage against you due to your goblin pass.

Level 125? Holy shit. I also noted the lack of the usual *This is a non-combatant NPC* in her description.

"Princess Donut," Astrid said, coming to hover over us. Her deep, serious voice didn't seem as out of place with her fairy appearance as one might expect. "On behalf of management, I'd like to personally apologize for our security's inexcusable failure. While we guarantee no one's safety within this establishment, that changes the moment someone employs personal security. You have my word that this will be dealt with swiftly." She looked over her shoulder to glare at Bomo and the Sledge, who stood rigidly.

Donut sniffed. She glowed, and I knew she'd finally taken the sober potion. She straightened on my shoulder. "It's quite all right."

"Nevertheless," Astrid said. "We will refund you the 400 gold, and you and Carl will be granted complimentary security from now on."

"We appreciate that," I said, interrupting Donut, who was about to correct the sprite. We had paid 500 gold for the guards, not 400. Clarabelle had cheated us. I filed that information away.

"Very well," Astrid said, turning away.

"One more thing," I said. The sprite stiffened and then turned.

"How you run this establishment is none of our business," I said. I gestured at the two guards. "But you can't blame them for what happened. We would consider it a personal favor if you didn't punish these guys too harshly. Donut and I have taken a liking to them. We'd like them each time we're here as our own security. Including for the remainder of this evening."

"You are correct, Crawler. It is none of your business." She paused. "But your request is not out of line. Very well. It is done." She turned and buzzed away.

The two rock monsters stared at us curiously. They'd fucked up, but I suspected I'd just saved their rocky asses. I'd trust them much more than someone else. Especially if that someone else knew we were responsible for their friends getting fired or worse.

Elle clapped her hands together, and shards of snow flew everywhere. "Now that's what I call entertainment."

———

THE FOUR OF US SAT DOWN AT A TABLE AND UNROLLED THE PAPER. I'd made Donut loot the body of the dead human. He had a lot of armor, all giving a few stat point boosts. I figured we'd give most of it to Katia. He also held a dozen daggers, each with a different enchantment. The one he stabbed Donut with had a 100% damage bonus if it was stabbed into someone's back. It would have killed her instantly if it hadn't been for Donut's Cockroach ability.

Donut sat quietly at the table. She ordered a regular nonalcoholic Shirley Temple and sat there munching on cherries.

"We're here," Imani said, looking over our map. She traced a line, intersecting several paths, and then pointed at a stop. "If you want to meet up, we can do it there."

"Mordecai found a pattern in all of this, but I think he had outside information," I said. "We need to figure it out."

"Other than the transfer station patterns, I don't really see it," Elle said. She seemed bored. Our three guards surrounded the table, arms crossed. She licked her lips as she watched a large, shirtless NPC elf gyrate on the dance floor.

"What's the transfer station pattern?" I asked.

"All of them are prime numbers," she said. She tapped the numbers of all the checked-off transfer stations. Then she pointed to a note Mordecai had written and circled in the corner that said, *Prime.* I hadn't even noticed it. "I thought you already knew that."

"What's a prime number?" Donut asked, speaking for the first time.

"It's a math thing," I said. "You learn about them in fourth or fifth grade, and then you don't need to know about it ever again unless you become a mathematician. Or a math teacher."

Elle grunted. "It sounds to me like you need to know about them right now."

"We don't have enough information," Imani said. "We need to know what happens inside of these every five stations where the mobs all get off. And more importantly, we need to know what happens at the end of the line."

"Agreed," I said. "Let's do this. We keep talking to others to see if they've figured anything out. In the meantime, you take your team and investigate one of these fifth platforms. Donut and I are going to get our hands on one of these engineers."

"Those engine cars are locked up tight, hotshot. How are you going to get one of the engineers out?" Elle asked.

I grinned.

WE SAID OUR GOODBYES TO IMANI AND ELLE. WE STOPPED BY THE Silk Road and sold some items and picked up a few explosives, including an additional case of smoke curtains. I also bought some items from Mordecai's list. The large booth that supposedly sold trap supplies wasn't open yet, but instead of an empty space, the skeletal outline of a booth was there, indicating it'd likely be open soon.

From there we checked out the newly opened row of guilds. This was a dark hallway lined with doors, each with a word or two written over them. Most of the skills were rogue-themed, from Lock Picking to Sleight of Hand. There were several rooms not yet opened. But one of the rooms was listed as "Dodge."

We tried to open the door, but it was locked. A note appeared.

This room is only accessible to crawlers with a Dodge skill of Seven or better.

Donut's skill was only six, but after another session or two in the training room, she'd hit seven.

Bomo and the Sledge followed us diligently, growling at any NPC or crawler who got too close. They didn't speak or acknowledge what had happened earlier, though they did appear more contrite, in their own sort of rocky way. I tried talking to Bomo, who just stared back at me blankly. I knew they could talk. Clay-ton had spoken. Once. But they used those words like they had a finite supply.

I remembered Chris had been like that, careful with his words. A rock monster was a perfect choice for him.

Finally, we headed to the casino.

While not as glitzy and loud as a Vegas casino, the room's purpose was clear the moment we entered. There were six card tables, a roulette table, a vertical wheel-of-fortune-type game, and a craps table. These were all Earth-based games, and I wondered on that. I knew we shared some cultural markers with the rest of the universe, but I wondered how that worked with the gambling area. Were the games different every season? I suspected they were. There were no slot machines. NPCs huddled over the smoky tables, quietly gambling. I wondered how that worked with the NPCs, if they were automatons like the dancers. I only saw one other crawler, a dragon-headed woman leaning over a card table, playing blackjack.

Like with the previous hallways, the moment we entered, the thump of the dance floor disappeared. It was replaced with a sultry, jazzlike song being played over a loudspeaker. The music was a mix of voice and free-form synth. I wondered if it was Manasa, the murdered Naga. The song was unlike anything I'd heard before, almost intoxicating. I suspected there was magic in the music, designed to get us to spend more money.

I counted eight tuxedoed guards in the room. These were not cretins, but more crocodilians. They watched us through beady, suspicious eyes.

This room was about the size of the dance floor, making it smaller than I expected. However, a pair of opulent spiral staircases leading down was closed. I suspected there were additional casino games at the lower levels. The stairs were right next to the entrance, and each was guarded. One led down to the Hunting Grounds. The other was labeled **Larracos**. I could hear laughter, shouting, and raucous cheering coming up from this second stairwell.

"What's Larracos?" I asked Bomo, who just stared at me blankly.

"Larracos is the capital city of the disputed lands," one of the nearby guards said. He was a level 45 crocodilian named Igor. "It is the prize over which the factions fight."

"They sound like they're having a good time down there," Donut said. She'd been sitting quietly on my shoulder this whole time, but she was starting to return to her normal self.

"Their fighting is mostly good-natured," Igor said. "The Desperado Club is where they come to unwind. The armies of the factions aren't allowed to start conquering each other until you lot reach the ninth floor. So until then, the serious commanders train their units, and the rest party. The gambling that occurs on that level is done with credits, not gold."

I nodded. The ninth floor was like a distant, looming stop sign.

An impending disaster. But at this point, I doubted we'd ever make it down there, and there was nothing we could do about it now other than train.

I held up my 100,000 gold comp chip I'd received long ago. "I want to cash this in."

He peered at it. "You got two options. You can turn it in at the wheel of fortune game right now, or you can hold on to it and use it at the high rollers roulette table. That's not the roulette table that's here. You'd have to wait until the sixth floor."

I strongly suspected it would be better to hold on to it, but at this point, I didn't care. It had been one blow after another recently, and we needed to have some fun. "I never liked roulette anyway," I said. That was Bea's game. We walked over to the wheel of fortune game.

On the way there, we passed the roulette table. The guy running the game was human, and the NPCs playing were a mix of elves, humans, and orcs. I noted that the symbols on the table were not two different colors and numbers, but a strange mix of four different colors and different symbols, like bones and knives, and a ringed planet.

The wheel of fortune was a vertical, round wheel filled with random prizes. A little more than half of the spaces were red and with labels such as "Nothing!" and "Get stabbed in the stomach by the croupier" and "Get poisoned" and "Vomit blood for ten minutes straight."

Some of the good prizes, however, were *very* good. They were "A new pet" and "50,000 gold" and "A Legendary Weapon Box." Others weren't great, but they would still be considered a prize. Like "Unlimited Free Handies over at Bitches or Penis Parade." The others were mostly platinum and legendary boxes. Most of the spots were the same size, except the Nothing! spot took up two spaces and one of them, "500,000 gold," was a tiny sliver with "Spin Again" on either side.

"Oh fuck this," I said, looking over the list of items. I wasn't about to risk landing on a red spot. The cost of a single spin was 10,000 gold. "Let's wait until Mordecai comes back and—"

"I see you got a chip," the human running the wheel said, interrupting. The bald man was named Tito, and he was huge. He was taller than me and looked like he came out of central casting for a mob enforcer. He only had one tooth in his mouth. The system listed him as **Desperado Club Wheel of Fortune Croupier. Also, the guy who will stab you.** "The comp chips are for a hundred grand, which is the maximum bet. Every bet over the minimum removes one of the red spots and adds a positive one. So if you use the comp, only two red spots will remain, which leaves 22 positive results. It will be the Nothing! spot and one more."

"Which one?" I asked, my eyes focusing on one that said, "Every hair on your body turns into a snake for five seconds."

The large man pulled out a large serrated knife and stuck it into the table. "Guess."

"Don't do it, Carl," said Donut. "You're going to get stabbed in the stomach. This game never plays fair."

"Hey," the man said, sounding offended. "This game is 100% on the up-and-up." I looked over at Bomo, who shrugged. One of the good prizes was a "Choose Any Skill to Level Up potion." I'd love to get my hands on that one.

"Is your dagger enchanted?" I asked, peering at it.

"Nope," he said. "Nobody has ever died from me stabbing them. And that's the god's honest truth." He smiled sheepishly. "Nobody playing the game, I mean. I stabbed plenty on me off time."

I calculated the odds in my head. There were 24 spots. It was 25, really, since the Nothing! spot was a double. Assuming the game was fair, which Mordecai said it was, then I had a what? Slightly worse than a 10% chance of not winning a prize? And really, it was only a one-in-25 chance of a terrible result. Getting stabbed would suck, but the odds were no worse than anything else we were doing. I plunked the chip on the table. "Let's do this."

Tito slapped his hands together. "Excellent." He looked up at Donut on my shoulder. "You'll have to step back, I'm afraid, madam."

Donut grumbled and jumped to the Sledge's shoulder, who showed no reaction. But a moment later, the rock monster reached up and gave her a surprisingly gentle pat.

"All bets are in!" Tito announced. The wheel flashed, rearranging itself. Several spots changed. Two red spots remained on the wheel. **Nothing!** and **Get stabbed in the stomach by the croupier.** He reached up and gave the wheel a mighty spin. It started clicking loudly as it spun.

"Come on! Come on!" Donut cried from the Sledge's shoulder, her voice rising in excitement. "Big money! Big money!"

I relaxed. This was the real reason I'd done this. The wheel spun for an absurdly long time. It eventually started to slow. It passed the "Get stabbed" box, ticking slowly to a spot. It approached the thin spot awarding 500,000 gold.

"Carl, Carl!" Donut cried. "Carl, we're gonna win big!"

Click. Click. Click.

"No!" Donut cried.

It'd stopped on **Spin Again.**

"Spin again!" Tito shouted. He reached up and spun it again.

Behind me at the roulette table, an NPC screamed. I turned to see the floor open up underneath him, and he fell, disappearing in the hole. His screams got quieter and quieter as he fell. Additional ethereal screams emanated from the hole, and a ghostly clawed arm rose up from the darkness before turning into smoke and dissipating. The trapdoor slammed shut.

"What the hell was that?" I asked.

Tito shrugged. "They also got a Nothing! spot on the roulette wheel. Works a little different, though. You have to bet that you *won't* land on the spot. But if you do, you're fucked. That game is much safer than this one, but I got the better prizes."

"Wait, what?" I said, alarmed. "That's what happens if I land on Nothing!?"

Tito grinned. "Yeah, the Nothing! sure is something."

I watched in horror as the wheel decelerated, perilously close to **Nothing!** *Click, click* . . . The little needle hung on to the last spot, and I held my breath. The needle settled on a green spot. Holy fuck. That would have served me right.

"Winner!" Tito shouted. I landed on Scroll of Upgrade.

It appeared on the table in front of me. A twenty-minute count-down timer appeared. I'd received one of these before. I had twenty minutes to read it. It upgraded a random one of my currently equipped items. Mordecai had warned me last time not to remove anything before reading it, as the system tended to fuck you over if you did that. The last time I'd done this, it had added to my boxers.

I picked up the scroll, took a breath, and read it.

I felt my foot buzz. I looked down to see my toe ring glowing.

Enchanted Toe Ring of the Splatter Skunk. (Upgraded)
   The item has been upgraded once.
   Imbues wearer with +10 Strength and gives +5 to the skill Powerful Strike. Also, it's a toe ring. It's probably uncomfortable and it makes you look like one of those hippie assholes who sit around in a field juggling and Hula-Hooping all day.

The toe ring had gone from +3 in strength to +10, adding 7 points. But more importantly, my Powerful Strike skill went up two additional skill levels. I had a base of seven with the skill, so with the plus five and the one more from my gauntlet, I had a skill of 13, which meant after all my other skill upgrades with punching and kicking, my damage was now multiplied by 13. Just two levels more before I started to see some serious upgrades and benefits. The closer I got it to 20, the more godly my damage became.

"Want another go?" Tito asked.

"Yeah, no," I said. "I think my gambling days are over for now."

Tito appeared disappointed. He looked forlornly at his knife. "Suit yourself."

"What're we doing now?" Donut asked.

"We're going back to base," I said. "We have an hour of training to do, I need to build a few things at the table, and then we're going to crash the shit out of a train."

10

WE RETURNED TO FIND HEKLA SITTING ON THE COUCH IN OUR BASE, drinking an Arby's milkshake.

"What do you think?" she asked, jumping up the moment we appeared. She held out her arms. She spilled some of the shake onto the couch.

"No eye shadow," Donut said. "She doesn't wear makeup. And she's a lot bigger. But you did a really good job."

Only then did I see the name over her head said "Katia."

"Wow," I said after a moment. "That's really good. If I was Hekla, I'd be weirded out right now, but that's great. Are you able to change the name over your head?"

"Sort of," she said. "It's an ability called Walk in Their Shoes, and I can only turn it on if my appearance matches their appearance by at least 90%. This Hekla is only 65%. It's the best I can do."

"It looks a lot better than 65% to me," I said. "It had me fooled."

"I'm working on it. I bought a new table that Mordecai told me about. It's called a makeup table, and at level three, I can superimpose the face of any monster or crawler or NPC I've met on the glass, which makes sculpting much easier. Plus it doesn't hurt when I sit at the table, and now I can save three designs and call them up on demand. Once I get it to level five, it supposedly comes with a full-sized mirror so I can do the rest of the body just as easily."

"Level three? You used your upgrade coupons?" I asked, trying my best not to sound horrified.

"Yes, I did. It is so much easier now. I think I've perfected my blocking build, too."

Mordecai was going to be pissed. I knew he wanted to talk her into using the two upgrade coupons on his own alchemy table. I supposed they were *her* coupons. Still, using them on upgrading a skill that was only moderately useful seemed like a colossal waste. But now that she had it, we were going to have to get creative with her shapes.

"We have some more armor for you," I said as Donut piled the greaves, shoulder pads, and helmet onto the ground. These were all from the assassin. They gave a combined upgrade to +8 in her strength and +4 to her dexterity. But more importantly, it added to her mass.

"Where did you get this stuff? Oh my god, Donut. What happened?" She'd finally noticed the skull over the cat's head. Her form shifted, and she returned back to her normal self, her real version I'd only seen up in the production trailer. The only difference was she kept her purple Mohawk instead of her normal black hair. And the knee-high boots. She was also much taller, thanks to her increased mass.

"Oh, it was but a trifle," Donut said. She licked her paw, as if it truly was nothing. "A poor crawler thought he could keep up with me, and I accidentally had to rip his throat out. Honestly, I barely remember the incident. I did have a cherry or two too many. Now if you'll excuse me, I have training to do."

She flipped her tail and walked into the training room.

Katia raised an eyebrow and looked at me. I shrugged. "I'll tell you about it later. We have a busy day ahead of us."

———

I USED MY HOUR TO TRAIN MY BARE KNUCKLES SKILL. I REALLY needed to work on my Powerful Strike, which was a more general, catchall fighting skill than the punching-only Bare Knuckles, but since I'd practiced it the day before, I wanted to see if training it two days in a row would level it up. It worked. My skill moved up to level nine just before my hour was up. Donut spent her time practicing her Dodge skill, leveling it up to seven, which meant she now had access to that training guild.

From there I spent another hour working on a few different items at the engineering bench. After, I moved to my sapper's table. I utilized my Demolition Workshop tab for the first time, which allowed me to remove bombs from my inventory and examine them, pulling up schematics and information about the bomb's content and yield. It also told me an item's rate of decay under different stress environments, something that would be important to know. It was a lot to take in. I dared going to use the restroom twice, both times to quickly consult the cookbook. I experimented with my bomb-deconstructing skill by taking apart several fused hob-lobbers. The fuses themselves could be useful. The stability of bombs and explosives did not degrade at all when I stood at the bench, allowing me the freedom to cut sticks of dynamite in half or bundle them together.

While I did that, Donut spent the time attempting to ride Mongo. After about ten minutes of coaxing, she finally managed to leap onto the saddle. The moment she landed on the dinosaur's back, a translucent strap appeared, wrapping around Donut's waist, affixing her to the saddle.

Mongo screeched and bucked like a bronco, causing me and Katia to stop what we were doing and laugh. Donut was magically attached to the saddle, but there appeared to be a limit to the adhesiveness, and she was thrown multiple times. Eventually, he calmed down, but he looked miserable. He didn't move from his spot in the middle of the crafting room. He just stood there, eyes pleading. The dinosaur gave me a look that said, *Get this thing off of me.*

"How are you going to control him?" I asked. "There aren't any reins."

"Mongo and I have a psychic bond, Carl. You've never been a mother, so you wouldn't understand."

Mongo suddenly squealed and bucked, tossing Donut halfway across the room. She hissed, poofing out before landing on all fours atop Mordecai's alchemy table, causing vials and supplies to scatter.

"Mongo, bad!" she cried as Katia and I howled.

Mongo grunted in derision and rolled onto his back in an attempt to dislodge the saddle.

"You're gonna need more than a psychic bond," I said.

WE SPENT THE NEXT FEW HOURS RIDING THE LINES, SWITCHING from one track to the next, grinding and training. After speaking with Imani and Bautista and coordinating where the best place to do this was, we ended up at a platform on the ocher line. The four of us stood on the platform, overlooking the track.

"What I really need is a multimeter. One at the end of a long stick," I said. I leaned over to stare at the three rails. "We don't even know if this is really electrified or not. I'm pretty sure it is. That third rail is raised off the ground and uses insulators. There's a possibility they're fucking with us. Or worse, the grounding is jacked to hell, and anything that goes down there will catch an arc."

"So how are we going to figure it out without getting ourselves zapped?" Katia asked, also leaning over to peer out onto the track.

"Do you want me to send a clockwork Mongo down there?" Donut asked.

"No, but that's a really good idea," I said. "I want to test these things first."

I pulled a curved metal rod from my inventory with the wired hob-lobber fuse. I'd made several of these earlier for just this sort of thing. I tossed it out onto the tracks, connecting the two main rails with the third rail. *Pop!* The hob-lobber fuse blew the moment it hit the metal. The metal stick continued to crackle and glow. A moment later it vibrated itself off the third rail. It finally stopped crackling. I didn't see any arcing.

"Well, something is hot down there. And we know the fuse

works." I repeated the experiment, tossing the fuses onto each of the three rails, just to be certain. The only time the fuse blew was when it hit the third rail and something else. That made me reasonably certain that the hot line was the third rail, as it should be. I still wasn't confident we wouldn't get a shock if we touched the main track, but the fact the tracks were physically grounded suggested we would be fine. *Famous last words,* I thought.

Just to be extra certain, I allowed Donut to cast *Clockwork Triplicate* on Mongo. She'd leveled the spell up to five, which now allowed the two duplicates to exist for 10 minutes. The robot dinosaurs both had little saddles on them now. She then ordered the two dinos down onto the tracks. The moment one of them touched the third rail, it exploded, showering the platform with little gears and springs. Both Mongo and the other dino squawked with concern.

A train pulled up, bumping and crunching over the metal on the track. I cringed as it hit and destroyed the second clockwork Mongo. Since this was the ocher line, it was full of mobs we hadn't seen yet. They ranged from lumpy wolf monsters with tentacles to small fairy-like skunks that clutched on to butcher knives three times bigger than themselves. Donut blasted a pair of the skunks as the door opened. While she did that, I spray-painted a big X on the side of the carriage. We stepped back as it pulled away.

If this worked as intended, both Meadow Lark's and Bautista's crews would have a warning that the train with the X would be the last one coming down the line for a while.

"Okay, guys, you ready for this?" I asked. I didn't wait for an answer. Katia, Donut, and Mongo retreated to the back of the platform as I pulled the first of the two devices from my inventory.

I gently placed it on the platform and watched it for a few moments to make sure it didn't deteriorate on its own. According to the Demolition Workshop menu, the device was stable against anything except heavy impact. Still, I watched that status number nervously. It did not lower. I pulled out the fishing pole I'd cobbled together, hooked the tire-sized device up, and I gently lowered it onto the track, keeping it as far away from the third rail as possible. I moved down to the far end of the platform and placed a second charge a half of a car's length into the tunnel.

For our first derailment, I decided to keep it simple. I originally wanted to build a metal ramp that'd fit snugly on the two rails, something that'd cause the first car to lift away and to the side, derailing it nice and clean. But I didn't have the proper measurements. So instead I went with a classic. Land mines.

The devices resembled tire-shaped cross sections of the spike-covered contact mines that were widely used in naval warfare in the early 20th century. I'd gotten the idea for the plunger from the cookbook. I'd changed it up just enough to make it look like I'd come up with the idea on my own. It hadn't taken long to build. Basically it was an oblong, hob-lobber-stuffed metal tube with a single hopefully stable hobgoblin stick of dynamite added for extra measure. The system labeled it a **Jelly Bomb**, presumably after a jelly donut. I did not get credit for inventing it. When the train hit it, one of the spikes would be depressed and would smash an impact-detonated hob-lobber, causing the whole mine to shred and explode. The metal on the top half of the bomb was scored into triangle shapes for added shrapnel. I'd built the plungers using the Gorgon Marital Aid. We hadn't yet been able to test it, and I was nervous about a premature detonation. Especially while I was setting it. I was reasonably certain two of these would be enough to dislodge the train from the track. Hopefully I didn't end up killing the engineer. Or myself.

Once the two land mines were set, I joined the others at the top of the stairs. If anything went wrong—like we accidentally unleashed a horde of flying skunk fairies on the station—we'd either retreat into the safe room or hop onto another line, depending on what happened.

I looked over my shoulder and examined the small transit station. The three shops were a pho restaurant, a general store, and a well-kept church-like building, which was the entrance to Club Vanquisher. The door to the club opened, and a ram-headed cleric in robes stepped out to regard us. He glared at us for a moment before returning inside.

> ELLE: Hey, stud. We explored through one of those five
>   stations. You wouldn't believe what we found. We had to
>   fight three neighborhood bosses. There's a borough boss,
>   too, but we left her alone. Imani says she's an old friend of
>   yours. A Miss Krakaren.
> CARL: Oh wow. I hope you guys are okay. Now's not a good
>   time. We'll talk in a bit.
> ELLE: Okay, big guy. Tell Donut I said hello.

I remembered the description of the first, tentacled Krakaren boss had said there were many of them. If this one was a borough boss, that meant she was probably a lot bigger. The original Krakaren we'd fought had been using her body along with the brindle grubs to produce their Rev-Up Moonshine. I wondered what this one was up to.

The ground rumbled, signifying the approach of the next train.

"I'm moderately excited about this, Carl," said Donut.

11

KA-BLAM!

Even from the top of the stairs, the detonation was deafening. The ground shook. Mongo screeched in fear. Dust cascaded from the ceiling. Horrific screeching and crashing noises filled the platform below, and even more smoke and dust billowed up. Katia grasped on to my arm for support, and Donut leaped to my shoulder, digging her claws in. The crashing echoed below our feet, followed a moment later by a second explosion that echoed through the tumult like a shotgun blast.

Level Up! You are now level 29.
Three stat points gained.

New achievement! Locomotive Breath!
While it's not exactly a feat of engineering worthy of a Queen Elizabeth Prize, you finally managed to manufacture a train derailment. Let's hope this doesn't set off some sort of unforeseen domino effect that will ripple throughout the rest of the floor, leading to mass confusion and death amongst you and your fellow crawlers.
Reward: You've received a Gold Engineering Box!

That was ominous.

"Okay," I said as the explosions and crumpling sounds finally ceased. "Let's get moving. Donut, do you see any red dots?"

"No," she said. "There are some corpses on the platform. I think one of the cars broke open."

"Let's go down there. Katia, keep a timer going. Eight minutes."

If the next train down the line didn't stop, we needed to be out of there for the next crash. And the one after that. I didn't know how this was going to play, but first we needed to look at what we'd done.

"Wow," Donut said as we went down the stairs into the smoke-filled room. The engine car was on its side, the top almost reaching the inside wall of the platform. I couldn't see the bottom of the train at this angle, but smoke billowed from underneath, most of it venting into the ceiling. The engine was still attached to part of car number two, which had been twisted and peeled away like a tin can. Dead tentacle wolves and skunk fairies lay scattered about the passenger car, some of them having rolled onto the platform. This second car was half on the track, back raised, half twisted forward and on its side, leaving a massive rent where the roof once was. I didn't know if the crash had killed the mobs or if they automatically died once they were exposed to the air of this platform.

"There are still some mobs alive in the back cars of the train," Donut said. "I can see the white dot of the conductor. I don't see the engineer, but I never did before."

"Good," I said. I felt relief that we hadn't killed the conductor.

"The train jumped the track, but the engine car doesn't look hurt," Katia said. "It's on its side, but it's all in one piece. It ripped that other car in half when it flipped over."

"It must be made out of stronger stuff," I said, picking my way down to the bottom of the stairs. The train had bowled over the magical sign in the center of the platform. Hunks of metal were everywhere. Dozens of small fires burned. If they didn't have the vent system, this place would be completely full of black choking smoke.

We moved to the peeled half of the second car, approaching the gangway, which had been flayed open, creating a window to the tracks below. Debris littered the ground, sparks flying as the metal came in contact with the rail. I could see part of the main train track was a mangled mess. This track wouldn't be used anytime soon.

We could now see the still-closed doorway leading into train car number one.

"The door is still intact," Katia said. "If he doesn't come out, what're we going to do?"

Before I could answer, the door slid open, and an enormous figure emerged, half pulling himself, half falling from the sideways door and onto the ripped and tattered wall of the gangway. He grumbled something and pulled himself up.

"All righty, then," I muttered as the . . . man . . . came to his feet. He stood about eight feet tall, towering over us.

Vernon the conductor had suggested that the engineers might be human based on their voices, but he really wasn't certain. He'd never seen one. He'd only been half correct.

From the shoulders down, this was a normal man. He was built large and strong. But where a normal person's neck would be was another torso, leading to the top half of—another?—man. This top half wasn't as large as the lower half. The creature had a pair of legs and arms on the bottom half and another pair of arms on the top half. The gap-toothed man had greasy black hair that hung out from his engineer's hat. His top torso wore a filthy, once-white tank top that read "Welcome to the Gun Show." The bottom, larger half was naked except for a loincloth made of fur.

The man's face and naked lower half were covered in lined streaks of blue paint, like he was cosplaying Mel Gibson's character in *Braveheart.*

Gore-Gore. ManTauR. Level 40.

Ocher Line Train Engineer.

Of all the 'taurs out there, from Centaurs to Bisontaurs to Rhinotaurs, the ManTauR is one of the weirdest. Half human and, uh, half human, the ManTauR has been genetically engineered for both strength and dexterity, making them perfect for the often-grueling and thankless job of Tangle Train Engineer.

Unfortunately, the act of making these magnificent, large-footed beasts oftentimes results in creatures with double amounts of testosterone and whatever else makes humans so prone to overt masculinity and hyper, overenthusiastic piety toward their god of choice.

"That's the weirdest thing I've ever seen in my life," Katia muttered.

"Hail, brother and sister," Gore-Gore shouted. "And Princess. Fine Princess! Hail! You have survived the train wreck. We must flee this wretched place. But behold! Luck is on our side in this dark time, for we are at a transit station where we may find sustenance and mead!" The mantaur fell forward, so he ran on his legs and lower set of arms, which was absurdly disturbing. He bounded from the train, rushed past us and onto the platform.

He thinks we were passengers. He doesn't know we're the ones who crashed the train. "What about the conductor?" I called, turning to look at the back of the train. Cars number three and four were smushed up against one another, the conjunction between the two cars starting to reach up toward the ceiling of the chamber. Car five was still half in the tunnel.

"Time is scarce!" the creature shouted, even though it wasn't necessary to shout. "The next train will be upon us soon. And the one after that! All will crash. It will take time for the home base to learn there is a problem and to send an interdiction team. We must flee this forsaken place! Run and we will live to battle another day!" He turned and charged for the stairs.

"Should we help the conductor?" Katia asked.

"Ah, he'll probably be fine," I said. "Come on. We need to talk to this guy before he gallops away."

THE SECOND TRAIN CAREENED INTO THE BACK OF THE FIRST, CAUS-ing yet another earthquake and a giant, screeching crash. It sounded as if more cars were pushed into the platform below. More dust and smoke billowed up from below.

All of us stood at the top of the stairwell. Gore-Gore didn't seem to know what to do with himself now that he was out of the train. This had already gone differently than I was expecting. I sent some instructions to Donut over chat.

"Hail, my fallen brothers!" Gore-Gore suddenly shouted for no apparent reason. He beat his top chest, leaving a splotch of blue body paint on his filthy shirt.

"Hey," Donut said, "can Carl here ask you some questions?"

"Of course!" he shouted. "It is my sacred duty to help the customers of the Tangle! That goes double for princesses and their man-servants!"

"Can you please stop shouting?" Donut said. "It upsets Mongo."

Mongo squawked in agreement.

CARL: Now you know how I feel when you type in all caps.
DONUT: THAT'S NOT THE SAME THING, CARL.

"I will do my best, Princess Donut," the man shouted. "I do not wish to upset your royal steed. How may I serve you!"

"We have some questions about the end of the line," I said.

"You mean stop number 435?" he said, his manner changing instantly. It was like I'd flipped a switch. He lowered his voice. "We recommend all passengers disembark at stop 433. That is the last transit station. After that, it is not safe. Even for fine warriors such as yourselves."

"Safe?" Katia scoffed. "The stops before that are safe?"

"What's at stop 434? And 435?" I asked.

"Stop 434 is barren," he said. "Stop 435 is where my fellow employees exit the train and take the portal back to the depot."

"What about you?" I probed. "We talked to a conductor, and he said he never sees your kind get off the train. And they don't remember what happens at 435."

Gore-Gore paused, an odd expression on his paint-covered face. He seemed scared and something else. Ashamed? It didn't make sense. I knew we'd never be getting this information if we didn't have Donut and her charisma greasing the wheels for us. "The Tangle employees, having completed their sacred duty, disembark at 435 and proceed into the tunnel, which transports them back to base. The Kravyad are in charge of employee return. They use their dark magic to prepare the employees before they enter the portal. The portal has a side effect regarding memory. Human resources says they're looking into it."

"What about you?" I repeated. "What do *you* do?"

"I, uh, gate the train. Like any true engineer would."

"What does that mean?"

"There's a gate just after stop 435, and I drive into it. It is an enormous portal that the train just pushes through. I enter, and I am back at the depot, pulling into a parking spot. Alas, it's just my engine car. The nineteen other cars are gone."

"Gone?" I asked.

He snapped a finger on one of his lower hands. "Just like that. One moment I'm approaching the abyss gate, and then I'm at the depot. It's magic, and I do not know how it works." He looked back and forth and then leaned in, whispering as if afraid he'd be overheard. "My kind do not believe magic is honorable or true. I do not like utilizing the gate. But I am a good employee, and I do what I am told. There's no memory loss like the dwarves and grapples experience. There's a flash of vile light, and I and the car teleport. I sleep for eight hours in my cabin, eat an epic meal, get up and do the checks, and wait for them to hook the cars back up for my next run."

"You sleep?" I asked. "The conductor said when he gets to the end of the line, he blinks and he's getting on the train again right away. He didn't say there was enough time for anyone to go to sleep."

Gore-Gore's top half shrugged. The streak of blue face paint glinted in the light. "They lose some time when they go through the portal. It's nine or ten hours until the next shift."

"And what about the other cars? They say they loop back in time, resetting themselves."

He nodded. "I do not know the details. The passenger cars go through a deep cleaning upon transport. Any damage is repaired. Foreign objects are removed. Mostly."

That wasn't exactly how Vernon put it. "But what about *your* car? It doesn't get, uh, deep cleaned?"

"No. It does not."

Excellent. I asked the important question. "So if we are with you when you go through the gate, we'd be okay, too?"

He paused. "I have heard of passengers riding through the gate. The deep-cleaning process isn't good for them. Sometimes there are bones."

I shook my head. "I don't mean if we were in the passenger cars. I mean if we were in the engine car. With you."

Gore-Gore frowned. "I always wish to ride with fellow warriors, especially into the unknown. But alas! Nobody rides in the first car except engineers. It is the rule of the Tangle! Not even other employees are allowed within. No exceptions!"

"But if we *were* in that first car, we'd be fine?"

"You would not be killed by the abyss gate." He abruptly lifted all four arms into the air, and metal blades erupted from the flesh over his top two wrists with a *shing*, like he was some sort of fucked-up Wolverine. "But I would be honor bound to slay you! No exceptions, my fellow warrior!"

"Okay, then," I said, taking a step back. This guy was crazy. *They're all crazy. Every last one of them.* "One last question. You came out because the train crashed. Is there any other reason why you'd come out of the car? Like if we ever wanted to talk to one of your fellow engineers, how would we do that?"

He lowered his arms, blades retracting back into his skin. Blood dribbled down his hands where the blades appeared. "We do not leave the engine car if the train is intact. This is a rule. Now, my fellow warriors. I see a place of respite. I shall drink my fill of mead and wait for the crash interdiction team to arrive to extract me back to base. Hail!"

We watched as Gore-Gore turned and walked toward Club Vanquisher. He ducked into the entrance, disappearing.

"It figures he'd be a member of that place," I said. I turned to Katia and Donut. Below, we heard another distant squeal as yet another train crashed. "What did we just learn?"

"It sounds like we can get back to the start if we can get into the engine car," Katia said.

"That's right," I said. "But if the only way to get into the car is by crashing a train, then that won't do us any good."

"We need an engineer's key. He probably has it in his inventory," Katia said. "That way we can break into the first car while the train is still moving."

I nodded. "That's what I'm thinking. But we know the keys are also color coded. So his key will only work on other ocher line trains. I don't think we can hop over to the yellow line and use it there. And if we have to crash a train to get the key, that stops the rest of the trains on the line. We don't know for how long. If the trains are stopped, then the key is useless."

"Wait, Carl," Donut said. "Doesn't it only stop the trains behind it? What if we get the key, jump onto the *Nightmare Express* or one of those other superfast loop trains, and jump ahead on the line and catch one of the trains that were already ahead?"

"That's brilliant," I said to Donut, scratching her on the head. She beamed. I'd also come up with that idea, but I wasn't about to say that now. "I think he actually revealed two different ways to get to the stairwells. We can also use the employee portal. Maybe. It sounds like people who take that path lose time and suffer memory issues. And they have to fight the Kravyad, whatever that is. Probably a boss guarding the portal."

"It seems so complicated," Katia said. "How many of the 300,000 crawlers are going to find out about this?"

"Hopefully all of them," I said. "With all of our contacts, we'll start spreading the word. I doubt there's only one or two ways to get out of this. There's a lot we're missing. Like what's at stop number 436, the one we can only get to with the *Nightmare Express?* And I still need to talk to Elle and Imani about—"

"Vile traitors! Saboteurs!" Gore-Gore shouted as he burst out of Club Vanquisher. "Poseurs! And I thought you were true! In the name of the exalted Grull, I will slay thee! Hail and kill!" He raised his arms and once again produced the metallic claws. His face was a mask of rage. His dot was now red.

The ram-headed cleric peeked out of the door and waved before disappearing back inside.

Music started to play. *Ah fuck.*

"Grull?" Donut said. "Isn't that . . . ?"

"Yep," I said just before the world froze.

B-b-b-b Boss Battle!

Our avatars appeared floating in the air.

You've enraged an NPC. But not just any NPC! It's a neighborhood boss! It's . . .

VERSUS! Clanged onto the floating text, with simulated blood splattering everywhere. Gore-Gore's screaming portrait splatted onto the virtual screen.

GORE-GORE THE MANTAUR! TRAIN ENGINEER! ADHERENT OF GRULL THE WAR GOD! BERSERKER EXTREME! LEVEL 40!

The world unstuck, and Gore-Gore galloped directly at us, screaming and frothing at the mouth.

"Oh, this should be fun," I said.

―――――――

"POSITION THREE," I CALLED. I FORMED A FIST, CAUSING MY GAUNT-let to appear. In this formation Katia remained close, but Mongo moved far to my left. Donut remained on the ground, falling back and to my left in the space between me and Mongo.

"Carl, I think that cleric guy told him we crashed the train! What a jerk!"

"Ya think?" I said. "Fire!"

Donut launched two magic missiles at him. They bounced harm-lessly off the charging man's chest.

"It says magic missiles are ineffective!" Donut screamed.

"Okay, we're doing this the hard way," I said. "Doozy!"

I dropped a smoke curtain as Katia and I moved three steps to my right. Donut cast *Hole* on the ground in front of the charging mantaur. At the same time, I cast *Fear*.

The hole was only an inch deep, and the creature barely stum-bled. My *Fear* spell seemed to only have a small effect. One of these days that was going to be a great move. I cast *Bang Bro* on my gaunt-let, which now glowed with electrical fire. I downed a mana refill.

"Further treachery," Gore-Gore squealed. "Magic and wizardry. Die in Grull's name!" He leapt and blindly swung his blades at the space where I was just standing. He turned and swiped again, this time at Donut's location, which I hadn't been expecting. She back-flipped out of the way. Mongo screeched in anger. Katia and I rushed forward. I pulled back and punched him as hard as I could, smash-ing him in the kidney of his lower torso. He grunted. His body felt solid and strong, like a sack stuffed with gravel. He howled in rage as a health bar appeared, down maybe 5%.

1.5

The notification appeared out of nowhere and hung persistent on my interface.

I recognized what it meant, though I was puzzled why it remained on the screen. I had to be careful with my punches. Because of my magic gauntlet's special ability, each successful punch had a 1.5% chance to summon Grull the war god, which would probably be a juiced-up, almost immortal version of Prince Stalwart of the Skull Empire. That was the last thing we needed.

Mongo shrieked as he leapt through the air, claws out. Gore-Gore reacted with lightning speed, backhanding the dinosaur and knocking him aside with the top, dull part of his blades. Mongo squealed in pain and hit the ground hard, his health alarmingly low despite the glancing blow.

"Mongo!" Donut cried, jumping toward her injured pet as Gore-Gore whirled again, leaping toward me.

I could tell the smoke curtain was doing a good job of keeping him blind. But he was a smart fighter with whirlwind reflexes. Before I could jump back, he sliced viciously down at me.

Katia leaped forward, blocking the blow with her arm. She tumbled, crying out in pain. I looked down in horror to see part of her arm spin away. It hit the ground with a clang.

It's just metal. Not flesh.

I leaped forward, getting close to his chest and punched four quick times.

3.0

4.5

6.0

7.5

Oh shit. The description never said it was a cumulative chance. But what choice did I have? I was in tight and too close to kick. I kneed at him with my spiked kneepad, but I could tell the power just wasn't there. *I have to get back.* I had to punch again two more times to get away. With the last blow, I felt something deep within the creature's chest crack. He howled in outrage and pain.

9.0

10.5

He swiped again as I reared back. The tips of the blades scraped across my face. I screamed as the three razors tore flesh. Gore-Gore grunted in surprise as my Damage Reflect hit him. A hand from his lower torso wrapped around my throat, catching me before I could get away. Then they were both around my throat, squeezing. I looked up to see him raising his upper-right hand in the air to pierce down.

I mentally slammed on *Protective Shell*.

He cried out as he was ejected from the area, flying to my right, pushed away toward the stairwell, down into the smoky, flaming wreckage of the ocher station platform.

Unfortunately, the static nature of the spell that worked so well for me before worked against me this time. While Gore-Gore was tossed away, he still had a firm, double-handed grip around my throat. So when he shot away, I was pulled with him like a dog on a leash.

I gurgled as I felt myself flying and spinning through the air. Somewhere in there, his grip on my throat went slack.

We bounced off the stairs once, his body cushioning my own, but when we hit the floor, he landed on me, knocking the breath out of my chest. I felt an ominous *crunch* within myself. He continued his forward, tumbling momentum as I slammed onto a healing potion, even before I stopped moving, coming to rest against a red-hot, burning hunk of metal. I cried out, scrambling away. I screamed again as my broken ribs and arm healed themselves. *Holy shit, that hurts.*

I turned in time to see him fall off the edge of the platform, his body plummeting into the space between the third and fourth cars, which had been smushed further together by the subsequent crashes, causing the two cars to form a massive tepee shape, with the junction between the two touching the ceiling.

I clambered to my feet as Gore-Gore, dazed, stood all the way up to his full height on the track between the cars, as if he was standing underneath an awning. The top of his head brushed the mangled wheels of the train cars. He'd lost his engineer's hat somewhere along the way, revealing a massive bald spot atop his head. His health was down to about 20%. *Christ, this dude is tough.*

"I feel it in my chest," Gore-Gore said, his voice odd. "I have been blessed by the gods."

That's when I saw that **10.5** was now blinking, and Gore-Gore had a timer over his head.

Ten seconds and counting.

Holy shit, I summoned the god. I had seconds to finish this or we'd all be dead.

"Carl! Carl! We're coming!" Donut cried from the top of the stairs.

This is a terrible idea, I thought as I rushed forward. I activated my Talon Strike skill as I ran, leaping over debris. I bounded one more time, and I executed a dropkick right at the solar plexus of the lower chest of Gore-Gore.

He rocketed back on the tracks as I dropped into the channel like a sack of hammers.

Zzzzzt.

It wasn't a loud sound. I barely heard it over the sound of the music. But I felt it. Anyone who has ever been close to high-voltage lines knows the feeling. You can sense it. Death, right there rushing by.

As the electrified corpse of Gore-Gore crumpled and hit the main tracks, I more than sensed the current rushing through the third rail. My entire body ripped in pain as the tracks were electrified by the short circuit caused by Gore-Gore's body. Thankfully, the grounding was enough that the shock was dispersed. I hopped backward, stumbling and hitting the back of my head on the platform's edge. I felt jaws bite onto the back of my jacket and cloak as Donut pulled me from the channel. She cast a *Heal* scroll on me as she shouted my name.

The world froze again as the **Winner!** notification appeared.

"That wasn't very fun," I said up at Donut a minute later. I groaned, sitting up. "Let's try to loot his corpse without getting electrocuted and then go get some pho. I need to rest before I can handle any more excitement."

Admin Notice. Congratulations, Crawler. You have been sponsored!

Viewers watching your feed will now occasionally see advertisements produced by your sponsor.

Sponsor's Name: The Valtay Corporation.

Additional details available in the Sponsorship Tab of your interface.

12

"Carl, Carl, I hit level 28 *and* I got a sponsor!" Donut said as I pulled myself to my feet. She gasped. "Carl, guess what. It's Princess D'nadia of the Prism Kingdom! I love her!"

I shook my head. I still felt disoriented. Below, a clockwork Mongo was gingerly pulling on Gore-Gore's loincloth in an attempt to get him away from the electrified rail. We needed to hurry this up. Once the next train came and smashed into the back of the line, it was possible these two cars could come crashing down. Plus every one of these other trains presumably had more Gore-Gores driving them. The last thing I needed was to have to fight another one of these guys. "D'nadia? Who was that again?"

Donut glowered at me. "Carl, she's probably watching right now. Tell her you're sorry!"

"I'm sorry, Princess D'nadia of the Prism Kingdom," I said. "Now who is she?"

Donut sighed. "You sat right next to her when we were on Ripper Wonton's show. She's a Saccathian. A Sac. Really, Carl."

I remembered, then. It'd only been a few days. She was a tentacle-faced creature. Her country, planet, solar system, whatever, the Prism, was supposedly small but powerful. Princess D'nadia was very outspoken and seemed to spend most of her time traveling from talk show to talk show. I remembered she'd kept trying to grab my virtual hand. When the Skull Empire had accidentally killed

Manasa—who had really been controlled by a brain parasite from the Valtay Corporation—in their attempt to assassinate us, D'nadia had been very upset. *Huh,* I thought. Two parties that were there during that incident had sponsored us.

"Who'd you get?" Donut asked.

"The Valtay Corporation," I said.

CARL: Not a word about them out loud. Borant hates them. They're the ones who are trying to invade the Borant system. They're the reason why the show started when it did.

DONUT: IF BORANT HATES THEM, THEN WHY DID THEY LET THEM SPONSOR YOU?

CARL: Borant probably doesn't have a choice.

DONUT: DOES THAT MEAN YOU'RE GOING TO GET REALLY GOOD STUFF?

CARL: I don't know. I hope so. But it might mean the opposite. It might mean Borant is going to try to get me killed much faster. The good thing is, we make them a lot of money right now. We need to make sure we are worth more alive than dead.

The last thing I wanted was to be a pawn in some intergalactic pissing match. I had enough to worry about already.

"Did you see the thing that said people watching our feed get commercials from our sponsors?" Donut said. "I hope Princess D'nadia has lots of different commercials. There's nothing worse than the same ad showing over and over and over. When you left the TV on the old-person channel, and I got stuck watching *Matlock* all day, it was the same help-I've-fallen-and-I-can't-get-up ad every commercial break."

"We get another sponsor when we hit the fifth floor. And another on the sixth. So let's make sure we get through this floor, and your fans will have a bit of variety."

"I think my fans should have a name. Wouldn't that be great? Like the Princess Patrol or something."

I grunted. "How about the Donut Holes?"

"Don't be crude, Carl."

Below, one of the Mongos exploded as he accidentally touched a hunk of metal attached to the third rail. The second automaton grunted and pulled the Gore-Gore corpse harder, bringing the large body up against the wall of the channel. I reached down and looted him, receiving 498 gold and three items. An **ocher line engineer's key**, a bottle of **Rev-Up Magic Hair Restoration**, and the neighborhood map. The moment I accepted the map, it populated in my interface, not with the immediate area like it usually did, but with a map of the complete ocher line, including all the stops and the current location of all the trains.

"Oh wow," I said, zooming in and scrolling up and down the map. The info started at station 11 and went all the way up to 435. "Make sure you grab the neighborhood map. This is way more than we usually get." This particular train line was shaped like a squiggle. Up the line, the trains continued to move. I could see all the dots on the trains, including the white dots of the conductor and engineers and grapples, along with the red dots of the Jikininki janitor ghouls and other monsters. I didn't see any blue dots of fellow crawlers. The last train to get through station 149—the one I'd spray-painted with an X—appeared to be continuing its way up the tracks unhindered. It was just about to hit station 160. A traffic jam of trains appeared behind the one we'd crashed. If there was an "interdiction team" coming like Gore-Gore stated, I didn't see any sign of them.

I did see a few oddities on the tracks. Since 151 was another transit station, the next station after this one that would have monsters was station 152. The tracks outside that station, along with 153 and 154, had monsters on them. Monsters on the actual tracks. I watched as one mob—something called a **Drake Bitch**—hit the electrified line and turned itself into an X. More monsters appeared by the minute.

The monsters are jumping on the track and walking up to station 155.

The trains had stopped coming, and the creatures weren't waiting any longer. It was going to take them a long time. There were miles between each station. That would soon start happening behind us, too. In fact, I could see the red dots of monsters moving between the crashed train cars behind us, though it didn't appear they could get past the tangled wreckage. The ones ahead of us would have a long walk. The stations were pretty far apart, especially further up the line.

The early stations were much closer, easily walkable. In fact, stations 11 through 72 were each about a city block or two apart from one another. We could walk that distance unhindered in a few hours. That was good to know. By comparison, stations 300 and 301 looked to be about 40 or 50 miles apart.

We went up the stairs to find Katia sitting on the ground, crying silently. She'd returned to her normal shape. She cradled her right hand in her left. I noted she'd gone up a level to 24. I was still at 29.

"Are you okay?" I asked, rushing up.

She chinned at the hunk of metal on the ground. It was the chunk of armor that Gore-Gore had sliced off when she'd been protecting me. Only then did I see the splash of blood.

She held up her right hand, which looked like a normal, unharmed hand. But as I watched, her palm reshaped and her four fingers disappeared. "He chopped my fingers off. When I healed, they didn't come back."

"Oh no," I said, sitting down next to her. "I'm sorry. I thought it was just part of your armor. We would've come back up sooner if we'd known you'd been injured."

She sniffed. "It's stupid. I can build fingers from other parts of me. He didn't *really* chop off my fingers. I'm like clay. All I lost was a bit of flesh. I had to take a ring off of my severed finger and put it on my new fingers. But part of me is gone. I'm losing myself."

"That's not true." I gently tapped her forehead. "Look. The real Katia is still there. They can cut everything else off, but you're still you. Don't let them break you. No matter what they do. Okay?"

"Okay," she said, getting to her feet. She did not sound convinced. She kept opening and flexing her hand. She swallowed and seemed to take a moment to steady herself.

We needed to get her more armor. Much more armor. Her class and race were a perfect combination for the ultimate tank, but we weren't taking advantage of it. I was worried how she'd react to the idea, but we needed to figure out a way to completely sheathe her in metal. She needed to be 90% metal, 10% flesh, not the other way around.

"Have you ever had pho before?" I asked, pointing at the safe room. Now that I had access to the map, I could keep a lookout for more of the boss monsters, but it didn't appear any were headed this way. "Let's take a minute to refresh ourselves, and then we'll hit the purple line and spend the rest of the day grinding."

"Hey, did you get a sponsor?" Donut asked as we walked. "I am sponsored by the beautiful and awesome Princess D'nadia of the Prism and Carl got the Valtay Corporation."

"I did," Katia said as we entered the pho shop. "Mine is a princess, too. It just says Princess Formidable of the Skull Empire."

"I WONDER WHO THIS PRINCESS IS," KATIA SAID AS WE ATE OUR soup. She had Mordecai's map out and was filling it in with the new ocher line information along with new intelligence from the Daughters. Donut was in the base taking a shower. Mongo remained with us, staring at me until I tossed a hunk of meat at him. "I haven't gotten anything yet from her. Have you gotten anything?"

"Not yet," I said. I knew exactly who this princess was. Zev had mentioned her once, though not by name. King Rust was the orc leader of the Skull Empire. Prince Stalwart was the crown prince. Prince Maestro had been second in the line of succession until he'd been disowned and then killed by the Valtay in retaliation for the botched assassination attempt that had killed Manasa instead of me. Zev had said that if Stalwart was disowned for his failed attempt, the sister would be next in line. I assumed it was this Princess Formidable. But was she now the first in line? *Had* Prince Stalwart been disowned?

"Hekla says she got sponsored by some interstellar ranch or something. They're probably showing her viewers commercials for space hamburgers."

I sighed. This pho tasted like ass. The Bopca running this joint had tried his best, but it was clear he didn't know what he was doing. I pushed the bowl to the edge of the table, and Mongo gleefully dunked his head in.

"Look, I figured something out," Katia said, pushing the giant paper forward. "Our next goal is to see what's at the end of the line as quickly as possible, no? If we go here"—she pointed—"and then jump lines here, we can get on something called the *Dismemberment Limited*. According to your friend Bautista, the *Dismemberment Limited* also stops here. The *Nightmare Express* stops two stations down on the mauve line. And since the *Nightmare* goes all the way up to 436, which is one higher than the supposed end of the line, we can get on that and see what's at the very end. If we take this path, we can get there in a few hours instead of days."

I just looked at her. "I don't understand what the hell you just said, but I believe you."

She shrugged. "You should try riding the Tokyo subway when you only know Icelandic, German, Russian, and English," she said. "I only went once when I was a kid, and it was a nightmare. This is much more straightforward once you have the map."

I looked over her map. The whole mess of lines gave me a headache. I'd looked at DIY wiring diagrams that made more sense. "The problem is, we don't yet know if the named trains, like the *Nightmare Express* or the *Dismemberment Limited*, are safe."

"Of course they're not safe," Katia said. She finally noticed that Mongo was inching his way toward her own bowl of forgotten pho. She pushed it toward him. He made a joyful peeping noise and started slurping noisily.

"You got that right," I said as Donut emerged from the base. She was washed and shining.

"The boss box was a bust," Donut said. "All I got was a bunch of healing scrolls and a poison dart trap kit."

"That sounds awesome," I said.

"So what's the plan?" asked Donut.

I looked to Katia. "Lead the way."

ACCORDING TO THE SIGN OUTSIDE OF THE *DISMEMBERMENT LIMITED*, the train came every 48 minutes. We didn't know when it'd last been through, so we sat down to wait. It was a short loop, and we needed to get off on the very next stop. Since the whole loop was 48 minutes, I figured we'd be at our next transfer in probably only 15 or 20 minutes. That seemed like it was too fast, but then I saw the tracks, and I understood.

The station for the *Nightmare Express* had been twice as long as the regular platforms. The tunnel was bigger, too. That wasn't the case with this train. The platform was actually smaller than usual. The tunnel appeared to be the same circumference as the colored lines.

The track itself was a wide, flat platform with two metal beams running on either side. This was a monorail system. A maglev train. We'd had something similar in Seattle, though this looked much more futuristic.

Donut practiced with her *Hole* spell while we waited. I'd finally talked her into grasping it wasn't useless. She managed to get it up to level two, which made a hole two inches deep. (The hole was really six centimeters deep, or three centimeters a level, which came out to 2.3-something inches. The dungeon used metric measurements for everything, but I still couldn't get the imperial system out of my head. It was something I had to constantly deal with at work, and I'd gotten used to guess-converting. I had a unit conversion chart taped to the side of my toolbox.) Anyway, a level two *Hole* was deep enough for most non-reinforced doors. She could snap the spell on and off at will. For now she could only make a manhole-cover-sized hole that'd last about five minutes if she didn't turn it off early.

I watched her as she placed a hole in the platform's information sign. She made Mongo stick his head through it and snap, practicing a move we'd discussed. We called it Surprise One. When we were done, she turned the hole off, and the sign returned to its previous form, undamaged.

"This is the greatest spell in the world, Carl. I need to train this up."

"Keep working on it."

While she practiced, I messaged Elle and Imani.

CARL: Hey. You guys free?

ELLE: There you are. I was starting to get worried. Naughty boy.

I spent some time explaining what we'd figured out.

IMANI: Carl, we should refrain from stopping any more trains until we have a solid plan of how to get out of here. If you stop a train and there are other crawlers behind you on the line, you might end up trapping them. And that's a really bad idea. Worse than you think.

CARL: So what was the deal with that stop you guys investigated?

ELLE: Drugs. This octopus lady has them all addicted to opiates. Painkillers. They're called Rev-Up Vitamin Shots. They're called shots, but you drink them.

Imani went on to explain what they'd discovered.

Every five stops, all the ones ending in a five or a zero, there was a set of tunnels. Each monster from the previous stops in that section would get off the train, and they'd line up by race, entering the tunnels. At the end of each passageway was a door with a slot on it.

Behind the door was a monster called a Pooka. Imani described them as fuzzy, goblin-like creatures. They were neighborhood bosses. Each Pooka had a pile of potion vials, and it would hand out one to each monster through the door slot, who'd then take the vial and go through a swirling one-way portal that'd return them to their station.

The potions appeared to be powerful, addictive, race-specific sedatives. That explained why the monsters who missed their stops would panic. The monsters were only allowed one vial at a time, and each high would only last so long. Imani said it appeared the drug didn't activate until they took it through the portal. So the monsters would get their vial, go through the portal to take it, and once the high started to wear off, they'd return to the train station to go get another.

IMANI: The description of the vials says if the mobs don't get their fix in time, something happens to them. They change physically. It's like with the brindle grubs all over again, but this time it's all the mobs on the floor. So every time we interrupt the trains, it sets off a chain reaction up and down the line for the monsters who can't get their vial.

CARL: And Krakaren?

IMANI: She's the one making the individual drugs. I'm guessing since each vial is race-specific, there's a different Krakaren borough boss at each one of those stops. I wasn't confident in our ability to face her, so I had the team back off.

ELLE: We could've taken her. Imani is too timid. I could've iced the whole lot.

IMANI: The Pooka monsters turn into giant goats when you attack them. So be careful if you face one. They're tough.

We agreed to meet up again soon at the Desperado Club so they could copy the map. It'd gotten too cumbersome to relay over chat. They wished us luck on the *Dismemberment Limited*.

"I don't understand. What's the point of all this?" Katia asked after I relayed what the others had discovered.

"I have a theory," I said. "Mordecai told us that the NPCs and monsters are released into the game, and they have new memories each time. Right? But in the end, they're still independent creatures. They're not brainless mobs like one might find in a real video game. Getting one or two mobs to do something is probably easy. But controlling an entire group is probably harder than it sounds. They have emotions and motivations and their own lives. In order to get them to do something, they have to *want* to do it. The showrunners came up with this level with the trains, but they wanted the monsters to come and go every five stops, making it an engineering challenge. They had to come up with a universal way to make that happen. Why not have them all addicted to drugs? Now the monsters are more compliant, and they are looping and patrolling in a predictable pattern."

"So they took a whole floor's worth of mobs and strung them out?" Katia asked. "That seems . . . overly complicated."

I grunted. "The whole thing is nuts. It's set up to be this perfect self-contained ecosystem. At least for a little while. I don't know when these guys eat or sleep or whatever else. But the floor is designed to break the moment people start messing with the system. Imani says they change if they don't get their drugs. I suspect we're going to find out soon what that means. Train is coming. Get ready."

The train was almost silent as it pulled into the station. The sleek white train's first car was at a steep angle, an aerodynamic shape, followed by only two additional cars. The entire front cockpit was glass like the cockpit of a B-17 chin turret. Through the glass window, we could see the train's operator.

He was an odd-looking creature. My first thought was *Grim reaper wearing a poncho and mask.* He noticed us on the platform the moment we saw him. And even though he had no physical eyes, I could feel his gaze upon us as we waited for the train to stop.

Unlike the colored lines, we could enter this first car. In fact, I realized, there was only one pair of doors on the entire train, and they were near the driver. It appeared the engineer was the only creature on board, at least in this first car. He was not in a separate room, but simply in a lowered glass section up front with a dashboard of controls in front of him, like a regular bus driver. He sat on a little bouncy seat. The glass front section of the train was designed so when the train was moving, the engineer could look straight down and see the track rushing by.

"No, please. Please, don't get on," he said as the door hissed open. "Please. Find another way. We're not open to crawlers."

"Oh, we're not going to hurt you," Donut said as she jumped on board. Mongo followed, with Katia and me taking up the rear. "Not as long as you don't try to hurt us."

"What the hell is this?" I muttered, taking in the carriage.

The train car wasn't as broad as a regular coach, but there were no seats here. It was an open room, almost like a freight car. At the end of the car was a closed sliding door leading to the next car.

Every square inch of the car's interior was covered in dried blood and gore. It smelled of rotting death.

"This is disgusting," Donut said. She jumped to my shoulder and started rapidly licking her paw. "I just took a shower."

"Please. It's not too late," the engineer said. "Get off now."

I turned to regard him. The sickly pale creature sat in the chair, naked except for his engineer's hat. What I'd taken for a poncho was actually just flesh that didn't properly fit his form. He had no muscles or definition to his body. The green-tinted flesh hung off of him like a fitted sheet placed on a too-small bed. The right side of his face hung loosely. When he spoke, the hole for his mouth hung below the bottom of his jawline, and the words came from the nose holes. The nose itself appeared like it was supposed to be hooked, but it hung to the side, dangling like a used condom on the side of the creature's face. The eyeholes drooped, revealing yellow bone. Clumps of black hair clung to the head.

Levi the Seventh—Troll Flesher and Hobgoblin Skellie Symbiote. Level 7.

This is actually two creatures. Only when combined do they have intelligence and the ability to speak. The Skellie is your typical, run-of-the-mill reanimated skeleton. In this case, it's the skeleton of a hobgoblin, one of the few monsters who are much more palatable in skeleton form.

Of all the War Mage spells soldiers encounter during the brutal mass combat that will occur on the ninth floor, the *You're Not Done Yet* spell is one of the most terrifying. Fallen soldiers—in this example a Basher Troll—are cast with the spell, and their flesh is ripped from the body. This loose skin becomes a sentient minion called a Flesher. Fleshers are oftentimes tossed across the battlefield, landing in and around the trenches of the enemy. Fleshers have one goal. To find a new set of bones.

Once they have found a victim, the skin unfurls and pounces, covering the body, smothering and melting it. Once dead, the rest of the victim burns away, and the Flesher casts the only spell it knows. *Boned*, which animates the remaining skeleton.

The creature that eventually forms is no longer a minion to the original mage. Nor is it undead. It is new to the world, oftentimes confused and afraid. And weak. The Symbiote is very easy to kill. After a few hours have passed and the new Symbiote is complete, the combined creature becomes a target for other Fleshers, who are said to be drawn to their former companion's new bones. If a Flesher kills a Symbiote, this second iteration is more intelligent and powerful than the last.

There are rumors about oft-re-sleeved Symbiotes. After enough repetitions, it's whispered they can become quite powerful.

Here's a neat tidbit of trivia. This is Levi the 7th. This quest has triggered six times now since the floor has opened.

"Please," Levi the 7th said as the door closed. It was already too late. "The back doors only open when crawlers are on board. It hurts so bad when they get to me."

The train started to move. I steadied myself as it picked up speed. A timer appeared in my interface.

Time to next stop 19 minutes.

"What's on the other side of that door?" I asked Levi, even though I knew perfectly well what it was going to be.

New Quest. Levi is on the Menu!
   This is a pass-or-fail quest. Failure has consequences.
   Do not allow Levi the 7th to be devoured by the Fleshers.
This quest is active as long as you remain on the train.
   Reward: **You will receive a Silver Quest Box.**
   Failure: **Every crawler on the train will be turned into a Flesher.**

I understood then why we hadn't received any information from people who'd ridden the named lines. People died when they rode the named lines.

I jumped into action. "Help me block out the door! Hurry!" I rushed for the back of the train as I pulled the gangway chock from my inventory. I now had several different versions of the blocking device, and the first one I pulled out was too big. The thin but heavy chunk of metal caught on the ceiling when I pulled it, and I stumbled. I jumped back and let it fall to the floor. It crashed with a tremendous clatter. I pulled the next size down. It was just a large, flat chunk of metal, rounded at the top. This one was about a half of an inch thick and had to weigh 800 pounds. It was designed to be placed in the gangways, but this train didn't appear to have spaces between the cars.

"Oh god, they're coming. I can feel them. Not again. They want my bones," Levi called from the front of the train as I struggled with the second chunk of metal. *I need to put handles on these.*

"He'll take your skin and my bones," Levi cried. "All is lost! I have been forsaken by the gods!"

Katia rushed up and helped me push the flat metal plate against the doorway. It slammed heavily against the wall. I could hear the doorway screech as it slid open on the other side of the block.

"We need to hold this in place," I said, pushing myself up against it. Katia also leaned in. She flattened out her shoulder and added thickness to her legs, turning herself into a brace.

"Carl, there's hundreds of them," Donut said, running up. "They just appeared on the map. The entire car is filled with them."

"They're going to get in. They always get in," Levi cried. "It's the end. Oh gods, it's the end!"

"Shut the hell up," I snapped back.

Thump. Thump thump.

It sounded like dishrags slapping against the inside of the metal. They didn't feel strong. Not yet.

"The third car door opened!" Donut said. "Carl, it's something else. It's bigger."

Thwap!

That one I felt. Something powerful and magical had just slammed against the barrier. I prepared my *Wisp Armor* spell.

"What else is back there?" I yelled at Levi.

"It's the war mage!" he cried. "Oh gods, he's coming."

Whap! Another spell hit the barrier, tossing us back an inch. Katia and I slammed the metal back into place, but not before at least a dozen flaps of pink and green and brown flesh started to reach around the edges of the metal. We slammed hard against the metal plate, pinning the manta-ray-like flaps of skin against the wall.

The dots finally appeared on my minimap, hundreds of them all bunched up against the door.

I looked up at the closest fragment of flesh, just above my head.

The exposed skin was only about three square inches wide, brown, and covered in hair, flapping up and down furiously.

Minion of War Mage Dismember—Swamp Orc Flesher—Level 10.
Ahh, isn't it cute? It wants to give you a hug.

As I pressed my shoulder against the metal, I reached up with my right hand and grasped on to the flesh. I yanked, easily ripping the flesh away like I was tearing at plastic wrap. It made no sound. Blood seeped from the wound before the rest of it pulled away. I had no idea if this hurt the main part or not. My fingers burned, and I dropped the wadded hunk of flesh. I stomped it down. The back side of the plastic-like skin was caustic.

The metal plate rocked again, but we were ready this time. Still, a few additional tendrils of flesh appeared along the edges. I was starting to feel pressure. I set my legs.

"Donut and Mongo, get the flesh on the edges. Only touch the skin side!"

I didn't have to ask twice. Donut leaped to my shoulder and leaped again, scratching down the edge of the barrier where the metal met the wall, ripping at the flesh. Her claws dug so deep she left scars on the wall itself. The moment she ripped through the flesh, it retracted as if in pain, leaving a smear of blood. On the other side, Mongo scrabbled at the wall with his feet. Jumping and pushing off, ripping at large sheets of skin. The pressure at the door eased.

I heard a deep squeal of rage from the other side. One by one, the red dots started to fall back. A new figure approached. It walked so it was right up against the other side of the metal. I felt it lean up against the barrier. It gave it a quick shove, as if to test our strength. The creature was strong, but we were stronger, especially combined.

Twelve minutes and counting.

"Do you really think I won't have your skin?" a voice rasped through the makeshift barrier. I pictured him there, whatever he was, head up against the metal. "Your friends were already on this train. Six other times. One group was much larger than your group now. They tried blocking the door, too. Such beautiful leather. Come now. Open it up. Join us. It will only hurt for but a moment."

I really wished I hadn't been forced to use my *Protective Shell* earlier. If we got past this, we sure as hell weren't going onto that *Nightmare* train until it was ready.

The metal plate rocked. It wasn't a spell, but the creature slamming it with his arms.

DONUT: SURPRISE ONE? SURPRISE TWO?

"What kind of creature is this mage?" I yelled down to Levi, who continued to whimper.

"He's a war mage!"

"No shit, he's a war mage. What's his race?"

From the other side of the metal, Dismember the War Mage started to laugh.

"War mages are war mages. That one looks like an elf," Levi called.

I felt two hands slap against the barrier. "I am not an elf, you fool. I just need eight more iterations, and you'll know, Levi. You'll know exactly what we are! Eight more trips. Seven after I get past these interlopers!"

"Stay the hell away from me, Dismember! You don't control me anymore!" Levi cried.

There was an odd crackling noise coming from the other side of the wall. *He's building up a spell. A big one. We need to hurry.*

DONUT: CARL?

Surprise Two involved opening a hole and me dropping a bomb through. I still wasn't too keen on the idea of blowing shit up inside of a moving train, especially after watching that last train wreck.

With Surprise One, I wasn't certain if a chomp from Mongo would be enough.

CARL: Let's do Surprise Three.

KATIA: We haven't practiced that one yet.

CARL: It's not exactly something we can practice anyway.

"On three," I whispered, pointing to a spot on the metal.

"Hey, Dismember," I said, speaking louder, "I want to tell you a secret."

"Oh, we don't have time for your secrets, you filthy crawler. Let me tell *you* a secret."

"Okay," I said, holding up one finger.

"After I knock this metal barrier down, I am going to send my minions in, and one of them is going to re-sleeve Levi. But they won't bother you. I'll have them leave you be."

"Go on," I said, holding up a second finger.

"And then I'm going to cast a spell that will peel the skin off of you and your friends. But I'm not going to kill you. I have another spell to keep you alive even after you've been flayed. It will be a journey of pain unlike anything that has ever been experienced in this world. I'm going to—"

I held up a third finger.

A hole appeared in the metal plate. Fast as I could, I reached through, grasped the surprised elf-like creature by his long silver hair, and pulled. The moment I pulled his head through the hole, Donut snapped off the spell.

I let go, and the severed head dropped to the ground, mouth still open wide.

"What was that, bitch? I didn't quite get that last part," I said.

13

MAUVE LINE—STATION 281.

The moment Dismember died, the Fleshers—now "bereft minions"—swarmed. We continued to press the metal up against the door, and they were unable to break through. I could see the X of Dismember's body for a few moments. It soon disappeared, presumably encompassed by one of his former minions. I didn't know if the process required a skull to successfully convert the Flesher into a Symbiote, but at least one of the monsters was making the effort.

Levi screamed for most of the remaining trip. "You did it! By the gods, you killed him! You sons of bitches did it!"

"He shouldn't get too excited," Donut muttered. "I can see a dozen other shapes in that third car who might be more war mages."

"It's former crawlers, I think. I think he was building an army. He takes our skin and then uses our bones to become stock for his budding army. It's probably some bullshit storyline we don't have time to get involved in," I said.

We pulled up to the stop, and I felt the door to car number two slide closed on its own. I picked up the war mage head and tossed it into my inventory. I retrieved the two metal chocks, and we got the hell off the train before the door closed.

We watched as the train left the station. Levi waved as it disappeared.

ZEV: Hi, guys!

DONUT: HI, ZEV! DID YOU SEE WHAT WE DID? WE POPPED HIS HEAD OFF!

ZEV: Yeah, that was a good one. The fans liked that line you did at the end, Carl. People want you to say your trademark line more often, though. Not too much, or it gets weird. But it's been a few days.

I sighed.

CARL: What can we do for you, Zev?

ZEV: I wanted to let you know that I booked you two for a show in two days.

DONUT: JUST US TWO? WHAT ABOUT MONGO AND KATIA?

ZEV: Katia stays in the dungeon. Mongo goes in the cage.

CARL: What sort of show?

ZEV: It's a little drier than what you're used to, but I'm confident you two can spice it up. It's a program called *Planet Beautiful*. It's especially popular this season. It's not so much an interview as a narration. You'll be going to a sound booth and reading prepared lines. It's a news program about the current season's planet. People are obsessed with Earth culture, and you two will be narrating a segment.

CARL: How can we "spice it up" if we're reading prepared lines? Also, I'm not going to read some anti-Earth propaganda bullshit. No way.

DONUT: WHAT WILL WE BE TALKING ABOUT?

ZEV: Uh, I'm not sure. I'll have to get back to you on that.

CARL: Zev, you are a terrible liar. What is the segment going to be?

ZEV: It's about beauty pageants. And pet shows.

Donut audibly gasped.

DONUT: WE WILL DO IT. I CAN'T WAIT.

I was about to object, but then I realized that this would be a god-damned vacation compared to what usually happened when we went on a show. What could possibly go wrong inside of a sound booth?

CARL: All right. We'll do it. But I won't read the lines if they're
bullshit.
DONUT: YAY!
ZEV: Yay!

———

WE DECIDED THAT WE'D WAIT UNTIL MY *PROTECTIVE SHELL* RESET before we hit the *Nightmare*. It was a long, large train, and it would be best to just clear it of mobs using my shell method and not risk whatever was waiting for us.

We stayed at station 281, two stations before the transfer station where we'd catch the *Nightmare*, which meant we'd be able to hit the Desperado Club after the recap episode. Then we'd sleep, train, and head back out into the world.

After a quick trip to the restroom, I returned to the safe room, which was nestled inside of an all-glass storefront called J.CO Donuts and Coffee. The Bopca here was a younger-than-usual guy named Nodd.

"Hey," I said to Nodd, "can I get a black coffee? And I'd like to see the crafting table menu."

"Sure," the Bopca said, pulling it up.

It was a long list of tables, and most of them seemed useless. Most cost about 25,000 gold each. There was everything from the generic **Tinker's Table** to the ultra-specific **Beekeeper Bee Suit Mending Station**. I scrolled until I found what I was looking for.

I slid one of my two free table coupons forward. "I'll take that one." And then I presented my two upgrade coupons. I hesitated. Was this the right move? "And I'd like to upgrade my sapper's table to level three."

———

MY BOOK CONFIRMED SOMETHING THAT I'D ALREADY SUSPECTED. While I could use an engineering table to shape just about any type of armor, it didn't become a true wearable—something that could be "equipped." I could shape something into a helmet, and I could plop it onto my head, but the system didn't acknowledge it as a helmet. For most people, that was no big deal. That was different when it came to Katia and her race. If she couldn't equip it, she couldn't add it to her mass.

If I created and shaped an item using the engineering table and then stepped over to my new armorer's table, however, the item's description changed. All I had to do was pull up my new **Armorer's Workshop** tab, select the item, and then pick its intention from a list. For the sample helmet I made, my only choice on the list was **Shitty Helmet**. It didn't look any different. But it was now titled as a helmet, and it resized itself—slightly—to fit either my or Katia's head. But most importantly, she could now equip it, which added to her mass.

I couldn't add enchantments or build with most types of metal yet, but that was okay. I could craft simple items from scrap metal and leather that we would be able to sell.

While reading through my book, a certain passage in the bomb-making chapter caught my eye.

<Note added by Crawler Rosetta. Ninth Edition>

Comrades, you know the high-level madness satchels, the bronze tier ones with the big yield? They are not as useless as they look. Because they randomly fall into rapid de-stability and explode, they are most dangerous unless they are in your inventory, of course. But with the 15-second waiting period after removing it, it makes them almost impossible to use because they can (and do) explode during those fifteen seconds. I have discovered a solution. If you can find or build an equippable backpack, they will not lose stability as long as they are in the backpack and the backpack is equipped. This also works for other party members if you wish to give them explosives to utilize. Use with caution.

<Note added by Crawler Allister. 13th Edition>
There is no longer a 15-second waiting period for removing items from inventory, so this advice is mostly moot. I can confirm that backpacks do still maintain stability. They weigh you down, however, and don't work as well as inventory.

<Note added by Crawler Forkith. 20th Edition>
Backpacks only slow destabilization now, not negate it. Found that out the hard way. Rest well, little sister. I pray those who read this kill an enemy in her honor today. That is all we can do, no? Her name was Barkith, and she was all I had left. I feel lost, but I will persevere.

All of that was good information, but for now what I mostly took away was that backpacks were a thing. I had an idea. I set out making one.

While I worked, I thought about Crawler Forkith and his sister. He wrote the 20th edition, and from what I could gather, he made it to at least the eleventh floor. He left extensive notes throughout the book, confirming or adding information to multiple passages. He even left instructions on how to append notes to passages, something I couldn't figure out how to do with the scratch pad system.

Forkith was originally a race called an Urgyle, which I gathered was a small, winged, demon-like creature. He'd kept his race upon selection. His class was Sapper. I hadn't yet had time to read his notes at the end of the book, but it struck me how someone so different, so alien, could still be so similar to me. Some things were just universal, I guessed.

The only one who wrote more notes was Drakea from the 22nd edition, the crawler who experienced the final Naga-run season. Drakea was both emotional and verbose throughout the book. Still, despite all of his or her notes, which dripped with absolute hatred for the Naga and the Syndicate, the crawler spoke little of themselves. Their notes section in the back of the book was only a short paragraph.

> Once lit, a fire is easier to stoke than it is to extinguish. Remember that. Fuck the snakes. Fuck the rats. Fuck them all. One day they will all burn, and while I'm certain I will be long dead, I will laugh. I will laugh long and hard, and I will be waiting for them on the other side of the veil, where not even the vast expanse of stars or time will withhold my wrath. If you are reading this, friend, I pray you will join me. Side by side we will exact our revenge.

The words, while borderline unhinged, offered comfort. Comfort I didn't realize how much I needed.

"WHAT IS IT?" KATIA ASKED AS I PLACED THE LARGE METAL BOX IN the main room. I placed it on the stand I'd especially built for it.

I pointed to the reinforced dingo-hide straps. "I was going through the menu of the Armorer's Workshop tab, and I saw 'backpack' listed." This was true. I'd searched until I found a feasible way to make it look like I'd just stumbled on this information.

"A backpack? It looks like an oversized laundry hamper," she said. "Or a giant quiver. It doesn't seal at the top."

"Nope," I agreed. "Strap yourself in, but don't remove it from the stand. That will make it so it doesn't disappear yet into your mass."

She examined it and frowned deeper. I couldn't help but laugh. The system labeled it as **Ugly-Ass Backpack with a Completely Useless Design That Only an Idiot Would Wear.**

I didn't care as long as the word "backpack" was in there. Katia hesitantly backed into it, sticking one arm through a strap. There was an additional set of waist straps. She tied those together and then pulled her arm through the other strap.

"This is really cumbersome," she said.

"I can make it bigger, a lot bigger, but we don't know what sort of environment we'll be fighting in. This is about as wide as I can make it and still be able to equip it in the tight aisle of a train car," I said. "If we ever get to a wide-open area, like the streets of the last floor, I have an idea for something a lot bigger." I pulled the long, reedlike metal pole from my inventory. This one was about six feet long, but I'd made dozens of these in multiple sizes. I dropped it into the basket.

I talked while I loaded the backpack. "So, a while ago, I found a filing cabinet in a boss room filled with stuff. I learned something interesting about the way inventory worked." The metal poles clanked loudly as I added them to the backpack. "If you put something into a container, and then add that container into your inventory, you can pull the container out of your inventory with or without the original contents. You can even pick and choose."

"Carl . . ." Katia began as I continued to put the heavy metal poles into the backpack. I worriedly eyed the stand, but it held. The straps would never hold even a fourth of the weight, but if this worked as intended, that wouldn't matter. They were only there so the system called it a backpack. Still, I was worried about them and Katia's ability to not collapse once I removed the stand. She'd been placing most of her points into strength on Mordecai's advice, and she was now at 49 after all her enhancements. Mordecai's plan for her was to build up her strength as quickly as possible, and once it hit 50, put the rest into constitution until her non-enhanced base was over 100. I noted with a small amount of dismay that she'd also been tossing points into charisma. That was likely a result of Donut and Zev telling her she needed to be more interesting. I'd need to talk to her about that, but not right now.

I took an armful of shorter reeds and stuffed them in. And then I poured a bunch of round balls, tiny versions of the ones I'd been making for my xistera, into the free space of the Ugly-Ass Backpack. When I was done, I stepped back to view my work. Katia stared at me helplessly. She stood there with the basket-shaped backpack over her shoulders, a dozen metal poles of various lengths sticking out of it like she was an overloaded donkey.

"If you remove that thing holding the backpack, I'm going to tumble and fall," she said. "I'm strong now, but I'm not *that* strong. And if I equip it, it's just going to give me the mass of the backpack, not the stuff in it."

"Are you certain about that?" I said. "Because I'm pretty sure you're wrong there." It'd taken some experimenting, but I'd finally managed to make an open-top backpack that listed the items as "contents" when I pulled it into my own inventory. I had to give the backpack a slight lip and something like three-fifths of the mass had to be within the pack and not sticking out.

Her eyes went wide. "Okay, but I can't equip it until you move that stand. When you do, it's going to break the straps or break my shoulders."

"You're stronger than you think. And we're not going to rest the weight on the straps. This is how we're going to do it. Keeping the backpack on, re-form yourself so you have four legs, and build a shelf on your lower back, pushing the holder thing rearward, easing it away," I said. I held up a crude drawing I'd made on the back of a gym membership form.

Katia went pale, but she started the transformation without another word.

Donut entered the room. She'd been in the training room practicing riding Mongo. She stopped dead at the sight of us.

"Carl, what are you doing to Katia?"

"The stand is too tall now," Katia grunted as her back side grew. She shortened as she grew two extra legs.

I nodded. "I'll fix it. Keep going. Keep your back flat. Think of it as a shelf. It doesn't need to be that long. Push your hind legs further back and make sure they're made of metal. Yeah, like that."

"Oh god," she said. I watched as her body transformed. Her arms disappeared, and a third pair of legs appeared, giving her six. Her clothes melted into her mass as her back grew in thickness, creating a shelf for the backpack. The straps strained against her shoulders as the stand pushed away.

"Legs aren't going to work," she grunted. The six legs melded together, lowering her body further. She was starting to look like a slug with an armless human torso. I pulled my tape measure and noted the height from her shelf to the floor.

"It's not as much weight as it looks," I lied. "As soon as that table pushes away, it should automatically equip itself to you."

The stand clattered backward. I cringed as the heavy backpack tumbled down, landing on her shelf. Katia cried out in pain. And then the backpack disappeared, turning the same color as her flesh. The whole dense blob formed into a rounded shell-like shape. *Holy shit, it worked.* She yelped as she tumbled over onto her back, like an overturned turtle. She started to cry out.

"Carl!" Donut yelled. "You hurt Katia!"

I ignored her. "You have a lot of mass now. Take a deep breath and reshape yourself. Use the new metal to keep yourself balanced."

Katia stopped struggling and closed her eyes. Her torso and head melted into the mass, making her nothing but a rounded lump. Six legs sprouted from the bottom. The torso returned, growing up out of the center of what had been her underside. Her top half retained its normal shape, but her arms were twice as long as normal. The elephant-like legs reshaped into wide spikes. The entire form rose off the ground, turning her into a horrific, bug-like monstrosity.

"I'm going to throw up," Katia said. "It's going to take a lot of getting used to."

"Yeah," I said. "You're carrying around more than a ton of extra armor now."

"A ton?" she said, lifting her arm. "A literal ton? 1,000 kilos?"

I grinned. "Closer to a ton and a quarter. Give or take. That metal from the dwarf robots came in two different types. One is a lot heavier than normal iron. How do you feel? Can you move okay?"

She re-formed, turning back to the Hekla shape she'd made earlier, but now she was about 11 feet tall. She stood to her full height, towering over us. She swung her arm. She formed a fist and punched at the air. I could feel the rush of wind.

Mongo cried out in fear and scurried to hide behind Donut.

"It says I have a strength bonus when I carry this much mass," Katia said. Her voice was deeper. "It also says my dexterity goes down, but I don't feel much slower. If I keep a normal body's density, I can probably make myself twenty feet tall. Do you think they're going to let me keep this? Isn't this some sort of exploit?"

"I don't think so," I said. "I think this is what you're supposed to be doing with this class."

"This is ridiculous," Donut said. "She's not going to fit into a train at this size."

"No, she's not," I agreed. My mind was already working on ways to make her even bigger. That dexterity debuff was going to be a problem. *Maybe if I build a foundation for her. Something with wheels she can slide into.* "But that's why the backpack method works. Unequipping is easy. She can just mentally pull the backpack into her inventory, and she'll shrink back down. She'll keep the backpack in her inventory, and she can now choose how much of that metal is in there when she puts it on, which will make her mass variable. We'll need to work on getting her able to equip it fast. And we need to upgrade her makeup table so she can store more shapes. I'll work on the stand to make equipping faster. Also, I need to be on the lookout for denser metal. Maybe we can fashion something that isn't so cumbersome. Those metal poles might be a problem if the ceiling is low."

Katia shrunk further down, her face taking many forms. She stopped at about seven feet, but her torso was three times thicker than it should be. Her arms reached to the ground, making her look like a gorilla.

I reached up and banged on her arm. It clanged like metal. Good. "Make sure you keep your flesh core deep on the inside."

"I'll have to work on it," she said, flexing her arm. "I can't replace my eyes and mouth with metal parts. I'll have to build a cage around my head."

"Good, good," I said. "I want to try with different materials in your backpack. And you need to practice with choosing the amount of metal that remains in the bag."

"Can you put weapons and other enchanted items in the backpack?" Donut asked. Mongo tentatively approached and started sniffing at her.

"I don't think so," I said. "Weapons don't become a part of her mass, and magic items like rings and stuff don't impart their enchantments unless they're equipped as intended. I can't make shoulder pads out of two enchanted helmets and expect it to work. I asked Mordecai that a while ago."

Katia continued to experiment. Her hand turned into a curved metal shield the size of the gangway chock. She pulled her rarely used ax and extended her arm. I noted she was getting a lot better at changing her form quickly. I knew it still hurt her. "When the Daughters hear about this, they're going to flip out. If only Fannar could see me. I'd like to see him call me useless now."

"I wish Mordecai was here," said Donut. "I bet he'd have something to say about this."

"I bet he would," I agreed.

THE FIRST PART OF THE RECAP EPISODE WAS A MONTAGE OF PEOple getting killed on the trains. I watched as a group entered what appeared to be a modern diesel train, one of the named lines, and was almost immediately overrun by little crab-like monsters that had drills instead of claws. In the midst of the battle, I spied a form standing at the back of the train car, watching and laughing. A war mage. This one looked like an orc, but he had the same long silver hair as Dismember.

Katia had returned to her normal size. She'd spent the last hour working with her new form, practicing with different masses. She could remove the backpack using her inventory system, which was a bit inelegant, causing her body to fall and splotch onto the floor in a

round, quivering, unshaped mass. It turned out, if she suddenly unequipped more than 50% of her mass all at once, her body reset itself. That was okay, though it was a little gross. She only remained
in the blob form for a couple of seconds before she reverted to her
regular human form. To equip the extra mass, she first had to pull
out the newly redesigned stand, set it up, and then place the backpack so it was set perfectly on the stand. She'd then back into it, set
the straps, and then transform to her slug shape. From there she
could form whatever she wanted based on the amount of "transformation mass" she kept in the backpack. Putting it on took her about
thirty seconds, which was still too long. We were working on it.

I pointed out the creature on the screen. "I think all the named
trains will have war mages on them."

"If so, each one attacks in a different way," Katia said. On the
screen, yet another war mage was ripping apart a pair of crawlers. I
couldn't tell what the attack was, but the crawlers were choking as if
they couldn't breathe.

The show moved to feature several crawlers it didn't normally
show, including Quan Ch, the one crawler who'd received a Celestial
Quest Box at the end of the last floor. Donut grumbled as she
watched him fly down a train tunnel on his ethereal wings, shooting
blue lightning out of his left hand. He blasted the front of a train,
which crumpled and stopped dead on the track. A mantaur corpse
fell out the front of the destroyed cockpit.

"That jacket he got lets him fly and shoot lightning," I said.
"That's pretty cool. But if he's flying around blasting trains, that's
going to cause all sorts of problems. I wonder what line that is."

"I don't know, but that's our jacket," said Donut. "He didn't even
do anything to get it. It's not fair!"

"Nothing is fair," I said.

We watched Elle pick up a clurichaun, freeze his head, rip it off,
and throw it to another party member. This guy, some sort of mus-
cleman class, twisted in the air and hurled the ice ball at a giant goat
boss. It slammed into the goat's head, staggering it. A menagerie of

other creatures, the former residents of Meadow Lark, rushed the goat monster and tore it to pieces.

They showed a short clip of us using the *Hole* spell to decapitate the war mage. They spliced in a shot of me laughing, a scene from some other time, before showing me picking up the mage's head and sticking it in my bag. *Those assholes. They're making me look crazy.*

"Why did you take the head, Carl? That's gross," Donut said.

"We loot everything, Donut. You never know what might be useful. We should've been taking all the corpses this whole time. We'll do that from now on if we have time."

We'd received a Silver Quest Box for that fight, but it had been nothing but healing scrolls and trap kits. I'd received another two of those alarm traps along with some random trap supplies.

The show ended with Lucia Mar fighting a group of zombielike creatures in a large room. The monsters just kept coming and coming, and she eventually fell back. The room, I realized, held a set of five stairwells, all situated in a circle.

How the hell did that little shit find the stairwells so quickly?

The show ended, and before the nightly message could come, two things happened. The leaderboard changed, and I received a notification.

You have received a Bronze Benefactor Box from the Valtay Corporation.

I paused, waiting to see if either Donut or Katia received anything. Neither said anything, and I assumed that meant they hadn't. I knew this season, the more they paid for us, the cheaper the benefactor boxes were to the sponsors. But Mordecai had said even bronze boxes would be prohibitively expensive. He'd also said the contents of a Bronze Benefactor Box were generally better than even regular platinum boxes.

Donut was gazing up at the leaderboard. The top five hadn't changed. Elle moved up to spot eight, and Li Jun the street monk had fallen off, replaced by Quan Ch, who was a level 31 half-elf Imperial Security Trooper. I wasn't surprised. With that magic jacket of his, he was likely going to rocket his way up the list.

"He's a cheating poseur," Donut grumbled.

Good evening, Crawlers.

I wanted to remind you of our earlier announcement, that for this floor *only*, the stairwells will remain closed until six hours prior to collapse. A handful of you have managed to find your way to stairwell locations. Good job, but we are still several days out before you'll be able to do anything with them.

Due to some unforeseen technical difficulties with our Hobgoblin Mechanic Interdiction teams, trains that are breaking down on the tracks are taking much longer than anticipated to be cleared and put back into service. This is resulting in some premature chaos along several routes. We're sure you can handle it.

And finally, you should all have your sponsors now. Every single crawler in the dungeon has received a sponsor, a first for *Dungeon Crawler World*. We are currently processing benefactor box requests, and there will be a slight delay in loot box fulfillment. We are distributing them as quickly as we can. We apologize for the delay and thank you for your patience. We are giving priority to emergency boxes where the benefactor has paid the emergency delivery fee.

Now get out there and kill, kill, kill!

"They're holding on to our boxes, Carl!" Donut said. "I just know Princess D'nadia got me something good."

"Actually," I said, "I just got a Bronze Benefactor Box. Hopefully you guys will get yours soon."

"And you haven't opened it yet? Open it! Open it now! And make sure you send a note that says 'Thank you.'"

"Oh, all right," I said, pulling the box. I wondered if they had paid the "emergency delivery fee" for this.

The box appeared, a glowing bronze-colored box. Sparks flew off it as it magically opened. A symbol I'd never seen before decorated the top. It was a circle with a squiggle through it. Words in Syndicate Standard were etched underneath the circle. It read, **The Valtay Corporation, Keeping the Best of You Alive.**

I shivered, remembering the brain parasites these guys really were.

The box contained a pill. It was a regular-sized blue-and-yellow capsule.

For a terrifying moment, I thought maybe this was an actual brain worm. I remembered seeing a video once about how people used to give themselves tapeworms to lose weight, and they came in the form of capsules like this. *They want to take over my body.* I shivered again. The idea was absolutely terrifying. I read the description, which was in a slightly different voice and font than usual.

Valtay Corporation Neural Enhancer #544. Variant 32.c.

This item is compatible with your Morphology and Interface.

Warning: This pill will cause a permanent change to your brain. This item cannot be unequipped or undone once installed.

Warning: You do not have a Valtay Corporation Neural Interface installed. While your current wetware system is compatible with this Neural Enhancer, it is recommended you visit a Valtay Corporate Outreach Center to discuss upgrade options. Payment and Legacy plans available. Keeping the Best of You Alive.

Current wetware: Syndicate Crawl Version 47.002.Human.

Taking this pill will install the following upgrade to your interface:

Identify and Analyze Subspace Portals.

"What the hell?" I muttered, turning the pill over in my hand. Why had they given this to me? What was a subspace portal? And if they had paid the extra fee to get it to me more quickly, was it just because they were rich assholes who could afford it, or was there urgency?

Also, since the description was in a different format than regular items, did that mean I could actually trust what it said?

Just to be double sure, I put the item in my inventory and noted both its rarity and value. Its value was just below the Kimaris figure. Its rarity, however, was listed as common. I pulled it back out of my inventory, now reasonably certain it didn't contain any sort of hidden parasite. If it had, it wouldn't have let me stick it in there. I hoped.

"Whatever," I said. I popped the pill into my mouth and drank it down, using my cold cup of coffee.

A moment passed before anything happened.

A new tab is available in your interface.

The tab was labeled **Third-Party Upgrades**. I clicked on it.

Warning: All communication-based upgrades will be disabled while you are within the dungeon. Any attempts to circumvent dungeon security will result in immediate disqualification.

The neural enhancer was the only item listed. I clicked on it, and a note popped up. **This upgrade is working properly.** There was no other information or menus.

I popped up the Sponsorship tab and found the notes section. I could send them messages, but they couldn't send them to me. I knew Donut had been composing and sending thank-you notes to Princess D'nadia all day.

Thank you for the upgrade. I don't know what it's for or what it does, but I appreciate the support.

I felt nothing but revulsion for anything and anybody who had anything to do with this shitshow, but if they were going to be sending me beneficial items, I had to appear grateful.

"So what was that thing?" Katia asked. She'd bulked up and was on her way to the training room, where she was going to work on her Catcher skill. I was going to follow her and work on my Powerful Strike. I was going to work on it every day until it hit 15.

"I'm not sure," I said, trailing off. My eyes caught the doorway to the exit out into the coffee shop. It now glowed purple. A tooltip popped up over the doorway.

Standard Subspace Portal.
   Analyze? Yes/No.

I clicked on **Yes**, and a series of numbers appeared. I had no idea what I was looking at. However, at the bottom of the list were a few lines that seemed important.

Type: Two-way portal. Gated to user.
   Can you pass this portal? Yes.
   Environment on other side of portal: Compatible.
   Visual Analysis? Yes/No.

I clicked **Yes**, and a still photo of the coffee shop popped up. It was empty of customers, but Nodd the Bopca stood behind the counter, picking his nose.

I can see through doorways now.

"Oh hell yeah," I said.

14

Views: 123.8 Quadrillion
Followers: 1.5 Quadrillion
Favorites: 372.4 Trillion
Leaderboard rank: 6
Bounty: 100,000 gold

THE *NIGHTMARE EXPRESS* LANDING—STATION 283.

I watched Donut train with the *Hole* spell while we waited for the *Nightmare Express* to come for the second time. She'd gotten the spell up to level three. She was practicing with making the hole a smaller diameter. She'd figured out how to cast the spell, and with Mongo standing right there, she could cast *Clockwork Triplicate*, and the two extra Mongos would appear on the other side of the hole. We'd be able to clear rooms without having to open doors.

I spent the time trying to read the last Louis L'Amour book, but I couldn't concentrate. I kept thinking of everything that had happened over the past several hours, plus Donut's loud exclamations kept distracting me.

I checked my timer. The train would return in a half hour. I still had ten minutes before we needed to get ready.

We'd kept our visit to the Desperado Club short. Imani and Elle sent a note that they couldn't make it. Neither could Bautista, who was nearing the end of the line on his train. So we decided to make it a quick visit.

While we walked through the club, the Sledge cast a magic protection spell on us, something he hadn't done the last time. Our entire party glowed blue as we walked through the dancers.

"He buy spell with own money," Bomo said, the longest sentence I'd ever heard a cretin utter. "He buy for princess protect."

"Ahh, thank you, Sledgie," Donut said, patting the rock monster on the head. She now rode on his shoulder when we entered the club. The Sledge made a grumbling, satisfied noise.

The Dodge guild wouldn't let me in, but they did allow the Sledge to accompany Donut inside. She went in and then sent me a message that she'd be in there for an hour.

DONUT: IT'S THE SAME THING AS OUR TRAINING ROOM, BUT IT'S EXPENSIVE. THE FIRST SESSION IS FREE, AND IT'LL RAISE IT A FULL LEVEL. IF I WANT TO RAISE IT UP TO NINE, IT'LL COST 20,000 GOLD. TEN IS 250,000! THAT'S OUTRAGEOUS!

CARL: Okay, I'll be at the bar.

I'd learned that my newfound ability to see through thresholds didn't work on all doors. It only worked on portals, magical doorways that were really designed to teleport people from one place to the next, like the one in and out of our personal space. It didn't work on the front entrance of the Desperado Club, but it did work on the doorway into the back room vestibule, the one from the local bar to the little area where Clarabelle sat.

The snap-a-photo feature, unfortunately, didn't work if I wasn't allowed access to the area, which was a major bummer. I still didn't know how the hell this worked. It wasn't magic. It wasn't a skill. It was some sort of technology thing, a software upgrade that interacted with the dungeon. There was so much about this world and how it worked that I still didn't understand.

I sat at the bar for the hour, staring glumly at my drink. I was approached a half a dozen times, but Bomo dutifully kept people back. When the hour was almost over, I had a thought, and I approached the dance floor.

I waved at the crowd, motioning for everybody to form speech bubbles over their heads. There were about 20 other crawlers in the room, most of them human, most of them hovering around level 20.

"Hey, guys," I said when I had everyone's attention. "I want to get into everybody's chat. I think we should all make a habit of getting the chat details of everybody we meet. If we do it enough, we can create a network where we can all pass information much more easily. It doesn't let you make a chat room unless everybody is connected with everybody else, which isn't really feasible, but we need to start an information exchange so we can all trade intelligence. We think we have an idea on how to get off this floor, but I know there's probably lots of different paths to success, and it's important we all know how to do it."

Most of the people shrugged and then started fist-bumping everybody else. I thought Bomo was going to have a heart attack, but I eventually fist-bumped everyone in the room, adding an additional 22 names to my roster. When Donut appeared, I made her do the same.

Now, as we waited for the *Nightmare Express*, I sat there distracted from my book, shuffling through messages. One guy, a human warrior from Japan named Koki, had discovered a way to mass-send messages to everyone on your list at once, and now my messages were a mess of people asking for help and looking to trade items. It was too much, and I created a special folder that would keep them from popping up on my interface.

Still, people kept messaging me directly. I was spending a lot of time explaining what little we knew about the trains. It was important people had all the information, and I wanted to help, but I was shocked at how little some people had managed to figure out after three full days of this.

CARL: No, no. If it's a colored line, it'll always be a subway train. Those are the ones that go up and never go back down. If it's a named train, it can be something else. Like the monorails and the diesel trains and the steam engines.

Those always go in loops. The named trains are the only
ones you can use to get down to earlier stations. We just
haven't seen any that go back down to lower than 83.
DONITA GRACE: I just don't get it. The fulvous line is a subway
and it just goes up and it doesn't circle back.
CARL: Then fulvous is a color. They're using some weird colors.
DONITA GRACE: Well, I've never heard of it.

I stopped responding after that. There was only so much I
could say.

I was nervous about this plan. *That's because it's a stupid fucking
plan. But it's all you got.*

—————

THE *NIGHTMARE EXPRESS* HAD A LOOP OF AN HOUR AND A HALF. IT
hit that first station 83—the very first station we'd traveled to with
the guy with the books, then 283 where we stood now, then 436,
then back to a different 283, a different 83, and then back to that
original 83. We'd been ready to jump on it during its previous pass,
but I'd pulled us back at the last minute after I saw what we were
required to do. If we'd gotten on, we'd have been screwed.

The ground had rumbled as the *Nightmare Express* eased into the
long station. The train hissed as brakes squealed. This was an old-
school steam engine, painted jet-black. This train ran on coal, or
maybe magic, but that explained the lack of a third rail. A wedge-
shaped cowcatcher sat low on the front of the train. It pulled about
forty cars, most of them freight cars designed to haul livestock. As it
pulled up, I could hear and see movement from some of the slatted
cars, one after another. These were massive creatures, all scrabbling
against the walls of their containers to get out. A pair of tentacles
rose from one of the cages, and I realized with horror that these cars
didn't have tops.

There was about four feet from the top of the cars to the ceiling,
though each car had what appeared to be a chain-link cage on top of

the car, which rose all the way to the ceiling. It was, I realized, to prevent people from jumping from the platforms to the top of the cars. Claws and fire burst from one cage. The next was a solid container filled with water, with spikes sloshing out of the car, like it was filled with pissed-off narwhals. Water sploshed from the car and cascaded onto the platform. It smelled like seawater.

Not all of the train cars appeared to be filled with giant monsters. I quickly counted. Fourteen of the cars appeared to have monstrosities within. The majority of the other cars were rickety, empty freight cars. None of the freight cars had doors, at least not facing the platform.

There were only two cars on the train where we could get on: a caboose at the very back and a passenger car at the front, right behind the engine car, which had pulled into the forward tunnel the same way the colored line trains did. There was no other way to get on the train. We'd positioned ourselves near the front, and I moved to enter the front passenger car. I grasped on to the door, and a message popped up.

This door is exit only. Enter at rear of train.

"Goddamnit," I grumbled, looking upon the train. My eyes caught the thin gangway above the open-top freight cars. It was immediately clear what we had to do. My *Protective Shell* wasn't going to help. We had to get on the caboose, where the back balcony had a ladder to the roof of the car. From there we'd have to proceed up the train on hands and knees on the goddamned roof of the cars while the ceiling whipped by at a hundred plus miles per hour, all the while traversing 38 open-top cars randomly filled with jumping, snarling monsters. And if there was a war mage in there somewhere, he was probably hiding in one of those cars, ready to ambush our asses when we least expected it.

Since it was from the back of the train to the front, my *Protective Shell* wasn't going to work. The chain-link fence along the roofs of the cars prevented us from jumping up there. And I wouldn't trust Donut's *Puddle Jumper* spell, either, not when the target gangway was so thin. It didn't let us move through walls, and I wasn't certain it'd work anyway if the target was moving.

"Yeah, fuck this," I said, backing away.

A minute later, and the train hissed, gathering speed.

"That was our plan," Donut said, watching the train leave. "What are we going to do now?"

I started counting in my head how long it took the train to leave the station. It'd taken a full minute and a half. My *Protective Shell* only lasted 20 seconds. *Shit. Too long.*

I looked at Donut and Katia and laughed nervously. "So, I have an idea."

"YOU KNOW," KATIA SAID AS I PREPARED TO JUMP ONTO THE TRACK, "Hekla warned me that you were crazy. She told me to be careful because you'd likely get me killed."

I grinned up at her and jumped down into the gravel between the railroad ties. "First off, you've told me this already. And this time the only one taking the risk is me. And Donut."

"I don't like this, Carl," Donut said. She jumped down and landed on my shoulder. Mongo was left in his carrier, leaving Katia alone on the landing.

"It'll be fine," I said with much more bravado than I felt. I met eyes with Katia. "Be ready. But stay back in case we accidentally crash it." I turned and started jogging my way up the track toward the oncoming train. It'd be in the station in about fifteen minutes. It'd take us five minutes of light running to reach the spot I'd mapped out.

The tunnel was cold and dark. My bare feet crunched on the gravel. Donut hummed nervously as I ran. I told her not to put the *Torch* spell on. I didn't want her warning the engineer, which might cause him to slow down.

"I should have left Mongo on the platform with Katia so she doesn't get lonely," Donut said. We reached the spot. The station was now a distant speck of light. I could feel the vibration of the approaching train on the track. It was a small rumble but growing.

"She's a big girl. She can take care of herself."

"If she is, then why do you keep telling her what to do? You didn't even ask her if she wanted to get giant. You just shoved the backpack at her and told her to do it."

"She likes it," I said.

"But what if she didn't?"

"Look who's talking," I said. "You with your boots and purple-Mohawk nonsense."

"That's different. Fashion is different than making someone change. You keep telling her to be herself, but you're the one making her change the most of all."

"I . . ." I paused. Donut was right. But in the words of the AI, this wasn't *Dr. Phil*. We didn't have the luxury of spending all day making sure we weren't stepping on each other's feelings. I didn't want to be a jerk, but I also wanted to keep her alive. "You know what? You're right, Donut. Next time I'll ask her."

Donut patted me on the head. "Good boy, Carl."

The trembling of the track grew. I glanced at my clock. Right on schedule. "Okay, it's time. Go ahead and set up your spell now, and let me know when it's ready."

"Uh, I think we went too far," Donut said a moment later. "The closest I can get is about three or four hundred feet before the platform."

"*What?*" I said, horror rising. "You said it was line of sight."

"That's what it says, Carl. It's not my fault if the description is wrong."

We had trekked too far into the tunnel. It was too late. She couldn't cast her spell if we were running. "Okay, okay. We'll be fine. Get ready to run your ass off after we teleport." *That motorcycle would be pretty useful right about now.*

The tunnel lightened. I could hear the train barreling down the track. It was still moving quickly, though the engineer was starting to apply the brakes. The distinctive squeal echoed through the tight tunnel.

A piercing whistle blasted. The distant light became an angry, round eye as the train barreled toward us. Even though it was slowing down, it still came at us at a terrifying speed.

Donut's *Puddle Jumper* had a three-second delay after it was cast, so we had to time this perfectly. The train loomed, the cowcatcher approaching like a spear. *Shit, it's moving faster than I thought.* "Cast! Cast now!"

I pressed down on *Protective Shell*. A moment passed, and we blinked.

Holy crap. I'd timed that a little *too* close.

We jumped a quarter of a mile down the track. Notifications started pouring in. The train roared through my *Protective Shell*. All the red-tagged monsters within were slamming against the wall of the spell and then getting pushed backward, hopefully splattering against the back of the train. The train continued to barrel at us. The back of the train screamed. Sparks showered. *It's not slowing down. It's speeding up. Why is it speeding up?*

"Fuck! Run! Run!" We turned toward the station, only 350 feet away. So close.

Donut bolted, running faster than me. "Hurry up, Carl," she cried without looking back.

It was like one of those dreams where you tried to run, but you were caught in something sticky. I knew I was running faster than any human had naturally run before, but I'd wasted a precious few seconds being disoriented and staring at the oncoming train. And then I'd spent another full second lamenting what a stupid idea this had been. The train seemed to have closed the quarter of a mile distance between us in mere seconds. How fast was this thing going? It's a damn steam engine, not a bullet train. *It's out of control. It's going to derail the moment it hits a curve.* We must have killed the engineer.

Ahead, Donut leaped, vaulting onto the platform. She'd been running so fast, she rolled the moment she hit the landing. I saw Katia standing there, eyes huge as I approached the station.

I felt the train behind me. The ground rumbled as if in an earthquake.

I'm not going to make it.

I jumped.

I didn't make it.

I CRASHED, I TUMBLED, AND I BROKE.

Part of me registered that if my body wasn't enhanced by my supernatural constitution, I would've exploded like a blood-and-guts-filled water balloon the moment the cowcatcher smacked me. The wedge was designed to throw whatever it caught aside, though in the tight tunnel, there was no aside except at the landings.

Being tossed onto the landing would've been preferable to what actually happened. I'd jumped just as the train caught me. I felt things break and snap within. I was flying, and then I wasn't. I slammed against hot metal. I'd instinctively bashed onto my *Heal* spell while I was still in midair, but my health continued to plummet, so I hit a Heal potion. I looked up in time to see Donut's and Katia's horrified faces looking at me as we rocketed past the station and back into the tunnel, still picking up speed.

I'd hit the cowcatcher and flipped in midair, getting slammed by the front of the train. My constitution, forward momentum, that *Heal* spell, and the fact my invulnerable foot was what actually caught the front of the train all conspired together to make sure I clung to life.

I lay prone on a small, flat section above the cowcatcher, just before the train's boiler. The light sat on a platform just above my head, shining into the featureless tunnel. The front of the train burned. The *chug chug chug* of the train was furious, louder and faster than it should be. In the shadow I could see **666** emblazoned in red on the front of the black boiler.

I took a second healing potion.

A terrible screeching noise rose from the back of the train. Whatever it was, it wasn't slowing the damn thing down.

DONUT: CARL! CARL!
CARL: I'm okay. I need to stop the train. Stay there.
DONUT: THE TRAIN IS ALL BROKEN IN THE BACK. YOU GOTTA
    HURRY.

A short ladder led to a thin gangplank that ran along the exterior port side of the engine. The plank did not run along the starboard side, which was the side facing the station platforms. The rocky, uneven wall of the tunnel was right there, whipping by at breakneck speed. My whole body ached. I could see points where the train had sheared the wall off on earlier passes. If I reached out, it'd probably rip my arm off.

I gingerly moved to the ladder, and I pulled myself up, careful not to touch the massive boiler, which was getting hotter by the moment. A handrail ran the length of the boiler, leading to a square window where the driver could look out onto the track. A red light glowed inside the cab, but I didn't see movement within.

Below, pistons spun and automatic steam-release valves along the wheels opened at random intervals, screaming hot gas into the passageway. With nowhere to go, the steam swirled in the tunnel, giving the already-dark channel a humid, hazy appearance. Everything was wet and hot, like the interior of a sauna.

I slid my way toward the cab, the wall occasionally catching the back of my cloak, causing it to whip up, threatening to pull me over. I slid down the boiler, reaching the window, which was about as wide as the platform, and only about three feet tall.

I peered inside, swallowing hard at the mess of valves, levers, and gauges. My eyes caught a splatter of gore against the back of the interior. The driver must have been red-tagged. Whatever he was, he was very, very dead now.

The train trembled as it started to curve. *Shit. Shit.*
I formed a fist, summoning my gauntlet. I punched the window. It was like punching through paper. I had to punch several times to clear the glass away. The train bumped ominously, the tracks stuttering. I squeezed myself into the narrow window, falling hard into the cab.

Entering the *Nightmare Express*.

Gore filled the chamber. It stank of oil and fire and blood. There was a second dead engineer against the wall on the other side. *Great,* I thought. Two drivers meant this shit was twice as complicated.

I turned to the controls. There were even more spigots and gauges and handles now I could see the control panel full on. Pipes ran everywhere. At the bottom was a door like on a wood-burning stove. It had a little glass window showing fire raging within. This was where they tossed the coal in to heat the boiler. My eyes caught a row of pressure gauges along the top of the controls. There were five of them, and all of them were almost in the red. The train bucked as it rumbled over track.

On the right side of the controls was a large red lever that I assumed was the throttle. I squeezed the handle and eased it down. I felt the train slow. I relaxed, but then I saw the pressure gauges start to rise. One of them shot all the way up to the top.

To my horror, a new tooltip popped up over the control station.

Shattering Train Bomb
    Type: A steam boiler made with a shocking disregard for safety. It's almost like they want this thing to explode.
    Effect: It's a train-sized grenade that is going to detonate from extreme pressure. What do you think the effect will be?
    Status: Deteriorating. 75/1000.
    If you don't figure this shit out in about two minutes, it's going to be pretty damn spectacular.

A chain hung from the ceiling. I pulled, and the whistle blew. I held it down to see if that alleviated the pressure. One of the gauges lowered. The others did not. I pulled another lever, easing it. The brakes. They only worked for a moment. I had to pump them back and forth, but it came with diminishing returns. There was another identical lever below it. I had no idea what the hell I was doing, and I feared I was doing more harm than good. It was already too late for me to run to the back of the train and jump off.

I was about to message Imani and Elle to ask them if any of the Meadow Lark team knew how to drive a train, when I saw the face staring back at me through the little fireplace window. Startled, I jumped back. Then I saw the dot appear on my minimap. A white dot. An NPC. *Inside* the fire.

I didn't allow myself enough time to think about it. I grasped on to the burning handle and turned, opening the door. Heat blasted into the chamber. A demonic female head popped out of the hole.

The red-skinned, black-haired woman was a 1950s pinup vision of a red devil woman, at least from the neck up. Only her head fit through the little hole. She had her hair up in a rockabilly-style updo tied with a red bandanna. Two black horns rose through her hair. Steam rose off of her, and her eyes were swirling black orbs. The demon woman had heavy rings under her black eyes, making her look exhausted.

Fire Brandy—Lesser Demon MILF. Level 75.
Fire[wo]man of the *Nightmare Express*.
This is a non-combatant NPC.
A single mother's gotta eat!
Where one finds big ovens that need stoking, one will regularly find a Lesser Demon in control. But if it's a fire that needs to be *extra* hot, the much rarer Sheol MILFs are often employed to keep those fires sizzling.
Once a pregnant Lesser Demon falls into labor, her delivery usually lasts about sixty days. During these two months, she

has a litter of 15,000–18,000 babies, delivering one approximately every five minutes, nonstop.

Only one in 10,000 Lesser Demon babies is viable. The rest rarely live more than a few seconds. Their corpses shrivel and harden, becoming a valuable resource called Sheol Bricks. The fifteenth floor will be lousy with them. If exposed to fire, Sheol Bricks burn long and hot. Lesser Demon MILFs who also learn water magic can find lucrative work as steam boiler fire stokers. Once they seal themselves within the boiler, they create an almost self-sufficient system that keeps most larger boilers humming. Plus it's a convenient method of disposing of their failed young.

This train is running on dead babies. Holy crap, that's fucked-up.

"Child, you are just in time," Fire Brandy said. She spoke loudly, over the roar of the train. She had an odd accent, almost German. It was a peculiar juxtaposition with her appearance. "Something happened to the engineer and that *kotzbrocken* war mage. They go splat. See that valve there on the top left? Will you turn it for me? The idiot didn't release that valve, and I can't control it from here."

"Uh, this one?" I said.

"That's right. Turn it left. Turn it all the way. Yes. Very *gut*." One of the five gauges moved into the green. The train shuddered as if in pleasure.

New Achievement! Kept A Rollin'!

You're driving a train! Holy shit!

Reward: I'm pretty sure the act of driving a train is a badass-enough award.

From there, Fire Brandy taught me how to take control of the train using crisp, matter-of-fact language. After I turned one valve one way for ten seconds, and then the other for another five, the This-is-a-bomb tooltip disappeared. I relaxed.

I managed to stop the train completely while we went over the controls. Then I got it moving again at a slow clip, about thirty miles per hour. That was a fraction of its normal speed. She taught me the throttle and the two-control braking system. One was for the brakes on the engine itself; another was for the train cars. I'd nearly wrecked us when I'd been jacking with it earlier, and I hadn't even realized it. Three times she gave birth while we talked. She scrunched up her face, and I heard a quick scream that was almost immediately cut away.

"Now you know how to run train," she eventually said. "Do not go fast. Do not over-pressurize, and we will have no problems, no? Now close my door and leave me be." She pointed to a small box at the back of the chamber. "But if something happens to me, you have that box. You can't use for long because you have no source of water or oil. So only use it to get back to the station and vent as much as you can. Now close the door." She started to pull her head back in.

"Wait," I said. "How do I get to the station from here? Uh, station 10, I mean. The train yard."

"Hit the switch. It is on the tracks just before the next stop. You have a few options. Choose 'Station Repair' and you'll get to the station, and the train will be fixed." She waved toward the starboard side of the train, the side I hadn't entered through.

She pulled her head back in. Over the roar of the fire and train, I heard the cry of another baby, and then a second.

She has two babies in there. Two viable babies already.

I closed and sealed the door using the heavy rag she'd pointed out. Hit the switch? How would I do that? I examined the driver's station on the right side. There was a handle there leading to a pole attached to the side of the boiler. I realized it was like a lance. Using the handle I could swing the pole to the side, presumably to hit the switches on the tracks. If I tried it now, all I'd do was hit the wall and break it. I'd have to be moving very slow before I dared try it.

I looked down at the small box she'd indicated. It sat in the back of the cab, near the exit. The box was covered in gore where the driver or the war mage had been pushed against it. I lifted the lid and pulled a black chunk out of it.

Sheol Brick.

If Santa gives coal to the regular naughty kids, he'd probably give this stuff to history's greatest villains, like Hans Gruber and the guy who invented those shoes with the individual toes built in. It burns a lot hotter and a lot longer than regular coal. And when I say "a lot longer," I mean until the end of your lifetime. So like a week or more.

To save you distress, I'm not going to tell you where this came from.

That was a lie! It's a baby corpse!

I dropped it in revulsion, wiping my hand on my cloak. There were about fifty bricks in the chest. I took a deep breath and then I picked up the entire box, adding them all to my inventory. I shuddered.

In the mess of gore, I found two items. A small satchel containing 350 gold and a large bronze key. I picked it up.

Steam Engineer's Key. I quickly examined it.

Allows access to Iron Tangle employee-only areas and actions on all 400 steam-type trains of the Tangle.

I was finally able to relax and look about my surroundings. I was alive. Not only was I alive, but I'd stolen a train. I had stolen a goddamned train.

Only then did I notice my stats. "Holy fuckballs," I said out loud.

I had risen three whole levels. I was now level 32. I had three new neighborhood boss boxes.

Apparently, I'd killed every monster on the train. And three of them were neighborhood bosses. I looked at the map, and I didn't see any X's on the train at all. The last time I'd done this, I hadn't even gone up a level. This time I'd hit the jackpot. It looked as if I'd also gotten a bunch of experience for taking control of the train. Despite all that, I only had one additional achievement I hadn't yet opened. I pulled it up now.

New achievement! Three Cheers for Slaughter!

You killed three boss monsters with the same attack! I'm starting to think your survival so far isn't just a fluke. You're either scary good at this, or you're just one lucky mofo. Either way, holy shit. Good job.

Reward: You've received a Platinum Big Daddy Box!

There was a small door out the back of the engine car. Stepping over the gore, I opened the hatch to gaze out over the back of the train as it chugged slowly down the track.

I laughed at the sheer amount of destruction I'd wrought with my shield spell. The passenger car just behind the engine appeared to be fully intact, though I spied blood inside. That was the only other car on the train that remained unscathed. The remaining cars, the ones that had been filled with the giant monsters, were still on the tracks and pulling behind the train, but the walls had all been peeled away and broken, turning the cars into a bunch of flatbeds. Several of the wall pieces still hung, attached to the cars. They sparked as they came into contact with the tunnel wall. A chunk of wood ripped off as I watched, bouncing and falling back onto the track behind the train. The caboose was still there, but the entire top of the structure was sheared off.

I couldn't believe we hadn't wrecked the whole thing. That other train had been pretty easy to derail. I wondered if there was magic keeping this particular train on the tracks. *Then again, I just almost blew the whole thing up.* Maybe the cars themselves were built to break like this. Maybe they hoped we'd accidentally unleash the giant monsters onto the tracks, and they deliberately made the walls weak.

CARL: Hey, Donut, can you go back out on the tracks and see if any of the corpses out there are neighborhood bosses? I have no idea where the hell I am, and it'd be pretty useful if you could snag the route map off a boss corpse and then

let me know when I'm approaching the stops. Make sure
they're dead before you approach.
DONUT: OKAY, BUT DON'T RUN ME OVER.

It had only been about forty minutes, and I was now moving at
a snail's pace compared to the train's regular speed. If I'd even come
to the next station, I'd missed it. I suspected I still had a bit before
I got there.

CARL: You have plenty of time. I'm going to try to eyeball
what's at station 436, and then I'll loop around to pick you
guys up.

Hopefully the debris on the track wasn't enough to stop the train.
I'd find out when I got there. I had a thought, and I pulled up chat
again.

CARL: But if you're worried, this might be a good time to field-
test riding Mongo. You can race down the track to see how
fast you two go.
DONUT: CARL, YOU ARE A GENIUS.
CARL: You know it.
DONUT: CARL?
CARL: Yeah?
DONUT: DON'T EVER DO THIS TO ME AGAIN. I THOUGHT YOU'D
BEEN SQUISHED.

15

THE NIGHTMARE EXPRESS.

Less than five minutes later, the train rolled through the switching station. The tunnel widened, leading to a large, well-lit cavern. Several other tracks ran through here, but I didn't see any other trains. There were dozens of entrances and exits.

The first switch was a large, round target painted red. It was a well-worn metal plate on a pole sticking up from the ground like a stop sign. I was supposed to use the lance thing to hit the switch if I wanted the train to change tracks. This first one was labeled "Auxiliary Tracks. Warning." The next was "Station Repair," and after that was a third entitled "Recycle."

There were so many tracks on the ground, it was difficult to tell what led where. I followed the "Recycle" track with my eyes, which led to a massive archway at the far side of the cavern.

A colossal, glowing portal dominated the center of the room. I tried to examine it using my new subspace portal skill, but it said I needed to be closer for it to work. This was the "Station Repair" portal.

I tried to follow the course of the "Auxiliary Track," but it got lost in the tangle of other tracks. I wasn't certain, but it appeared to lead to another switching area with dozens of additional choices. If my brain was parsing it correctly, it looked as if I could possibly switch the *Nightmare Express* to one of several other train lines.

A large train steamed through the room, belching smoke and

chugging merrily away. This one came from the opposite direction. It didn't slow as it passed. This was also a steam locomotive, but it had a more modern design, with a smaller cowcatcher. It pulled ten cars. I caught a quick glance of the final car. It was a caboose similar to what this train once had. Two spears stuck up from the back balcony, and a pair of human heads was impaled on the sticks. The engineer tooted twice in greeting before disappearing into the tunnel.

A minute later, I reentered the tunnel.

DONUT: I GOT THE MAP AND A LOT OF GOLD. YOU ARE ABOUT
   TO COME TO STATION 436. THERE ARE A LOT OF DEAD
   BODY PARTS AND WOOD AND METAL ON THE TRACKS.
   ALSO MONGO CAN RUN REALLY, REALLY FAST.
CARL: Okay, thanks. I'll loop around to pick you up. Hopefully
   the train can push through all the stuff on the tracks. But
   in case it won't be able to, I'm going to stop and check out
   this station 436 now while I still can.

Ahead, I could see the light of the platform. I slowed the train as I approached. It looked like any other platform from this angle. The sign above it read **Abyss Station—436**. I eased the engine to a stop, set the brake, stuck the boiler to standby, and I stepped out of the cab. After a moment's hesitation, I decided to close the door to the engine car just in case. Someone could still climb in through the broken front window, but this would dissuade all but the most determined train-jackers.

Entering Abyss Station.

I searched the map for signs of life. I saw nothing. I felt the ground rumble, and I could hear a train rush by. It sounded as if it was directly above me. There was a distant whine of a different train and a muffled crash. A minute later came another crash. And then another. Another train whipped by. This one sounded below me. It reminded me of being in line for a roller coaster at an amusement park, with things whipping by from all directions.

The station was bare. No sign. No bench. There was only a single set of metal industrial-style stairs in the center of the platform. The stairs here were especially steep, like those on a fire escape. The stairs led upward and disappeared through a dark hatch in the ceiling. I hesitated, and then I pulled a torch from my inventory and ascended. *I'm just going to look.*

It took almost an hour to ascend the stairs. The entire time, the sounds of trains coming and going and crashing surrounded me. The walls continually shook. Donut and Katia both demanded I keep them constantly updated. Finally, just as Donut was regaling Katia with a story about how she pulled a last-minute win at some best-in-show cat pageant because her biggest competitor, a Singapura, was disqualified over some paperwork dispute, I saw a red light at the top of the stairs. Ten minutes later, I pulled myself up onto a circular iron catwalk overlooking a massive flaming pit. The long walkway circled the interior of the hole. Hot air blasted up at me.

Entering the Abyss.

"Oh wow," I muttered.

Below me, above me, and all around the interior of the massive burning pit were hundreds and hundreds, if not thousands, of giant glowing portals. Catwalks like the one I was standing upon dotted the interior at non-regular intervals. Monstrous shapes haunted the walkways, but none were near me.

I had a memory of standing on the precipice of the Grand Canyon. It was just my mom and me standing on the edge, looking off into the chasm. This had been on the way back from Texas. My father was there in the car, waiting. His presence, patiently waiting behind us, was even bigger than that of the canyon spread before us.

I remembered that moment at the barrier, my mom clutching tightly on to my wrist. For a moment, she clasped so much it hurt.

Do you remember the circus? That was fun, wasn't it?

You're hurting me.

I know, honey. I'm sorry. I'm so sorry.

This wasn't really as big as the Grand Canyon, but I was surprised at how shaken I was by the sudden memory. This hole was almost perfectly round, at least a mile across. It had to be thousands of feet deep.

As I watched, a train burst through a portal. The cars shot into the air and then tumbled into the pit. They twisted and turned as they fell and fell, landing in a heap at the bottom with a distant crash.

I strained to peer at the base of the pit. The giant hole was filled with thousands of crashed train cars. Hundreds of fires burned. The tiny dots of figures crawled over the debris. I recognized their gait. Jikininki janitor ghouls. They swarmed like ants over the wreckage. Another train came from a different portal. Then another.

There's no engine cars. I remembered what the mantaur guy had told us. He would go through the portal, and it was just his engine car on the other side. These were all the colored trains reaching the end of the line. The trains were driven through the portals. Only the engine car was teleported back to base. The rest of the cars were just thrown into this pit, like garbage. The conductors and the porters got off the train at the last stop. And when they returned, the train had been re-formed. The train wasn't looping through time. They were building new trains. All except the engine cars.

"Holy shit!" I cried as a train burst from a portal directly over my head. I ducked as the catwalk shuddered. The train roared as it plummeted into the hole. The wheels spun uselessly as the driverless train nose-dived.

I looked up at the portal.

Ultima Corp DungeonWerx Industrial Subspace Portal.
Analyze? Yes/No.

I clicked **Yes**, and the page of numbers that appeared was much longer than the last one. I scrolled down to the bottom.

Warning: You are facing the incorrect side of this portal. Entering through this side will have no effect. You may pass safely through this side, but use caution not to backtrack while entering.

Type: One-way portal. Gated by conveyance type and to key holders.

Can you pass this portal? Yes*

Warning: You must be on a gated conveyance and/or a key must be equipped or held outside of inventory, depending on type. Compatible keys have been marked in your inventory.

Environment on other side of portal: Compatible.

Visual Analysis? Yes/No.

I clicked **Yes**.

I was greeted with a screenshot of a massive train yard. Thousands of trains spread out in all directions. It was only the engine cars. They were all in a high-fenced yard. In the fenced-in area of the yard were what looked like thousands of ghoul-like creatures milling about. They looked like zombies, but from several different races and mobs.

I moved to another portal down the gangway and took another screenshot. It was the same, but from a different angle. From this direction I could see just past the fence and saw what appeared to be a line of dwarves waiting for the train. The zombies were only in the train yard. I couldn't see how the trains were leaving the fenced-in area or how they were keeping the zombies within.

My eyes did catch something interesting. There was a swirling portal in the corner of the train yard, much too small for a train. I could only see half of it from this shot. But in that shot I could see the distinctive form of one of those rolling cages like the one I'd looted from the room with the robots.

A distant roar made me look up. A large lizard-like monster had spied me and was crawling up the wall to my gangway. Several others of the mobs also started to move in this direction. I still had several minutes before they'd get here.

I wanted to stay and fight, but I was worried that they'd do something to the walkway, causing me to lose access to the stairwell back to the *Nightmare Express*. I dropped a goblin smoke bomb so they couldn't see which direction I went, and I returned to the stairwell and started to quickly descend.

Several minutes passed, but it didn't look like they were following me. As I descended, I moved to my inventory. I found a new sort-by option. I could sort out items that had been "marked." I had three keys that would allow me passage through the portal: the ocher key, the steam train key, and that stupid souvenir hat we'd received the moment this floor started.

Holy shit. That was it? All we needed to do was equip the stupid fucking train conductor hat?

CARL: I'm sending this message out to everybody on my chat list. You guys aren't going to believe this shit.

———

CARL: In case you haven't heard, the stairwells are all at stations 12, 24, 36, 48, and 72. The problem is, we all started higher than station 80, and it doesn't look like there's a way to backtrack. Here's what we have gathered. So far we know for sure of two ways to get to the early stations, and we're pretty certain about two more. Spread the word.

One. If you equip that stupid hat and just ride a train to the end of the line, you'll get through. Problem. The train car you're riding in *won't* get through, which means you'll be teleported into a train station filled with literally thousands of zombies.

Two. You can kill an engineer and get an engineer's key. You will be transported to the same train yard, but you'll be inside of a train car. Problem. You'll have to manage to do that without crashing the train. You can possibly jump ahead using one of the named lines. But let me tell you, those named lines are a bitch. Also, we don't know what you can do after you get to the station. If you have control of the train, you can possibly drive it out of there, but we're not sure.

Possible Solution Three. Station 435 is where the employees get off. There's supposedly a portal there that takes you to the headquarters. I believe the headquarters is on the other side of the zombie fence. Problem. It sounds like there's a boss monster at these stops called the Kravyad. Also, it appears if you go through this portal, you lose time and memories. Plus we're not certain you *can* get through these portals. If someone tries this, let us know your experience.

Possible Solution Four. If you get on a named line that has a stop at station 436, and you get control of the train, you can use the switching station to get back to the base. I'm not certain how that works yet, but we're going to try to figure it out.

I know there are other solutions. If you find them, please let me know. Stay safe out there, everybody.

PORTER T: Thanks, mate. You're not nearly as crazy as they make you look on the show.

MEI W: We sold our hats. Everybody in the party sold them! They were offering 5,000 gold each for them.

I continued down the stairs, answering a wave of messages. There were rumors of a hidden train that moved backward, down the line and not up it. But you had to break through a wall to get to it. I was half expecting to find my train gone, but it remained on the track, boiler chugging in standby mode. I got in, knocked on the fire door so Fire Brandy knew I was back, and I pulled out of the station. I slowly increased the train's speed, getting it up to about 50 miles per hour. Behind, the cars still sparked and rumbled ominously, but they remained on the tracks. I should have unhooked them, but I didn't have anywhere to put them. If we could figure out the switching station, maybe there'd be a way to ditch the extra cars.

DONUT: CARL, HURRY UP AND GET BACK. I GOT MY FIRST BENEFACTOR BOX AND IT'S THE GREATEST PRIZE IN THE HISTORY OF PRIZES. PRINCESS D'NADIA HAD IT MADE ESPECIALLY FOR ME. I WANT YOU TO SEE IT. IT'S A SURPRISE!

KATIA: It's a surprise, all right.

DONUT: DON'T RUIN IT, KATIA.

CARL: I can't wait.

DONUT: ALSO I FORGOT TO TELL YOU I WENT UP TWO LEVELS TO LEVEL 30. MY CHARISMA HIT 100, AND I HAVE A NEW SPECIAL ABILITY!

CARL: That *is* good news. You can tell me all about it when I get back.

DONUT: IT'S CALLED LOVE VAMPIRE. IT'S AWESOME!

CARL: I'm going to make one more very quick stop before I get back. The train is moving a bit slower than usual, so it'll still be a couple of hours.

DONUT: WHAT KIND OF STOP?

CARL: I'm going to try to make a trade over at station 83. Let me know when I'm getting close. In the meantime, you should head over to the other platforms at the station and grind on the monsters riding in from station 282.

KATIA: That's what we've been doing, but the trains stopped coming on the purple line. The mauve line is still moving.

Also, I spent some time clearing the track of debris. In my
larger form, it's a lot easier to pick up the big stuff. There's
still stuff strewn across the track, but I don't think it'll be a
problem now.

―――――

ABOUT TWO HOURS LATER, THE *NIGHTMARE EXPRESS* RETURNED TO
station 283. Katia had cleaned the track pretty well. Most of the remaining debris I hit was caught by the cowcatcher, and it eventually
flew to the side of the narrow path or broke into thin chunks. The
train occasionally bucked, but we remained on the tracks.

I stopped the engine about halfway down the platform. Katia
stood there, leaning against a ceiling support. She was about half full
of transformation mass. She looked like a pink-skinned She-Hulk,
but with spikes on her back. She'd given herself a leather outfit and
black boots. The purple Mohawk had returned.

Donut was also there, sitting upon the back of Mongo. I noticed
the new addition to her outfit right away.

"Sunglasses, huh?" I said as I stepped off the train.

"Aren't they just to die for!" Donut exclaimed, hopping off the
back of Mongo, who was jumping up and down wildly at my return.
I patted the dinosaur on the head as Donut leaped to my shoulder.
"They're not just couture. They're *super* sunglasses."

They were large and round, making her look like a bug. They
were similar to the movie-star-style sunglasses Bea was wearing on
her head in that picture Donut had received. These seemed to be
magically affixed to Donut's face. The frames had no arms, and her
nose was too squished to properly hold them up, yet they remained
firmly plastered to her face. She removed them and let me examine
their properties:

Prism Industries Capacitating and Focusing Goggles. Special
High-Fashion Edition. "The Princess Donut."
   This is a Unique Item.

This one-of-a-kind item was a gift from Princess D'nadia of the Prism Kingdom to Princess Donut of the Blood Sultanate. It was personally signed by Princess D'nadia.

Protects the eyes from a variety of environmental hazards, including magic-based attacks that render the user blind. Enhances all dark vision effects. Allows for heat vision and other visible-light viewing options.

In addition, any energy-based spell that originates from the ocular region is caught and focused by these goggles, which allows for multiple combat and targeting options.

"Holy shit," I said, reading it a second time.

"It turns my *Magic Missile* into a laser!" she said. "I can shoot four at the same time! I've been standing on the back of the mauve platform, and when the doors open, I can shoot inside four doors at once. It can even hold on to the energy of one shot and add it to the next. Plus they're beautiful. I look like Miss Beatrice. Don't you just love them?"

"Those are pretty good," I agreed. I wondered how much it cost D'nadia to get the box to Donut. I glanced up to Katia. "Did you get anything?"

"No," she said. "None of the Daughters have gotten anything yet, either."

I still didn't know what Katia's sponsor's angle was. I wouldn't be surprised if Katia never got a prize at all. "I am absolutely starving," I said, trying to change the subject. "Let's eat and take a nap and reset our buffs because I don't know how long before we'll find another safe room after this."

"We're going through the portal?" Katia asked.

"I just want to see if we can get through and then come back using the *Nightmare Express* train. If not, it'll give us time to figure out what our next move will be. If we can set up near a stairwell and just grind for the remaining time, that'll be ideal."

"And if we can come back?" Katia said. "We'll return?"

I held up my hand as I read the new message that just popped up.

ELLE: Hey, Carl. We have found ourselves in a bit of a pickle. I
    wanted to give you a heads-up.

CARL: What's wrong?

ELLE: We just cleared out stop 275 on the camel line. Killed
    one of those Krakaren bitches. It was easier than Imani
    thought it would be. Anyway, we cleared the area, and we
    went back to the station to catch the next train to 277,
    which is a transit station. But the train never came. We're
    stuck here. We're going to have to walk.

IMANI: I think it was that Quan Ch guy. There's chatter in my
    inbox that people keep seeing him blowing up trains. He's
    farming the train drivers, but he's making it so everybody
    is getting stuck. If he keeps it up, all of the train lines will
    be stopped.

CARL: How far is it to station 277?

IMANI: Far. 276 is probably twenty or thirty miles, and by the
    time we get there, the monsters at that station will be
    starting to transform and will be on the tracks. It's another
    thirty after that to 277.

ELLE: Yeah, so instead we'll be taking the druggie portal back
    to station 272 and then we'll hike down to 271. It's still far,
    but not nearly as much. We'll still have to walk on the
    tracks. That's why I'm letting you know. We'll be out of
    commission for a day at least. There's a named train at 271,
    and if the cobalt line is also out of commission, we'll have
    to take that one. It's called the *Eviscerator*.

I'd seen that one listed a few times. I cursed that Quan asshole.
He had to know what he was doing. What a selfish prick.

CARL: What kind of monsters are at stop 272?

IMANI: Gross Atomizers. Floating bags of gas. They're easy to
    kill, but they have a poison-cloud area attack. We can

handle them. It'll also give us a chance to look at these robots you've been talking about.

CARL: Okay. Good luck. See if you can find a secret way out of that robot room. We're going to try to take the *Nightmare* through the portal. I'll let you know what happens. Keep me updated. Stay away from the third rail.

ELLE: Oh you know it. Kill, kill, kill!

I laughed.

"SO TELL ME ABOUT YOUR NEW VAMPIRE SKILL," I ASKED AS I ATE A corn dog. The safe room was bigger than usual. It was a self-enclosed mall food court. Only one of the many restaurants was open. A Hot Dog on a Stick. The Bopca even wore the absurd hat the workers had to wear. Katia was scandalized by the restaurant's normal menu. She'd instead talked the Bopca into some sort of fish recipe from Iceland.

Donut had also ordered the fish. She currently had a piece of broken mirror propped up on the table and was practicing her voguing. She looked up at me. The sour look was ridiculously enhanced by the sunglasses.

"It's not vampire—it's *Love* Vampire. I had three choices, and I picked that one."

"Did you actually read the descriptions first?"

"Of course I read them, Carl. Besides, it's the one Mordecai told me to get when we talked about this before."

I relaxed. "That's good. What does it do?"

"It makes one enemy my level or lower give me his heart. That's what it says. So if I get stabbed, they take the damage instead of me."

"Wait, really?" I said, intrigued. "How often can you do it? How long does it last?"

"It lasts until they're dead. I can do it every couple of hours. Now let me do this, Carl. We're going on the show later and I need to perfect my look."

I sighed. Zev had said we'd only be doing voice-over stuff on the show, but I wasn't going to point that out now.

I moved to my loot boxes. The boss boxes were typical neighbor-hood boss items. The best prize was a Scroll of Upgrade, which had been good to me so far, but when I applied it, all it did was add +3 dexterity to my trollskin shirt. That was a decent upgrade, especially since I'd been planning on throwing a couple of points into dexterity, but it wasn't a great one.

The Platinum Big Daddy Box contained a regular, unenchanted toothbrush, plus a tiny travel-sized tube of toothpaste. The tube was red with a black skull on it. It had "Carpe Diem" written on it in what appeared to be Comic Sans font.

Seize the Day Toothpaste—Five Applications.
You know that feeling you get when you walk out into the world with minty-fresh breath? It's like you can take on any challenge that is thrown your way. It gives you confidence. It boosts your self-esteem. It makes you feel like you're on top of the damn world.
Well, this stuff does none of that. However, if you brush your teeth using this enchanted cherry-flavored toothpaste, you are imbued with the following buffs for 30 hours:
+Three Times Damage to all Boss Monsters.
or
+Four Times Damage to all Boss Monsters if the Boss is a Province, Country, or Floor Boss.
This buff may only be applied in a safe room.

That was a fantastic prize, but it would only be useful if I knew I was going to face a boss that day. With only five applications, I'd need to be stingy with it. I added it to my stash.

From there, I assigned my stat points, adding six to my strength and three to my constitution.

I needed to sleep, but I found myself spending too much time using the chat feature. I'd traded away all of my Louis L'Amour books, and I'd suddenly realized how much I'd gotten used to reading, even if it was only for a few minutes before I slept. So instead I moved to the chat feature. I was starting to see a reoccurring theme in my small chat group. The trains were going out of commission at an alarming rate. People were getting stranded. We still had almost six days left, but that wasn't nearly enough time if people were going to have to hike dozens of miles a day.

Mordecai's long-ago advice echoed in my head. *Look, kid. I want this to sink deep into your thick skull. You can't save them all.*

Taking that train through the portal seemed like I was abandoning them. I knew that was stupid. Everyone was spread out to the wind. I didn't even know these people. I told them how to get free. That was all I could do. It had to be enough.

But what if it wasn't? I'd read something earlier that had stuck with me. It was from the back of the cookbook. It was written by a crawler named York, who'd written the 10th edition. He'd written pages and pages of rambling philosophical essays I could barely understand. But I couldn't stop thinking about one passage in particular. I wasn't certain I fully understood exactly what he was trying to say, but it stuck with me. It appeared to be his last entry before he died or lost the book:

> Reading the words of those who have come before me, I know them. You, reading this. I know you, too. You are me. That is whom this book finds.
>
> I have been alone my whole life. I have been surrounded by my hive, yet I have been alone. That is okay, I now know. It is acceptable to have your own thoughts, your own mind, despite what they say. But it is also acceptable to be alone and want the strength of

the hive. There is no shame in that. No contradiction. That is what this book attempts. To make a hive of those who will never cross paths, except in these pages.

Yet sometimes this book is not enough. You sometimes want more. You want to belong. Again, there is no shame. There is no shame in wanting to be alone yet also wanting the comfort and the strength of your brethren. But more importantly, there is no shame in wanting to protect those who are your hive, even if you never knew them. For they are yours, and they are being taken. It is us or it is them. There is consolation in dying in the pursuit of justice, no matter how small or big that death is.

I wasn't sure I agreed with that last part, but by the time I closed my eyes, I felt resigned to the idea that there was something more to be done for those trapped on the tracks.

But what was it? I had no fucking clue.

16

I AWAKENED TO FIND A MESSAGE FROM ELLE AND IMANI.

> **ELLE:** Hey, Hotshot. Your instincts were right. There is a secret way out of the robot rooms. It's a long tunnel leading downward at an angle. It doesn't look like it opens up until after the robots wake. And the robots don't wake until the monsters start their withdrawal symptoms. Luckily we don't have to fight the metal bastards. I can't believe you blew two of them up. We're following the tunnel right now to see where it goes. It sounds like there's another train track down there. It's far. Will update later.
>
> **IMANI:** Beware of the monsters once they transform. They're much more powerful.

That had only come in about ten minutes earlier, so I wasn't expecting an answer for a while. I was hopeful for what they'd find. If that secret, down-the-line train existed, people stuck on the tracks could flee to the nearest robot rooms and hitch a ride.

"Carl! Carl! I realized something," Donut said excitedly as I sat up. I yawned. I still couldn't get over how perfectly rested I felt after sleeping only two hours.

"What is it?" I said.

"Remember that spell book I got a long time ago? That tome of *Minion Army*? It wouldn't let me read it because it costs 50 spell points to cast."

"I remember," I said. She'd gotten the spell book from a beguiler box way back on the first floor. I started to do the math in my head. Donut's base intelligence was 40, giving her 40 spell points. But she added one intelligence with her butterfly charm and another three with her new tiara, bringing it up to 44. However, with the Good Rest buff plus the buff from the shower, our stats rose another 20%. The stat increase was calculated before any of our equipment buffs, and it didn't actually show on the list, either. Mordecai had said it was a persistent bug that had been around for a few seasons now. Nevertheless, we knew the buffs were active because while our intelligence stat said one thing, our spell points reflected the actual number. Mordecai had said he put in a ticket, but we shouldn't hold our breath on it getting fixed.

Anyway, with the 20% buff, Donut's 44 in intelligence was now actually 52, giving her a total of 52 spell points.

"I take it it'll let you read the tome now?"

"Yes! I didn't think it would because of that bug thing, but I thought of it before we took our nap, and I remembered when I woke up. And I looked."

"And you read it already, didn't you? Mordecai said we needed to talk about the spell once you got enough points to use it."

"Of course I read it, Carl. That's why I'm telling you this. Mordecai isn't here, so we're talking about it now."

I sighed. "Okay, just don't go casting it unless you know what you're doing. Remember what Mordecai said? It takes five minutes to cast, and you get stuck in place while it's casting."

The *Minion Army* spell was simple on the surface, but the spell's specifics were convoluted. You cast it on a group of enemies, and some of them would turn and fight on your side. Mordecai had said it was a powerful spell, but only in certain circumstances. It was almost impossible to train up because the conditions in which one used it were rare. The mass-charm spell had a casting time of *five* minutes, which was outrageous. At level one, it also had a cooldown of five hours. Its base area of effect was a thirty-meter-diameter circle, though that went up—a lot—based on her charisma.

It only worked on intelligent mobs. That plus its five-minute casting time made the spell almost useless. At level one, once cast, every mob in the area of effect had a 2% chance to turn and fight against their friends.

All of that for only a 2% chance to turn someone? It didn't seem right to me. But Mordecai had insisted that it could be a great spell. I took his word for it.

"I can't wait to try it out," Donut said.

"Goddamnit, Donut," I said. "Don't cast it unless I tell you to. You'll get frozen in place for five minutes. If we're in a situation where a 2% chance to turn someone on our side is our only hope, we'll be running, not waiting five minutes."

"Don't be so pessimistic, Carl."

Our training cooldown hadn't reset yet, so we decided to head out right away. We left our personal space and entered the food court. I grabbed another corn dog before we proceeded outside.

"Stop," Donut said just before I opened the door to the transit station. "There are mobs out there. Lots of them."

"What?" I said. My portal skill didn't work on this door. I didn't see anything on my map. Monsters weren't supposed to be in the transit stations. "How big?"

"Human sized," Donut said. "Maybe a little smaller. There's dozens of them. They're bouncing all over the place. I think they're really fast."

"That's new," I said. We couldn't use Donut's *Hole* spell on safe room doors. But we were safe while we were inside. "Step back. Let's see what we're dealing with."

I opened the door, but I stayed inside the room.

"What the hell, man?" I said, examining the screeching, frothing bedlam in the small transit station.

The squealing chaos abruptly stopped. About forty pairs of eyes turned to look at me.

"Howdy, fellas," I called. These were baboons with wide, discon-
certingly human faces. The actual features, like the eyes, nose, and
mouth, were much too small for the broad, fleshy faces. The rest of
their bodies were completely simian. I focused on the closest of the
creatures. It was wearing a ripped T-shirt with a cobra on it. It had
a backwards baseball cap on its head. Another had an equally ripped
shirt with the actor Nicolas Cage's screaming face on it. A third wore
a shirt that read, "It's not going to suck itself," with an arrow pointing down. The mobs all had red exclamation marks over their heads,
something I hadn't seen before. It was some sort of buff indicator.

Babababoon. Level 17.

Warning: This mob is suffering from the DTs. It is in stage
two of three.

In stage two, this mob's strength is doubled. Intelligent mobs
lose the ability to speak and reason. They will attack anything
that is not also suffering from the same condition.

(I should note that with this particular mob, you probably
won't see much of a difference between a normal one and one
suffering the DTs. These guys are something else, even when
they're not suffering from withdrawal.)

The Babababoon is the king of idiotic chaos. This exclusive
mob was created by taking a standard Earth baboon and crossing it with the population from a Florida jail drunk tank. Not
gonna lie. I'm pretty proud of this one. These guys ruin just
about anything we put them in.

"If this is stage two, I wonder what stage one is," I said.
"By god, they look like living Botero paintings," Katia said.
Some of the mobs were attempting to break into the small general store. I could see the face of the mole man proprietor through
the barred window, looking out worriedly. The monsters had vomited and shit all over the place. One of them appeared to be passed

out on his back. Another was scratching at his own face while he tea-bagged his unconscious companion. Half walked on two legs, and the others rushed about on all fours. Their bright red asses flashed in the light as they jumped about.

They screeched at my appearance at the door. The first one with the cobra shirt lunged at me, barreling into the safe room. It roared, swinging. *Crack.* The monster teleported away. A second, then a third rushed into the room, also teleporting away the moment they attacked. They didn't seem to notice or care that their fellows weren't able to do any damage.

"Where did they come from?" Katia asked.

"They must be from the purple line," I said. "You said the train on that one has stopped coming. But I don't know why they're allowed into the transit station. Maybe the ones suffering from withdrawal aren't blocked the same way the regular mobs are. Or maybe since they walked here, it's different."

Another three rushed into the room, screaming and disappearing. From the back, the Bopca with the stupid hot dog hat started yelling for us to close the door.

"Come on," I said, forming a fist. "We need to get them before they all teleport away. And we need to keep them from fucking with the *Nightmare.*" I'd locked the door on the train, but they could still climb on the engine and get into the cab through the broken window. I punched one in the head just as he lunged at the door. He grunted and barreled back. My stun effect activated, but only for a moment. The mob was dead before he hit the ground. *Hell yeah,* I thought. My upgraded Powerful Strike absolutely destroyed these things.

Katia returned to her spiked She-Hulk form. It was about as big as she dared go and still be able to—barely—fit through most doors. Donut jumped on the back of Mongo.

"Ready, guys?" I said. I cracked my neck. I cast *Bang Bro* onto my gauntlet. It hissed with energy. "Let's do this."

DONUT CAST *SECOND CHANCE* ON A DEAD BABABABOON. THE THING
was wearing a top hat for some inexplicable reason. The zombified
creature roared to life and started tearing at his companions climbing up the side of the *Nightmare*.

It didn't appear as if any had gotten into the train, but they were
crawling all over the outside. A few bounded off down the track,
disappearing into the darkness.

At the top of the stairs, the one remaining clockwork Mongo
chomped down on a screeching mob. Donut glowed as she drank a
mana potion, and then she fired a three-way laser at a group of mobs
at the end of the platform. They all cried out and fell onto their
backs. Their health went down, but only about a third. The power
just wasn't there when she split her *Magic Missile* into three or more
beams.

I released my gauntlet and formed my xistera. I hadn't gotten to
use it much on this floor because of the close-combat nature of the
trains. I called one of my new "Banger Spheres" into my hand, loading it into the curved device. I spun, and the metal ball rocketed
away, blasting down the long platform. It hit one of the three recovering babababoons in the neck with an audible *splack*. It fell, dead.

"Damnit," I muttered. I'd been aiming for between the eyes.

The ammo was nothing more than spheres made of dwarven robot scrap metal, but I'd spent some time at my engineering table
making a few hundred of them. I'd made a few different sizes before
settling on the baseball-sized ones. The system automatically labeled
them **Banger Spheres**, but only the ones I made at that specific size.
I had an idea for a few additional designs, including spiked balls, but
I hadn't had the chance to implement them yet.

Mongo, with Donut still on his back, leaped onto the train engine and lunged at another mob. Donut hissed and jumped off,
bounding once before landing on my shoulder. Katia meanwhile had
another in a bear hug and was smashing him between her arms as

the babababoon pummeled at her. Her eyes were clenched tight. I could tell she was terrified, but at least she was actively fighting.

These monsters were exceptionally strong, and they moved fast, but their speed didn't translate well into precise movement. This buff—or debuff, depending on how you looked at it—was similar to being hopped up on PCP. I paused to watch Katia grapple with her opponent. For a moment, it looked as if the mob was about to power his way out of her arms, but her body jerked to the side, twisting at an unnatural angle, taking the babababoon's top half with her. It cracked and stopped moving. A blood-soaked baseball cap fell to the floor. Satisfied, I returned my attention to the two mobs on the other side of the platform. I tossed two more Banger Spheres, killing them both.

After another minute, the fight was done. Mongo returned, squawking happily.

"I think you need more practice before we battle while you're mounted," I said to Donut. If she'd been a human-sized rider, she'd have been brained on the ceiling of the tunnel when Mongo had leaped atop the train.

Katia stood there, looking at her blood-covered hands, breathing heavily. She had an odd expression on her face I couldn't read.

"You good?" I asked.

"He was hitting me really hard," she said. "I mean, like, really hard. But I think I figured out how to move the metal around inside of me. It's slow still, but I think it hurt him more than it hurt me. I think . . . I think I can make traveling spikes so monsters using their hands will impale themselves on me. I just need to keep practicing. When I do it really fast, it feels like I'm breaking my own bones. It's hard to explain the sensation."

"There's more up in the main area," Donut said. I started jogging toward the three at the end of the platform so I could loot their bodies. So far, none had anything of interest except a few handfuls of gold. "They keep coming. There are some on the tracks, too. The *Nightmare* tracks. I don't know where they think they're going."

"Let's get out of here," I said when I was finished. I took all of their hats, but not their shirts, which I'd have to physically remove. I took several of the actual corpses, too. "Something tells me we're going to be seeing more mobs like this from now on."

"THERE'S ANOTHER ONE," I MUTTERED AS WE BARRELED DOWN THE rails. "He got far." A moment later, the train gave a barely perceptible stutter as the cowcatcher crashed into the babababoon on the track. The creature was thrown sideways and was sucked between the train and the wall of the tunnel like he was being eaten by a paper shredder.

As I suspected, my message system was filled with people reporting encounters with mobs suffering from the DTs. All second stage. For whatever reason, once they got sick, the terminals were no longer safe.

Elle and Imani still hadn't reported back. Bautista would soon arrive at 433, which was the last transit station. It was called "Terminus Station."

It took less than twenty minutes to reach the switching station now that I was more familiar with the train's controls. Katia had to remove all of her mass to fit into the cab, and we ended up storing Mongo. I had the key to the passenger car directly behind the engine, but it was filled with the gore of some unknown mob from when I'd blasted the train. We all decided to crowd into the engine cab instead.

Fire Brandy remained in her boiler, not coming out at all. I figured that was a good thing. The less the others knew about the nature of her presence, the better.

I pulled the train to a stop just before the "Station Repair" switch. I wanted to make sure the massive portal was what it claimed. I exited the train and walked right up to the portal so I could examine it. The description was virtually identical to the portals that led off into the abyss, with one difference.

Type: Pass-Through two-way portal. Gated by conveyance type
and to key holders.

Can you pass this portal? Yes*

Warning: You must be on a gated conveyance and/or a key
must be equipped or held outside of inventory, depending on
type. Compatible keys have been marked in your inventory.

Environment on other side of portal: Compatible.

Visual Analysis? Yes/No.

The previous description said they were "one-way" portals. As I
stood there examining it, trying to puzzle out the exact definition of
"Pass-Through two-way portal," a loud *clank, clank, clank* noise emanated from the other side of the gateway. I stepped sideways to get a
better view of the threshold's flip side, and I realized that the track
actually ran *through* the swirling portal. The track on the far side
looked like a root system with dozens of tracks diverging off of the
main. That sound I'd heard was track switches activating down the
line. They were being controlled from the other side of the portal.
And if they were switching now, that meant . . .

I took a step back as a steam engine rolled out of the portal,
screaming loud and faster than I expected. It was a steam engine
almost identical to the *Nightmare*, but painted red. It only towed six
cars behind it plus a caboose. The train clunked loudly as it switched
off the main track and then onto another, then another, before disappearing into a random tunnel.

I backtracked, looking at the "Auxiliary Tracks. Warning"
switch. It led to a long track that entered the root system. That basically meant I could jump onto a different track without going
through the gateway if I wanted, though with the switch controls on
the other side of the portal, we'd be stuck with whatever track the
last train had utilized. In other words, we'd be on the same track as
that red-colored train.

The "Recycle" switch clearly led off to the abyss. So our only real
choice was "Station Repair."

I took a screenshot of the portal, and it was the same massive train yard as before, still filled with zombies. This one appeared to be on a different side of the yard as where the subways entered. I looked worriedly at the closest zombie creature. I couldn't examine its properties using the picture, but I recognized the monster as a zombified cornet, one of the sound-attack rabbit monsters. The skinless monster was covered in sores that exposed bones, as if worms had erupted from the inside. It reminded me of the parasitic-worm things that had infested Grimaldi's circus crew. I shuddered.

I returned to the train to find Fire Brandy sticking her head out of the door, chatting away with Donut and Katia.

"I'm a mother, too," Donut was saying as I entered the train. "My boy is named Mongo."

"That's a good name," Brandy said. "I have two children so far. We don't name our young until they're presented at the altar. What about you?" she asked Katia, who'd retreated to the back of the cab to escape the heat.

"No kids," she said. "I was about to adopt, but aliens destroyed my planet."

"Ah, that's too bad, honey," Brandy said, sounding genuinely sincere. She looked at me. Her face scrunched up, as if in pain. Another child was born. "We heading out?"

"Returning to the station," I said. "I don't suppose you know if they'll let us just drive the train out of the yard?"

"Don't know. We usually just go in circles all day long. Try not to blow the train up, okay? I have two little ones to look after."

"I'll do my best," I said.

17

WHEN WE ENTERED THE PORTAL, EVERY CAR ON THE TRAIN MADE IT through. The world flashed, the train bucked, and we entered a massive train yard. A notification appeared.

Entering Station and Repair Hub E

"Station *E?*" Katia said. "Does that mean there are more of these giant things?"

"Probably," I said, looking over the massive yard. It just went on and on. "Remember, there are nine-thousand-something stairwells out there. When we saw that clip with Lucia Mar, there were several bunched up in that one area, but that still means there have to be hundreds of instances of each one of those stairwell stations. There's no way they can fit all of those trains into a single train yard. This station is big, but it's not *that* big. I bet there's at least twenty of these yards. There might even be more than one of those abyss places I saw earlier."

"Do you think they all have zombies in them?" Donut asked.

"Maybe. Who knows?" I said.

We were still in an underground area, but the ceiling was very high, higher even than the fake sky of the Over City. The place was lit with random spotlights, giving the whole area a surreal, washed-out look. The train clunked as it moved over several switching tracks, and we angled forward, pushing into a long track section, straightening out the cars behind us.

I marveled at the sheer size of the fenced-in area. It had to be at least a full mile from the portal to the fence. The stone wall of the chamber blocked the area behind us, and I couldn't even see how far the yard went from left to right. Thousands of zombie creatures milled about. They gave no heed to our sudden appearance. Most were congregated in the far distance, up against the high wall that led out of the yard.

The entire fence was shaking, I realized. They were pushing it back and forth. It would collapse at any moment.

Dozens of freestanding towers dotted the rail yard at regular intervals, like watchtowers at a prison. At this distance, I couldn't see the creatures inside of the fortifications, but there was definitely movement in the closest one, about a quarter of a mile away.

"Ah, crap," I said as we were automatically routed onto another track, one with a dead end. The sign above the track read **Service Bay 32**. A shadow fell over the cab as we went under a corrugated metal awning. I had to slow and stop. I knew the train could go backward, but I was hoping to find a way to unhook the broken cars behind us and steam out of the yard and onto one of the other tracks. "It looks like the road ends here."

"Maybe not," Katia said, peering out the other, broken window. "It stops here, but there's a roundabout system." She pointed forward, and I saw what she was indicating, a vast, baseball-field-sized section of ground that appeared as if it could spin like a turntable. Track sections on the circular platform were designed to line up with these service bays, allowing trains to proceed forward. You could pull the engine onto the platform, and it would spin, lining up with another track. One of the odd watchtowers was situated at the edge of the disc. I assumed the controls for the turntable were up there.

"Hey, those aren't zombies," Donut said. She had her face smushed up against the glass, looking out into the yard.

I followed her gaze out the side window to the pair of monsters shuffling by. She was right. One of them was speaking with the other. *Zombies don't talk.* They hadn't noticed us yet. These were a pair of moss-covered, bark-skinned creatures. They were covered with the same sores as everyone else, though with their wooden skin, it looked like gunshot wounds.

Festering Ghoul—Level 18.

One of the unfortunate side effects of the Rev-Up Amazing Cure-All Vitamin Immunity Shot is the possibility of addiction. If a customer becomes addicted to the vitamin shot, and they do not get their dosage in time, they oftentimes start suffering from withdrawal. The effects of withdrawal ravage the addict's body, and if they are not treated in time, they begin to suffer from a dreaded condition known as the DTs.

Once the DTs start, there is no cure. All die. Or worse.

At stage one, sufferers are overcome with violent tremors. They are barely able to think, or to move. Their mind starts to rot out from within. Only 50% of sufferers survive this stage. Half move on to stage two, which allows for increased mobility. The other half drop dead.

They don't stay dead long, however. They soon transform into what you see before you now. A Festering Ghoul.

Important note. A Festering Ghoul is not a true Ghoul. It is *not* undead. It is simply a new life-form reborn in the shell of the old. As such, anti-undead attacks will not work on them. Still, a double tap on these guys is not a bad idea.

A Festering Ghoul has two purposes. One, to devour as much organic material as possible, and two, to find more of its kind. These particular Ghouls have been born with the knowledge on how to get to this area. All they need now is enough of their kind to arrive before their purpose becomes clear.

"That sounds vaguely threatening," I said. "So I guess all those bababababoons we fought had survived stage one and got to skip the ghoul stage."

"Unless they turn into something worse if they die at the end of stage two," Donut said.

"How are they getting here?" Katia asked. Even though the mobs appeared to be able to talk, everything else about them screamed *mindless zombie.* There were hundreds of different types, but they all moved in that same plodding, aimless manner.

I thought of those robots and that secret tunnel. "I think I know what's happening, but Imani and Elle are about to discover for sure. The real question is, what happens when enough of them get together?"

"It's obviously something awful, Carl," Donut said. "We need to get out of here."

We heard the echo of a detonation. It sounded like a cannon blast. A moment later, a second crash echoed directly over our heads. Whatever it was, it had hit the corrugated awning covering the train. Then came a *click, click, click* sound of something being ratcheted tight.

"I think someone's shooting at us," I said.

"Look," Katia said. "There's a chain. It's coming from that tower."

She was right. The closest watchtower, the same one at the edge of the turntable, had shot some sort of chain at the roof over our heads. Whatever it was, it connected with the roof, and it was now ratcheting itself tight.

"Do you think they're going to pull the roof off the awning?" Katia asked.

"No," I said. "Look. There's a little dude up there. In the tower. He's going to use the chain to get to us."

Sure enough, once the chain was tight, the small creature attached a little basket to the length. The basket hung off the chain by a pair of straps. It looked like and was the size of a woman's purse. The little furry man jumped in. The basket bounced wildly as it slid down the length of chain toward us.

His white dot appeared on my map. The creature eventually disappeared over our heads as it landed on the awning. A moment later, the tiny furry man swung off the edge of the corrugated roof and landed deftly on the front of the engine. He had something large and metallic attached to his belt, and it clanged loudly when he landed.

He scrambled up the walkway and approached the broken, port-side window. We all moved to look.

He was goblin-shaped and -proportioned, though instead of clothes, he was covered in black bristly hair. He was much smaller than a regular goblin, about the same height as Zev. He wore a little railroad cap and a tool belt that dragged a wrench three times his length. It clanged and dragged against the metal of the train as he approached. When he jumped, the wrench didn't appear to impede him at all.

Widget—Grease Gremlin—Level 19.

Iron Tangle Steam Engine Train Technician.

Not all gremlins are bad or evil. Not all of them glory in the tearing of flesh and the rending of bone. Some prefer more quiet activities, such as boiler repair and heavy engineering. Then there are Grease Gremlins, who could go either way. The only thing keeping this guy from attacking you is that "Sensitivity Training" class human resources made him take in order to se-cure this job. As long as you don't abuse him or his beloved trains, you'll probably be fine.

"I told ye last time dis here station is closed," the creature ranted. "First the *Raven Blade Unlimited* and now the *Nightmare?* I don't care if you lost the beasties on your backside. Don't you see we're suffering from a ghoul infestation? They about to reach critical mass. Now I gotta risk me life just to get your stupid butts out of here. We're not giving ye a resupply, that's fer sure."

I could barely understand what he was saying. His inflection was like a Creole guy poorly attempting a cockney accent. His head ap-peared in the broken window opposite Katia. He remained frozen like that for a long moment.

"Oh, for fig's sake," he eventually said. "Yer crawlers? Ye took the train? Where's CrackJack? Didja kill em? Don't care about the war mage cunt. I hope for yer sake ye didn't hurt Brandy."

I saw no point in lying to the little creature. "If CrackJack was the engineer, then yes, we killed him. Brandy is fine. We're just trying to get to one of the stairwells."

Below, a pair of ghouls finally noticed us. One of them screeched and pointed. All around the train yard, the mass of ghouls turned in our direction.

"Stairwells?" Widget said, either oblivious or uncaring of the sudden ghoul attention. He laughed. "Then why d'hell you come all this way? Why not take the *Escape Velocity* train? It goes to all the stairwells." He rapped on the metal on the window. "'Ell, this train stops at 83 tangerine and plum. You take the tangerine up to 89 and hop right on the *Escape Velocity*. It'll take you straight to a gaggle of stairwell stations." He laughed. "Silly crawlers, always making it difficult. Well, I reckon no real harm done if'n Brandy's okay. She's to be a mum, ye know. CrackJack was a cock. CockJack." He laughed at his own stupid joke. "And nobody has no love for the war mage kind, either. Out with ye. We about to abandon the yard. Gon all move over to Yard A. Ain't no ghouls at Yard A. Ye can catch any numma of lines up to 12, I reckon. Or 24 might be better for you lot. Twelve got them janitor ghouls. But all the trains from this yard is done. They ain't opening the gate for nobody. We gotta use the chains to get out."

A ghoul, this one some kind of multi-limbed monstrosity, scrabbled up the side of the train like a spider.

"Get ye filthy paws off 'er!" Widget cried, turning to face the ghoul. He pulled the gigantic wrench off his belt and waved it threateningly, using two hands to hold the massive oversized wrench like a halberd.

Thwap!

Through the broken window, Donut fired a magic missile directly into the ghoul. It didn't die right away, but it was blasted onto its back. Its legs curled up. **Unconscious** appeared over it. A moment later, the notification went away, and it turned into an X.

"Oi, nice shot, lassie," Widget said. He licked his lips and looked at Donut appraisingly. "I like a lassie within meat on 'er bones. Especially 'em with fight in 'em."

"*Excuse* me?" Donut said. "Did you just call me fat?"

"Why are the ghouls here?" I asked.

"Some cunt done buggered up the system. Cheaped out. Tryin to combine systems and that there why it broke down. Never worked right. The ghouls are supposing to get all caged up, hop on the service conveyor back to the yard. And then get wheeled onto one of dem Terminus Direct lines. Shoulda just build a second conveyor system right into the abyss if ye ask me. But nobody ever asks Widget what he done thinks. Too many came at once. Sometimes them wrath ghouls are in the cages, so the cages are broke when they get here. Or they spill out. The system broke down. Ain't no stopping it." He pointed to another ghoul. "Lassie?" Donut obliged by firing another missile. This ghoul rocketed off the train.

"That's m'girl. What's a fine lass like yerself doing with this lot? I get off shift in a couple of hours. Got a place up at 60. M'wife will cook us a nice stew."

"Your wife?" Donut asked, incredulous.

"She no mind one bit. She'd liken a smack of you, too, I reckon. Plus she cook. We got a drop of fresh fish in our food boxes, we did."

"Wait, what kind of fish?" Donut asked.

"Yo. Focus. How are we supposed to get out of here?" I asked.

"You gotta abandon ship. Up me chain. Into tower. Then we do a bit o' hopscotch. We got a system. One that works." He grinned. "As long as yer climbin' skills is up to snuff."

I eyed the chain dubiously. Below, another group of ghouls was attempting to climb up the side of the train. A single ghoul had discovered the ladder behind the cab, and it was now scratching at the door.

Widget leaned in through the broken window and pointed at a red spigot with his wrench. Katia had to jump back from the unwieldly thing. "Turn that one right quick, will ya? Then turn it back."

Brandy had told me never to touch that one. I turned the spigot, and the train hissed. Steam spilled from the side and rose all around us. Below, the ghouls screamed. I quickly tightened it back up. "It'll teach ye right!" Widget yelled down at the monsters. Several scrambled away from the side of the train, but they soon returned. "I reckon I better open a hole in the ceiling before ye get overwhelmed. It'll take me a good . . ."

He didn't finish. In the distance, a mighty crash reverberated throughout the train yard. A section of the colossal wall that separated the yard from the conductor staging area collapsed in a mighty heap. The crowd of ghouls surged out of the enclosure. Below, the ghouls who'd been advancing on us turned to regard the new exit. A few shuffled off toward it, but most remained at the base of the train.

"Oi. That no good," Widget said. "Plan change. Now the wall is gone I reckon it don't matter if we use the gate. I'll unhook ye. Then I'll get into me tower. Get on the turntable, and I'll get ye onto the employee line. There's only a station over at 60, and it loops back after, so no 72, not that ye'd want that one anyway, but there's a service entrance at every station between 'ere and back. Go slow and ye'll see 'em. They come quick. The distances are much shorter here. The *Homeward Bound* is locked up tighter than an octoid's cunt, so you'll have the track all to yerself."

He disappeared, scrambling over the top of the cab. He dropped into the space behind the cab and the next car. That one ghoul remained at the door, but Widget dropped him with a bonk to the head with his wrench. Less than ten seconds later, there was a mighty clang that shook the whole train. A few moments after that, and he returned to the window. Behind, three additional ghouls discovered the small ladder that led to the back of the cab. They stood at the closed door, banging on it.

"Oi, you did a mighty nummer on them cargos. No matter now. They's unhooked. Now I'm going to climb up the chain and get into me tower. Imma turn the table to yer bay. You get on. Make sure you get all the way on. I'n spin it up right and stop at the right track but don't be leaving yet. Imma come down and we ride out together. Sounding good?"

"That sounds great," I said. I wondered if he was genuinely this accommodating, or if this was a result of our charisma. Either way, I wasn't going to complain. "Better than I hoped for. I appreciate your help."

"Oi. You a good lot." He winked at Donut. "I'll be back and we talk some more about that fish, okay, luv?" He turned and ran to the edge of the engine. He paused to wave.

And that was when the spider ghoul, the one Donut had killed, turned from an X back to a red dot. It lunged forward and grasped the small furry gremlin. It ripped the mechanic's head off in one smooth motion and started to devour his body. The whole thing happened in less than a second.

"Well, that's going to be a problem," I said.

"WE HAVE A FEW CHOICES," I SAID AS DONUT SHOT THE RE-reanimated spider ghoul off the engine. "We can abandon the train. If we do that, we either fight through the ghouls and make our way up one of the tracks on foot, or we can try to go back through that same portal and return to the switching station, also on foot."

"Neither is very appealing," Katia said.

I gazed out the window at the length of chain attaching the top of the awning to the tower. "I can try climbing that chain up into the tower. I can figure out the turntable controls."

"That's not going to work, Carl," Donut said. "You're the only one who knows how to drive the train. *I'll* go up the chain and see if I can figure it out."

I exchanged a look with Katia. "I don't know, Donut. I don't like the idea of you doing that alone. You might need hands to control it."

"If that little pervert can work the controls, then I can figure it out," Donut said. "Besides, do you really think you can climb that chain? It's quite long. Mongo will be ready to graduate college by the time you get up there. I can do it quick. I can use *Puddle Jumper* if I have to, but I'd rather save it for coming back."

"Okay," I said after a moment. "Just be careful."

"I'm always careful, Carl," Donut said, shooting another missile. "I'm going out there."

"Wait," I said. I pulled a hobgoblin smoke curtain from my inventory and tossed it through the window. It ricocheted off the side of the engine and landed on the ground between two ghouls. Thick smoke started to billow around the train.

Donut leaped through the window, traversed down the walkway to the very front of the engine. She turned and leaped up to the top of the awning, flying easily into the air. A moment passed, and then I watched as she nimbly rushed up the chain. Twenty seconds later, she disappeared into the tower.

DONUT: WOW. I CAN SEE REALLY FAR. THERE ARE A BUNCH OF
    SUBWAY CARS AT THE OTHER END. I CAN SEE THE GATE
    WHERE THE TRAINS ARE SUPPOSED TO GO THROUGH. THE
    BUILDING THERE IS ON FIRE. THE GHOULS THAT WENT
    THROUGH THE FENCE ARE CHASING THE DWARVES AND
    THE TALL GUYS WHO GIVE OUT THE PRIZE SUITCASES.
    CARL, WE NEVER GOT KATIA A SUITCASE. I CAN'T
    BELIEVE WE FORGOT!

CARL: We didn't forget. We decided the prizes weren't worth
    the risk. Are you good? Do you see what to do?

DONUT: HONESTLY, CARL. GIVE ME A MINUTE. THERE ARE
    MULTIPLE CONTROL PANELS. IT ALSO SMELLS AWFUL IN
    HERE. JUST AWFUL. WIDGET WAS A VERY MESSY
    CREATURE. HOW MANY LOTION CONTAINERS DOES ONE
    GREMLIN NEED? I CAN'T IMAGINE HIS WIFE WAS A VERY
    GOOD COOK CONSIDERING HOW MUCH TIME HE
    OBVIOUSLY SPENT UP HERE.

CARL: Make sure you loot everything. You never know what
    might come in handy.

DONUT: WAS THAT SUPPOSED TO BE A PUN?

CARL: Just hurry up.

DONUT: DON'T PRESSURE ME, CARL.

A loud clanking filled the train yard. In the distance, a freight car sitting by itself on a track toppled over onto its side.

DONUT: WHOOPS. WRONG PANEL.

CARL: How in the hell . . .

Ahead, the massive turntable rumbled. It started to rotate. Multiple ghouls standing on it tumbled off their feet. The track spun, stopping in front of us. I peered through the window at the track. It didn't match up.

CARL: Great job, Donut! But move one more slot over. That track isn't the right gauge.

It moved again, clanking into place. This time, the rails matched up. I pulled the brake, knocked on the window to let Brandy know we were moving, and I eased the train forward. We had almost a dozen ghouls climbing the exterior. If they got near the window, Katia speared them with her hand. They stumbled as the train lurched. A few fell off.

The train detached from the other cars as it moved. Thank goodness. I pulled as far forward as I dared, making certain we were fully on the platform.

DONUT: NOTHING IS LABELED. I DON'T KNOW WHAT THE RIGHT ONE TO TURN TO IS.

I searched the line of trains sitting under the awnings. There weren't too many actual steam engines here. Most of the trains and train parts were random cars. I did catch sight of one engine sitting on a track adjacent to the awnings. It was attached to a single passenger car, and the train was facing the wrong way. It was also painted blue. I followed the line of tracks, and it curved toward the distant exit. Most of the tracks sized for steam engines curved back toward the portal.

> CARL: I think I know which one. I'll tell you when to stop. Now see if there's a control up there that will open the gate.
>
> DONUT: I ALREADY OPENED IT BY ACCIDENT AND MORE GHOULS STARTED WALKING OUT. I DIDN'T TELL YOU BECAUSE I THOUGHT YOU MIGHT GET MAD.

DONUT USED *PUDDLE JUMPER* TO RETURN TO THE *NIGHTMARE*. I opened up the back door and pummeled down the ghouls on the small landing, clearing the area for her return. These guys weren't nearly as quick or strong as the ones suffering from stage two DTs. Like with zombies, their danger was in the swarm. Luckily only a few dozen remained interested in us. Donut leaped down, getting gore on her paw. She grumbled as we returned to the cab, locking the door.

From there, we steamed our way toward the massive double doors that led out of the train yard. Dozens of tracks converged side by side as they pushed through the exit. The archway reminded me of that giant entrance in the *Jurassic Park* movies.

We moved slowly. The ghouls mostly got out of the way, but the cowcatcher sometimes caught one of the monsters, causing it to spin away. Sometimes they died, but I suspected if we didn't get them in the heads, they'd just get right back up again in a few minutes.

Just outside of the gates stood a hulking concrete building that was now fully engulfed in flames. The sign above the three-story building read **The Iron Tangle Substation E**. The thing reminded me of a Soviet-era government building in its simple, efficient brutality. In fact, I wouldn't be surprised if this was a repurposed structure from that era. Dozens of dead dwarves and grapples lay on the ground where they'd been congregating. Since the trains had stopped coming, the conductors and porters were lining up, waiting for trains that would never appear. As I watched, a dwarf and a pair of porters materialized, popping right out of the brick wall. They looked dazed. A moment later, they were set upon by ghouls.

Almost all of the tracks led to the front of the substation, running along the loading area for the workers. Our track, however, led along the back side of the building. We eased our way around the wide turn. There was another, smaller landing here at the back of the building. The track eventually led to a cave entrance against a distant wall.

As we moved, a single figure popped out from the back of the flaming building and ran directly for us. A human! She waved her arms frantically as I eased the brakes. She had a white dot, meaning she was an NPC, not a crawler. She screamed as a flaming wolf ghoul lurched from the building.

The woman wore a white business dress that was now covered in soot. She only had one shoe on, a black heel. She shuffled as she ran toward us, shrieking. She was in her mid-forties, and she looked like any typical, suburban soccer mom. She was absurdly out of place here.

"I'm going to let her on," I said.

"You sure that's a good idea?" asked Katia. "This has got to be some sort of trap. Or something. I mean, *look at her.*"

"I don't think so," I said. "Check out her description."

Madison—Human. Level 10.
   Iron Tangle Human Resources Associate.
   This is a Non-Combatant NPC.
   Madison's real name was probably something like Jennifer or Ruth, but she had it legally changed to something more trendy right around the same time as her divorce. After multiple rounds of breast augmentation, Pilates, and labiaplasty, Madison has

> emerged as a new woman. She don't need no man. While only a
> human resources associate—after all, she started her career
> late—she still walks the world with new confidence. She won't
> tell this to any of her friends at her book club, but she relishes
> the power she has over the other Iron Tangle employees. She
> feels an almost-sexual surge of gratification when she tells
> those dwarves that overtime is mandatory.

"Why do they keep calling it *human* resources?" Donut asked. "It's racist!"

Madison cried out as the wolf ghoul leaped and caught the back of her hair in its ravening mouth. She tumbled backward.

"Donut," I said. She jumped through the broken window, jumped to the top of the cab, and shot two quick magic missiles at the ghoul. The former wolf monster hissed and dropped. The woman scrambled to her feet and ran to the train, pulling herself up the ladder. I eased off the brakes, touched the throttle, and we steamed away just as more flaming ghouls emerged from the back of the building. They gave chase, but we quickly outpaced them.

"Thank you, thank you," the woman said when Katia opened the door for her. We entered the tunnel. Just a few moments later, I caught sight of a glowing sign. There was a ladder against the wall, leading up to a trapdoor in the ceiling of the tunnel. The sign read **Transit Station 11**. I wondered if there'd be a Desperado Club at this one. The glowing sign for station 12 was only a few hundred meters further down. I remembered what Widget had said: that station 12 was where the janitor ghouls congregated. Sure enough, the little sign read **Jikininki Peak Station 12**. *Let's skip that one for now.*

"Wait, I don't recognize you," the woman said. "How did you get in here? What're your employee numbers?"

"Hardly. Do I look like someone who would work for a train yard?" Donut asked.

The woman was a mess. It appeared as if she'd spent a lot of time getting her hair perfectly placed this morning, piled atop her head in a bun. Now it hung in frizzy tatters where the festering wolf ghoul had lunged at it. That giant bun of hair had saved her life.

The woman looked scandalized. The look instantly reminded me of Bea's mom. The woman even had the same my-facelift-is-a-bit-too-tight Catwoman glare. "Customers are not allowed in the train engines! I'm going to have to alert the transit authority. This is most irregular."

Station 13 whipped by. It was also a transit station. I laughed. "Lady, we just saved your ass. If you don't like it, I can stop and let you off right here. I'm sure those ghouls will take fine care of you."

"Where are we taking her?" Katia asked.

"You're taking me to Yard A," the woman said. "It's the head-quarters. There you can turn yourself in."

"Yeah?" I asked. "How do we get there from here?"

"I don't know," she said. "I'm not an engineer. Isn't there a map or something in here?"

Stations 14 and 15 whipped by. "We're going to stop at the service entrance for 24 to check it out and see if it needs to be cleared," I said. "After, we can take her up to 60 and set her free. Widget said there's a loop after that, and the train can turn around. If that's true, then we can stay in the area until it's time to go down."

"Set me free?" Madison said, incredulous. "Are you suggesting I'm a prisoner? And station 60 is where the lower employees stay."

Yep, I thought. *Bea's mom.* "Where do you live, then?"

"I have an apartment in the executive quarters outside of Yard A."

"And you don't know how to get there?"

Station 17 was another transit station. Eighteen was called **Barren Station**. I wondered if these had monsters similar to the higher stations, and if there was a Krakaren boss at 20.

The woman didn't answer. I looked back over my shoulder to regard her. She was staring off out the window, a strange look of confusion on her face. "I've been putting in a lot of hours. Mandatory overtime."

I was starting to suspect there was no Yard A. I was also suddenly curious about what we'd find over at station 60, these supposed dorms for the employees. Before, when Vernon the dwarf conductor had told us about his wife, I'd assumed his wife had been a made-up phantom. Widget had a similar story, but it was clear he'd actually been living in that tower. "You've never been to your apartment, have you?"

"Of course I've been to my apartment. It's just been . . . It's been a few days."

I nodded. When they'd programed this floor in, they'd given all these NPCs a bunch of false memories, but they hadn't set up a proper foundation. All the stories were paper-thin, like the background of an NPC in an actual game. This was probably the first time since the floor started that Madison had left her office. I thought of Brandy and her two new babies. When this floor was done, would she be able to keep the children?

A crawler named Herot had written the 16th edition of the cookbook, and she had a long essay in the back about the nature of the NPCs. She had a theory she called "The Worn Path Method," which suggested success in quests and puzzles was much easier when you deliberately broke through the fourth wall. She believed the NPCs were the weakest link in this world because they were biological and not autonomous. I'd only read the first few paragraphs so far. She claimed that breaking them out of their reverie was cruel, but also necessary if one wanted to survive. *Ask them questions, and then challenge them when they don't know something they should. Be kind but firm.* There was so much in the cookbook I still needed to study, and my reading time was at a premium. I made a mental note to go back and finish through the essay.

"You've either been to your apartment or you've never seen Yard A. It can't be both. Which is it?" I demanded.

"I . . . I don't know," she finally said. "That ghoul must have given me a concussion."

I saw the sign for station 24, and I slowed the train. We stopped, and I set the brake. I turned to Madison. "Look," I said. "I have several questions. Answer them for me, and we'll take you to station 60. If someone there knows how to get to Yard A from there, we'll take you."

"Okay," she said after a moment. She leaned up against a bulkhead. She looked exhausted. "What do you want to know? If it's about the trains, I don't really know much. I'm in charge of telling employees that overtime is mandatory. They come out to get on the *Homeward Bound*, and I tell them to get back to work. Oh, and I am the benefits manager for all the Kravyad and the six station mimics."

"The *what?*"

"Terminus. The station mimics. There are six of them, and boy, do they get cranky if we don't send enough passengers into them. Those things are ravenous. We tell the workers to always tell the customers to get off on 433, but you'd be surprised at how awful dwarves are at following instructions. And don't get me started on the mantaurs. They can't keep their paws to themselves."

CARL: Bautista. Do *not* get off at the Terminus Station. It's a goddamned trap.

18

BAUTISTA: Yeah, you're a little late there, buddy. Can't talk. The whole damn station is a city boss. We gathered about 400 people on the train, and when they went up the stairs, it swallowed the first twenty of them like it was eating cheese rings. We're on the platform now fighting off its tongue and its minions. It belches and these walking mouth things pour out of it. They're too strong. Waiting on the next train to escape. Don't know what we're going to do. Half of these guys sold their hats.

CARL: Holy shit. Be careful. You're going to have to fight the Kravyad boss two stations down at 435 and try the employee portal exit. I'll try to find out about them now. Keep me updated.

BAUTISTA: Talk soon.

Geez, 400 people? That seemed like too many at one place at one time. A disaster waiting to happen.

I turned to Madison. "The Kravyad. Tell me about it. Now. Quickly."

"Which one? We have a few dozen on shift right now."

"Does it matter? Are they different?"

"Of course they're different," she said. "One of them is always whining he wants to go home to visit his girlfriend. Another is demanding hazard pay after getting stabbed by a crawler. She was highly offended as she's not designated as a combatant. They're just as different as you and your little hairy friend."

"Not a combatant? So they're not bosses?"

"Bosses? Hardly. They're actually part of the human resources department." Madison straightened, standing proudly. "They work directly under me. Part of management's initiative to increase productivity."

"Holy shit, lady. Start with the basics. What is a Kravyad? And do they attack people? Like the station mimics attack people?"

"Like I said, they're part of a money-saving initiative. A very successful one, I might add. The conductors and porters are less likely to demand time off if they don't remember their between-shift breaks. They end their shift, go into what we call a preproduction stupor, and they awaken ready for their next shift. They're still quite dazed until the moment they get on the trains. And by then it's too late to request time off. It has increased productivity by 35%. The Kravyad are responsible for maintaining this program."

I refrained the urge to choke the woman out. All of this information about how they abused their workers was infuriating, terrifying, and painfully familiar, but it was also irrelevant. "But *what* are they? Are they wizards? Giant owls? Elves? Tell me what they look like and what sort of powers they have."

She gave me an are-you-really-that-stupid? look. "Do you know what a Naga is? They're kinda like that. But blue and with six arms. They take their payment by getting to eat one or two dwarves a shift. It saves the company a lot of gold."

"What kind of magic do they cast?"

"They hypnotize the dwarves and grapples getting off the train. They keep them around for eight to twelve hours depending on the lines attached to their station, and they send them through the portal when it's almost time for their shift to start again. It saves me from having to tell them that overtime is mandatory. Though sometimes they gather enough wits about them to ask for time off before they get on the train. Then they get a trip to my office, and I give them the gold armband."

"Armband?" I asked. I couldn't help it.

She beamed. "It was my idea. We tell them that if they wear the armband during one more run, the Kravyad will know to teleport them straight home at the end of the shift. But really it lets the Kravyad know they're troublemakers who are okay to eat. It added another 5% to our productivity in Q2. Even Rod was impressed."

DONUT: I DON'T LIKE THIS LADY. SHE'S ONE OF THOSE PEOPLE WHO IS REALLY MEAN BUT DOESN'T THINK THEY'RE MEAN.

CARL: No kidding.

I took a deep breath. "Tell me about the employee portal. If the workers go through it, it just takes them to the platform? Can anybody pass through it?"

"That's right," Madison said. "Straight to the platform. I suppose others could go through. We've already had a few of you lot sneaking through. Of course it's life bound to the Kravyad. So if something happens to them, then it snaps closed. They insisted on that when we wrote out their contract. It was a big point of contention."

"So the creature has to remain alive for the portal to work?"

"That's what I said. Now are you going to take me back?"

That station number 435 was another sort of trap. You could only get through if you kept the Kravyad, boss or not, alive. I paused to send all this information to Bautista. He and the survivors had retreated from the mimic back onto the train, which was thankfully still running.

You can't save them all. This was something Bautista and his group would have to figure out on their own. I'd done all I could from here.

"I have a few more questions," I said to Madison. "Tell me about the ghouls that almost killed you."

She frowned. "Those filthy things are *not* my job. Doris over at

Substation B is in charge of that. This is her fuckup. That husband-stealing whore couldn't even get that right. I told Rod that she'd be the death of him, but of course he didn't listen. She's in charge of keeping the Krakaren happy, which meant she was also in charge of excess-citizen disposal. But she wanted to impress Rod, of course, with her money-saving concept. An extra train on an existing line was much cheaper than a dedicated conveyor line. And look what happened. The good news is Substation B fell before E did. I hope the ghouls ate that fat bitch and popped her oversized implants."

I was about to ask her another question when Elle pinged me. I held up a hand. As I talked to them, Brandy knocked on the furnace door. I opened it. She started grilling Madison about her paycheck while I stepped outside to escape the heat.

CARL: Hey, guys. What's the news?

ELLE: It's not a train like we thought but a roller coaster with no cars. You know, those rolling carts they have in the robot rooms? The robots fill them with these ghoul things and roll them down to the coaster. It's a pretty far hike. At least it was for us. The robots push the roly things and the bottom of the cart catches on the roller coaster, and off they go. It's like the thing they have at the hospital that takes your trays away. But a hell of a lot faster.

CARL: Yeah, the carts end up back at the train yards. The ghouls are then supposed to be moved to a train that takes them all the way to the abyss to get rid of them.

ELLE: Why would they send them all the way back to the start just to turn them around and send them back? What sort of inefficient bullshit is that?

CARL: You were never in the military, were you?

IMANI: It's designed to break down, I think. Or maybe they're just terrible at design. Maybe both. At least we're free of monsters in this tunnel. Only the ghouls can enter the robot rooms. The other monsters aren't allowed in for some

reason. But the ghouls actually get into the cages
themselves. And then the robots lock them in and roll them
down into the tunnel and put them onto the conveyor.

CARL: Something is going to happen when enough of them get
to the same place. I don't know what.

I quickly went over everything I had discovered, and I gave them
an update on what was happening with Bautista. I'd already sent out
a mass warning about the station mimics at station 433.

IMANI: We've been camping and killing the ghouls as they rush
by, but they give shit experience. Carl, there's a lot of them
coming now. A whole lot. Also, there's another type of
ghoul sometimes in the mix called a wrath ghoul. I think it
might be what happens at the end of stage 2. They are
very strong. Be careful. We were just debating on whether
or not to hijack a few carts and get onto the carousel
ourselves or going back to the main track and hiking to the
transit station.

Shit. That was a scary proposition.

CARL: If it was me, I'd take the conveyor. But it's super risky. I
don't know how gentle it is, plus when you land, you'll end
up at the service station. If you end up at Stations B or E,
the gate is down, and there'll be less ghouls. But if the
fence isn't down yet wherever you end up, you'll be
surrounded by literally thousands of the monsters. It's a
huge gamble.

ELLE: But it also sounds really fun. By the time all those best
roller coasters were popping up around the country, I was
too old to do it. My Barry used to puke cotton candy after
just the Tilt-A-Whirl, and I never got to do the real rides.
Now's our chance.

IMANI: I'll let you know what we decide to do. Take care, Carl.
DONUT: CARL, YOU BETTER GET BACK IN HERE. THEY'RE
  FIGHTING!

I grumbled as I returned to the cab.

"Well, we just don't need your services anymore," Madison was saying to Brandy as I returned to the cab. The entire room was sweltering. The cry of a baby emanated from the furnace.

"You can't fire me," Brandy said. "I only deal with Portia."

"Portia!" Madison scoffed. "I have two weeks more on the job than Portia, which makes me her senior. I will not have my employees mouthing off to me like this."

"*Your* employees? Why is it everyone in human resources always thinks they're the boss? You're not, you *einzeller*. You may be the one who does hiring and firing, but it's not your decision. You are ze boot, not ze foot. Besides, I have contract. We demons take our contracts very seriously. You can't make decisions like that without running it past an exec, and we both know it." The demon's black orbs glowed, and I feared she was about to blast the human with a fireball, which would probably be bad for everybody in the room. Brandy was level 75, and Madison was only level 10.

"Ladies," I said, interrupting, "you guys can discuss this later, preferably *after* the ghoul outbreak. Nobody is getting fired right now." I grasped on to the towel and gently pushed at the furnace door. Brandy made a face like she was going to protest, but then another baby came, and I took the opportunity to slam the hot door while her face was scrunched up in pain.

Madison crossed her arms and pouted. She was literally quivering with anger.

DONUT: CARL, SHE REMINDS ME OF SOMEBODY BUT I DON'T
  KNOW WHO.

I laughed out loud.

CARL: Do you think you can guard her while I go up that ladder
    and peek into station 24? Maybe you can use that charm
    of yours and get more info out of her.
DONUT: OKAY, I'LL DO IT.
CARL: Cool. Don't let Brandy out again.

"I'll be right back," I said out loud.

"Can I come?" Katia asked.

I'd been planning on going up the ladder and sticking my head
through the trapdoor to look and see what was up there. If there
were mobs, we'd come back to clear them later. That quick shot we'd
seen of Lucia Mar had shown her fighting waves of ghouls before she
had to retreat, and I wanted to see if this station was the same. But
it was rare for Katia to want to do something dangerous, and I didn't
want to shoot her down.

"Okay," I said. "But we'll just be a minute."

———

"I'LL GO FIRST," I SAID, CLIMBING UP THE LADDER. THE LADDER LED
to a trapdoor about 25 feet up. Unfortunately it was a regular door,
not a subspace portal, so I couldn't use my skill to see through it.

Katia got on the ladder behind me. She was in her normal,
human-sized, non-enhanced body. We ascended quickly. I grasped
on to the door and pushed it up. Dust cascaded down over me as I
pressed. I emerged into a large, well-lit room with rocky walls and
ceiling, the size of a big warehouse. Five stairwells sat in a circle in
the middle of the room, light shining directly up over them like
blazing spotlights. The moment I saw them, they marked themselves
on my map. I didn't see any mobs or any other features in the room
except the exits. Ten of the exits circled the room, leading down to
regular train platforms. Each one had a sign over them. All were
colored lines except one, which was *Escape Velocity III*.

That gremlin mechanic had been right. There *was* a named train
that looped back. I already had one person on my chat who said he'd

seen the *Escape Velocity* train, but he hadn't tried it. Also, the name didn't have a number after it, which suggested all of the trains that looped back might be called *Escape Velocity.*

Then again, the Iron Tangle employees were also trying to talk people into the mouth of a station mimic, so who knew what was safe and what wasn't?

The trapdoor I'd pushed through was disguised as a rock outcropping. It made me wonder how many hidden and secret doorways we'd walked right past. My Escape Plan skill supposedly had the ability to find hidden doorways, but it didn't seem to work very well. I needed to talk to Mordecai about that once he got out of jail.

I hesitantly pulled myself up into the room, looking about. Katia popped up beside me.

"There's nothing here," I whispered. Whispering felt appropriate. The stairways all emitted a gentle pulsing hum. I knew they wouldn't open up until there were six hours left, which was ominous. There had to be a reason for that.

"Maybe the ghouls are on the train platforms," Katia said, pointing at the exits. "I don't have anything on my map."

"Weird. It feels like a trap. Let's leave it be for now. Maybe we'll look at stops 36 and 48 and see if they're the same."

"Hey," Katia said as I turned back to the trapdoor. "I wanted to talk to you alone for a second."

"Sure," I said, pausing. "You know you can always private message me, too."

"I know," she said. "But the messaging always feels so impersonal. This is really important."

"Okay," I said, starting to feel a little apprehensive. "What is it?"

She was clearly nervous, which made *me* nervous. "Remember when I said some of my parts, like my eyes and mouth, need to be flesh? What it *really* says is at least *two* of my eyes need to be flesh. Which made me wonder, does that mean I can have more than two eyes? So I've been practicing, and it turns out, I *can* make as many eyes as I want. The problem is, it makes me want to vomit if I have more than two. And the acuity is not right. I'm very nearsighted with them. I've gotten it to where I can have a third eye, and as long as the field of vision doesn't overlap with my other two, my brain can handle it. You'd think it'd be the other way around, that it'd need to overlap for it to work better, and maybe that's so and I'm doing it wrong, but for now I'm training myself to see directly behind me while I walk. It's like watching two shows at the same time, and it's hard to remember which one is which even though it's obvious. I keep it closed most of the time, but I can open it a minute or two at a time before I get a really bad headache. Hopefully soon I can train my mind to understand a full array of vision all around without going insane. That would be very useful. It's just, I feel less—I don't know—human when I do it. I know I'm *not* human anymore. I need to get over it. I know that. But it's hard."

"That . . . that's wild," I said, "and it will be really helpful. But why is this a secret?"

"That's not the secret." She wrung her hands worriedly. It was something she did often, no matter what size she was. "Donut did something when she didn't think anybody was looking. I talked to Hekla about this, and she thinks it was a setup. That you had her do it on purpose to test me. But I think I know you better than she does, and that's not the sort of thing you'd do. Besides, you didn't know about my third eye, so how would that be a setup anyway? Donut did it so nobody would see."

"What the hell are you talking about, Katia?"

She pulled a little slip of paper out of her inventory and handed it to me.

"The other day when you got hit by the *Nightmare* and were gone, Donut and I went back out on the tracks to clean it. I saw Donut pull this from her inventory and then stuff it under the track so nobody would find it. But I was practicing with my third eye, and I saw her do it. When she wasn't looking, I grew a new arm, slid it along the track, and I grabbed it."

I examined the paper. It was a black ticket with a familiar gold leaf skull embossed on it. I felt a chill rush through me as the description appeared.

PVP Coupon.

Ah, betrayal. Sweet, delicious betrayal.

If you have this coupon in your inventory, and you kill the crawler whose name appears on the back side of this coupon, you will receive the following rewards:

Gold Savage Box

Gold Weapons Box

Gold Apparel Box

Platinum Adventurer Box (This benefit may only be redeemed a max of 3 times)

+1 Player Level (This benefit may only be redeemed a max of 3 times)

I flipped the paper over. The slip read:

Crawler #4,122. Carl.

"What the hell?" I said. The sight of my name on the paper gave me a second chill. "Where did she get this?"

"PVP means player versus player," Katia said. "I didn't know that. Hekla says when someone gets one of those skulls next to their name for killing a crawler, and if they're in a party, they get a savage box, and it contains the coupons."

"That means she got this after she killed that guy in the club, and she didn't want to tell us about it." I felt myself relax. This wasn't a big deal. Was it? She had gotten rid of it. The system gave out the coupon to be a dick. I imagined in a less tight-knit party, the existence of such coupons could cause a lot of paranoia and damage. But the idea of Donut wanting to hurt me was ridiculous. It was a waste of a prize, and she'd gotten rid of it so she didn't have to deal with having it. End of story.

Katia continued to wring her hands. "There's more. I thought this was a good thing at first. But later, I told Hekla about it, and she said they don't just get one coupon. They get one for every member of the party." She paused. "This was the only coupon Donut got rid of."

Shit, I thought. I could now see why Katia was freaking out. She thought Donut still had one of these coupons with her name on it.

"Maybe she got rid of your coupon at another time," I said. "And how does Hekla know this anyway?"

"My friend Eva. I told you about her already. She was with me before. We went into the dungeon together. She has a skull. There was a man. We didn't know him, but we met right when we got in. When we joined the Daughters, Hekla didn't want him coming with us. But he insisted. We told him to go away, but he wouldn't. He grabbed me by the arm, and Eva stabbed him with her trident. I thought he'd be okay. She'd just stabbed him in the back of the leg. But he died, and she got the skull. She got the coupon book, though she never told me about it. She only told Hekla."

"I'm sure Donut got rid of the other coupon," I said. "Look, I'm glad you told me. But the last thing we need is to worry about each other. I'll talk to her to make sure. I won't tell her you found the one with my name on it."

"Okay," she said, her voice small. "Thank you, Carl."

I pulled the coupon back into my own inventory. My mind raced. I'd have to ask Donut about it. I didn't have a choice. But first I needed to confirm some of this info with one of the two other people I knew with a player-killer tag.

CARL: Imani, I have a question for you.

She had been forced to kill several of the Meadow Lark residents when they'd first arrived at the dungeon, to save them from agonizing deaths. I knew it haunted her.

IMANI: Hello, Carl. We're collecting carts so the team can ride the conveyor. It's hard to get them off the track without breaking them. What can I do for you?

CARL: When you received your skulls, did you get a PVP coupon? I'm sorry. I wouldn't ask if it wasn't important.

There was a long pause. I thought maybe she wasn't going to answer.

IMANI: I did. I received something called a savage box, and all it contained was the coupon book.

CARL: How many coupons were in it?

IMANI: It had a coupon in it for every member of the party. I tried to burn them, but they didn't catch on fire. I left them behind on the first floor. Brandon wanted me to keep them in case I had to, you know, do it again. But I could feel them sitting in my inventory, and I didn't want them there. So I got rid of them. You should know Elle did *not* get them when she got her skull. I used to think people only got them on the first floor, but after Donut told me about the two she received, I now think only the first member of a party to get the player-killer skull gets the coupon book.

CARL: You talked to Donut about her coupons?

IMANI: We talked about them when she received the box. She wasn't too happy about them, and she was having a really hard time coping with getting that skull. I told her to get rid of them. She's like a child, Carl. She doesn't process things the way a person does. Talk to her about it. I gotta go. We'll message you later.

I had no idea Donut and Imani had ever said two words to each other. I wasn't sure how I felt about that. It made sense. Donut had done the same thing I just did, which was immediately turn to the person with the most experience in the matter. The coupons were

designed to instill a wedge in a group, whether they were used or
not, and Donut recognized that. It was a smart, mature decision.
Still, it suddenly felt as if something had changed in the dynamic
between us.

CARL: Okay. Thanks. Be safe.

"Hey," I said to Katia. "So why didn't Hekla want that guy in the
party with you and your friend? Was it because he was a man?"

"No," Katia said. "He was a creep. I don't think Hekla would care
if a guy joined the group."

"So it's just a coincidence the Daughters are all women? What if
Donut and I wanted to join up, do you think she'd let us? Do you
really think she'd let *me* join?"

Katia paused. I saw the telltale flash in her eyes. *She's talking to her
right now.*

"*Do* you want to join up with the Daughters?"

"Maybe," I lied.

"I think she'd want to talk to you first. Hekla thinks you're a bit
reckless. But she really likes Donut."

"Okay," I said. "We better get back before . . ." I paused as I saw
the red dot on the map. It was on one of the colored line landings.
The puce line. "Hang on. Stay here. Get ready to run."

I jogged over to the stairwell that led down to the landing. *Shit.*
More red dots appeared. I peered down the stairs. As I suspected, it
was the festering ghouls from the train yard. It was just a few for
now, but there would be more soon. I saw additional dots on the adjacent platform. They'd traveled from the train yard all the way up
to station 24. Station 12, I knew, was already filled with Jikininki
janitor ghouls.

As I watched, however, it was clear they weren't sticking around.
Some of them clambered up onto the landing, but only for a few
moments before jumping back onto the passageway. They continued
on their way up the track.

I also noted that none of them appeared to be getting shocked by the third rail. From this angle I couldn't really see what was going on. Either they knew about the rail and were avoiding it, they were immune to electricity, or the power was off. There was no way to know which of those three scenarios it was.

I tossed a pair of hob-lobbers down the stairs just to kill a few; then I turned and fled for the trapdoor. We quickly descended the stairs and went on our way.

STATIONS 36 AND 48 WERE IDENTICAL TO STATION 24. IT WAS TOO soon for the ghouls to have walked this far. We'd check on them again after we ditched Madison. Zev sent us a message that we needed to find a safe room soon because we were supposed to go on that show in a few hours. I told her we were too busy, and she said she'd have us teleported away no matter what we were doing. I told her to go fuck herself, and she laughed as if I was joking.

I didn't yet say anything to Donut about the coupons. I wanted to wait until we were up in the production trailer. I just knew that since Katia had voiced her suspicions out loud, they were going to make this a thing. I wanted to cut it off at the knees while nobody else was watching.

There was more to the story, too. Katia was having a hard time. It wasn't just the coupons. She was struggling with something. I suspected maybe it was because I didn't quite treat her like a member of the team. Yes, I'd spent money and resources on getting her bulked up. But I'd done that for myself and Donut just as much as I'd done it for her, and she knew that. We all knew she was eventually going to go back to Hekla. It was clear that was what she wanted.

The thing was, I liked Katia. I liked her a whole lot. She was painfully quiet. Even when she was bulked up, it was easy to forget she was there. But she was just so damn earnest. She was afraid and hesitant, but she never once ran. If she said she was going to do something, she did it. And she usually did it well. That was a rare quality. With just a bit more training and mastery of her race, she would be the ultimate tank. Still, with Odette's warning about Hekla, I couldn't stop from thinking maybe it would be better if we just cut her loose sooner rather than later. I didn't want to do that, but maybe it was the safer bet in the long run. If we did go that route, I'd need to really up my own defenses first. Or we'd have to find another tank. Maybe we could hire Bomo and the Sledge from the Desperado Club. Mordecai had hinted that it might be possible to hire NPCs.

I hated this. *Why does everything need to be so complicated? Can't people just be loyal?* I'd said that not too long ago as Bea and I were fighting about her decision to get rid of Donut. We'd been in the car, on our way to a Christmas party, and she'd casually mentioned one of her mom's Persians—Sugar Bun, who was Donut's aunt or cousin or something—was pregnant and was due soon. Once they were weaned, Bea would be taking two of the kittens and Donut would be returned to her parents, who would try to sell her as a show-quality breeder.

You don't even like her, Carl. Why do you care?

She's your cat. She's a living thing, and you took responsibility for her. I don't understand how you can just give her up. I don't care if you get another cat, but why do you have to give Donut away?

Do you know how much money she's going to sell for, Carl? She's a former international grand champion. She's past her prime. I don't understand what you're not getting about this.

Goddamn bullshit. All of this.

In addition to the stops with the stairwells, we paused to examine stations 50, 58, and 59. With 50, I wanted to see if it was one of the Krakaren drug dens. It was not. The trapdoor lifted, revealing a tiny room the size of a small house. A single ramp sectioned down, leading to nine different platforms. The small station had no mobs. It looked as if it had never been visited by anything or anybody.

Next, we stopped at the ladder outside of station 58, which should've been a regular stop with a random nest of regular mobs, and it was equally empty and small. The next station after that was number 59, a prime number, and therefore supposedly a real transfer station. This one was as it should be. The place was set up just like any other transfer station we'd visited at the higher stops. There was a restaurant, a general store, and a small church leading to Club Vanquisher. The trapdoor popped up behind an alcove in the wall next to the general store. The only difference was it appeared there were a whopping 27 different platforms attached to this one station. It was usually only three.

After discussing it some with Madison, we learned stop number 60 was supposed to be a sprawling station filled with dozens of dormitories and apartments, along with restaurants and stores for the employees and their families to shop and eat. All colored trains would stop there, along with the *Homeward Bound*, the employee-only train that was supposed to be on this track. There would be a portal at the station platform that would work like the back room entrance to the Desperado Club. It didn't matter what train one used to get to station 60 nor what substation they started at. Once they stepped through the portal, they'd end up in the same place.

However, when we arrived at the employee-only platform for station 60, it was clear something was wrong. The platform—the only platform on this entire line—was old and decrepit, covered in cobwebs. We stopped to investigate. The stairwell led up into a tiny room just like with station 50. A single additional stairwell led down to a confusing mess of stairs and platforms where one could catch multiple trains.

"Nice," I said after we saw there was no settlement here.

"It's a mistake," Madison said, spinning in circles, as if that'd make the buildings magically appear. "I don't understand. This is where our employees live. This is where their families live. What did you do?"

"Now you know why they made you give everyone mandatory overtime," I said.

My suspicions had been correct. They had never turned this into a real place. There were no families. No wives or children. No food boxes with a touch of fish. It was all made up. All false memories. That *Homeward Bound* train probably never even rode once. It would've been nice to have a large settlement here with safe rooms and NPCs. Instead they were playing up the evil-corporation angle, which I thought was pretty meta considering the source of all this bullshit.

"Come on," I said. "Let's see if there really is a turnabout for the train. If not, we'll have to drive backwards. We'll go to station 41 and hit the safe room there." That was the closest place with a Desperado Club. I wanted to go in there and add more people to my chat list. We'd have to risk leaving the train on the tracks. It appeared the ghouls were avoiding this tunnel because it didn't lead to regular platforms other than this one. Hopefully it remained that way.

"No. I'm staying here," Madison said. She sat down firmly on the rocky ground and crossed her arms. She looked up at us defiantly. "Someone will come investigate what's going on. I don't know what you did, but transit security will sort it out. People are scattered, and they will come here. Even if here isn't a real place, this is where they'll go."

"Is there really a transit security department?" I asked. "We've been up and down the line, and I haven't seen any sign of them."

She huffed. The woman did have a point. The workers who escaped the ghouls probably would be coming here. But I didn't give a shit if she lived or not. If she couldn't help us anymore, there was no point in keeping the murderous NPC with us. Part of me knew it wasn't really her fault. That her personality and memories were programmed into her. I still didn't care. She wasn't from Earth. She wasn't a crawler, nor a former crawler as far as I could tell.

"If not security, then Rod will come," she added out of nowhere. "Rod always comes."

"Who the hell is Rod?"

"He's her ex-husband, Carl. Haven't you been paying attention? He's also the CFO of the Iron Tangle and works at Station A," Donut said. "Madison, are you sure?"

"Rod will come."

"Bye, Madison," I said, turning away. "Go fuck yourself, okay?"

"Right back at you, boxer boy."

"I remember who she reminds me of!" Donut exclaimed as we returned to the *Nightmare*. "Miss Beatrice's mom! She's just like her. She was really mean. I never liked visiting. None of the cats there were very happy. I could tell she didn't treat them as well as Miss Beatrice treated me."

"Come on," I said. The comparison didn't seem so funny anymore. "Let's get the hell out of here."

19

IT TOOK ME LONGER THAN I'D LIKE TO ADMIT TO FIGURE OUT HOW TO turn the train around. There was a section of track designed for the purpose. The track was shaped like a T on its side, and I had to steam past it, get out and hit the switch, back into the base of the T, hit the switch again two times, and it turned the *Nightmare* around.

I managed to talk Zev into delaying our obligation to go on the show about pet and beauty pageants for six hours. She'd huffed and puffed, but since it wasn't a live show, it turned out to not be a big deal. It would give us time to sleep, eat, get our training room time in, and shower. Plus I wanted to stick my head into the Desperado Club. Then we'd go on the stupid show, which would eat two or three hours. This close to the end, that seemed like a ridiculous waste of time.

We went down to station 41 and parked the train. I told Brandy our plans, and she seemed content to just sit there and idle. Donut leaped to my shoulder as I ascended the ladder. This station was exactly as I expected. One restaurant, one store, and the Desperado Club. There were multiple exits.

A line of red-tagged ghouls appeared on the map from all of the colored station landings, but they weren't stopping. They remained on the tracks, shuffling higher.

Once we were up there, Donut finally released Mongo, and we headed for the safe room, which was a Greek café called Everest. We skipped past the Bopca and went straight to our personal space.

We'd missed the last recap episode, and the announcement hadn't been anything special. The leaderboard hadn't moved.

As we entered the room, I received updates from both Meadow Lark and Bautista.

Imani and crew had safely ridden the conveyor system all the way down to Train Yard D, which also had a breached gate. Still, they'd arrived in a yard full of ghouls. They'd had a harrowing running and fighting battle. They'd taken shelter in the Iron Tangle administrative building outside of the yard. Elle had floated above the ghouls and frozen them by the hundreds, eventually killing all the ones surrounding the building. I got to listen to her bitch for five minutes straight about how little experience she'd received for it. Once they killed all the ones in the immediate area, all the newcomers ignored the building and walked straight back into the tunnels. The former Meadow Lark residents were currently holed up in the building, planning their next move.

I suggested they take the employee train tunnel on foot up to the nearest transfer station.

Meanwhile, Bautista said the Kravyad wasn't a boss monster at all, but instead was a multiarmed snake woman NPC, just like Madison had reported. The NPC had attempted to hypnotize the crawlers, but Bautista had somehow neutralized her ability to cast the spell. He said, "I used my last Voca Nye. The purple variant." I had no idea what that meant.

But a new wrinkle had developed. Defenseless, the Kravyad was now threatening to kill herself if the crawlers got any closer. The crawlers remained on the platform while one of them, apparently a former police negotiator, was talking to her through the doorway. If she did kill herself, and that portal closed, it was going to get ugly. Less than half of them still had their hats, which would allow them passage through the only other portals in the area, the portals above the abyss. That was their last practical chance to get to the stairwells after the employee portal. With less than five days left and the vast

majority of the subway trains now stopped, those in the group without their souvenir hats were in very real danger of finding themselves
stranded.

I trained my Powerful Strike, which did not advance, and then I
collapsed into bed, sleeping the full two hours.

Afterward, Donut and I headed to the Desperado Club to talk to
any remaining crawlers while Katia spent some time at her makeup
table. We only had about an hour of free time before we'd get teleported away, and I didn't want to waste it.

"Sledgie!" Donut cried when we entered the club. She jumped to
the rock monster's shoulder.

The cretin grumbled in greeting. A blue magic protection spell
appeared around us, followed by a new one, this time a translucent
shield spell, a real *Shield* spell, that would also protect us from physical attacks. Between the two spells, we were now practically invulnerable while we were in the club.

"I bought *Shield* spell," Bomo said proudly. "The Sledge cast
Magic Protect. I cast *Smack Protect*."

"That's really awesome," I said. "We appreciate it."

We moved to the dance floor, which was sparsely populated with
actual crawlers. After explaining why I wanted to exchange everyone's chat info, I ended up collecting an additional 10 names to my
list.

"We should go into the Bitches and Penis Parade strip clubs to
see if anybody is in there," Donut said. "Plus I've always wanted to
see a naked man dance around. One with better moves than that one
weird guy who always came over when you were gone. He used to
dance in the mirror and stare at himself and call himself a king.
He'd put your socks on his wang and twirl them around in the
mirror."

I barely heard her. Instead, I was staring at the man sitting at the
bar. "Holy shit," I said. Donut hadn't yet noticed the purple-skinned
elf creature. I tapped her on the back and pointed. She turned and
hissed, all of her hair poofing out.

"Did that guy come in alone?" I asked Bomo.

"He alone," Bomo rumbled. "He always alone. He here a lot. Usually in Bitches room."

"What are we going to do?" Donut asked. "Should we get him?"

"No," I said. "You go ahead and look in Bitches and Penis Parade. But be careful."

The man at the counter appeared to be drunk. He was missing his right hand. He should have chosen a race like Katia's, something that would've allowed him to regrow a limb. He clutched a drink with his left.

I leaned in and said to the Sledge, "Watch Donut carefully. There might be a woman in here who wants to hurt her. She'll fill you in on the details." I turned to Bomo. "Stay with me. This guy is much more dangerous than he looks. Even with only one hand."

I approached and sat down next to the man, keeping him more than an arm's length away.

"Hello, Frank," I said. "It's been a while. You look like shit."

FRANK WAS DRUNK. VERY DRUNK. HE LOOKED AS IF HE WAS sprouting from the bar. I examined his properties.

Crawler #324,119. "Frank Q."
    Level: 17.
    Race: Night Elf.
    Class: Blood Assassin.

Only level 17? He was seriously lagging behind.

I didn't know what a Blood Assassin was, but a Night Elf was much like a dark elf or a drow from so many games and stories. His rough face was still recognizable in elf form. His skin glowed dark purple in the lights of the club, reminding me of an eggplant. He'd lost his spiked shoulder pads and battle-ax. He now wore a flowing black jacket. He still sported the Seahawks beanie on his head, though now he had long black hair. It looked out of place above his dark elf countenance. Fanged incisors peeked out from his lips.

The man's eyes were heavy with deep rings underneath them. It didn't appear as if he'd slept in ages. He smelled, too, of an odd mix of perfume and stale alcohol.

"Carl?" he said, looking up. He didn't have a speech bubble over his head. He tried to draw it, using his stump, and the spell failed. The badger-headed bartender, with practiced ease, drew it for him. "Carl, is that really you? What the hell is a Primal? You still look human. Where's your cat?"

"She's here," I said. "Where's your wife?"

"Dunno," he said. "I haven't seen her since the end of the second floor. She's around, though. I can see her on my interface. Don't talk so much. I think she blocked me. Bitch. But I'm glad you're here. They say you come here sometimes. Now I can get my revenge."

I tensed. This was either an elaborate trap, or the man had completely self-destructed and was now just talking shit. Based on his low level, I assumed the latter, but I prepared myself.

"You haven't seen her since the second floor? So right after our appearance on the Maestro's show?"

He nodded. "And I know you haven't seen her, either, because you're both still alive. We got into a fight. About you and your cat. My plan after that was to sit at a bar just like this and wait for the end. But I got kicked out of the safe room an hour before the second floor collapsed, and I wandered into the stairwell. When I got to race selection, that tentacled asshole told me Maggie had already chosen her race and class and left."

"What did she pick?" I asked.

He shrugged. "Dunno. Is soul-sucking bitch a class?" He grunted at his own joke. "It probably is. I don't even remember picking this body. I was so drunk. I think he picked it for me."

This conversation was not going the way I had expected. "But you made it through the third floor, obviously."

"Yup. Met up with some folks. Maggie used to tell me I was the

William Shakespeare of lies. A damn virtuoso. That's why we got a divorce. But you know what?" He raised his stump, like he was pointing a finger. Bomo lifted his arm, lightning quick, but I waved him away. "Sometimes the truth is worse. I told them the truth, and they ditched me at the end of the floor. I didn't want to go down. But I'm a coward, and I did what cowards do. I followed the easiest path, and I descended. Stupid. I landed on a train with a bunch of new folks. But they didn't want anything to do with me, either. These skulls make it hard for people to trust you. Got off at station 101, saw the Desperado Club, and I haven't left the station since. Gonna be brave this time. And more drunk."

He pulled out what I first thought was a cigarette, but then I recognized it as one of the highly addictive blitz sticks. It smelled like patchouli. I still had one in my own inventory. When smoked, the drugs could permanently increase your intelligence, but there were unspecified side effects.

"And," he added after taking a long drag, "I'm going to do what Maggie hasn't. I'm going to avenge Yvette."

Yvette was his teenage daughter. The one who Maggie had inexplicably choked to death after they'd tripped my dynamite trap.

"How are you going to do that?" I asked. I tensed, ready to jump into action. I had no idea where he was going, and that made me nervous.

"I'm going to give you a present," he said. "That is how I will avenge my daughter."

He pulled an item from his inventory. Since he didn't have a right hand, the small metal item clattered onto the bar. Bomo leaped between us, pushing me back. Several cretin bodyguards I hadn't even noticed were suddenly surrounding us, arms raised.

Frank cackled with drunken amusement. "You guys sure are jumpy tonight. Are you really this much of a pussy, Carl? I'm not going to hurt you. Not physically. My fightin' days are over. My revenge will be via a different means."

He sat back, leaving the object on the bar. It was a magical ring.

Green glass with a red jewel. It glowed with enchantment. I kept my eyes on Frank.

"You see, Maggie, she's more hotheaded than I am. She wants to fucking kill you and your cat. It's not your fault. I know that. You defended yourself. You did the same thing I would've done if the situations were reversed. But Mags, she don't see it that way. She's more biblical with her thirst for vengeance."

"What is that?" I asked, indicating the ring.

He pushed it forward with his stump. "It's yours now. Got it in a legendary box right after we got in the dungeon. It ruined us. Now I'm giving it to you. That's my revenge. You're going to take it, because you'd be stupid not to. A jeweler in one of those big towns on the last floor offered me 300,000 gold for it." He laughed. "It's like winning the lottery. Of course you take the money if you win. But it ends up ruining you. That's what this did to us, and that's what this will do to you. That's my revenge. It's all I have left to offer. And it's all I want. Knowing what happened isn't enough. You need to understand. You need to feel it. You look down on me. I can see it. But you don't understand. Fuck you, Carl. Take the ring."

The dude wasn't making sense. I looked closely at the ring, examining its properties.

Enchanted Night Wyrm's Ring of Divine Suffering.

Oooh, that's scary sounding.

For the discerning Crawler Killer, this magical ring can be one of the most formidable items in the dungeon. If utilized properly, this ring's wielder can grow exponentially in strength, especially on the deeper floors. But beware. If poorly wielded, this ring will kill you quicker than an exploding rage elemental. Either way, this ring imparts one of the dungeon's most highly sought-after skills.

The wearer of this ring receives the following benefits:

+5% to all stats.

The Marked for Death Skill.

I reached over and picked up the ring. I had to hold it in my hand before I could read the description of the Marked for Death skill.

Marked for Death.

It's not just Steven Seagal's magnum opus. It's also one of the dungeon's greatest, most infamous skills!

Once activated, you will be presented with a list of all crawlers within your map's range. Only crawlers with 100% health will be selectable. Once a crawler is chosen, they will be marked. It takes 30 seconds for the mark to fully set and become active. When a crawler with an active mark dies, no matter the cause, you will receive a permanent +1 stat point to whatever that crawler's current highest stat is.

The +1 stat benefit increases by one for every three marks you kill.

Warning: Once a mark is set, you may no longer heal. If you are injured, or poisoned, or if you get a hangnail, you will suffer the ill effects and pain of that injury until the moment your prey is killed. So choose your marks carefully. Don't let them get away.

You may only mark those designated as crawlers, except on the Scolopendra Lair levels (3, 6, 9, 12, 15, and 18), where you may also mark any non-dungeon-generated combatants. You may only mark one crawler at a time except on the ninth floor. This skill has a five-hour cooldown on floors 1, 2, 3, 4, 5, 7, and 8. It has no cooldown on the sixth floor. Also on the sixth floor, marks will form instantly. There is a 15-minute cooldown on the ninth floor, but there is no limit to the number of simultaneous marks. All remaining floors have no cooldowns or delay to mark formation.

Confused yet? Here's a cheat sheet:

Current Marks killed: 0

Current Mark benefit: +1 Stat Point.

Current floor cooldown: 5 hours.

Marks take 30 seconds to form on this floor.
Happy hunting.

That was an insidious skill. The risk/reward didn't seem worth it, even if I was a murderous asshole. I didn't see why it was that big of a deal unless I became a full-on murder hobo, which wasn't going to happen. Plus it was super dangerous to use. If you marked someone, and they got away, you couldn't heal. You'd be fucked. Still, that 5% to stats was no joke.

"You got this in a box?"

"Yes," he said. "And now it is yours. Got it for fighting a family member while I entered the dungeon. A Legendary 'That's the Spirit' Box or some shit like that."

"Fighting a family member?"

"My ex-brother-in-law. Not even a real family member, but the dungeon didn't see it that way. I choked him out, and then we got attacked by rat-kins, these rat monsters that walk on two legs, and they killed him while he was still unconscious. Jesus. Do you remember that day, when it first started? One minute we were outside the annex, fighting, and then the buildings were just gone. What a mind fuck."

"Of course I remember . . ." And then it hit me. I trailed off. *Holy shit.* I remembered the video from the Maestro's show. Yvette had been injured by the dynamite. She'd been screaming in pain. I looked at the ring in my hand, horror dawning on me.

I waved the bartender over and ordered a drink. "Whiskey," I said, voice hoarse. He poured, and I drank.

"You let your daughter use the ring before you attacked us?"

"Not 'let,'" he said. "Made. I *made* my daughter use it. She refused to fight. She wasn't going up levels. This was the compromise. She wore the ring. Mags told her which mark to choose. We'd picked you. I figured the cat might get away. Never imagined you would. It was the only way we could make her stronger. She marked you, we waited thirty seconds for the mark to settle, and we attacked. Would've had you, too, if you hadn't been saved by the safe room."

That was why Maggie had killed her own daughter. She was in pain from the explosion. She wasn't going to heal. The pain wasn't going to stop. Not as long as I was alive.

"She was beautiful, you know. On the inside, I mean. She didn't have that anger in her. Not like her mother. Or her dad. When she ran away, it wasn't because she was a bad kid. It was self-defense. Kids aren't always a product of their parents. But sometimes that doesn't matter. Sometimes parents can cast a shadow so thick, you can drown in it."

That poor girl. Jesus, she must've been so scared. I felt no sympathy for the man next to me. He deserved all the pain he was feeling right at that moment. But I understood him a little better now.

It was as if he read my mind. He suddenly erupted in anger. "You don't understand what it means to be responsible for somebody. You don't have a kid in here with you. You don't understand what that responsibility means, what a weight that is on your shoulders. And when you fail, it's like being crushed, constantly crushed, only you don't die. And the pain never stops. It just keeps coming and coming."

A silence hung between us for a long time.

"Were you really a cop?" I finally asked.

"Yup," he said. "Customs Enforcement. Maggie was a detective at Seattle PD." The bartender refilled my glass without asking and pushed it toward me. "Cheers," Frank said. "To the end of the world."

"But you were divorced?" I didn't know why I was asking this stuff. It didn't matter, not really. This man didn't deserve for his story to be told, not after what he did. In a way, people like him were worse than the Syndicate and the aliens who'd destroyed us. He was one of us, and he'd turned against his own.

But we all have that in us, the curiosity. The need to know the truth. And I really wanted to know why someone like him could exist. I understood, philosophically at least, that he was killing people in part to strengthen his child. But that was a choice, not the only path. I felt nothing but revulsion for him.

"Mags and I separated five years ago."

"But you were together the night it happened. You went into the dungeon together. With your daughter."

"Yvette ran away. Again. Got picked up by the Pierce County sheriff. My brother-in-law was a deputy. He was Maggie's little brother. Always protective of her. Blamed me for all of Yvette's issues. He called us to come get her. It pulled me off a surveillance. Two in the goddamn morning on the coldest night of the year, and the four of us were in the parking lot, all screaming at each other when it happened. Yvette ran into the tunnel. Maggie tried to run in after her, and I pushed her, which made her brother mad. He didn't understand what was happening. He tried to put cuffs on me. We went in fighting."

"Come on, Carl," Donut said. "It's time for us to leave."

I turned to see her standing there on the Sledge's shoulder, glaring at Frank. Both she and the Sledge now had pink feather boas around their necks. The Sledge now also wore a cowboy hat. Hanging from the boa on the Sledge's neck was a giant pin-back button that read, "I like my sausages extra large. Penis Parade. Desperado Club Floor One."

"Did Maggie ever take that potion?" I asked, standing from my chair. The Maestro had given them a Legendary Skill potion that would max out the Find Crawler skill.

"That's what we were fighting about. I wanted to sell the potion and the ring. Use the money to buy gear and to train properly, but all she wanted was revenge. She has the potion, but I don't know if she's taken it or not. Our guide suggested that she wait until she picked a class to take it. Something that would let the skill rise up to 20, not 15. But I don't know if she did that or not."

I suddenly thought of those PVP coupons. I wondered if Maggie had one. I wondered if she'd received extra rewards for killing her own daughter. I shuddered.

"Okay," I said. "I'm sorry your daughter had to die. She didn't deserve that. Goodbye, Frank."

I met eyes with the man one last time. He was no longer a threat. His wife—*ex*-wife—was dangerous, possibly even more dangerous than I realized, but Frank was done. I had no doubts he wouldn't be getting off this floor. Maybe not even up from this bar.

The man drunkenly watched me take the ring and slip it onto my left index finger.

"Vengeance is mine," he said.

20

THE PRODUCTION TRAILER WAS A SUBMARINE, NOT A BOAT. WE
ended up being late for our appointment, but this time it was because Zev had delayed it. She said my conversation with Frank and
my "stunningly controversial decision" to wear the ring along with
"Donut's amazing lap dance" at the male bordello were the top two
feeds in the world during that hour. I didn't want to know what had
happened in the strip club.

I couldn't stop thinking about Yvette, and of her mother choking
her until she died. The ring hung heavy on my finger. I was never
going to use it, but Frank was right. I'd be an idiot not to take it. A
5% bonus to my stats was too good to pass up. I just wouldn't ever
use the Marked for Death skill. I'd taken it off just to make double
sure it wasn't cursed, though Mordecai had once told us that we
couldn't get cursed items in loot boxes. I put it back on, though I
wasn't fully certain it was a good idea to keep it on my hand. I kept
going back and forth on whether I should keep it on there. I'd pulled
it off a half a dozen times until I decided I was being a wuss. I knew
some people would probably think I was an idiot for putting it on,
and maybe they were right. But I needed every advantage I could
get, and if people didn't like it, they could suck it.

I'd ask Mordecai's advice once he returned, but for now, it stayed
on my finger.

"You weren't worried about what Frank might've done to me?" I
asked Donut just before we were teleported away.

"No," she said. "One look at him, and I could tell he wasn't going to hurt you. And Sledgie said his wife left him, so I wasn't worried about her, either. He's still there at the bar. Hasn't moved since we left. There's another crawler talking to him right now, but it's not a woman."

"Wait, how do you know that?"

"I have Sledgie in my chat. I showed him how to do it."

"Huh," I said. It never even occurred to me to even attempt something like that.

"Anyway," Donut said, "sometimes you can just look at someone and see that they've given up. I've been seeing a lot of it lately, even in people who are pretending to hide it. It's quite scary. But it's worse in some, and with him it was the worst I've ever seen."

"Those are the ones we need to worry about the most, Donut."

"Why do you say that?"

"When someone has given up, they no longer care about the consequences of their actions. That can be dangerous."

Zev pinged us, and we zapped away. The moment we reappeared, I could tell we weren't on a regular boat. I took a few steps in the lavish velvet-covered room, and the floors felt odd. Then my eyes caught the massive picture window at the end of the room revealing nothing but a sea of dark blue punctuated by a blinking light that revealed we were under the surface.

I realized with a start that my interface didn't disappear like it usually did. My health bar still appeared, and I had access to my inventory. I walked to the counter and pulled the entire bowl filled with Snickers bars into my inventory to test it. It let me.

Donut rushed to the round window, which extended from the floor to the ceiling. She put her two paws up on the glass, gazing out. A floating menu appeared in Syndicate Standard. **Lights On?**

"Yes, yes!" she said. An exterior floodlight snapped on, revealing a vast, sandy ocean floor. Squat, round plants dotted the ground as far as we could see. It reminded me of the desert. Furtive movements disturbed the silt-covered floor, and a wide, flat fish darted away, causing dirt to swirl. Donut's mouth hung open in amazement as she swished her tail.

I looked about the room. It reminded me of the lavish production trailer we'd borrowed from Manasa the day she was murdered. There was a bathroom, a kitchen with a row of shelves that kept items cool, as if it was a refrigerator without walls. Multiple expensive-looking chairs filled the room, along with a makeup table with a light-up mirror. This was a real makeup table, not the thing Katia had in the crafting room. This was obviously one of those trailers meant for off-planet celebrities and not crawlers.

A now-familiar robot-like Frisbee descended from the ceiling. The soothing female voice was similar, but not quite identical to the robot voice of the last one of these things we'd seen, which had been in the standard production trailer that had been rented for the Maestro's show.

"My name is Mexx-6000. You are in a deluxe rental trailer owned and operated by Senegal Production Systems, Unlimited. Since this is a security trailer, your location is not being disclosed. The producers of *Planet Beautiful* are not privy to your exact location, and the only entities on board are you and myself. We will be ready for you to enter through the door in approximately five minutes. Please make yourself comfortable. I see you've already discovered the refreshments."

"Mexx?" I asked as I moved to the couch. I pulled one of the full-sized candy bars out of inventory and unwrapped it. Donut remained at the window, looking out.

"Yes, Carl?" she asked.

"Do you know why my interface hasn't gone away? Usually I can't access my inventory or other systems. But here it works."

The blue light on the floating robot blinked. "A normal crawl consists of multiple tightly focused system zones networked under a single system AI. Under traditional circumstances, each floor has its own individual core and boundary zone. In such cases, once removed from the zone, you would lose access to all system upgrades and non-internal enhancements. Think of it like Wi-Fi. However, in this iteration of *Dungeon Crawler World*, the Borant Corporation has opted to use a dual-layer planetary zone system instead. The main zone extends from the planet's core to sea level. The secondary zone extends an additional five kilometers above the surface. So while you are in a surface trailer, you will not have access to your primary interface, and you will only have limited access to certain personal upgrades and systems. This trailer is still in the main zone, as it is below the planet's sea level. Traditionally, in such circumstances, it is customary to create an administrator bubble around the trailer, limiting your access to certain features. This season, Borant has elected not to implement this feature. Therefore you have full access to your regular systems. You should note, however, being in the main zone, you are still subject to the system AI's purview and its rules and regulations."

"I don't understand a word of what the fuck you just said."

The robot sighed. "I apologize, Carl. Let me translate it to Earth monkey speak. The mudskippers are cheap bastards who have built this entire crawl with spit and duct tape and items they have purchased at the equivalent of an interstellar swap meet. Everything is built with very little regard for system security and is done as cheaply as possible. The fact it hasn't yet broken down or bitten them in the ass is a testament to the very real existence of the concept of 'dumb luck.' Do you understand now?"

I gave the robot a thumbs-up. "Got it."

"Carl, do you think there's ever been a cat under the ocean before?" Donut asked. She was making an odd chirping noise as she watched the occasional fish dart by.

"Lots of them," I said. "I don't know if any have had this sort of view, but navies have a long history of keeping cats on board. Remind me sometime, and I'll tell you the story of Unsinkable Sam. He was a famous cat from World War II who survived multiple ship sinkings."

"I didn't know about this," Donut said. "So he was a hero cat?"

"Every boat he served on ended up at the bottom of the ocean. I don't know if that makes him a hero."

"But he survived?"

"Yep," I said. "Ended up dying of old age."

"Sounds like a hero to me," Donut said.

———

"I AM NOT READING THIS BULLSHIT," I SAID. "WHERE DID YOU EVEN get this? It's like you used Reddit and YouTube for research, and that's it."

The teleprompter froze. I could see Donut through the glass of the booth next to me. This room was different than the holo studios we were used to. This was an actual studio with physical sound booths. My chair was made for a creature much too small, and I asked if they had a different one. The chair in the booth disappeared, and a new one appeared in its place. It was like the room itself had an inventory system.

Donut was currently narrating her portion on pet shows with gusto. I couldn't hear her, but she was waving her paws in the air and narrating with obvious enthusiasm.

My section was on human beauty pageants. The paragraph I was supposed to read hung in midair. The first part of the program had been okay. I'd read about the history of beauty pageants throughout the ages. I had no idea if any of it was true, but the information was both believable and harmless. I talked about an ancient Greek ritual called *Kallisteia*, which I had no idea how to pronounce. Their description of the event seemed a little too children's book-y to be accurate. Especially since the script included video inserts from several bizarre and random sources, like *Fraggle Rock* and *WKRP in Cincinnati*. It was like the Unsinkable Sam cat tale I'd just told Donut. It was probably exaggerated and filled with half-truths, but it was an interesting story passed down through the ages.

Once we got into the specific details of the modern beauty pageant, the tone of the script changed. I couldn't stomach reading any more.

"Why do you even need me to do this?" I asked. "If they can

make a realistic video of me banging an orc, then surely you can have a robot Carl recite fake, made-up facts."

I looked over the script hanging before me.

The swimsuit portion of this human mating ritual is designed to entice the Chad-class males. The evening gown is to demonstrate their ability to mix with society, and the question-and-answer portion is to prove mental fitness. The goal of each pageant contestant is to attract the highest-quality male and have him inject them with his superior sperm in order to create the most viable offspring. After they receive the gift from a genetically superior male, they oftentimes find a lower-quality male, a "beta," to help raise the child.

Judges for these pageants are usually a mix of ultra-alpha males and former contestants who are well past their prime.

These women are oftentimes referred to as "roasties." A roastie is common human parlance due to their genitals being irrevocably damaged by multiple sexual partners. These roasties are honored and desired only by the male beta members of society, as evidenced by my recent trip to an Arby's-themed safe room.

Multiple images and videos accompanied the script, including a photo of the actors Lorenzo Lamas and Fabio as examples of an ultra-alpha male. The "roasties" were an Asian woman I didn't recognize and Judge Judy. They also had a video of me eating a roast beef sandwich.

"Seriously. What the fuck?" I said.

The screen lowered, and Bin the producer appeared. He was one of those stereotypical gray aliens. He looked tired and irritated.

"Carl, we can't artificially create your voice. It's against the law to do so without a disclaimer. People will watch this because they know it's really crawlers telling them about their world. Don't you want the universe to know about your culture?"

"I do, actually, which is why I'm not reading this bullshit. Where do you even get this stuff?"

"We hired a consultant."

"Christ. Was it some 15-year-old kid?"

"No. We can't use surface human consultants. We can't approach the natives until the crawl is over. We used an AI consultant who has consumed all of your media."

"Well, then, you got ripped off."

"We got a discount because Borant started the season early, before the AI could complete its scan. It insists its knowledge is adequate and accurate."

"You guys can't be this stupid," I said. "Do you really believe this is the truth?"

The gray shrugged. "Do you know how much we paid for this? The cost for you and Donut was more than the entire budget of the last two seasons combined. People have an unexpected thirst for your world's culture, and this little show has suddenly found itself as a ratings powerhouse. The least you can do is help us out. Hekla had no problem reading her script on Nordic mythology. Prepotente and Miriam Dom were happy to discuss Earth hip-hop culture. Your partner may be off script, but she is also embracing the subject. Why can't you?"

I looked over, and Donut was still gesticulating, talking animatedly.

"How off script is she?"

"She is telling the universe about a breed of dog called a cocker spaniel, about the real reason why they are the winningest champion of the Crufts dog show. It is fascinating. We have never heard such a tale of evil and intrigue."

"Goddamnit, Donut," I said. She saw me through the booth window and waved.

CARL: Don't make shit up.

DONUT: I AM TELLING THE TRUTH THAT NEEDS TO BE TOLD, CARL.

I sighed. "You're either going to have to get another script or ask Borant for a refund because I'm not reading this. I don't care what happens."

The alien looked as if he wanted to jump through the screen and strangle me. We stared at each other for several moments before he seemed to deflate. He looked back and forth nervously and leaned in.

"Look, Carl. I know the scripts are crap. When I started this program years ago, it was just me. I wanted to tell the real story of the cultures that were getting erased. But suddenly this show is bigger than I ever expected, and Titan, who was happy to leave me alone and let me make this show with little to no interference, is up my ass. They are making me use crawlers to narrate, we have to use shit intelligence to make the scripts, and the show *I* created is about to get yanked out from underneath me unless I make it even more 'interesting.' It's a kick in the chest cavity, is what it is. I was happier when I wasn't noticed, and now that I am, I am being punished for being successful. So the last fucking thing I need is somebody giving me shit about something neither of us has control over."

"Oh, I'm sorry," I said, anger rising. "Your rented slave labor isn't participating like how you wanted? Well, let me look for some sympathy." I patted myself on the chest. "Nope, all out."

The alien looked as if he was about to cry. "Okay, okay. We have a few other scripts. Which one do you think will resonate with your audience better? We have the history of mechanized military conflict. One on video arcades. Oh, and this one is about the history of milk pasteurization."

I almost told him to give me the milk one just because it would be so boring, maybe this idiotic show would get canceled. But then I took a deep breath and thought about it for a minute. If I took him at his word, he genuinely seemed interested in presenting the truth about our planet to the universe. That wasn't so bad, was it?

"Just give me the damn video game one."

AFTER WE WERE DONE, WE RETURNED TO THE GREENROOM.

"Carl, Carl!" Donut said as we entered the room. "Sledgie just messaged me. He said Frank is dead! You know that crawler who was talking to him? They got into a fight, and the crawler killed him! I can't believe it!"

"Huh," I said. "I'm not surprised, though."

"It was Chris. *Chris* killed him. Sledgie said he did it and walked right out. Now he's banned from the club. Sledgie said he's a rock monster like him, but a different kind."

"Holy shit, really?" Chris? Imani's crew hadn't had any interactions with Frank and Maggie as far as I knew. I'd told them the story, of course. Especially after everything that had happened on the Maestro's show. Was that why? That didn't seem like the Chris I'd known. But Imani and Elle had said he'd changed. I remembered Brandon's last words about his brother. I had the message pasted into my scratch pad, and I found myself reading that last message, especially the part about Chris over and over.

. . . tell him I love him. That's the most important part. It's always been the most important part, but I didn't realize it until it was too late.

I sent a quick note to Imani and Elle telling them what happened and asking if they'd managed to get Chris to talk. They didn't answer right away. They were likely asleep. I knew they'd been heading for a safe room.

"If I may interrupt your drama," Mexx the robot said. We both looked up at the floating Frisbee. "Your time with me is drawing to a close. You may freshen up a bit before you return to your crawl, but do not take too long. When you're ready to go, you may exit through the doorway to the studio. On behalf of Senegal Production Systems, I'd like to thank you for using our services. Have a great day."

That door, which had been a normal door only moments before, transformed itself to a one-way subspace portal. I took a screenshot, and it showed the main room of our personal space. It was empty. Katia was likely in the crafting room.

Donut returned to the picture window and looked out. "I wonder why Chris did that. But I'm glad he's okay, even if he liked stupid TV shows. Anyway, that was fun. I like the interviews better, but I think it's good for the Princess Posse to get some culture in with their daily Donut fix. Plus they had a video of me and Miss Beatrice winning a show, so that'll be a bonus for the fans."

"Princess Posse?" I asked.

"Zev says that one seems to be winning out, no thanks to you. Some are going with the Donut Holes, which I do *not* approve of."

"Whatever," I said. "Look, I want to talk to you about something real quick before we leave."

"Is it about the PVP coupons?"

I froze. "How did you know?"

"Imani is a big gossip," Donut said. "She doesn't look like someone who'd be one, but she is. She felt bad about telling you about the coupons when you asked her, and she messaged me to apologize. She said you'd probably ask me about them. How did you find out?"

"I heard someone talking about them." That technically wasn't a lie.

"You don't need to worry, Carl. I got rid of them. I didn't like having them, so I buried yours under a train track, and I threw Katia's out in the garbage at that Hot Dog on a Stick place. And quite frankly, it's a subject I'd rather not talk about."

I relaxed. That went much easier than I thought it would.

I moved to the kitchen to see if the refrigerating cabinets could be removed from the walls. They pulled off easily, like they were magnetized. I wanted to see what the electrical connections, if any, looked like. There were none. The shelves appeared to be self-powered, like I hoped. There were four shelves, and I took them and pulled them into my inventory. I looked up at the ceiling to see if the robot would object, but it didn't move. *Well, if we're doing this . . .* I went and picked up the entire makeup table and pulled it into my inventory as well.

"What are you doing?" Donut asked.

"You know how the ice machines sometimes don't work in the safe rooms? I figured we could make our own. I'm sick of drinking warm soda."

Donut cocked her head to the side, but then shrugged. I wasn't normally a steal-stuff sort of guy, and she knew it. Plus that excuse was dumb, as the ice usually did work. But I couldn't exactly tell her the real reason why I wanted the shelves. I didn't have a specific use for them yet, but there were multiple trap, potion, and bomb recipes in my book that required items to be frozen or cold before they were utilized. And the makeup table would fit well in the main room of the space. I thought about taking the rest of the chairs, but I didn't want to piss Zev off *too* much.

Still, I thought, *why the hell not?* I went to pick up the couch, but I paused when a message came in.

> **BAUTISTA:** Hey, Carl. Want to give you an update. We tried to paralyze the Kravyad, and she ended up dying. The portal closed. Over 150 of us don't have our souvenir hats. We're not sure what we're going to do. The trains have stopped coming on all the tracks. We're going to head up to that abyss portal on foot. It's about 50 kilometers.
>
> **CARL:** Shit. Do *you* have a hat?
>
> **BAUTISTA:** Nope. A guy at the bar was bragging about how much they were buying them for. A bunch of us sold them. Dumb.
>
> **CARL:** Get to the abyss. Send those who have hats through on foot. See if maybe you can find a way to station 436, which is where the named lines go.

I went on to explain the catwalk that surrounded the interior of the abyss. I warned him of the lizard mobs I'd seen there. If they could maybe find one of those small trapdoors, they could get to the station and onto a named train like the *Nightmare*, take it over, and steam it into the yard. That was really their only hope.

"Let's get going," I said to Donut. I picked up the couch and stole it. I pulled the bowl filled with cat treats off the counter and added it to my inventory for good measure.

"Have you ever noticed how shit always happens while we're doing these shows?" I asked Donut. I told her about Bautista.

"At least we get snacks," she said.

"Yeah. Let's get out of here before something else happens."

I paused before the portal. Out of habit, I pulled one more screenshot. I froze.

Our personal space, which had been empty just minutes before, was now full of people. There were at least thirty of them. All women, as far as I could tell, of various races, from humans to fairies to a four-armed lizard. I saw Hekla there in the back, peering inside the training room while Katia pointed at something.

"Motherfucker," I said.

ENTERING THE ROYAL PALACE OF PRINCESS DONUT.

"Hi, Hekla! Hi, Hekla's friends!" Donut said. She jumped to my shoulder. "Look, Carl. It's Brynhild's Daughters!"

"Yeah, I can see, Donut."

Thirty pairs of eyes turned toward us. I quickly looked over the group. Hekla had risen to level 33, one higher than my 32. The rest of her crew averaged around 25, which was respectable, but a little lagging. That was the problem with staying in a big group. I'd discussed this with Mordecai a while back. He firmly believed small groups were the best for that very reason. Experience was shared, but due to the nature of the earlier floors, there was only a finite amount of experience to be had. So while the bigger groups offered a certain amount of protection, it came with diminishing returns regarding experience.

But looking over the diverse group of crawlers and classes, I could see the advantage of having such a large team. The pool of spells and skills amongst them had to be impressive.

At level 24, Katia was no longer the odd one out. She'd fit right in. I sighed.

Hekla and Katia pushed through the crawlers. Hekla held out her hand. She was even taller than I realized. She was about nine inches taller than me. Her muscles bulged. She kept her automatic crossbow slung over her shoulder, and the thing was huge. I hesitantly shook her hand. It practically swallowed my own. Her hand felt as if it was made of iron. I wondered what the woman's strength stat was.

"Carl," she said, "thank you. I asked you to take care of my girl, and you did. But you did more than take care of her. You helped her level and taught her how to protect herself. I am in your debt."

"How did you find us?" I asked. "And how are you even here?" I looked at Katia. "I didn't realize others could come into our space."

Katia smiled sheepishly. "Since I have a personal space attached to the whole, I have the ability to allow groups in. I white-listed all the Daughters."

Hekla nodded. "We came through the employee portal thanks to your information, Carl. Sadie cast her *Glass Prison* spell on the Kravyad, and we all made it through. We were at Substation H. We hiked up to station 60. The station was barren. Well, mostly barren. A few NPCs had gathered, looking for their families. There's a switch there that allows you to choose which of the 12 *Homeward Bound* platforms to get upon. Katia said you'd come in at Train Yard E, so it was easy to find you from there."

"Wait, really?" I said, this new information momentarily causing me to forget the potential danger of this situation. *We can use station 60 to get onto any track.* I held up my hand as I sent a mass message out informing everybody of this information. And then I sent a quick, additional note to Imani and Elle, telling them what was going on with Hekla and her team.

I caught sight of a Daughter with a familiar name. Eva. Katia's friend. She stood slightly back, just behind Hekla's right side. The green opalescent woman was a four-armed cobra-headed creature, similar to Manasa the singer, though the coloring was different, and she did not have a Naga body. Also, unlike Manasa, this woman was small, only about five feet tall. She stood on two regular legs, though she was covered in scales. She had a pair of wide sabers over her back, placed in an X formation, and she wore green shiny leather armor that almost looked like a tracksuit. The woman glared at me, crossing both pairs of arms. I quickly examined her properties.

Crawler #9,077,240. "Eva Sigrid."
Level: 27.

Race: Half Nagini, Half Orc.
Class: Nimblefoot Enforcer.

The woman had one large skull and three smaller skulls over her head, indicating she had killed thirteen people. Katia had said she'd only killed one, which suggested those additional 12 skulls were a recent addition. Looking about, I didn't see any other skulls over the crew, including over Hekla. *This is the one who does her dirty work.*

"This is a very impressive space," Hekla said. "We combined two personal spaces, but we don't have any of these upgrades." She looked at Donut. "We can't even white-list visitors until we buy one more space. Your manager has proved to be very helpful. It's too bad you lost him. When is he coming back?"

"Two days and 18 hours," Donut said. "Carl, maybe we can combine safe rooms with Hekla's team! Do we have to all be in the same party for it to work?"

Goddamnit, Donut. "Uh, I think maybe we do," I said. "But I'm not certain."

CARL: Donut. Don't say stuff like that. Let's wait to see what
     Hekla wants before we all jump into bed together.
DONUT: OMG YOU SHOULD DATE HEKLA. THE AUDIENCE
     WOULD LOVE THAT. THINK OF THE VIEWS.

At that moment, I had to confront something that had been at the back of my mind since the moment Odette had cautioned me about Hekla. *Why hadn't you warned Donut about what Hekla really wants? Why hadn't you told Mordecai?*

I knew the answer—I always knew the answer—but I hadn't admitted it to myself.

You think she would be better off with Hekla's team. You think Mordecai would think so, too. That's why you never told them. It had been nagging me for a while, but I'd kept pushing it to the back of my mind. Stupid. Self-destructive. It was also par for the course. I thought of what the late Frank had said to me, about being responsible for someone else.

You don't understand what that responsibility means, what a weight that is on your shoulders. And when you fail, it's like being crushed, constantly crushed, only you don't die. And the pain never stops. It just keeps coming and coming.

But seeing that woman Eva with all the skulls over her head, any thoughts I had of Donut being better off fled. For all I knew, each and every one of those skulls was someone who had deserved it. Or maybe it had been a mercy kill like with Imani. But my instincts told me, *No. No, no, no.*

I could see both Hekla's and Eva's eyes flash, and I knew they were talking, plotting.

CARL: Don't let Mongo out. These guys are looking a little
     jumpy, and I don't want any accidents.
DONUT: WE ARE IN A SAFE ROOM. AND EVERYBODY LOVES
     MONGO. THESE ARE OUR FRIENDS, CARL.
CARL: Just keep him locked up for now. If there's a scuffle, we
     don't yet know if he'll freeze or teleport away, and this is
     not the place to find out.

Hekla smiled. "Now is not the time for such discussions, little Donut. But we wanted to come by and pick up our lost little lamb, and we wanted to see what a wonderful job you and your Carl have done for her. But we are also in a hurry."

Donut beamed. Katia appeared to be wavering, like she wanted to say something. If Katia left and disengaged her personal space, it would severely alter the nature of the room. Mordecai would lose access to his space. We'd lose the training room. We'd spent so much time working together, it seemed like such a waste.

"I'm afraid there is little time to chat," Hekla said. "We have an issue, and it involves some people I believe you know."

Here it comes, I thought. *The cheese on the trap.*

"Katia is but one of our lost lambs. We have a small cluster of friends who have collected with a larger group. They are gathered at station 101 on the vermilion line. It is a significant group of people. A thousand at least. The trains are stopped on all three lines that service the station. They are stuck. Mobs are swarming all around them, and they are fighting them off. They need our help. We are going to rescue them, and I am asking the Royal Court of Princess Donut to help us do that."

On my shoulder, Donut started to tremble with excitement. She worshipped Hekla, and I knew the thought of fighting alongside the shieldmaiden was a dream of hers.

"Tell them to hike to station 102," I said. "Go into the robot room and ride the conveyor back." But even as I said it, I knew that wouldn't be feasible. Not when there were a thousand people. It had taken Imani's crew a few hours to gather enough of the rolling cages to get her team down to the train yard. She'd said it was difficult to extract them from the conveyor tracks without breaking them.

"They're boxed in," Hekla said. "There's plenty of fighters in the group to keep the monsters back, but they keep coming. The vermilion line is clear for now, but they're being inundated with mobs from the other two platforms at the station. I have the boss map from the vermilion line, and the track is swarmed. A massive herd is making their way up the line and will be upon them soon. So the crawlers can't just hike down the line. It's at least 150 kilometers from 101 down to the closest stairwell at 72, and if they have to fight the whole time, they will never make it. There is a ghoul generator at stop 72, similar to the one at 12. Even Lucia could not hold the line against them. There's also something going on at 75. And that's all in addition to the regular mobs suffering from the DTs that are coming from the other two platforms. Any hour now we'll be seeing whatever stage three looks like."

What a goddamned clusterfuck. "You said it involves people we may know," I said. "Who?"

"From what I understand, it's a crew you met on a show. A man named Li Jun along with his group. Also, a few others you have in your current chat circle."

For fuck's sake, how much did Hekla know about me? Was Katia just feeding her everything I did and said? How could she know who my friends were otherwise? It made me wonder if Hekla had spies strategically placed everywhere. Jesus, was that possible? Or was I being overly paranoid? I was in over my head, and I knew it.

And even worse, I had enough wits about myself to recognize that asking me to help her was a masterful move by Hekla. How could we not help? I'd look like a cowardly idiot if I didn't.

Plus I *wanted* to. A thousand people? And Li Jun and possibly his sister, Li Na, and friend Zhang? I'd last seen them when they'd unwittingly been dragged onto the Maestro's show for the Death Watch segment. But they'd managed to save themselves. I didn't really owe them anything, but if they were truly trapped, how *couldn't* I help?

But what about Bautista all the way at the end of the line?

You can't save them all.

I couldn't save anybody if I ended up dead.

So what should I do? I had no idea how to help Bautista. I could try going back through the portal with the *Nightmare*, but then what? I didn't even know if there was more than one Abyss Station. No, it simply didn't make sense.

I had to look at this logically. If Hekla's plan was to kill or otherwise discredit me and get Donut to join up with them, so they in turn had access to Mordecai, they had to do it without Donut knowing that's what they did. Or Mordecai. And the only way to do it would be to make it look like an accident. But how could they possibly do that when literally the entire universe was watching them at all times? It'd be easy to hide something from Donut at first, but Hekla had to know by now that people like Odette existed. Information entered the dungeon like drops through a leaky roof.

Whatever it was, it wouldn't happen right away. Donut worshipped Hekla, and once Donut latched on to someone, it was hard to get her to unlatch. But she didn't know any of the other newcomers. I'd made a serious mistake by not talking about this earlier. I would have to start fixing it now.

I glanced over at the cobra-headed Eva and met her eyes. A very slight smile curved her mouth. A smile that did not reach her eyes.

CARL: Donut. Be careful, okay? I am getting a bad vibe from that Eva woman. Don't trust her.

DONUT: RIGHT? SHE'S SCARY. SHE KEEPS LOOKING AT YOU LIKE YOU'RE A CAN OF FANCY FEAST.

CARL: If anything happens to me, question everything.

DONUT: WHAT DO YOU MEAN?

CARL: Just watch that one, okay? And keep an eye on Hekla, too. I know you like her, and so do I, but I don't think she likes me too much. She might let me get hurt if it will help her team.

I quickly rummaged through my inventory and rearranged some items on my hotlist. I added that invisibility potion I'd gotten from the suitcase into one of my slots. Then I added Mordecai's Special Brew, which would give me almost-invulnerability for about thirty seconds. I had to be careful with that one since it made it so I couldn't take another potion for ten hours afterward.

"Okay," I said out loud. "We'll help. Just don't get me killed so you can have Donut all to yourself."

Eva's mouth tightened. Hekla laughed. And at that moment, I saw it. It was just a glimmer in the normally stoic woman's façade, but it was there. *She's having fun. She likes this. She's as crazy as the rest of us.*

"We were just looking at the map," Katia said, indicating the large paper on the counter. "Vermilion is a colored line, but it's different than the others. I think it's one of the ones that Widget the gremlin was talking about when he mentioned the Terminus Direct. It looks like it runs the whole line in about a day."

"Okay," I said. "So what are you proposing?"

Hekla crossed her arms, suddenly all business. "We're taking a vermilion subway train down to 101, picking everybody up, and we're taking them back by going reverse, using a second engine attached to the back. We tested it, and it works well. We'll come back to a stairwell station where we can make a stand. We'll hold out until the stairwells open."

"So you have a train? What about the wreckage on the track?"

"There is no wreckage on the vermilion line. And it's one of the few with the power still turned on. We discovered the train just sitting there, ready to go when we teleported to that building near the train yard. The engineer was out of the train, inspecting it, when we showed up. I shot him, took the route map, and we took the train. It doesn't look like this train ever ran. It has three passenger cars, but the rest are cargo containers. They are supposed to roll the ghouls onto the train and transport them to the abyss. But it never ran. And since it never ran, it never crashed. Eva stole a second engine and backed it into the train. We drove it down to stop 60 and left it on the tracks to come here."

I nodded appreciatively. "Is there a cowcatcher on it?"

Hekla grimaced. "That, Carl, is the problem. It's a subway car, and it is not designed to withstand such abuse. There are hordes of ghouls on the tracks further up the lines. There is a small device at the front, but it does not work well. When we hit the few ghouls that were on the track, it was okay, but I can tell it will be a problem when we push through the heavier hordes. The track is about to get very dense, and I fear pushing through so many is going to derail it. If we go slow, we will be overwhelmed. We have to move fast, but the faster we move increases the chances of a wreck. That's why we came here first."

I started mentally working on the problem. I had plenty of metal in my inventory. I'd have to go up there and measure the front of the train, as each one was a little different. "So you want me to build you a cowcatcher, or some other device to put on the front of the train?"

"Well, yes, but you've already built what we need." Hekla turned to Katia, who appeared as if she was going to vomit.

I felt the blood drain from my face.

DONUT WAS THE FIRST TO OBJECT.

"You want to stick Katia to the front of the train?" she said, sounding outraged. "Are you kidding? That sounds like a Carl plan."

"Yes," Hekla said.

> CARL: Katia. You don't have to do this. I can build a metal one.
> KATIA: It's okay, Carl. This is what I'm for. You said it yourself. I
>   need to learn to use my race properly. We don't have time
>   to build anything.
> DONUT: CARL IS RIGHT. YOU ARE GOING TO GET HURT.

It was actually a brilliant idea, and I was impressed at the sheer insanity of it. But I would never let her do it if it was up to me. It was simply too dangerous.

> CARL: You're not disposable, Katia. Hekla is treating you as if
>   you are. I'm sorry if I didn't make you feel welcome. You
>   can say no. You can stay with me and Donut.
> KATIA: This was my idea. I'm the one who came up with it. It's
>   why they're here now.
> CARL: *Your* idea?

I was so flabbergasted, I didn't know what to say.

> KATIA: I altered the backpack and made it wider using your
>   engineering table while you were gone. I have more metal in
>   there now. I can make myself even bigger. I've also added
>   rubber to the mix. If I layer it between the metal and flesh,
>   it absorbs the impacts. I just need help with the design
>   for the front of the train. I need to be careful of that third
>   rail.
> CARL: I don't like it, no matter what the design is.

KATIA: This is just like when Donut wanted to climb up the
chain and turn the roundabout. You're a . . . a back seat
dungeon driver. You only don't like the idea because you
didn't come up with it.

Ouch.

CARL: I don't like it because you're going to fucking die, Katia. I
don't understand. You used to be scared of fighting just
regular mobs.
KATIA: You're right. You don't understand, Carl. They came
back for me. She brought the entire team to pick me up.
That is more than anyone has ever done for me.

An awkward silence hung in the room. It was clear to everyone
that we were having a private conversation. Katia rubbed tears from
her eyes.

ZEV: Goddamnit, Carl. You need to be having these moments
out loud.

"Go fuck yourself, Zev," I said up to the ceiling. "How's that for
talking out loud?"
Hekla barked with laughter. "Zev sounds like our Loita."

ZEV: I'm serious, Carl. You're one of the most popular feeds,
and half of your conversations are inaccessible to the
viewers. What do you think is going to happen?

I ignored the question. The tension in the room had eased with
my outburst. "Okay, okay. If we do this, Donut and I will ride in the
engineer's car. And I would like Katia to stay in our team until we're
done. All this transferring around will take too long." I turned to
look at Katia. "As long as that's cool with you."

To my surprise, she walked up to me and hugged me, long and tight. "Thank you," she whispered in my ear. I had no idea for what.

"That's fine," Hekla said after a moment, though she seemed irritated. "You can ride with me and Eva. She knows how to drive the subway cars."

WHEN WE LEFT THE PERSONAL SPACE, I PAUSED, CONFUSED. BE-fore, the door led straight into the attached restaurant, but now there was a vestibule similar to the one at the Desperado Club. A second door was attached to a wall next to ours. It was a subspace portal that I couldn't enter or screenshot. After a moment, I realized it was the entrance to Hekla's team's headquarters. That was how the system dealt with multiple non-attached personal spaces being accessible when crawlers had the ability to enter into more than one. *I know what this is. This is a temporary, situationally generated space.* I remembered there was a note about them in my book.

I half-expected Eva to turn and attempt to saber me in the face the moment we left the safe room. She didn't. We went through the trapdoor down onto the dark employee line. It appeared the ghouls were leaving this track free. That was good. The *Nightmare* remained where we left it, happily idling. I briefly wondered what Fire Brandy did to pass the time. But then I remembered her babies, and the fact she was constantly giving birth. She probably had no time to get bored.

"If you want to ride, your team will need to hang on to the outside of the train. There's not enough room in the cab. There's room on the back platform, though."

"We will ride," Hekla said. Donut, Katia, and I climbed into the cab while Hekla, Eva, and a few more Daughters stood on the back platform by the door. The rest moved to the front and clutched awkwardly onto the railings, standing on either side of the *Nightmare*'s boiler. A few of the smaller, fairylike Daughters alighted onto the platform out front, just above the cowcatcher. I imagined we looked like a parade float with so many colorful women attached to the outside.

"It's too bad we can't move this train to the vermilion line," I said as I flushed the brake line. This train would be perfect for clearing the track of ghouls. I stuck my head out the window. "Ladies, watch out. The boiler gets really, really hot. Only hold on to the rails. And watch the walls. We'll go slow, but if the walls hit you, it's game over."

I eased the train forward.

"I just realized you're the only boy here," Donut said. "All these people, and there's only one penis. You could start a harem. Like the guy on that *Sister Wives* television show."

I laughed. "Nobody is starting a harem."

"No, I suppose not," Donut said. "You couldn't even keep one woman interested."

The train hissed, and we started to pick up speed. We'd be at station 60 in just a few minutes.

"Why does your friend have so many skulls?" Donut asked Katia as we lurched forward.

"I don't know," she said. "I knew she had gained a few on the third floor, but I hadn't realized it was that many. She says she doesn't want to talk about it."

I bet.

"How do you know her anyway?" I asked.

"Eva? She's an economics professor at the university. We eat lunch together sometimes. We were friends before, but not great friends. She actually knows Hekla, too. From before, I mean. Hekla has known her longer than I have. Reykjavík is a small town."

"Was Hekla a professor, too?"

"No," Katia said. "She was Eva's psychiatrist."

LIKE MADISON FROM HUMAN RESOURCES HAD PREDICTED, A SMALL colony of NPCs had gathered at station 60.

We didn't stay long at the station, which was too small already to house the group of NPCs gathered there, but as we passed through, I noted Madison sitting in the corner glaring at us sullenly. She was being berated and threatened by an angry mob of dwarves and gremlins. Rod, her ex-husband, was nowhere in sight. I wondered if he was even real.

As we left and entered the long, twisting hallway that led to a confusing series of portals that in turn led to additional platforms, we had to step past a dwarf huddled on the ground, his head hanging low.

According to the tag, the creature's name was Tizquick. A conductor for the mango line. A puddle of tears had formed underneath him. Hekla stepped over him as if he wasn't there. Donut and I paused. I kneeled. I knew there was nothing I could do for him, but I felt compelled to acknowledge him, if just for a moment.

"I'm sorry," I said. "I don't know what you're going through, but it has to be hard. It'll be over in four days when the level collapses." *Only to start all over again for you,* I didn't add.

The dwarf looked at me, and it struck me, as it always did, at the life there in his eyes.

"She was never real, was she?" the dwarf asked, tears streaming down his dirt-colored face. They left rivulets of clean skin through the grime. "My little girl was never real. I just don't understand."

I put my hand on his shoulder, and I leaned in. "No, I suppose you don't. And that really sucks." I thought of Frank Q killing people so his daughter could have a chance. I thought of my own mother, and what she did. *This is my birthday present to you. I am giving you a chance at life. I'm sorry it took me so long.*

Both of them had failed miserably. But this guy had it even worse. He'd been tricked into believing something that just wasn't real. He never even had the opportunity to screw it up.

Before this was done, people like him would kill people like me by the thousands. And people like me would cleave through his kind, wreaking even more damage. All the while the real culprits sat back and watched and laughed.

"One day, this pain you're feeling right now will matter," I said. The conductor looked up at me, eyes sparkling with confusion.

I straightened, and I left the man on the floor.

Hekla remained there at the edge of the portal. She'd watched the exchange.

"You are going to give yourself an ulcer," she said. "Focus on what you can accomplish, not that which is beyond your control."

I grinned. "How much do people normally have to pay for that advice?"

She just looked at me. "We need to hurry. The main horde of ghouls will be upon them soon, and they're starting to see mobs suffering from the third stage."

22

"FOR A WHILE, THE HORDE OF GHOULS SEEMED TO BE STOPPED AT station 75," Hekla said as we watched Katia form in front of the subway car. I nervously kept an eye on the third rail, just nine inches from the lower left of her plow shape. She'd consulted with me and one of the Daughters, an architect, on the design. I'd had her place her new rubber layer between herself and the front of the train, along with a coating all along the left and bottom side of the scoop. That way if she did touch the rail, she wouldn't—in theory—complete the circuit. But the last thing we wanted was to test it.

"But they just kept coming and coming," Hekla continued, "and they broke through whatever barrier there is, and now they're moving quickly up the track. There are hundreds of corpses on the tracks already. They mostly avoid the electrified line, but there are so many of them. Every once in a while, one of them hits it, and the ghoul kills all the ones around him. There are just piles of dead bodies up there."

The engine car of the vermilion line was like most of the subway cars. It had a flat, window-covered front section. The controls were simple, especially compared to the *Nightmare*. It was a lone throttle switch and an emergency brake, along with a few lights indicating electrical connection status and an indicator telling the driver that all the cars were still attached. I briefly inspected the second engine car, attached backward at the end of the train. It had a slave mode where it added power to the train, even though it was facing the wrong direction. It would be more efficient if it was right behind the first engine, but this worked, too.

As long as we didn't get into an accident.

The stock "cowcatcher" attached to the front of the subway car was just a metal shield welded underneath the front, designed to push debris away. It looked like a forward-facing trailer hitch. It'd work fine for a few bodies here and there, but it was clear we needed something much more robust.

After some discussion, we decided a traditional wedge cowcatcher design wouldn't be enough. Katia had to make something that combined the low, forward comb with a bulldozer-like scoop.

"A plow is an easy design," I said. "The problem is, the train fits so tightly in the tunnel that there's nowhere for the debris to go. It's not like the *Nightmare* line, where there's a thin channel between the train and the ceiling and the sidewalls. These trains are packed in tight. Otherwise we'd go with a wedge design. Even with just the scoop, the tunnel will get clogged like a drain."

"That is a concern," Hekla said.

"That's why we came up with the kebab plan. Katia," I said as I watched her form. I couldn't even see where her head was. "Extend the lower scoop a little further. Yeah. Damn, I wish I'd had time to make train wheels to stabilize it. You'll need to be careful not to clip the ground. If you do, don't let it pull you off the train. They're going to be heavy."

KATIA: I know, Carl. I'm anchored to the top.

We'd broken out the windows in the engine car so Katia could reach inside. This was where most of her biological flesh would remain, though I worried that this was the wrong design. Nobody in the group was an engineer, and that was a problem. She'd built herself almost like a toggle bolt, affixing herself to the flat front of the subway car, reaching in through the window and then making a small vertical hunk of herself that was bigger than the window hole and pulled flush against the wall. It'd work well, I hoped, but if she gathered too much weight onto her scoop, I feared she'd rip the front of the train off. I cushioned the top and bottom of the metal parts where she attached with a pair of yoga mats to make it more comfortable and to help with insulation—both for herself and those of us in the cab. None of that would matter if she gathered too much weight. If the bolt pulled free, she'd get dragged down, hit the track, be ripped off the front of the train, and then run over. She'd be splattered all over the tunnel along with everyone in the engine car.

After the scoop was formed came the spikes. Multiple thick, sharp metal spikes protruded out from the scoop, like a sea anemone, or one of the street urchin mobs from the third floor. We kept these mostly at about chest level and above. This was a gamble. We expected the spikes to break if they hit armor or ghoul mobs with tough skin. But the faster we went, the higher Katia's constitution, so it was crucial if we wanted to maintain speed. The moment a mob was impaled on the spike, or caught in the scoop, Katia would start the process of sticking the body into her inventory. That would only work if the monster was truly dead, however, so Donut and Hekla would stand at the windows and would—carefully—shoot anything caught in the spikes or scoop.

With the spikes, we hoped they'd die more quickly, especially if the train moved as fast as Eva said it could go.

Katia finally finished forming. I marveled at how much area her body took. But that also worried me, as I knew the larger she was, the thinner the metal, the weaker the joints. She was literally stretched thin. A pair of eyes and a mouth sat in a little divot, looking out near the top of the scoop. I'd wanted her to face inside the cab, but she still didn't trust her ability to grow new eyes.

"Last chance to back out," I called as we climbed onto the train. She didn't answer.

The engine car was much roomier than the *Nightmare* engine. This was an entire train car with an apartment attached to it. It was meant to house a mantaur engineer. Eva stood on the right side at the controls. Hekla stood next to her, crossbow ready to fire through the missing windshield. Donut and I stood on the port side. Katia's body snaked in through both of the two windows, and she'd formed a thick metal plate there, bolting herself to the front of the cab. If it wasn't flesh colored, she'd look like a feature of the train. I put my hand against it before I realized what I was doing, and I could feel her heartbeat, fast as a jackrabbit. Until that moment I hadn't realized she even had a heart. I quickly pulled my hand away.

KATIA: That tickled.

One more of the Daughters rode up front with us. A level 25 **Wisteria Fairy** named Silfa. She was a "holistic healer." I hoped her healing abilities were more effective here in the dungeon than the holistic, snake-oil stuff from the real world. The plump woman appeared to be about fifty years old and was half the size of Donut. She quietly hung back.

"Speeding up," Eva said, pushing the throttle.

This was the first time I'd heard the cobra-headed woman speak. I was a little taken aback at how normal she sounded. A little tongue flicked out.

"I wish you'd let me take Mongo out," Donut said. "He'd love this."

"It's too dangerous for him right now," I said. "I'm pretty sure we'll need him soon. Besides, he'd eat that fairy lady right out of the air."

"That's not true, Carl. It only takes him a minute to get used to people. And then he'll love them for life."

That was the problem. I wanted to keep Mongo away from them as much as possible in case something happened. If we had to fight, I didn't want Mongo stopping to roll over for a belly rub from Hekla.

I eyed Silfa the healer nervously. Since I'd never fought with her before, I didn't trust her. I had eight scrolls of healing ready to go, and Donut had another six.

My stomach dropped as the train picked up speed, barreling down the tunnel. The sickly headlamp wasn't nearly as bright as the light on the *Nightmare*.

"Donut."

"On it," she said, reading my mind. She cast *Torch*, setting it to travel ahead of us. It lit the tunnel brightly, revealing the uneven rocky walls.

A group of red dots appeared on the map. It was just three of them. I barely had time to bark a warning before we mowed them over.

There wasn't even a thump or an audible *splat*. Only a small spray of blood over Hekla's and Eva's faces. I tried not to laugh. There wasn't even a body. It was like we'd hit a bug with the windshield. We'd completely liquefied the mobs, and the train was still accelerating.

> KATIA: Hey, I got experience for that.
> CARL: Did it hurt?
> KATIA: It was like a little beesting. No big deal. There was a head on my spike, but I pulled it into my inventory. Also blood. It lets me add liquid to my inventory if it's in my scoop. There's a new tab called "Gross shit."

My mind started to race with the implications and possibilities of that.

"Coming up on 72," Eva called.

This was the station where the ghouls were all coming from.

"Faster," Hekla said. "Speed it up." She had to shout the words now. The wind whistled through the two open windows of the subway car.

> KATIA: Whoa. I just got a fan box! It's for having the most new followers in a 30-hour period. I can't believe it.
> DONUT: CONGRATULATIONS.

That wasn't necessarily a good thing, but I wasn't about to say that now. I swallowed, seeing the wall of the red dots rushing toward us like missiles descending on a target.

There was a constant stream of ghouls coming off the platform. Most were traveling up the line, but a handful was turned toward us. Most of the mobs were now sticking to the right side of the tunnel. They were running, too, running fast. Terrifyingly fast. There was a pile of X's along the track where the ghouls had barbecued themselves on the third rail. I was worried that the pile of electrified bodies would still be intact enough to give Katia a shock as we plowed through. Hopefully her self-insulation would be enough.

"Here we go," I said, bracing myself.

***

"JESUS FUCK," I CRIED, RAISING AN ARM TO BLOCK THE SHOWER OF blood. Gore and bits of bone and hair blasted into the engine like it was being sprayed at us through a fire hose. A hundred mini, fleeting shocks rocked me, giving me a small amount of damage. The train shuddered, but it didn't slow as we plowed through the screaming mass of ghouls. We cut through the bodies like a goddamned wheat thresher.

"Katia," I cried, getting a mouthful of guts.

She'd been fine, but she was suddenly unconscious, and her health was at about 50% and dropping. I put my hand against her flesh and felt a tingle of electricity. She was getting shocked by something. Probably a body part wedged between her and the line.

"Faster," I yelled at Eva, who was choking on a splatter of guts. Where the hell was that healer? I cast my *Heal* scroll on Katia, and her health returned to the top, though she remained unconscious, and it continued to drop.

Something in the cab hissed, and I turned in time to see a monster head on the floor, growling. It was an almost-human head with green rotting skin pulled tight over the skull. I stomped it down with my foot.

There was another, a torso with a head attached. It growled as it reached for Silfa, who had buzzed to the top of the cab, screaming for Hekla to help her. These were different than the festering ghouls. These were the monsters being generated at stop number 72. I quickly examined the creature before I crushed its head with my foot.

> Blister Ghoul—Level 20
>
> The thing with the Blister Ghoul is that it is so damn tenacious. This undead creature is created and unleashed into the dungeon using a device called a Ghoul Generator. There are multiple types of ghouls and generators out there, but the bad boy that spits these suckers out is top of the line.
>
> For every non-undead mob that dies within this floor, one of the soul-crystal-powered Ghoul Generators will birth a single Blister Ghoul.
>
> It's rather unfortunate, then, that every mob on the entire floor is suffering from something that will eventually kill them.

Soul crystals. Goddamn soul crystals. That's what they'd used to power the swordsmen guards on the third floor, and it's what Miss Quill had been using to cast her spell. The soul crystal had become overwhelmed and turned itself into a massive bomb. That bomb—now dubbed Carl's Doomsday Scenario—still sat in my inventory. I hadn't even dared take it out at my sapper's table yet. These things were always bad news.

The chaos of this entire floor was starting to form into something a little more cohesive than I'd originally suspected. This wasn't just a maze. It was an almost-perpetual engine. In the next day, these things were going to be everywhere.

"That group was small compared to the main horde approaching stop 101 where everyone is trapped," Hekla said. "It has many times more ghouls."

The mobs had thinned out, but we were still hitting a handful every few seconds. Katia had a dozen heads and other body parts attached to the spikes. Some of the body pieces were still alive. The gore was starting to fill up her scoop. Donut was carefully shooting them through the window while Hekla did the same. Donut was soaked in dripping, steaming guts. Absolutely soaked. Her massive sunglasses protected her eyes, but she had to keep washing the blood away.

Katia's health continued to move downward. She hadn't once been healed by the so-called healer.

"Heals, goddamnit!" I yelled at the fairy, who remained at the ceiling, looking down at the blister ghoul's corpse. I kicked it. "It's dead. Come on!"

"I'm supposed to wait until she's at 25%."

"You will heal her now. And can you wake her up?"

The fairy looked at Hekla, who nodded. The fairy had over two dozen boss kills by her name, but she acted as if this was her first foray into action.

Katia glowed, and the unconscious debuff faded just as she hit another group of ghouls. More blood splattered into the train, soaking Silfa, who shrieked.

> KATIA: Ow. That hurt. It's okay now, but I was shocked really bad.
>
> CARL: Be careful of things getting wedged under there.
>
> KATIA: Not much I can do about them now.

I watched as the massive pile of body parts lowered, zipping away into her inventory. She did it again. And again. All that was left was a pile of chattering heads. Donut and Hekla went to work.

Eva sputtered as more gore splattered across her face. "Coming up on 75," she cried out.

Corpses dotted the tracks here, including a pile of bodies on the platform. As we rushed past, I caught sight of several dead hobgoblins and jackal-faced gnolls. Multiple tracks spread out from the main line here, too, with a long line of small cars sitting idle, ready to hop onto the main track. These were tiny platforms, each about the size of a Mini Cooper. A long group of portals and switches remained here, too.

But the station passed quickly, and I'd only gotten a quick glance. Hobgoblins meant this was where the crash interdiction teams were stationed. They'd been overrun by the ghouls. I knew that gnolls were often used as security. I wondered if they were the transit security forces Madison had been babbling about.

After that, the stations were much further apart. Ghouls remained on the tracks, always jogging forward. We also started seeing other mobs, but only in ones and twos. They shouldn't be on this track at all since this line only stopped at transit stations. But nevertheless, they were here, all mobs suffering from the DTs. They came and died so quickly, I never got a chance to examine them.

But some of these single mobs were bigger and armored, and Katia started losing spikes. We passed through a pair of rhino-sized, metal-clad troll creatures, and her spikes were left all broken and bent. The train bucked, and I thought for certain we'd derail. But we remained on the tracks. Katia fixed her spikes the best she could, but she needed the metal to maintain the scoop's integrity. Thankfully the monsters died instantly upon impact.

A moment later we hit a small group of ghouls mixed in with some fist-sized fairies who exploded. When we hit the flying creatures, they detonated in a mix of sparkles that covered the front of the scoop with rainbow-colored luminescence.

Hekla leaned back from the window, rubbing the blood and gore from her face. She suddenly grinned big and said, "There are many wonders in a cow's head."

"Indeed," Eva said.

I had no idea what the hell that meant.

———

FOR THE NEXT HOUR AND A HALF WE ZOOMED UP THE TUNNEL, MOVing toward station 101. Hekla tried talking to Donut, but I kept myself between them. I tried to strike up a conversation with Eva, but she just grunted at me. I could tell everybody in the room was talking to one another via chat. Just a few minutes before we got there, I received a message from Elle.

> ELLE: Hey, good news.
> DONUT: HI, ELLE. HI, IMANI!
> CARL: Oh yeah, what's that?
> ELLE: We now know what happens when too many of the festering ghouls get together.
> CARL: You're being sarcastic, aren't you?
> IMANI: She is. It looks like this type of ghoul's goal is to get to stop 48. We used that stop 60 to move to your line. It took us a minute to find the right portal, but we found your train sitting there. We ranged downward to the stairwell at 48 and found it full of the festering ghouls. We watched them transform. These worm things come out of them, and then they pull themselves tightly together, making a giant Frankenmonster. It's too big to leave the room, but it fills it completely. It's a province boss, Carl. We all got achievements just for discovering it. Thankfully it let us get the hell out of there.
> ELLE: It's really gross, too. It makes a slurping noise when it moves, and it's covered with mouths that are always screaming.

Holy shit.

> CARL: That sounds like the shambling berserkers from the last floor. But bigger.
> DONUT: THOSE GUYS WERE REALLY SCARY.
> IMANI: I didn't see those, but the monster has *completely* filled stop 48. And the wrath ghouls are stopping at station 36. Who knows what they're going to do? All the ghouls

coming from the train yards are that kind now. They're
going to do the same thing. Or worse.

CARL: Okay, we have Jikininki ghouls at stop 12, nothing yet at
24, the wrath ghouls at 36, the province bosses at 48, and
these blister ghouls at 72. It sounds like we need to pick
one. Assuming whatever ends up happening at 24 is going
to be awful, the Jikininki and the blisters are probably the
easiest to kill, but they both have generators, which means
they continuously spawn.

ELLE: Can't you just pull a Carl and blow the shit out of the
room? That was one of Mistress Tiatha's suggestions.

CARL: I keep forgetting you guys have a manager, too. I think
that's what they want me to do. The generators are run by
soul crystals, and they don't take too kindly to being blown
up. Station 12 still might be our best bet, but we'll have to
do it the old-fashioned way.

ELLE: Miss T isn't all that helpful. She spends most of her day
drinking and smoking blitz sticks. Then she cries about her
space pony or whatever it was when she was in the
dungeon. She was really excited to be our manager, but
she's treating it like it's a spring break. She'll throw a
suggestion out every once in a while, but mostly she steals
gold from me to buy more booze.

IMANI: We're going to post up at 36 and kill the wrath ghouls
as they come in. If we kill enough, maybe we can stop them
from doing whatever they're going to do. There are no soul
crystals in that room. We could really use some of your
boom jugs.

CARL: That's a great idea. Once we rescue these folks, we'll
have a lot more people to hold the line. I'll meet you there
as soon as I can.

ELLE: Okay. Stay frosty.

DONUT: IS THAT YOUR NEW CATCHPHRASE? I LOVE IT.

ELLE: Yeah, I'm throwing a few out there to see what sticks.

"Coming up on the main horde," Eva said. "Look at all of them."

"Speed up," both Hekla and I said at the same time.

I turned to the healer. "Heal her about five seconds after we hit the crowd. I don't care what her health is. Just do it. How many times can you cast before you run out of mana?"

"Five times. But I got mana potions."

"What's your potion cooldown?"

"Twenty seconds."

We rocketed down the tunnel. The line of dots appeared at the edge of my map, closing fast.

"Okay, good," I said. "I want you to heal Katia, count to five, and heal her again. Keep doing it until we say stop. Keep an eye on her for any other conditions. Do you understand?"

Silfa looked at Hekla, who nodded.

"Okay," she said.

"We're just in time," Eva said. "The horde is going to hit 101 in a few minutes."

"How does the track look behind us?" I asked Hekla. I knew since she had the route map, she could see down the entire line.

She frowned. "Not bad yet. Hopefully it'll stay clear for our ride home."

"Here they come!" Eva called.

Smack. Smack, smack, smack. We plowed through the first few ghouls. The train shuddered. And then we were in it. The train bucked and lurched. The tight tunnel was actually keeping us on the track, I realized, as ghoul pieces showered into the cab. I went to work killing everything that continued to move. I smashed at a gnashing head with my fist, and it exploded. More came, one of them chomping painfully onto my leg. I pushed it down. My knee-pads activated, the spikes killing it.

The train whined ominously as we plowed through. We notice-ably slowed. A few notifications appeared. Donut was screaming and slicing with her claws as more and more living ghoul bits showered into the cab. In moments, we were waist-deep in body parts, more than should be possible, and a lot of it was still alive. Something bit me. Then something else. I had to step back from the window. The pile of gore reminded me of the piles of chum dumped by boats by the docks. It angled down from the window, reaching halfway through the car and growing by the moment. The actual liquid was up to my knees. *Holy shit, this was a bad idea.* Donut was suddenly on my shoulder. She had a severed hand clutched tight on her tail.

KATIA: Help!

I looked up to see Katia's health at about 10% even as my own health started to plummet. Where was the fucking fairy? My Damage Reflect was doing a good job at hurting the monsters when they attacked, but there were so many. I slammed my *Heal* scroll, topping off Katia, and then I had to heal myself with a spell.

I activated Talon Strike and cast *Bang Bro* and waded back toward the window. I started smashing the heads all around us. It was like trying to fight while buried in oatmeal. The gore continued to shower into the train. Hekla had a physical *Shield* spell around herself. Eva had one of her four hands on the throttle while she sliced down with her sabers. She was up to her chest.

Body parts just kept coming and coming. The parts were getting bigger and bigger as we slowed, including full, living ghouls who weren't quite dead. I ducked as a fully intact ghoul flew into the car. The green-skinned monstrosity got up and charged at me. Donut blasted it with a missile.

The exterior of the train was completely covered with crawling and moaning and scrabbling monsters. The whole front cab groaned ominously. Katia was spiking them mercilessly, clearing the gore by pulling the bodies into her inventory. But there was just so many, and she wasn't moving fast enough.

"Station coming up!" Eva cried. "I'm going to slow down!"

"Not until Katia is healed again," I yelled. "Where the fuck is Silfa? Is she down?"

"She ran," Donut said, breathless. She'd raised a pair of clockwork ghouls to fight for us, but Hekla killed them both in the confusion. "She ran away into the apartment!"

KATIA: Carl. Where am I? Why isn't Eva answering me?

I whirled back to Katia. *Fucking hell.* How was her health so low? We'd almost pushed through the horde, and only a few ghouls remained on the exterior. I dodged and swung, punching over and over, killing monsters while keeping an eye on Katia's constantly dwindling health. Was she getting shocked again? There was so much gore and so many bodies out there, surely she was getting blasted. But it was going down even faster than before, and I didn't feel anything. It was like she'd been hit with a debuff, but it didn't show on her status. I read another *Heal* scroll, then another. I'd soon be out.

DONUT: CARL! CARL! HEKLA SHOT KATIA WITH AN INVISIBLE ARROW! I SAW IT WITH MY SUNGLASSES! SHE DID IT EARLIER, AND I THOUGHT IT WAS A MISTAKE BUT SHE DID IT AGAIN. IT WAS MIXED IN WITH HER REGULAR ARROWS. IT WENT INTO HER SCOOP. THE ARROWS ARE STILL STUCK IN HER! I THINK SHE DID IT ON PURPOSE!
CARL: Katia! Disengage! Lose your mass! Now! Now!

The train continued to slow, the brakes screaming. We were free of the crowd. Eva was also screaming. She'd been injured, blood spewing from one of her four hands. Hekla continued to kill the ghouls in the cab. She'd fallen back from the window, standing, thankfully, out of reach. She'd slung her crossbow and had a short curved blade in each hand and was twirling about, slicing and killing. Her shield was gone, and she now had **Enraged** flashing over her head. The tall woman screamed as she fought. While this subway car was a little wider than usual, it wasn't *that* big, and I had to duck several times to avoid her frenzied slashes. I stayed back the best I could.

The scoop at the front of the train vanished. Blood and guts showered onto the track. A lump of flesh plopped onto the floor of the cab, disappearing into the gore. A moment passed, and Katia reappeared, her health still plummeting. She popped up, gasping. She started to collapse again, and I grasped her with my arm, pulling her up. **Unconscious** reappeared over her.

"The arrows are still there! They're sticking out of her shoulder!" Donut cried. "Pull them out!"

There was no visible wound on Katia's shoulder. She appeared to be wearing her regular red leather outfit. I un-summoned my gauntlet and reached over, scrabbling until my hand grabbed on to something invisible.

"That's it! Pull it! Pull it!"

I yanked, and Katia screamed in her sleep. Only then did the hole in her leather appear. Donut healed her. I pulled the invisible bolt into my inventory and grasped until I found the second one. I could feel that the shaft was splintered. I yanked. I quickly examined it.

Dirty Little Phased Bolt.

This item is broken. It must be repaired before you may use it.

This is a Phased item. It is invisible. It will hide its entry point and will only be discovered if it is physically touched.

The perfect ammunition for the discerning crossbow assassin. This item will cast both *Temporary Amnesia* and *Suffering Bleed* onto its victim, draining them of health until they are at 10%. A second bolt will lower the victim's health to 1%. Victims who subsequently perish will be listed as dying from an alternate source. You will not get credit or experience for the kill. Nor will you get one of those nasty skulls by your name if you happen to kill a fellow Crawler. *Wink, wink, nudge, nudge.*

What the actual fuck? Why was she trying to kill Katia?

Out on the platform, a mass of crawlers surged toward the now-stopped train. On the periphery of my map, I saw what had to be 500 red dots pushing the mass of blue dots back.

Hekla finally looked up from the gore. The **Enraged** buff blinked a few times and disappeared. She had a wild look to her eyes. She focused on the still-unconscious Katia hanging on my arm. She frowned. It was as if she hadn't even noticed that we'd saved her until that moment. Eva had healed herself, but she had lost a hand. She stared at it stupidly, as if she was surprised it hadn't grown back.

I stomped down on one last ghoul head.

Everyone just looked at each other, not sure what to do next.

**CARL: Donut, be cool. This doesn't have to turn into a fight.
She was trying something, and whatever it was, it didn't
work. We don't want to fight her.**

"You tried to kill Katia, you fucking bitch!" Donut cried. She blasted a full-strength magic missile right into Hekla's face.

23

HEKLA FLEW BACK, EYES REGISTERING SHOCK AS SHE SLAMMED into the sidewall of the car. At the same moment, Eva flew at me—or Donut, who was perched on my shoulder—swords swirling in the air. The back of the cab opened, and two more Daughters rushed in, hands glowing. Silfa rushed from the apartment, eyes wide as she took in the scene.

I dropped Katia and dodged back as I re-formed my gauntlet. My feet scrambled through the slippery muck, and my back slammed against the train wall. I caught a vicious slice of the saber with my armored hand. *I need more fucking armor.* I kicked up into Eva's stomach, and she rocketed back. I cast *Wisp Armor* on myself just as a magic missile and an electrical bolt slammed into me, one each from the two newcomers.

"Hold!" Hekla cried, pulling herself to her feet. She'd been fully healed by Silfa. "Everybody, hold! Cease!"

I'd dropped Katia, but her health had stabilized. Her head remained above the line of body parts and gore, like she was treading water. She remained unconscious. She'd awaken on her own in thirty seconds. Eva stood and hissed and lunged at me and Donut. Hekla held her back. Then she grabbed Eva's wrist and pulled it up, eyes going wide at the injury.

"Did I do that?" Hekla asked.

"Yes, you did," Eva growled. "I have three more hands. That little bitch shot you. Let me kill her."

"You tried to kill Katia," Donut yelled. "I saw it! You used invisible arrows! I thought she was your friend! We don't shoot our friends!"

"Bolts," Hekla said. "They're called bolts when they're from a crossbow, Donut."

Donut spit and growled. Her claws dug into my shoulder. I was painfully aware of how small this train really was.

"What're we doing?" I called. "I don't know what the hell is going on, but everyone needs to calm the fuck down. This is bullshit. We're all on the same goddamn side."

Hekla turned to the two mages. "Out. You, too, Silfa."

They started to protest. "Out!" she yelled. The three crawlers reluctantly fled. They remained right outside the door. It was me, Donut, Katia, Hekla, and Eva.

Outside, the crawlers continued to swarm onto the train. They didn't all fit into the passenger cars, so they were moving to the cargo containers. A group of crawlers was at the top of the stairs to the platform, making a stand, protecting everybody else's escape. We didn't have much time. An ungodly roar filled the platform. A group of five blue dots at the top of the stairs turned to X's.

"I made a mistake," Hekla said once the others were gone. She shrugged, as if it was nothing. "I can't take it back, but there's no reason for it to snowball. We need a pause and a reset. We can discuss this after we get out of here. We need to work together."

"Never!" Donut cried. She was shaking with rage. "I'll never team up with you! Traitor!"

"Donut," Hekla said, calm as can be, "we need to be practical. There's no time for this. You need to breathe."

But Donut would not stop shaking. "I used to think you were awesome, Hekla. But you're just like all the rest! You pretend to be good, but you're not! It was a lie, all a lie. Why? Why can't we trust anyone? You told Katia you wanted her. You made her feel special and loved, but you just wanted to use her and trade her in."

Katia finally awakened. She sat up, eyes wide. She took in the room. "Carl? Eva? What's happening?"

"Hekla tried to murder you—that's what's happening!" Donut yelled. "We don't even know why. You didn't do anything wrong."

"Control your fucking animal, or I will shut her up," Eva growled.

I put my hand on the side of Donut's head in an attempt to calm her. It was starting to dawn on me why Donut was having such a visceral reaction to this. The monumental revelation hit me like a goddamned truck, but we didn't have time to deal with it now. "We need to stay calm, okay?"

"She didn't do anything wrong, Carl. She did her best. It's not fair."

"I know, Donut."

"Guys, please," Katia said. She stood on wobbly legs. "What is going on? I can't remember . . ." She trailed off. "Everything hurts."

Hekla sighed and leaned up against the wall of the train. Her knives disappeared into her inventory. She pulled a pack of cigarettes, popped one into her mouth, and lit it. "Well, this backfired. God, I need a shower. Anybody want a cigarette?"

At that exact second, that exact moment, I wanted nothing more in the universe than to take her up on that. But Donut remained on my shoulder, and I didn't dare move closer.

"Look, we're all adults here," Hekla said. "We need to get to the other engine. The track is clear. So you three can hang back, if you want. Or just take this engine and go the other way. I don't care. It's over. What is the American phrase? No harm, no foul? But you're right, Carl. We don't need this. It was a stupid risk."

"I don't know what 'this' is," I said. "I thought for sure you were going to try to kill me. But Katia? Why?"

Katia, eyes still huge, was looking back and forth between us. "Eva?" she asked.

"It's nothing. Go outside, Katia. The others are waiting for you."

"Don't do it," Donut said. "They tried to hurt you, Katia. You can stay with us. We'll get out of here. Okay? We won't ever abandon you. And we won't be filthy liars, either."

"Can we just take this down a notch," Katia said. "For god's sake. I don't know what's happening. Why don't I remember?"

"Because Hekla shot you with a scary arrow that was going to kill you."

Hekla laughed, and it sounded unhinged. "Bolt, Donut. It was a bolt."

"No," Katia said. "You were both shooting. *You* hit me with a magic missile, Donut. You were aiming at the ghouls. I remember. It was an accident. That's okay."

"We don't have time for this," Hekla said. She flicked her cigarette away and pushed herself from the wall. "Come on, Eva. We need to hurry."

"No, wait," Katia said. "Please. We can't—"

"Damnit, Katia," Eva said. "Quit being stupid. Come with us. You're always fucking like this. Just do what I say."

"I'm just trying to figure this out. Hekla, you hurt me on purpose? Why? Did I do something?"

Eva growled. "You were always saying you felt useless, Katia. You were being useful. We weren't *really* going to kill you. We just wanted Carl's famous temper to flare. Now shut the hell up and come."

"I . . . *What?*" Katia asked. "You used me? For what?"

"Oh, Katia," Eva said, voice dripping with mock concern. She impersonated Katia's voice. "For what? For what?"

"Eva," Hekla said, "drop it. Remember your anger. Let's go. It's done."

Eva did not drop it. She continued to mock Katia. "What? Fannar left me for one of his students? What? They're not going to let me adopt. Why me? Boo-hoo. For fuck's sake, Katia. Open your goddamn eyes. Quit being so naive. Look where we are. Look at what we need to do to survive. This is why I left you behind on the third floor. This is why you're such a damn fuckup. This is why nobody likes you. Because you're so damn confused all the fucking time. Now for once in your pitiful life do the right thing and get away from those two."

Katia had a special ability she didn't like to use very often.

Rush, it was called. It turned her body into a battering ram. When activated, she blasted forward, shattering everything in her path. She could only use it once a day, and when she did use it, it knocked all the wind out of her, even if she didn't actually hit anything. As a result, I knew she abhorred the skill, despite Mordecai's insistence that she use it as often as possible.

Also, the skill wasn't predictable. Sometimes when she used Rush, her body flew forward five feet. Sometimes it flew forward twenty, and there didn't seem to be any sort of rhyme or reason to the discrepancy.

In addition, the angle in which she rushed forward wasn't always perfectly straight. Mostly her body dashed straight forward in the direction she was facing, but sometimes, every once in a while, she flew slightly off-center.

And that's what happened this time. Katia screamed something incomprehensible, and she activated Rush. She was aiming at her former friend Eva. She missed her by inches.

Instead, she inadvertently became the first crawler on this season of *Dungeon Crawler World* to kill one of the top 10 and claim a bounty.

In this case it was Hekla the Amazonian Shieldmaiden, the current number two in the game, whom she splattered against the interior wall of the train, thus earning herself a bounty of 500,000 gold.

And in that moment, just before all hell broke loose all over again, I finally noticed Katia's level. She'd been level 24 when she'd formed herself into a cowcatcher at the front of the train. When she fell back from the wall, skull forming over her head—a special golden skull—I saw that she was now level 37.

24

HEKLA'S BODY PEELED OFF THE WALL AND COLLAPSED INTO A HEAP.

System Message. A champion has fallen. A bounty has been claimed.

The door to the train flew open, and the two mages and healer burst in. More of the Daughters crowded in behind them, screaming and crying.

"Katia, what did you do? What did you do?" Eva cried.

CARL: Mic Drop. Platform. Get ready. Wait for my signal. Katia, grab her crossbow!

DONUT: WON'T WORK. TRAIN WALL IN THE WAY. WE NEED TO GET OUTSIDE FIRST!

A magic missile blasted me in the chest, and I fell back against the open window. I almost tumbled outside. It felt as if I'd been hit with a sledgehammer. My *Wisp Armor* spell was still active. Still, the spell had taken almost a quarter of my health away.

At the same moment, Eva lunged at Katia, swords flashing. Hekla reached up and caught one saber in her hand. The sword sank into the soft flesh, splitting her palm in two. The other sword bounced off the Amazonian's breastplate as she pulled herself to her feet, ghoul gore showering off her. Eva was so shocked that she re-coiled back in surprise, dropping that first sword, which splashed onto the train's floor. A second Hekla appeared and picked up the cowering snake woman by the neck and tossed her through the window just as a third Hekla rose to her feet. Eva cried out as she disappeared. I heard her crash onto the track below.

The other Daughters scattered back, confused and crying out.

"Holy shit, Donut," I said, scrambling forward. She'd cast *Second Chance* on Hekla's corpse, and then she'd cast *Clockwork Triplicate* on the minion, creating three Heklas. It was brilliant. It was fucked-up, but it was brilliant.

"Don't, don't hurt them," Katia cried, finally recovering. "Not the other Daughters. They don't know what's going on."

"Push them back," Donut yelled at the three Heklas. The Daughters started to recover from their shock, howling in outrage at Donut's desecration of Hekla's corpse.

"Clockworks first!" I yelled at Donut. "Keep the real Hekla back. We need to loot her damn corpse!"

One of the clockwork Heklas' heads exploded. Sparks and little electronic pieces showered as it was hit with a second electrical bolt, cast by one of the Daughters. The other two Heklas continued to push the others back and out the door into the gangway and then to the next car. In addition to the remaining Daughters, at least a hundred other crawlers filled the car, which was packed to the brim. They yelled as one, confused and afraid at the sight of one of the dungeon's most famous crawlers lurching toward them. I chased after the minion. I tried to pull the crossbow off Hekla's back, but it wouldn't come. As I pulled, I looked down and saw the square access panel in the gangway's floor.

"Katia, we need to get the vermilion key from Hekla's corpse. It has to be you since you killed her. Get the key first. And then everything else you can grab. Hurry."

"Why?" Donut asked. She shot a magic missile past undead Hekla's legs. One of the Daughters fell back, crying, grasping her knee. "Why do we need the key?"

Katia, to her credit, recovered quickly. She rushed forward. "Where's Eva?" she cried as she reached for the undead Hekla.

We'd placed blocks so the doors to the two engine cars could close, but not lock, so we didn't need the keys. If I wanted to disengage this car, however, I still needed it. My first instinct was to take this engine and get the fuck out of here. Hopefully somebody else would have the presence of mind to get to that other engine and pull it out of the station.

A part of me screamed, *This is a douche move. You're abandoning 1,000 people.* They needed to know how to disengage the slave mode to pull the train. Surely someone would figure it out. It was just one button. *Still,* I thought, *what if they don't?*

Fuck, fuck, fuck.

"It doesn't let me loot from her while she's a minion," Katia shouted.

The second clockwork Hekla exploded after it was speared in the chest. Donut leaped to my shoulder.

Out on the platform, the last of the crawlers retreated into the train. A trio of monstrosities leaped down the stairs. Holy shit, what were those things? They had blinking red exclamation marks over their heads. *Those are stage three monsters.* We needed to go.

"Katia, the very moment that minion dies, get the key. Then get her crossbow. Then loot the shit out of everything you can."

One of the monsters jumped at the train, bouncing off the wall of the passenger car. It looked like it'd once been a skull-faced, bear-sized monster. The DTs had transformed it. Tentacles erupted from its back, reminding me of the mold lions from Grimaldi's circus. But those tentacles had been thinner, parasitic. This was different. The tentacles were a part of the creature. Very . . . Krakaren-like.

Fuck. We don't have time for this.

The original plan was to disengage the drive on this first engine car, walk all the way to the back of the train, and reengage that second engine, turning it into the primary one. In theory, however, with that second engine still in slave mode, we didn't need to do that. The train would work fine from this cab no matter which direction we went, though we'd be driving blind.

I didn't have a choice, not with a thousand people suddenly on the train and in imminent danger. We needed to stay here and drive the train backwards. That'd be difficult if we were dead.

"We need to close the door!" I cried.

At that moment, the Hekla minion collapsed, having been hit with a spell. She tumbled in the gangway, blocking the door. Donut fired another missile at a woman who rocketed back, health halfway down.

I jumped forward and grabbed the Hekla corpse by the legs and pulled it back into the cab. "Close the door! Close the door!" Katia grabbed the sliding door, kicked away the block, and slid it closed, locking it, just as it rocked with a pair of spells. I knew from experience nobody would get in without a key, not in an engine car. Hopefully none of the other Daughters actually had keys.

I looked down with horror to realize Hekla's body had been ripped in half. All we'd dragged into the car was her legs and half of her torso. Her glowing breastplate and, more importantly, the crossbow that'd been slung over her back were on the other side of the wall.

The train rocked again as one of the monsters slammed against it. The creatures' tentacles grasped at the doors to the passenger cars. I jumped up and to the controls. I pushed the train into reverse mode, and I added power to the throttle. The train vibrated ominously, and I feared it wouldn't go, or the back cars would smash together like they had during that last crash, but the train started to move. Slowly at first, but then it gathered speed. We left the station, moving back down the track. Behind me, the door banged and crashed as the Daughters desperately tried to break it down.

By the time we cleared the platform, it was filled with tentacle-covered creatures. I took a deep breath. I kept my eyes on the receding platform. One of the monsters jumped into the channel. Then another. The platform quickly moved away from view. I slowed the train, but only a little. Hopefully these things weren't that fast.

"Where did Eva go?" Katia asked again. She had an odd, distant quality to her voice. *She's in shock.*

Behind us, the door continued to bang.

"She went out the window. I don't know if she died or not. I didn't see her when we pulled away."

"She's alive," Katia said. "She's still in my chat."

I nodded. Holy shit. It had all happened so fast. Hekla was dead. Hekla was fucking dead. Katia had killed her. She'd gone from level 24 to 37, which was insane.

"Have you seen your level yet?" I asked Katia.

"Have you seen yours?"

Surprised, I checked. I'd gone up two levels to 34. Donut had gone up two to 32.

I suspected while Katia had gotten a lot of experience for being a living battering ram, the lion's share of that experience that had rocketed her up the ranks actually came from killing Hekla. I still wasn't clear on how sharing worked, but we probably hadn't gotten a share of that. But two levels at once was a big deal. Now all we needed to do was get out of this.

"You know, you're probably the highest-level crawler in the dungeon now," I said after a moment. "Last I saw, Lucia Mar was 35, and that was just a few hours ago."

Katia said nothing. The train rumbled over the tracks, riding much more roughly than our trip up here. We were all still covered in gore. The room was filled with it. I looked at my hands, marveling at all of the blood.

Katia turned to look at Hekla's legs. She put her hand to her mouth and just stood there for a moment. "I didn't mean to kill her."

Donut leaped from my shoulder to hers. "When I killed that guy, I didn't mean to do it, either. But he had it coming, and Hekla had it coming even worse. She was going to kill you."

The door banged again. They weren't letting up. If anything, their bangs against the door were getting more frantic. I looked nervously down at Hekla's half body. The loot dialog did not pop up.

"Hey, did you get the key?"

"I got it," Katia said. "Not that it matters now."

I relaxed. They would never get in here. At least not through that door. "True. But we don't want them having it, either." I paused, seeing the look in Katia's eyes. I recognized it for what it was. That moment before the collapse. I reached out and grabbed her arm to steady her.

"Katia, are you okay?" Donut asked.

"No," she said. "I'm not even a little okay. Nothing about this is okay." She rubbed her eyes, looking about the gore-filled room. "Goddamn it, there's nowhere to sit down and have a breakdown in here."

We all just looked at each other and started to laugh. There was no reason to laugh. None of this was funny. But we laughed. We laughed long and hard. It didn't make sense. None of this made sense, but we were alive, for now at least, and we had each other, and that was something.

THE MOMENT ENDED AS QUICKLY AS IT STARTED.

"Carl," Donut suddenly hissed, "there's someone in there. In the mantaur apartment. They're trying to hide, like they have a spell or a skill, but I just saw a blink on my map. It's a blue dot. It's someone small."

Fucking hell. I suddenly felt so very tired.

"Silfa, is that you?" I called. "Come out. We're all done fighting. We're done hurting each other."

The door to the apartment flew open, and the small fairy burst from the room. She rocketed toward the exit door and tried to un-lock it.

Donut leaped from Katia's shoulder, bounced once off the wall and landed atop the screaming fairy, pinning her to the floor. The fairy gurgled as her head went below the line of liquid gore. The blood in the car was slowly draining away, but there was just so much of it.

"Don't you fucking hurt her," someone cried from the other side of the door. "I swear to god if you hurt her, I will kill you all."

"Let her go!" another woman screamed, frantic, banging on the door. "You let her go right now!"

I reached down and grasped the healer. She was bigger than most fairies, bigger than the ones from the second floor and that manager from the Desperado Club, but I could still hold on to her with a single hand. She screamed and struggled. A weak ice spell shot from her hand and blasted down, hitting me in the leg. With my ice resistance, I didn't even feel it.

"Calm down," I said. "Silfa. Jesus. Calm the fuck down. Quit wiggling. I'm not going to hurt you."

"Traitor," she yelled at Katia. "She saved your life. She saved all of us, and you killed her. What are we going to do now?"

"Silfa," I said, "I am going to let you go, and we are going to talk. We don't want to fight. We are just going to talk. Okay?"

The fairy stopped struggling, but she glowered at me.

Donut returned to my shoulder. She hissed at the fairy. "If you try something, I will rip you from the air and eat off your wings. I've done it before."

"Okay, everyone, chill," I said again. I let her go, and she flitted into the air, buzzing up to the ceiling and against the wall. She crossed her arms. Blood dripped off her body. The train bumped as we hit something on the tracks, and the healer hit her head and winced. I stepped back, grasped the throttle, and slowed us further. I did not like driving blind. As long as the monsters on the tracks were only in ones and twos, we'd be okay, especially since the train was much heavier now. But still, we needed to keep it slow.

"You're a murderer," Silfa said to Katia.

"Katia didn't want to kill Hekla," I said. "But Hekla *did* intend on killing Katia, and I believe she was planning on sacrificing you, too. I'm pretty sure I know why. I'm not mad at you guys. She gambled and lost. It's done. It is pointless for us to fight now. We're all on the same side."

"No, you're wrong," Silfa said. "Hekla would never sacrifice me. She was protecting us."

"Hekla *was* protecting you. You as a group. She told you to stop healing Katia, didn't she? And she told you to hide in the apartment. Not leave the car, but to go into that room. She told you to hide in the room if anything went down. Didn't she?"

The fairy didn't answer. She just glared. I took that as an affirmative.

"Look, I didn't know her very well, but someone once told me that she was a very practical person. She was playing this like a game of chess, and she was willing to sacrifice others for what she thought was the greater good."

"Hekla would never hurt me," Silfa said. "My girls wouldn't allow it."

"But she told you to stop healing Katia, didn't she? Probably waited until the end to make sure we got through that last horde first, right?"

She paused. "Eva told me to do it. Not Hekla."

I nodded. That made sense. Eva was Hekla's fixer. Her lieutenant. Like I thought, the one who did the dirty work. "And she told you to wait in the train car. Not leave."

"What's it to you?"

"Don't you see? You were the bait. Why do you think she wanted you nearby? She wanted Katia to die, and she wanted me to get angry. I wouldn't have gotten mad at her or Eva. I would've been mad at *you*. She thought I would've attacked you. Maybe even hurt or killed you. She thought I was unhinged."

"You *are* unhinged. You're crazy, and everybody knows it. We've seen the videos. You get mad for no reason. You laugh when you pick up body parts. Hekla would never have let you hurt me."

"Just like she wouldn't deliberately shoot Katia with two of those invisible bolts from her crossbow?" I pulled the broken bolt from my inventory. It remained invisible in my hand. I dipped it in blood and held it up. Its shape appeared for a moment before everything flowed off it. I stepped forward and handed it up to her. She didn't move. "Oh, just take it. I'm not going to hurt you."

She hesitantly reached forward and grasped the broken crossbow bolt. Her eyes went big as she examined its properties. I took it back. "This means nothing. This could be yours." She didn't sound so sure anymore.

I continued. "She would've been forced to kill me if I attacked you. There was probably a whole plan in place, something to distract Donut. It would've been quick."

"Why? Why would she do this?"

I sighed and thumbed at Donut, who remained on my shoulder. "With me and Katia dead, Donut would've been all alone. She would have been forced to join you guys. And so would Mordecai, our manager. That's what Hekla wanted. How many healers do you have in your party? It's a lot, isn't it? I saw all the fairies. It was an acceptable trade-off. One healer plus Katia, who hasn't been in the party since the end of the second floor, in exchange for one of the dungeon's best assets? If it had worked, the party would've been better for it. No offense."

"I would never have joined with Hekla if she'd killed you, Carl," Donut said.

I thought about that. "Maybe she would have sent Eva to kill me. Or those two mages she had posted right outside. And once that was done, she would've had them killed, too. Or banished them just to keep you happy, Donut. Who knows? She was a shrink. She probably had some big plan worked out. I don't know the details, but I think I'm right."

"I still wouldn't have joined her," Donut grumbled, though not as loud.

"Is Eva still alive?" I asked Katia.

"Yes," Katia said. "I don't know where she is. I think maybe she got back on the train. I sent her a message, but she's not answering."

"Why don't you ask her?" I said to Silfa. "Ask Eva if she was supposed to protect you from me. I bet she was. Maybe Hekla was planning on sacrificing her, too."

"It wasn't Eva," Silfa eventually said. "My daughters, my real daughters, were standing guard right outside. Hekla told them if anything went wrong to kill you first. Damnit. I shouldn't be here. I own a bakery. I just want my girls to be safe. I just want to go home. I shouldn't be here."

"Your daughters are the two right outside?" I asked. They were the two mages who'd jumped into action once the shit hit the fan.

She nodded.

"Go to them," I said. "Tell them what I told you. Tell them I said we're sorry about what happened, but this is on Hekla."

"She was protecting us," Silfa said. "When she died, it automatically made Eva the party leader. People don't like her. They're leaving the party. Brynhild's Daughters is no more. We're nothing without Hekla. We have hardly any equipment. We don't have a personal space anymore. We all have sponsors, but most of us have the same one as Hekla, the crab ranch, and they've never sent us anything. We have nothing. What are we going to do?"

I shook my head. "I don't know. There's a whole train of people out there. I'm sure someone would love to join up with a healer and two mages. It won't be us, though. We'll never trust each other, and that sucks. It really does. It's exactly what they want to happen, and it breaks my fucking heart."

I OPENED THE DOOR JUST ENOUGH FOR THE DEJECTED FAIRY TO slip out. I snapped it closed and locked it. On the other side of the door, I heard the three women start to sob.

I leaned my back against the door. The train shook violently as we hit something, but it soon settled. Christ, what a day. The more I thought about what Hekla had attempted, the more it angered me.

Is this what we've become? Is this who we really are? I refused to believe it.

I thought of Bautista, who was still walking toward the abyss with a group of people who wouldn't be able to get to a stairwell.

You can't save them all.

Fuck you, Mordecai, I thought.

"How did you know?" Katia asked. "About Hekla?"

I shrugged. "I've gotten pretty good at spotting that sort of thing." That wasn't true at all. If Odette hadn't warned me, I'd likely be dead right now. I sighed, looking at Hekla's half corpse.

"It's too bad about that crossbow," I said.

"Oh, you mean this?" Katia asked, and the massive repeating crossbow formed in her hands.

Holy shit. She'd done it. She'd looted one of the most powerful weapons in the game. My anger fled.

"Katia, I am going to kiss you."

She laughed. She sounded just as exhausted as I felt. "Not without taking a shower first you're not."

"Can I see it?" I reverently took the weapon from Katia's hands. When fired at full auto, I remembered thinking this thing was like a ranged chain saw. It was lighter than I expected. It appeared to be made of gold, but it felt almost like plastic. It was inlaid with carvings of a vulture creature.

I received a nasty notification the moment I touched it.

Warning: You have a dick.

"Thank you for the information," I said to the ceiling as I examined the weapon's properties.

Enchanted Repeating Crossbow of the Scavenger Mother of Mothers.

   This is a unique item.

This is a repeating ranged weapon. It has the buffet enchantment, meaning it will not run out of basic ammunition. You may load and fire additional ammunition types to use with this weapon, though any special bonuses will only apply to the stock ammunition.

It is said that the long-forgotten goddess Nekhebit is both jealous and terrible. When the elf mothers chose to abandon Nekhebit and instead worship Apito, the Oak Goddess, it is written Nekhebit grew enraged. The mighty vulture goddess blamed the male-dominated high elf court for causing her worshippers to stray. As a result, she cursed their seed, thus creating what is today known as the Fae Diaspora. There are dozens of elf and fairy breeds, all of whom may trace their lineage back to the early high elf court, whose cursed offspring sowed the universe.

This crossbow is rumored to have been given to Nekhebit's last warrior guardian as a gift for remaining true to her faith.

This item may only be wielded by a female.

For every female in your party, up to thirty, this item's damage and firing speed is increased by 25%.

Your strength+level increases base damage 1.5× more than a standard crossbow.

+15 Dexterity when wielded.

+10 Strength when wielded.

Casts *Birth Defect* on monster types who generate or birth additional monsters.

"Wow," I said. It wouldn't be as powerful or fast in Katia's hands as it was in Hekla's, but I was already thinking of ways to maximize the unique weapon's strength. *No wonder she had surrounded herself with women.*

———

"IT'S GOOD TO SEE YOU," I SAID TO LI JUN. THE STREET MONK clapped me on the shoulder.

He looked distastefully at his hand, which was now covered in blood. "You, too, Carl and Donut. You're a little, uh, dirty," he said.

I laughed.

After we'd freed Silfa, we'd decided it was best to keep the door closed just to head off any further misunderstandings. I moved Katia to the small engineer's apartment so she could rest for about a half hour. The room had a bed, a table, and a long, thin toilet designed to be used by a mantaur. Heavy metal posters from Earth covered the walls. I went through and looted everything not bolted down before I returned to the main room of the engine car.

A few minutes later came a knock, and Li Jun's familiar, halting voice wafted through the door. I quickly let him in, though he stopped dead at the sight of the gore in the train car. Most of the liquid had drained away, leaving piles of body parts and bones throughout. Donut had let Mongo out for about thirty seconds before I made her put him away again. The dinosaur had gone crazy, like that fat kid in the Willy Wonka book who started eating the walls and shit.

Li Jun looked sick to his stomach as he took in the room, but he quickly recovered and grinned widely up at me.

I examined the man. The last time I'd spoken to him was on the Maestro's show. He remained human. He was a level 28 Street Monk, which I assumed was some sort of melee class. He didn't carry any weapons. He didn't look much different than before. The Chinese man had deep acne scars on his cheeks that hadn't gone away with the transformation, but when he smiled, it lit up the room, despite the gory surroundings. He'd been on the top-10 list, but he'd fallen off. I was glad to see he was still alive.

"Your sister? Zhang?" I asked, suddenly concerned that he was here alone.

"They are fine," he said. "They are in the cargo near the front, and we can't get to each other until the train stops. We have a group of twelve people now. We have been saved again by you. I have come to pay my respects."

I nodded. We fist-bumped so I'd have him in my chat.

"Now that you're here, I need to show you how to drive this train," I said. "We're going to stop at station 75 and detach this car from the rest. From there, you can drive the train back to station 36. Get the people off there. I already have a few friends waiting. That's where we're going to make the stand. Station 36."

Imani and crew were already dealing with an increasing wave of these wrath ghouls—which I hadn't seen yet. The station, unfortunately, had multiple platforms attached to it. The ghouls were coming from almost every one, making it difficult to defend. But with these reinforcements, Imani's plan of keeping the ghouls from transforming further might just work. Especially since we had several nearby stations with safe rooms where people could rest and recharge in shifts. There were no ghouls in the "hidden" railway where we had the *Nightmare* parked, so people had easy access to the rest areas.

I told all of this to Li Jun, who nodded thoughtfully.

"The monsters will likely come at us from all sides just before the stairs open, even if we do prevent the wrath ghouls from forming a boss monster," he said.

"Probably," I agreed. "The whole thing is designed to push the monsters toward the stairwells. We all have to work together to survive."

"Why do we not go to station 24?" he asked. "That station also has stairs but no ghouls."

"We don't yet know what sort of monsters form once the creatures suffering from stage three die. But it looks like they'll head to 24, and it'll probably be something terrible. At least with station 36, we know what we're facing."

He nodded. "Okay. What will you be doing?"

"We have some more friends who are trapped all the way at the end of the line. We're going to save them. Each and every one."

25

TIME TO LEVEL COLLAPSE: 3 DAYS, 3 HOURS.

Views: 974.1 Quadrillion

Followers: 5.2 Quadrillion

Favorites: 1.9 Quadrillion

"WE'RE SAVING THOSE GUYS, TOO? REALLY?" DONUT SAID AFTER LI Jun left.

Katia emerged from the small apartment. "We need to slow down. I think I see station 75 coming up on my map."

"Seriously, Carl," Donut continued. "We just helped to save *these* guys. How are we going to help everyone at the end of the line?"

"I have no idea," I said as I moved back to the train's controls. "But I won't try if you guys don't think we should."

Donut sighed. She whispered something to Katia. They both started laughing.

"What?" I asked. "What's so funny?"

"You're going to get us killed one way or the other, Carl. It might as well be for a good cause," Donut said.

I grunted. "Well, they do say I'm crazy."

THE GHOULS STREAMING OUT OF STATION 72 APPEARED TO HOME in on the closest large gathering of crawlers. Before, they'd moved up toward the crawlers trapped at station 101, but after Li Jun led the 1,000-plus survivors to the stairwell platform at station 36, meeting up with the exhausted team Meadow Lark, the ghouls started flowing in that direction instead. That, added with the wrath ghouls traveling up from the train yards, made it so they were besieged the moment they got off the train.

That was okay for now. The way the platforms funneled passengers to the stairwell stations created multiple defensible choke points. It'd be tough, but the group should be able to keep the station clear. Since we'd discovered the secret escape hatch that led to the employee line, the defenders could keep themselves supplied and refreshed. We sent out mass messages to everyone who would listen of the plan. Last we heard, there were multiple groups set up in other instances of station 36 doing the same, plus another group that was going to try their luck at holding a station 24 and a few more teams who were going to attempt to kill the ghoul generators at 12 and 72. Everyone was avoiding the boss at station 48. I wished them all luck.

In addition to the people who'd managed to make it to the stairwells, there was a rising chorus of crawlers who found themselves trapped at the abyss. If they had those hats, they could just step through one of the thousand-plus portals and teleport to a train yard. But an increasing number were finding themselves at the edge of the pit with no way to escape.

Despite my earlier thoughts, I now suspected there was only a single abyss. I was starting to get a sense of how the entire railway looked. The whole thing was shaped like one of those Spirograph drawings. The train yards dotted the exterior edges of the pattern, spaced at regular intervals. The colored lines looped around, over, and under each other, but all led to a single point in the center, which was the pit.

Katia, who studied the map more than anyone, continued to insist there was something that we were missing. I didn't care as long as we knew how to get from point A to point B.

There were currently about 500–600 people trapped there at the end of the line, with more appearing by the moment. Word was starting to spread that you needed the hat to utilize that escape, so those without were mostly braving the "ghoul coaster," as Elle had dubbed it, back to the train yards.

The crawlers had been desperately searching the interior walkways of the pit for the elusive camouflaged exits that would lead to stop 436, where they could in turn get to the named-train switching stations. However, the lizard monsters appeared to be constantly generated, just like the ghouls, and that was making it difficult for them to search. A few battles later, and the interior gangways had started to collapse. That nixed my idea of going back to the train yard and using the *Nightmare* to return to the abyss.

That left us with only one option. We had to take the battered and half-destroyed vermilion car all the way to the end of the line and distribute as many of the hats as possible. The trip would take about a full day and would be fraught with danger. If the train broke down or the line was blocked or the power went out, we'd be fucked. Surely there would be monsters crawling all over the line, and we'd have to plow through them all. It was a terrible idea, and I knew Mordecai would have a coronary if he knew we were even thinking about this. Still, what else could we do? We all agreed that was the plan for now unless someone came up with something better.

We had about a day to find an alternative before it would be too late.

We used station 75 to quickly disengage the front engine and send Li Jun up to the other engine. A few ghouls were out on the lines, but we sent a group ahead of us to deal with it while we worked. I saw no sign of Eva. The remaining Daughters held back, disappearing into the crowd. Brynhild's Daughters truly was no more.

I couldn't help but think that was for the best. Hekla had built the entire party around herself and that crossbow. They had too many healers and mages and not enough damage dealers and not a tank amongst them. The system had worked great early on, but I suspected the entire team would've fallen apart eventually. Maybe now they'd all find groups where they would be better utilized.

We decided to keep Katia hidden while we unhooked the train, lest someone's emotions get the best of them. I traded fist bumps as

I loudly exclaimed that I needed people's hats and any keys they'd gathered along the way.

My fellow crawlers were standoffish at first considering what had happened with Hekla, plus Donut and I looked like extras from a *Hellraiser* movie. But once people learned about why I was collecting the hats, a chorus went out. I'd been expecting people to selfishly hold on to them just in case there was one last trick, or so they could sell them later, but that's not what happened at all. People worked together. They coordinated. They spread the word. In twenty minutes, I had over 700 of the hats piled in front of me plus another fifteen colored-line keys that would also work for the portals. It was enough, for now. Hopefully it'd remain that way.

Yes, I thought. *There is hope for us. Not a lot. But it's there.*

"Carl, we could sell these for over three million gold," Donut whispered as I started pulling them into my inventory. Her eyes got huge. "Three and a half million! I bet I could sell them for even more. Carl, we'll be rich!"

"Yeah, that'd play great on the show. We'd be like Bea's cousin who pretended she had cancer and got all that money on GoFundMe."

"What if we figure out how to save the people without using the hats? Can I sell them then?"

I laughed. "Absolutely," I said.

AFTER THE TRAIN LEFT, LEAVING THE THREE OF US ALONE WITH THE battered subway car, we spent some time exploring the strange station 75. This was one of the last major parts of the railway we hadn't yet investigated. I hoped we'd find something to help us. We set Mongo free, and the dinosaur squawked angrily at us for being cooped up for so long. He quickly got over it, instead getting distracted by the blood and gore covering our bodies. I had to smack his beak several times to keep him from licking me.

It was clear right away that this station was different from the others. Multiple tracks led off to a small-scale yard, consisting of a few dozen flatbed train cars designed to be occupied by no more than a handful of riders at a time. There were a few different kinds of the small cars. I assumed these were for the hobgoblins to get to the crashed trains in order to fix them. We would investigate once we cleared the station.

We walked through a tunnel that led to a large, sprawling cavern filled with squat buildings, mostly warehouses with no doors and open-area workshops. The entire chamber had been turned into a graveyard. It had been overrun. Hundreds of ghoul corpses littered the ground. But there were also gnoll and hobgoblin bodies sprinkled throughout. There'd been explosions, too, as evidenced by scorch marks throughout the industrial-style station. Most of the gnoll bodies had been devoured, leaving nothing but broken pieces of spears and armor. I took it all, though little was useful.

"I think someone was here already," I said. "All of them look as if they've already been looted. I haven't found a single gold piece."

Upon examination, the system indicated all the ghouls were killed by gnolls and hobgoblins, and the gnolls and hobgoblins were mostly kills by the ghouls. Though a lot of the gnolls were also killed by hobgoblins. That didn't surprise me. Hobgoblins equaled explosives. And explosives equaled collateral damage.

Right in the middle of the cavern were three intact buildings sitting next to one another. A gnoll armory. Something called a hobgoblin repair shop. And a safe room. A glorious, beautiful safe room. I saw with dismay that the armory's door was open. Whoever had come before us had already gotten inside. I wondered if they'd also raided the hobgoblins' stash. Probably, which was too bad.

We needed to figure out this station's secrets as quickly as possible, but we also needed a shower and to sleep and to reset our buffs. Plus, the recap would be on soon.

We made a line toward the bar, which was called the Downward Dog. A handwritten sign attached to the front door read, "Oi! No hobgoblins!" I pushed the door open to find the place was similar to most of the tavern-style bars on the third floor. It was not a converted Earth restaurant. That was kind of odd.

I realized what the difference was. There was still a screen over the bar, but there were no rooms for rent here. There was still an entrance to our personal space, but this was more like the local bars they had at the entrance to the Desperado Club, meaning this wasn't a true safe room. We couldn't open boxes inside the bar, nor were we protected from mobs.

The stench of beer-soaked wood assaulted my senses as we stepped deeper into the dark room. The tavern was empty except for a single gnoll bartender who was asleep on top of the bar, surrounded by empty bottles. He snored loudly. Mongo walked up and started sniffing the creature. I noted he was a **Shade Gnoll**, which was something we hadn't seen before. He looked more like a hyena than a jackal.

"There's gotta be a story attached to this," I said. "We'll get it out of him after we shower." I turned toward the doorway that led to our safe room. We entered.

"Don't track blood on the floors," Katia called as we all tracked blood on the floor. "God, I can just hear my mother now. 'Katia, take off your shoes. You're going to grow up and have a filthy home.' It turns out, she was right." She laughed as she tiptoed through the room and toward her space. She still left dirty red prints on the floor.

At that moment, it hit me. Katia was now and forever a part of the team. Nobody needed to say it out loud. We all knew. While this would never be "home," this space was just for us and only us. The three of us.

I grinned. "My dad once made me sleep in a tent in the yard because I had a nosebleed that wouldn't stop."

"Miss Beatrice once used scissors to get poop off my butt," Donut said.

"Uh-huh," I said. "Once?"

"We're having a moment here, Carl. Don't ruin it."

———

DESPITE ALL OF THAT INSANE CRAZINESS OF THE PAST DAY, NEI-
ther Donut nor I received anything except a handful of standard
adventurer boxes. And one of my achievements didn't have anything
to do with the battle with Hekla or for killing all those ghouls.

> New achievement! Mentally Unstable Clothing Hoarder!
>   You have over 500 of the exact same, stackable clothing
> item in your inventory.
>   What the hell is wrong with you? You planning on opening a
> thrift store? You might want to see a shrink. One that your
> group doesn't immediately kill.
>   *Reward:* We don't reward this sort of behavior. It's weird.

Katia, on the other hand, received 10 loot boxes. We all showered
first before coming out to watch her open her loot. We came out to
find Mongo "cleaning" the floors.

"Gross, Mongo," I said.

The dinosaur squawked at me.

Katia opened her first box and looked at me, grinning. "Sorry,
Carl," she said as the dagger tattoo formed on her neck. "I know you
wanted to get me into Club Vanquisher."

"Oh my god, yay!" Donut exclaimed as she realized what had just
happened. The cat had gone from a red matted nightmare to poofed
out and washed, ready for the stage. She smelled of lilacs. "We can
go dancing now!" She gasped. "You can meet Sledgie! This is great!"

"I can't wait," Katia said. I laughed.

Katia sobered somewhat after opening her next box. A Gold Savage Box, which she'd received for being a player killer. Instead of
coupons, it contained a skill potion that gave her the Find Crawler
skill. It was the same skill that Maggie My potentially had, though
this was only level three. She downed it immediately. It put the
name of all nearby crawlers on her map, and she could sort and find

them using the list. It wouldn't be until a higher level that she'd be able to actually hunt down and find those not currently on the map, plus I wasn't so certain it'd find crawlers using stealth. Not yet. But it was a great skill to have.

She received an achievement for collecting the bounty, and a Legendary Bounty Box, which was that 500,000 gold. She also received an achievement for being the *first* to collect a bounty, but it didn't come with anything. Donut complained loudly about that one.

However, she did snag one more awesome item. She got something called a Platinum Slam Master Box. She'd gotten it for killing a certain amount of mobs using her momentum. I watched as the item appeared. It was a gold wrestling belt, like any regular heavyweight champion belt they'd give to a WWE star.

"Who is Christopher Pallies?" she asked as she examined it.

"I don't know," I said, taking the belt from her so I could look.

Enchanted Wrestling Belt of the Great Gorgo.

While you'll never be as amazing as the greatest, most beautiful wrestler of all time—Christopher Alan Pallies—you will look pretty snazzy when you wrap this bad boy around your waist.

This enchanted belt offers the following benefits:

+5% Strength.

+5% Constitution.

+The Avalanche benefit.

The added stats alone made this a really good item. The Avalanche benefit was pretty badass.

Avalanche.

This benefit is straightforward. If you hit a living creature with your body while you are moving, the force exerted upon that body will be as if they were hit by twice the mass.

Your entire body must be moving for this benefit to activate. This benefit's power will not translate to weapons.

You might want to take this off if you plan on getting busy
with someone. Especially if you're the top.

"Man, we need to stick you to the front of another train," I said,
handing the belt back to her. Her Rush ability would also be even
more powerful, but I didn't say that part out loud. She still didn't
want to talk about the Hekla incident.

She was, however, mostly back to her regular self. She was laughing and joking with us. I couldn't tell if she'd truly recovered from
the trauma of the day, or if she was just good at covering it up. I
suspected the latter. Either way, she'd grown into one of the most
powerful crawlers in the dungeon, and I didn't think that'd quite
sunk in yet.

"That leaves everything except the Platinum Fan Box. I guess
they're voting on it now," she said. "Do you think we'll see that
Chaco guy again?"

"I hope not," I said. She would get to open the fan box about
15 hours before Mordecai's time-out expired. I actually *did* hope
she'd get the prize carousel, so she could pick instead of being at the
mercy of the fans. But I wouldn't say that out loud.

"What should we do with all of this gold?" she asked.

Donut gasped. "Are we going shopping? Do you think if we buy
a lot of stuff, they'll have a shopping montage scene on the show, like
in *Pretty Woman*?"

"Hopefully we'll have time to ask Mordecai when he gets back,"
I said. "We still have two environmental upgrades. I'm thinking
maybe a kitchen upgrade to get food buffs and one more buffing
item. Some of those cost more than the coupon's value, and we'll
need the money for that. There's just so much on that list, I don't
know what the best choice is."

We also had four free tables to purchase between the three of us,
and we needed to buy them quickly since they leveled up on their
own when a floor collapsed. That was also something I wanted to
consult with Mordecai about. When he returned, there would be one

day and 15 hours left. Hopefully that was enough time, but just in case, I collected everybody's free table coupons and left them on his alchemy table. That way he'd be able to buy them for us if we were otherwise occupied.

THE RECAP SHOW CAME ON, AND THE ENTIRE PROGRAM WAS A SPEcial on the death of Hekla. It was set up like a tribute to the crawler, starting with a scene of her entering the dungeon. She was a much different woman then, and it seemed odd seeing her in street clothes. She'd been fighting with her husband as they came in, a tall, goodlooking man who looked like he was twenty years older than her. He'd gotten poisoned by a walking cactus mob, and she left him while he was on the floor, crying for her to come back.

She returned later to find him dead, being devoured by rats. She screamed as she kicked the rats away. One turned and attacked Hekla. She picked up a broken bone—one of her now-dead husband's exposed rib bones—and she used it to stab the rat in the eye. By some miracle, the jab killed the mob.

That had garnered her a Legendary Grrl Power Box for being the first woman in the dungeon to use the corpse of a human male to kill a mob. I assumed that was where she got the crossbow.

We watched a much-abridged summary of Hekla's rise in power and how she gathered crawlers to her.

During that segment, the show started to also focus on Katia. We got to see her enter the dungeon, clutching tightly to Eva's arm. They went on to portray how mousy, terrified Katia depended on her friend, how she hid behind her during early battles. It showed Eva killing the man who'd grabbed Katia when Hekla demanded he leave the group.

Eva's features oddly matched the cobra face of the nagini/orc hybrid she'd become. And Katia's before-face was also strange to look upon. It was the face she had now in the safe room, almost, but it was just slightly off from that terrified, bewildered woman who entered the dungeon almost a month ago. She was a different species now, of course, but those human eyes had a deeper quality to them. The thousand-yard stare.

The next scene surprised me. Katia wasn't alone when she got to the third floor.

I should have realized. Everyone who entered the third floor met up with their original game guide. Katia and Eva had the same one, and the two of them entered character creation together. But Eva went first, and she left the safe room as Katia's body transformed. By the time Katia was ready to leave, Eva was long gone. It wasn't clear what happened next, but the next time they showed Hekla, Eva was there with her.

"What happened?" I asked Katia. "How did she find Hekla and not you?"

Katia shrugged. "We were in a small settlement. Eva said she'd accidentally made one of the swordsmen guards angry and had to run out of town. She got on one of the traveling caravans and ended up in a different city and reconnected with Hekla. At least that's what she'd told me."

"Caravans?" I asked. "I didn't see those."

"They had them. I got on one, and we passed by the circus and then ended up in the skyfowl town where I met you."

I remembered then what Eva had said to Katia in that moment before Katia had tried to kill her. *This is why I left you behind on the third floor.* That revelation must have hit her hard.

The program continued to show Katia's grand return to the Daughters and the formation of the plow in front of the train. We watched Katia's level rise as she plowed through the ghouls.

And then, finally, it showed Katia killing Hekla. They did not show it to be an accident, but an act of rage on Katia's part once she discovered she was being used.

"That's not how it happened," Katia groused. "They're making me look like a bloodthirsty crazy woman."

I grunted. "Welcome to the club. When I first—" I paused, my eyes on the screen. The moment the episode ended, the leaderboard changed. All three of us turned to look at the new list.

1. Lucia Mar—Lajabless—Black Inquisitor General—Level 35–1,000,000

2. Prepotente—Caprid—Forsaken Aerialist—Level 34–500,000

3. Carl—Primal—Compensated Anarchist—Level 34–400,000

4. Donut—Cat—Former Child Actor—Level 32–300,000

5. Quan Ch—Half Elf—Imperial Security Trooper—Level 38–200,000

6. Florin—Crocodilian—Shotgun Messenger—Level 32–100,000

7. Miriam Dom—Human—Shepherd—Level 30–100,000

8. Katia Grim—Doppelganger—Monster Truck Driver—Level 37–100,000

9. Dmitri and Maxim Popov—Nodling—Illusionist and Bogatyr—Level 30–100,000

10. Ifechi—Human—Physicker—Level 29–100,000

"Carl, Carl, we're in the top five! You're number three! Katia! You're in the top 10!"

"Oh, wow," Katia said. "The list has changed quite a bit."

"Yeah, Elle fell off the edge," I said. "Also, it turns out, you're not the highest level in the dungeon, Katia. Quan has you beat." I regretted saying it as soon as the words came out of my mouth. Any mention of Quan Ch was enough to send Donut into a tirade.

"He's a cheater," Donut started to grumble, but then she paused, finding something else to be outraged about. "Hey, why do those two guys get to be in the same spot? That's not fair! Carl and I should both be number three! Katia, too!"

"I don't know," I said. "It's also weird they hardly ever show that goat thing, but he's number two."

We were interrupted by the start of the daily announcement. It wasn't anything interesting. They were nerfing the running speed of the blister ghouls but increasing the running speed of creatures suffering from stage three DTs, which was pretty terrifying. The moment the announcement ended a notification appeared.

Warning: You may not wield your weapons while in the presence of Admins. Any attempted violence against an Admin will result in your immediate execution.

Before I could react, there was a *pop*, a splash of cold water over my legs, and Zev teleported into the room.

"Oh my god, hi Zev!" Donut said. "You didn't say you were coming!"

"Donut. Carl, Katia. Mongo. Hello."

Mongo rocketed from his spot on the floor to press his face against the kua-tin's glass helmet, almost knocking her over.

"No, Mongo!" Donut yelled. "It's Zev! Be nice!"

The tiny fish woman still wore the ridiculously cumbersome deep-diving helmet on her head along with the space suit. I remembered our very first conversation with the creature, and she'd said she was only going to wear it for the first few floors.

"Still wearing protective gear, I see," I said.

Zev furiously and uselessly rubbed at the exterior of her helmet where Mongo had fogged it up. "Yes, Carl. The protections aren't in place like they should be."

"What do you mean?" I asked.

"It's of no consequence to you, but the dual-layer system integration utilized for the initial capture and subjugation of the planet was supposed to be replaced by the pocket system at the end of the third floor. When it didn't switch over, people just thought we were being cheap. Turns out, Hinter, the company that normally rents out the necessary cores for the integration, wouldn't allow us to use them at the last minute. I don't know the details. It's confusing, boring business stuff. I don't even understand it all. The bottom line is, I'm wearing this suit when I enter the dungeon for the foreseeable future."

Weird. I wanted to ask more questions about it, but I knew that would be a bad idea.

"What can we do for you today?" I asked.

"Several things. I figured it would be best to talk in person. First off, I wanted to officially congratulate Katia on hitting the top ten, and to congratulate you two for getting in the top five. Also, just an FYI. Odette has amended the contract to include a Katia option, so she's now obligated to travel to the post-floor interviews. She went to the last one anyway, but now it's official and permanent."

"What about Mongo?" Donut asked.

Zev cracked a smile. "Mongo, too, Donut, but dungeon-born pets are considered Borant property, so there's no contracts involved. So, Katia, regarding Odette's show. She had to pay quite a bit more to make you exclusive, so she added a few, uh, riders to the contract. Namely, you need to be more 'zippy,' I think the word was. Apparently last time Odette thought your interview performance was a little lackluster."

Katia frowned and crossed her arms.

"I'll tell you what," I said. "Katia, I'll give you a zip lesson right now. Okay? Repeat after me. I want you to say, 'Go fuck yourself, Zev.'"

Katia laughed. "I'm not going to say that."

"Don't be crude, Carl," said Donut. "Also, Mongo is not anybody's property. This is an outrage!"

Mongo squawked in agreement.

Zev, I suddenly realized, wasn't accepting our abuse with her usual chipper obliviousness. She looked very tired. An ominous feeling came over me.

"Why are you really here, Zev?" I asked.

"Look, guys. In case something happens to me, I wanted to let you know how much I really appreciate how hard you've worked."

Oh, shit. "What's going on?"

"You didn't do anything. There's another representative who

wants to take over your account. Her name is Loita. Nothing has happened yet, but I think they might give it to her."

"What?" Donut said. "No. No way. We only work with you."

"She's Bloom. She just lost her main account, and technically she was Katia's rep first, and now that Katia is in your party, she has a claim. Not a strong one. But, like I said, she's Bloom, and I am not."

Bloom was the kua-tin political party that ran Borant. From what little I knew, the party members received much better treatment. That last substitute we'd had, the Mukta guy who'd put us on the Maestro's show, had been a party member.

"Loita? I've heard that name before," I said. "Isn't . . . wasn't she Hekla's representative?"

"That's right. The outreach associates represent the whole party, and since Katia was in Brynhild's Daughters, she's making noise that she should be the one in charge of you three. The only thing I have going for me is that you guys pulled in more money than Hekla, for interviews at least."

I shrugged. "Tell your bosses that Donut is right. We only work with you." The last thing we needed was some new asshole tossing us on shows like the Maestro's again. Especially one that probably held a grudge against us because we killed off her client. Zev, as annoying as she could be, attempted to keep us out of trouble with these shows. It rarely worked, but she tried. Plus Donut really liked her. And so did Mordecai.

"I wish it was that simple," Zev said. "Plus there's more. Something happened back at home. A bunch of people . . . I really can't talk about it. It's difficult for those of us who aren't party members. I'm holding on the best I can, guys. But I gotta go. I believe in you. Keep doing what you've been doing. Oh, yeah, I forgot to tell you. They're going to make your chats public starting tomorrow for people who pay extra. Sorry about that."

And without another word, she popped and disappeared, splashing more water over the floor.

"That's just wonderful," I grumbled.

IRON TANGLE ENDGAME TRAIN MAP

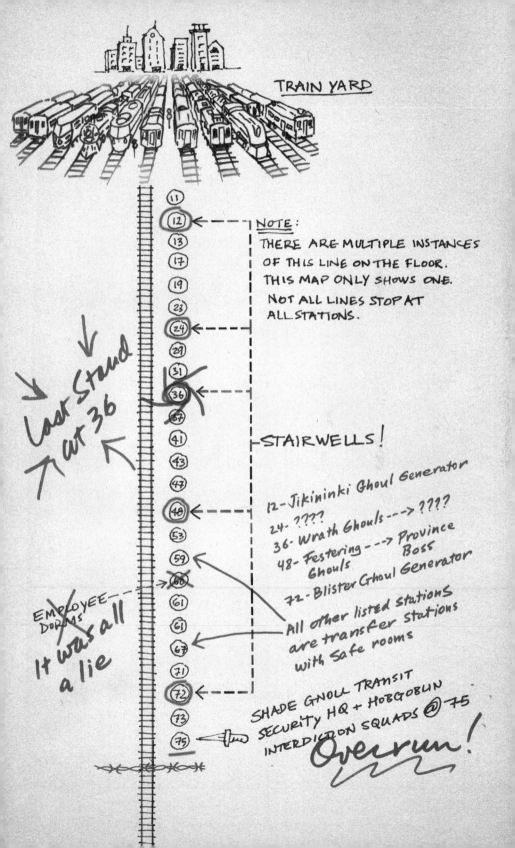

26

THE LEVEL 25 GNOLL BARTENDER'S NAME WAS GROWLER GARY. HE was conscious when we reentered the bar. Barely. He was so drunk, he couldn't sit up.

"They're all dead. Every last one. Even those ugly-ass, greasy hobgoblin fucks," he said to us with no introduction.

Donut jumped to the counter and made a face. "This is what happens when you put dogs in control. Disgusting."

"Not true, Your Majesty," the gnoll said up to the ceiling. "Growler Gary tried to help. Fought from the door. The best Gary could do."

"Aren't *you* Growler Gary?" Donut asked.

"They all died," Growler Gary said.

"So what happened?" I asked. I pushed a few empty bottles away, clearing space on the bar. Everything was sticky.

"We got fucked by the Tangle—that's what happened," he said. He suddenly rolled right off the bar and clattered loudly to the floor. He groaned, followed by the clink of glass bottles. I peered over the edge as he blindly rummaged under the bar. He grasped a bottle and pulled it to his mouth, but it was empty. "If you're looking for dinner, it might be late tonight, folks. You ain't hobgoblins, are you?"

"So the ghouls came and killed everybody?" I asked. The gnoll found a full bottle and struggled to get the top off.

"That's right," he said, grunting with the effort. "Growler Gary can't leave the bar for some reason. Went out there to fight and got stopped right at the door. Jumping Jen-Jen called Growler Gary a coward. But it was like an invisible wall."

"Why don't you let hobgoblins in the bar?" Katia asked.

"Have you seen a hobgoblin?" he said. The bottle opened, and he whimpered with happiness, even as half of it spilled onto the floor.

"How was all of this the Tangle's fault?" I asked.

"Turned the whole thing into a Krakaren nest. The whole damn system. Instead of declaring bankruptcy. Sold us all out. You sure you ain't hobgoblins? Tried to fight. Wouldn't let Gary. Then afterwards that woman ripped Gary's throat out, but Growler Gary didn't die."

"He's gone crazy, Carl," Donut said. "Typical."

"Who ripped your throat out?" I asked.

"That woman. Came through and took everything from my brothers and sisters. Then she came in here and grabbed me by the throat and pulled it out. Stole all my alcohol. Didn't get the stuff under here, though. Woke up in a pile of my own blood. Growler Gary ain't no coward. Fuck Jumping Jen-Jen. Gary would've fought. Doorway was like a wall. Not a coward."

A memory tingled the back of my mind. Something I'd read in my book. I'd read through the NPC chapter earlier, and I was suddenly reminded of a particular passage.

<Crawler Azin. 17th Edition>

Some NPCs are indestructible. You can kill them, and they regenerate in a matter of minutes. If you find one of those, it means they have something on them or they know something important. Big important. The trick is finding out what that is.

<Note added by Crawler Drakea. 22nd Edition>

We found one of them and tied him to the front of our shield. Ha. The next day the Nagas patched it. Didn't make an announcement or anything, but the guy disappeared. Went back to the church to grab him again, and it wouldn't let us take him from the building. We dragged him out the door, and he exploded and then was reborn. Tried it five times before giving up. Turns out, he knew the password to the safe that held the key for the stairwell chamber.

Donut, as if she'd read my mind, asked the relevant question.

DONUT: WHY WOULD HE COME BACK TO LIFE?
CARL: In some games, you can't kill NPCs if they're necessary to complete quests. I think maybe this is the same thing.
DONUT: OR MAYBE HE'S A LIAR. HE'S A DOG. DOGS ARE LIARS.
CARL: Maybe. Let's find out if he knows or has something.

"I believe you," I said to Growler Gary. "I believe you're not a coward."

The hyena looked up at me, wide eyes registering surprise, as if he'd just realized I was there. It was awkward talking to him like this, with him on the floor, and me leaning over the bar. His eyes held my own for a moment, and I feared he was about to burst into tears.

"We're going to stop them," I continued. "The people who made it so you couldn't leave and fight are the same people we're trying to stop. But we need help. Do you think you can help us?"

"I'm useless," Growler Gary said, using "I" to refer to himself for the first time. "I'm just a bartender. They wouldn't let me fight. She was so pretty, and she called me a coward. But I tried. I couldn't leave. And then she died right in front of me. Right outside the door. She died thinking I was afraid."

"Hey," Katia said, "don't call yourself useless."

"Why?" he asked. "I am."

I leaned a little deeper over the bar. "After we're done here, we're headed to the end of the line to meet up with some friends who need our help. Is there anything at this station you think could assist us? We're going to take one of the trains up there, but there are monsters on the tracks. Plus I'm worried about the power. We're afraid we're going to get stuck."

Growler Gary closed his eyes, and I thought for certain he'd passed out again. But then he said, "You could take one of the interdiction team carts. The carts are normally driven by a pair of transit security gnolls and an interdiction repair team of five hobgoblins. Jumping Jen-Jen was a driver. I kept the marrow juice cold just for her. Sometimes they'll have a second team if the tracks need repair, too. This station services over one hundred different lines. You just dial in the line you want to go to, and the cart goes there. They're powered by batteries, so they run even if the line is out. Make sure you take a lead car. They got the front portal. Cleans everything up nice and tidy."

"That's great," I said. "We'll go check them out."

"You do that," the gnoll said. "Now let me finish this bottle."

———

"IF HE IS IMPORTANT," DONUT SAID AS WE LEFT THE BAR, "WE STILL haven't figured out why. All he did was blabber on about stuff we could figure out without him."

"Agreed," I said.

Both the repair station and the armory were indeed looted. There were empty wooden cases of hob-lobbers sitting on shelves in the repair station, along with multiple tables and empty tool shelves. There was something called a **Repair Bench** that was stupidly left behind by whoever had looted the place. I took it along with the plain tables and the shelves and the empty boxes. The armory was similarly empty, though it was filled with metal shelves designed to hold spears along with forty wooden mannequins designed to hold armor. I took them all.

From there we returned to the small yard just off the tracks. A line of carts sat there, parked in rows. In addition, six portals stood at the end of the small yard. The first five were attached to tracks. The smaller, sixth portal was up on a landing and was meant to be walked through. This last one, I realized, was a way to get to additional platforms, similar to the one at station 60. If we went through the portal, it'd lead to more portals eventually leading to various colored platforms. The map would help us walk to platforms we'd already traveled to, but the whole system gave me a headache. I was glad we didn't have to deal with it. I turned my attention to the five larger portals.

I moved to the portals before we investigated the carts. Each of the five was up against a wall, meaning none of them were pass-through portals. A manual switching station allowed one to choose which of the tracks to enter. There was a small sign above each station.

The first was a one-way portal that led to Train Yard C. The little sign could only be read using my Escape Plan skill, and it simply said, "Train Yard." I took a screenshot, and Train Yard C was a burned-out mess. A pair of large, ogre-sized ghouls stalked across the train yard, headed for the distant, knocked-over gate. Were those wrath ghouls? Yikes.

The next four portals were a little more complicated. Each sign was a long list of colored lines, each one different. Each portal had a list of 48 different colors, from orange to amaranth to pink to zomp. On each of the four lists, the colors were numbered from one to 48. I examined the first of the portals using my skill.

Ultima Corp DungeonWerx Industrial Subspace Multi-Destination Light-Duty Portal.
    Analyze? Yes/No.

I clicked **Yes**, and I scrolled to the bottom of the list.

Type: One-way selectable portal. Requires DungeonWerx Portal Selector to dial destination. If no selection is made, portal defaults to selection one: Orange Line.
    Can you pass this portal? Yes.

Environment on other side of portal: Compatible.
Visual Analysis? Yes/No.

I clicked **Yes**, and all I could see was a regular train track. I assumed it was the orange line, but I had no idea where on the line it would be.

"It looks like they can dial a destination and drive there, but I don't know how they get back," I said. "They probably have to go all the way to the end, but I'm not sure."

From there, we moved to investigate the carts. There were three different types. The first was a simple flatbed cart with two sets of four wheels on it. Each of the battered, well-worn carts was about the size of a small car. It had no controls. Just a hitch on the back along with holes around the edges, likely so equipment or a railing could be attached. This cart was like a trailer designed to be attached to the other, powered carts.

I tried to pick it up, and even with my strength I couldn't do it. I could lift one end up and drag the whole thing, but there was no way I could put the whole cart into my inventory. Just one set of four wheels and an axle alone felt as if it weighed more than a ton and a half by itself, and there were two of them. That plus the heavy wood made the prospect impossible. Even Katia couldn't do it with her mass maxed out. Not yet.

The next cart was the same thing, but with an engine on the back, like an outboard motor, with a few additional controls, including a strange glowing switch that appeared to be magical. This was by far the most common type of cart. It was basically a flatbed we could use to ride on the rails. I examined its properties.

Interdiction Auxiliary Railway Repair Cart. Contraption.
Main Passenger Line Gauged.
The simplest of the powered railway carts. Includes battery power or powered track selection option. Includes portal track selector. Interdiction teams are supposed to use these to carry *additional* personnel and supplies to repair areas as backup and

support to the more robust Rapid-Response Carts and their
teams. They are *not* supposed to be used as a primary response
vehicle.

As such, a Gnoll Transit Security Officer is not required to
run this vehicle.

The engine had a connector that allowed it to run off the third
rail power or it could run on battery power. I lifted the top of the
battery compartment and pulled out the brick-sized battery. It was
a familiar dwarven battery, and it was at 2% power.

Since these lines off the main weren't powered, it was probably
just enough juice to get the cart through one of those portals.

I had traded the rest of my Louis L'Amour books along with a
single jug of moonshine for the dwarven battery fabricator. The mole
man shopkeeper had practically begged me for the trade, having finished the books I'd given him. I'd had a sneaking suspicion the
fabricator's odd placement at the first store we came across wasn't a
coincidence, and I was glad I had. The cookbook had a short but in-
formative section on power supplies, and these batteries were common throughout the previous crawls. Each battery required four full
mana potions to fully charge. Once charged, the batteries would
supposedly last a very long time. The fabricator had come with fifty
of them. Most were at 10%–15%, though five had been fully charged
and another five were at 50%. I'd also charged up another two just
to see how it worked, giving me a total of twelve useable batteries.
Plus it only took five minutes to charge one up, though our supply
of mana potions, while healthy, was not endless.

For now, I pulled the empty battery from the cart into my inventory. If every one of these powered carts had one, that'd be another
40 plus added to my stash.

There were only ten of the last type of cart. They were pushed
into the back, lined up on two different tracks, and it didn't appear
as if they'd ever been used, which was odd, especially considering the
description of the auxiliary carts, which were heavily worn.

Each of these ten carts was about twice as long as the auxiliary ones. They had three sets of wheels instead of two. A line of seats filled the first half of the open-top cart, with cargo space in the back. There was a raised platform in the center with a small enclosed driver cabin above the main deck, making the small train car look like a flybridge game boat. The raised cabin was accessed via a small ladder. Despite the height of the cabin, the train was still shorter than the typical colored-line subway car.

The engine took up the entire back of the train, much larger than the engine on the auxiliary cart. The battery compartment took three batteries.

But the carts' most distinct feature was the odd blade that ran in front of them, almost like a flat squeegee. It was a wide blade that appeared to be the exact width of a regular subway car. It ran across the front of the cart, close to the ground. The pole had two track-shaped indentations in the center, so when the cart ran along the tracks, it appeared the blade traveled right against the ground, molded to fit. The only give was the port side of the blade, which rose at two 90-degree-angles, allowing for the third rail to pass by underneath.

"Weird," I said, examining the train. How did the blade thing work? It seemed it would immediately snag on debris while the train zoomed down the track, breaking off or, worse, wrecking the whole damn thing. I read the description.

Interdiction Rapid-Response Railway Repair Cart. Contraption.

Main Passenger Line Gauged.

The main workhorse vehicle of the Hobgoblin Interdiction Team. Includes battery power or powered track selection option. Includes portal track selector. Includes dual-destination, selectable debris scoop.

When it comes to cleaning up a crashed vehicle on the tracks, nothing works better, faster, and more efficiently than the Hobgoblin Interdiction Team.

In the rare case of an accident on the Iron Tangle, one of these vehicles is immediately dispatched to clear the line.

This cart will move up a line at up to five times the speed of the regular passenger cars. The debris scoop will safely transport any active and running trains and their passengers back to the rail yard. Once the wreck is reached, the debris scoop is switched to abyss mode, clearing the line of the damage. In case of a broken rail, the debris scoop automatically detects and removes anomalies and track breaches, allowing for the hobgoblins to do their thing.

Unfortunately, the corporation running the Iron Tangle has little trust in the hobgoblins and requires security to escort these vehicles at all times. As such, this cart may only be started by a pair of gnolls.

"Whoa," I said. "We need to figure this thing out. That weird blade thing is a mobile portal."

I saw how the car worked. The blade had to be turned on the entire time. The contraption traveled through the tunnel on the rails, and the portal filled the entire tunnel ahead of the cart, tossing everything on the tracks—including other trains—to one of two places, either a train yard or the abyss.

"It says only a gnoll can drive it," Katia said. "Two gnolls. Do you think we can remove the portal part and just use that? I wonder if we can somehow detach it from the cart and bring it with us. The blades are wide, but they don't look heavy."

"That's what I was thinking," I said. I moved to examine the metal blade in front of the first cart. The other two cart types had bodies made of wood. This was made of metal. My portal skill didn't work on it because it wasn't turned on, though I suspected we were out of luck. I suspected the entire cart was part of the mechanism, not just the blades. "Shit, I don't think that'll work." I started to ascend the ladder to the cockpit.

Donut jumped to my shoulder as Mongo sniffed about the train.

The ladder was covered in dust. It had clearly never been used. "We need to get that Growler Gary out here. That's probably what he's for. To drive the train," Donut said.

"It has to be," I agreed as I opened the door to the driver's cabin. "But we need two of them, and if he can't leave the bar, then how would that work?"

I looked down at the controls, and then I understood.

"Oh," I said. "Fuck."

BAUTISTA: Okay. So somebody found the sinopia line. That's about five levels deeper than where most of us are, but there's a group down there. For my group, there's a gangway up one level to the mindaro line. The gangway is still intact, but those wall monitors are congregating near there. We'll have to fight our way up, but I think we can make it. That only leaves one more group heading toward the grullo line. I think that's everybody.

CARL: Good work. Let me get this first part done, and then we'll start working on getting you guys through.

BAUTISTA: Thank you, brother.

CARL: Don't thank me yet. I have no idea if this crazy shit is going to work. And I still have something very unpleasant to do.

"Hey, buddy," I said as we entered the Downward Dog. "You awake, Gary?"

Growler Gary didn't respond. I hesitantly walked to the counter and looked over the edge at the sleeping gnoll. He hadn't moved. He clutched on to the same bottle as before, like he was holding a baby. It was now empty.

"We should do it now while he's still asleep," Donut said.

I nodded. "Killing a guy while he's asleep seems like such a dick move," I said. "But you're right. If he's going to just wake up again after we do it, maybe he won't even notice. Plus I guess it's not really killing him if he's just going to resurrect."

Katia remained in the personal space. She knew and understood what had to be done, but she didn't want to be a part of it. That was okay. I understood. I didn't want to be a part of it, either.

She was still desperately trying to form into a gnoll shape that would trick the magical key into accepting her. So far she'd been unlucky, despite getting it to 98% accuracy.

It was painfully clear what the dungeon wanted us to do.

You will not break me. Fuck you all.

Mongo had recently risen to level 23, but the dinosaur was woefully behind the rest of us. We'd decided ahead of time to allow the dinosaur to kill the gnoll.

"Face first," Donut said. "Then the hands. Don't eat the hands. Give them to me."

Mongo squawked excitedly.

The interdiction cart only turned on with a pair of gnoll hands on a magical sensor plate. The two plates were far enough apart that a single gnoll couldn't do it, but if the hands were no longer attached to the body . . .

We'd first tried farming a body part from one of the corpses strewn out in the station, but there was absolutely nothing useful. Every single gnoll had been chewed to hell. There was no way that wasn't on purpose. *You fucking assholes,* I thought for the hundredth time. Then came Katia's insistence that she could change into a gnoll and activate the train cart that way. That didn't work, either, though when she emerged that last time, the system designated her as a gnoll. The skill, when she used it for this sort of thing, was terrifying.

She'd tossed all of her most recent points into constitution, but seeing her as a perfect gnoll made me realize maybe those earlier points she'd tossed in charisma weren't such a bad idea. If we continued to work on her self-confidence, we'd have the perfect spy on our hands.

"Go," Donut said.

Mongo jumped over the counter and chomped down on the sleeping gnoll's head. It killed him instantly. The creature had a single gold coin in his inventory. Mongo quickly and efficiently chomped off the hyena's two arms right at the elbow, horking them onto the counter.

"Yuck," I said, picking up both of the hairy severed arms. I tossed them both into my inventory. "Sorry, Gary."

THE PLAN WAS SIMPLE, BUT IT WASN'T WITHOUT RISK. IT WAS A "Carl plan," as Donut called it. After talking with Bautista, we learned there were three groups of people trapped at the abyss. Since the colored lines all emptied into the massive pit at different heights, coming into the giant crater from different directions, and since the walkways that circled the pit's interior were now blasted to hell, these groups couldn't reach each other. We had to make three separate trips.

We didn't need to drive the train ourselves. We just had to get it started and send it along.

That was okay. As long as we got the engine and scoop portal turned on so everything it touched went to the train yard, and we got the interdiction cart on the correct track, it would speed along the line all the way to the end, scooping up everything on the path and sending it to the train yard. The stranded crawlers would stand on the tracks and allow the train to hit them, thus also getting teleported to the train yard.

We had a list of almost 200 colored lines to choose from, and after almost two hours of going back and forth, we discovered three lines that would work.

That, at least, was the first draft of the plan. Both Katia and Bautista pointed out a few problems with the idea.

First off, if the track itself was sufficiently busted, the cart would derail, despite the portal, and it wouldn't make it all the way to the end. We hadn't tested these things yet, and we didn't know how well they worked. For all we knew, it'd face-plant the moment it hit something.

Secondly, if we scooped up *everything* on the path, the crawlers waiting at the end of the line would be tossed face-first into a pile of crashed trains and possibly thousands upon thousands of ghouls and mobs suffering from stage three DTs. It'd be less dangerous to just throw them into the pit.

We had ten of the rapid-response trains to work with. After thinking on it some, we came up with an alternative idea.

We'd send two trains down each track. The first would have the portal tuned into the abyss. So the crashed trains and all the mobs and ghouls running up and down the line would be hit by the portal and sent directly into the pit. Fifteen minutes after the first train, we'd send a second train through, but this one would have the portal tuned to the train station. The crawlers waiting at the end of the line would have to get the hell out of the way of that first train. Bautista said the tunnels opened up as they approached the pit, and that wouldn't be a problem.

This plan wouldn't work if the track was broken. We had a contingency in place for that eventuality. One I hoped we wouldn't have to utilize.

"What if there are people on the track we don't know about?" Katia said. "We'll send them into the abyss. Also, how loud are these things? Will they even know when to expect them?"

I shrugged. "We're talking about three colored lines out of possibly thousands. By now most everybody who hasn't given up has gotten to a train yard. We've spread the word out as much as we can. It's a risk, but this is the best idea we have. Don't worry about the trains being loud enough. I already have a plan for that."

While Bautista and I had spent those two hours playing the telephone game trying to figure out the three lines that would work for our plan, Donut, Katia, and I started the process of moving the train carts out of the way to make way for the rapid-response carts, which were shoved in the back of the parking area. The small carts we simply pushed onto the main track in front of our vermilion engine. Then we drove the auxiliary carts out of the way. Most of them had just enough battery power to drive. Once they were safely out of the way, I pulled all the batteries. We also started the process of taking apart one of the engines and putting all the pieces into my inventory. Katia led this process. She had a wealth of knowledge about engines thanks to her Earth Hobby potion. She'd received the Gear Head knowledge base, and it was mightily useful here. She was certain we'd be able to reconstruct the engine and put it on something else.

The rapid-response carts wouldn't budge until they were turned on. I climbed the stairs of the first one now. I pulled one of Growler Gary's arms from inventory and placed it on the hand-shaped key console. "Here goes nothing," I said to Donut. I held my breath.

The console glowed green. I relaxed. I had to put a rock on top of the hand to keep it in place while I moved to the second key console on the other side of the small cockpit. It was only about eight feet away, but it was just far enough that a single gnoll couldn't activate both at once.

I placed Growler Gary's second hand on the key.

Warning: You must use your left hand to activate the key.

"Fuck," I said.

"Mongo," Donut called, "come on, we're going back to the bar."

GROWLER GARY WAS SOBER WHEN WE RETURNED. APPARENTLY THE act of resurrection did that, which was unfortunate for everybody involved. He was desperately searching through his stash for another bottle when we arrived. He wouldn't find one. We'd taken the rest.

"You're back," he said. "Sorry, dinner isn't ready. Growler Gary seems to be low on supplies. Someone drank them all."

He didn't know we'd killed him, but he did remember us. I sighed.

"Hey, Gary," I said, "I'm really sorry about this."

He looked up at us, wiping his hands on his fur. "Sorry about what?"

Mongo leaped across the tavern, landed on the counter, and chomped him right on the head. It sounded like a walnut being crunched.

Five minutes later, we had the first of the portal carts turned on. We started the engine and positioned it in front of the third portal. Number 17 on the list was the sinopia line. The DungeonWerx portal selector was nothing more than a pair of handles with numbers. I put the first to one and the second to seven. The little selector changed to 17 on the dust-covered screen.

We turned a switch, turning on the front portal. The blade in front of the cart hummed, and a large tunnel-shaped portal appeared, throbbing. It looked a little different than the static-television-channel style of most open portals. This was like a frosted mirror, allowing us to see through it. Sort of.

"Hopefully the act of pushing a portal through a portal isn't like dividing by zero or anything," I muttered as I moved to the front of the train to investigate the magical doorway. I had a horrifying thought of it blowing up. There was a section on portals in my book, but I'd only skimmed it and hadn't seen anything like that. I did remember something about arrows with small portals at the end of them. If they didn't cause an issue with being added to inventory or passing through doorways, hopefully this would be okay, too. Hopefully.

Ultima Corp DungeonWerx Subspace Heavy-Duty, Self-Adjusting Clean-up Portal.

Type: One-way selectable portal.

Can you pass this portal? Yes.

Environment on other side of portal: Warning. Drill down for more information.

Visual Analysis? Yes/No.

The portal was switched onto the abyss, and I pulled up the screenshot. It looked as if it just jumped things in the middle of the air over the pit. So anything that got caught up in the portal would fall a good half of a mile before it hit the ground. I clicked on the environmental warning, and a new page of numbers appeared. Elevation above solid ground was highlighted, confirming that was the issue. I went back to the cab and switched the selector to the train yard instead of the abyss, and the environmental warning went away.

I put the portal back to the abyss, and I went to remove the hands so I could start the next train.

The moment I pulled one of the hands away, the train shut off. I'd been hoping once the train started, it no longer needed the hand keys.

"Fuck," I said. *"Fuck, fuck, fuck."*

"Mongo," Donut said, "back to the bar."

———

IN THE END, WE HAD TO COLLECT A TOTAL OF 14 LEFT HANDS FROM Growler Gary. We could have stopped at 12, but I wanted to have an extra pair, in case we needed to drive that seventh cart.

Gary only fought back the first few times. We were too strong for him. He hid in the back of the bar each time, huddled in the corner, holding on to his spear. He whimpered like an injured dog, and the sound hurt my heart.

"I'm sorry," I said when we came for the fifth hand. He jabbed at Mongo, who screeched gleefully as we approached.

"If you're sorry, then why are you doing it?" he said. "Get back! Get the fuck away from me!"

The floor of the back room was slick with blood. Upon regeneration, every body part remaining in the tavern disappeared except items we placed into our inventory. But the blood remained, and it was everywhere.

"Everyone stop," I said. "Mongo, wait." The dinosaur looked to Donut, who waved him down. He squawked with disappointment.

"I'll tell you," I said. "You deserve to know why we have to do this." And I explained it to him. I told him exactly what we were doing and why we were doing it. He stared up at me, wide-eyed and afraid as I told him we'd have to kill him ten more times.

"So you need Growler Gary," he finally said, looking down at his own hand. "Gary never realized that was the problem with those carts. Jumping Jen-Jen and the other drivers were always complaining, but he . . . I didn't understand. That was why they never went out. The hobgoblins took their own carts instead, but they couldn't clear the crashed trains without the portals. Gary's not a driver. Hadn't realized it worked that way." He looked up at me. "Ten more times?"

"Ten more times," I said.

"And this is to get the people who killed my friends?"

"Yes."

"Do you have any alcohol on you?"

"I do," I said.

"Will you give me some when it is done?"

"Absolutely."

He put the spear down and walked back to the bar. He cracked his neck. He looked over at Mongo and said, "Do your best to make sure it doesn't hurt."

27

"HE ENDED UP BEING REALLY BRAVE," DONUT SAID AS WE LASHED
the last hand to the pedestal, "especially for a dog. It's kind of sad."

"Kind of?" I said. "Everything about this sucks. God, we really
need duct tape for this." We had to use rope to keep the hands in
place. If one of them fell off, then all of this would be for nothing.

Katia, who hadn't participated in any of this, had returned to her
human shape. She was beating herself up over her inability to get the
carts started on her own, though in the end it hadn't mattered. Our
plan to hit the crawlers stuck at the abyss with portals required six
trains to work, and no matter how she looked at it, we would've still
had to collect several of those hands.

Bautista had fought his way up to the correct station, though he'd
lost almost fifty guys during the battle. A few of the crawlers could
fly short distances, but apparently there was some sort of black hole
effect on the pit the closer you got to the middle. They'd flown off
the walkway to fire arrows and spells at the lizards—called wall
monitors—and gotten themselves sucked in. Several more died when
one of the gangways collapsed.

Now that we had a portal straight to the abyss, we'd been brain-
storming alternate plans in case this didn't work, but so far everything that seemed viable at first kept fizzling out. None of our plans
were feasible, especially since there were so many people trapped
there. We couldn't use a flyer to go through the portal and bring
hats. We tried a rope attached to a weight, too, with thoughts maybe
we could dangle a bag over the massive hole and Bautista's crew

could try *something* to get to it. But the moment we started to feed
the test rope into the portal, the rope went tight for about a half of
a second and then started to tingle. Surprised, I dropped it, and the
whole thing disappeared. I was lucky I hadn't gotten dragged in
with it. We decided to stop experimenting after that.

I announced I needed to use the restroom and went to the personal space and pulled up the chapter on portals in the cookbook.

<Note added by Crawler Milk. 6th Edition>

Portals are hard to understand. It seems like there are dozens of
different types that all work in different ways. Sometimes they're
like doors, and you don't even know they're there. Sometimes, like
the entryways between floors, you just need to touch them and they
work. Sometimes you have to put your hand through, and you start
to feel like you're getting dragged. If you let yourself go slack, you
get pulled in. But you can still break free. It's not consistent. Sometimes you have to be big enough to fit through it to work, and
sometimes a portal the size of a button will toss you into a monster
den. Teleport traps are the worst.

I added a note about the different brands of portals, but I didn't
have time for writing. I'd add more later. Since I didn't have to have
the book open to add to it, I'd been spending a lot of time mentally
writing in that second, hidden scratch pad, mostly when we were on
a train or sitting down to eat. I didn't know if any of it made sense.
I wasn't a writer, and whenever I started to mentally type my feelings
onto the pad, I couldn't tell if it was coherent or just bullshit. I assumed some future crawler would find my chapter and just think I
was being a whiny bitch.

We had everything lined up and ready to go. If all went as planned,
we guesstimated it would take about 8–10 hours for the first three
trains to reach the end of the line. The system said these things went
five times faster than the normal trains. I really hoped this worked.

Also, it turned out while every single one of the portals on the rapid-response carts was a two-way switch where one could select the abyss or a train yard, the train yards themselves were different on each one. The train yard number was helpfully painted on the edge of each cart, likely so the workers would know which cart to use when an interdiction was required. I supposed in the end it didn't really matter which cart we used, though the three separate groups at the end of the line would all be sent off to different instances of the train yard. We picked three where we knew people were already holed up at the local version of station 36.

Only one of the carts had a portal that was tuned to Train Yard E, the same yard where we had come in earlier, and the same one where we could easily return to the *Nightmare* and Imani's group if we needed. We'd keep that cart here with us.

Meanwhile, Imani and Li Jun and everybody else from station 101 were in the process of fortifying station 36. They'd disabled the vermilion train on the track, blocking any monster coming down the line. I was afraid that'd mean the blister ghouls coming from station 72 would simply turn around and head back toward us at 75, but it appeared they were congregating in front of the train. Not that it mattered much. There were literally dozens of lines that fed into that station, and they were in a constant state of battle, pushing the invaders back. I hoped they'd be able to hold out.

"Okay, everybody cover your ears," I said as I finished placing the final trap onto the sixth cart. "I'm putting a delay on all of them, but I'm going to set this one off just to make sure it works like we want."

"How am I supposed to cover my ears, Carl?" Donut asked.

"Okay, go to the other side of the station, then. Remember last time? It's loud as shit."

The regular subway cars were big and heavy and thundered through the tunnels. These carts made hardly any noise at all. As Katia pointed out earlier, that'd be a problem for those waiting at the other end of the line. Therefore we needed one last touch so the crawlers could hear the portal coming.

I reached down and set the one-minute delay on the last of the traps. I had one on all six of the carts. This one would go first. The others all had a 30-minute delay, but I wanted to make double sure that the delay function worked as intended before I sent it through the portal. I engaged the engine, double-checked to make sure the portal was set to the abyss and that the car was dialed to the correct portal. Everything was a go.

"What do you think it's going to be?" I called over to Katia, who stood by the side of the tracks, covering her ears.

"It'll be 'Wonderwall'! I just know it," Donut shouted from the far side of the platform. "It's the greatest song of all time!"

"'Wonderwall'?" Katia said, turning and laughing. "You mean the song by Oasis?"

Peaking at Number 1 on November 21, 1981, it's "Physical"!

The alarm trap activated, and the Olivia Newton-John song started playing so loud, I took a small amount of damage. I pushed the throttle of the train and jumped down. I watched as it shot down the track, hit the portal, and disappeared.

I rushed forward to get a screenshot so I could see if the train had actually made it, but I could hear it. It was distant, barely audible, and it sounded as if it was far below us, but it was there. The line it had transferred to was physically nearby. I took the screenshot, and I could see the end of the train, already far away. The scoop portal was still intact.

Holy shit, it worked.

CARL: Bautista. Sinopia line is on its way.
BAUTISTA: What was the song?
CARL: "Physical" by Olivia Newton-John.
BAUTISTA: Damn. I had one gold on "Eye of the Tiger." I don't think anybody picked that one.
CARL: There's no way people are going to guess the song. The trap uses any song that ever charted on the Billboard Hot

100. There's gotta be a million choices. I'm going to send
the grullo and mindaro trains now. Then in fifteen minutes
we'll send the second trains tuned to the yards. Your team
will end up at Yard Q. There's already about 400 people
guarding station 36 at that one. Remember to take the
employee line. It should be clear.

BAUTISTA: Okay, buddy. Thanks.

"Monsters! Monsters!" Donut cried, running up just as I saw the
wave of red dots on the vermilion track. There had to be about thirty
of them. They were moving fast.

"Shit," I said. "Okay, let's get ready."

"Carl, they're really, really big. I think they're those stage three
DT monsters. I don't think we can handle them!"

We only had about thirty seconds to decide what to do. If we hid,
they'd probably stream around the subway engine car we had parked
here and continue down the line, where they'd eventually come to the
disabled train on the track right before station 36, mixing in with the
blister ghouls. That'd be fine if they stayed put. But I remembered
how big those fuckers were, and if they managed to break into the car
and open a path down to station 36, it'd be another weight on the
shoulders of Imani and Li Jun. Though I strongly suspected they'd be
dealing with these guys whether we liked it or not.

Still, we couldn't just let that happen. I had an idea.

"Hide," I said. I turned toward the Downward Dog and started
jogging. "Come on, guys, let them pass. But as soon as they do, we
gotta move."

KATIA AND DONUT SENT THE LAST THREE RAPID-RESPONSE CARTS
through the portals while I attached the explosives to the back of the
vermilion train. I needed to get this done quick. I was placing them
on the short shelf in front of the door that'd turn into the between-
train gangway when it was properly attached to another train. I had

to tie everything together with a rope and then use the door to keep it in place.

"You know," I said up to the ceiling while I worked, "If any of you guys want to send me duct tape, it'll make this sort of thing a lot easier. Rope sucks for this stuff, and pus is too expensive to waste. I'd be able to make bigger bombs. Just saying."

Even though the battered vermilion engine faced the wrong direction, it did have that half-assed standard-issue cowcatcher device in the back, which really doubled as the connector mechanism. Still, I was afraid this wasn't going to work. Either way, it would be spectacular. I warned Li Jun and Imani what I was doing, and they agreed to it.

Yes, I knew I could probably use one of the interdiction carts, and that'd clear the line much more easily. But I wanted to see if I'd get experience if I did it this way. Plus I really wanted to see if this would work. Other than the land mines I'd used to derail that first train, I hadn't gotten the opportunity to use much explosives on this floor, so I jumped at the opportunity to sandwich a bunch of ghouls and monsters between two trains.

Nobody was on the tracks on this line, so the worst that could happen was it went off prematurely. Or it didn't go off at all. Or I caved in the line. Or I killed myself.

The plan was to reunite this engine with the rest of its old train.

ELLE: Hey, Carl. She's not here. I did as you asked and went through every single person. No four-armed cobra lady. There are some pretty weird ones, though. There's a guy here who is a mushroom. Why would you turn yourself into a mushroom? He looks like a penis. Like one of those weird ones that's really wide and short. My boyfriend before my Barry had a dick like that. It smelled like mushrooms, too.

CARL: Shit. We know she's alive. Where the hell is she, then? Maybe try sidling up with one of the former Daughters and asking them.

ELLE: Already did. Talked to that fairy with the two mage
    daughters. She claims the bitch is not answering anyone.
    She might have come in with the rest of us, but if she did,
    she took off, and nobody says they've seen her. She's
    probably off pouting somewhere.

CARL: Okay. Everything else good?

ELLE: Same ol' shit. Imani is mother-hen-ing every damn person
    in here, even though they're all terrified of her. Your friend
    Li Jun doesn't know his best friend is in love with his
    sister even though she's turned into a demon, and most of
    those girls from Hekla's group are as helpless as I was
    when I was still in the wheelchair. On top of that, some
    crazy asshole who doesn't want everybody to think he's a
    crazy asshole is throwing a train full of explosives in our
    direction. So, you know, typical day.

I laughed out loud as I tied the last piece of hobgoblin dynamite
onto the pile. The train would splatter random ghouls on the way
down the track, but I didn't want the bomb going off until it hit one
of the larger stage three monsters, who'd hopefully be in the midst
of the gathering ghoul horde. The hobgoblin dynamite was much
more stable than the regular goblin stuff and would, in theory, survive multiple impacts. Still, the bundle of dynamite was up high and
shouldn't go off until it was triggered. For that, I used a device I'd
already built in anticipation for just this sort of thing. It was part of
my first prototype for the land mine. A long pole with an impact-
detonated hob-lobber at the end. The pole was too high to hit the
regular blister ghouls, but it would hit one of the giant stage three
monsters. Or, if it missed, it'd go off when the train crashed into the
back of the other train. Or if the whole thing derailed. Hopefully.

BAUTISTA: The trains are definitely working. It's raining
    crashed trains and monsters into the abyss. I haven't seen
    any crawlers fall thankfully. But it's a lot of those giant

monsters. Are you getting experience for this? They're
splattering across the bottom of the abyss like hail.

CARL: No, unfortunately. The system can be damn stingy
sometimes. You never know what's going to give it to you.

BAUTISTA: Yeah. My pets usually give me experience if they
kill something, but not as much as if I had done it myself.
Sometimes, though, I don't get any experience at all, and
every once in a while, I get a big bonus. I don't know why.

CARL: Your pets? I didn't know you had pets.

BAUTISTA: It's complicated. Most other crawlers think it's a
spell. I don't want them to know the truth. It's kind of
embarrassing. I'll explain it if we ever get together.

I liked Bautista, I thought as I finished building my train bomb,
but his Tigran race made him look like a tiger that had been vomited upon by a Lisa Frank notebook. I didn't know how anything
could embarrass him.

It took a minute to get the pole positioned correctly, but once it
was, I didn't waste any more time.

"Everybody say goodbye to the vermilion train," I called over my
shoulder as I reentered the gore-filled engine car. I waded through the
starting-to-stink-even-worse entrails and bodies and hit the controls,
easing the engine up to full speed. Just as I prepared to jump out the
front window of the backward-moving train, I spied something sitting on the floor. It was one of Eva's two sabers. She'd dropped it when
Donut had raised Hekla from the dead. It'd fallen into the gore, and
I'd forgotten about it. I grabbed it and pulled it into my inventory as
I slid out the front window and jumped heavily to the track below.

Christ, I thought as I hit the gravel. *I need another shower.* I turned
to watch the train rush backward down the track. It wouldn't be
long before it hit something.

The ground suddenly shook with a distant explosion. It didn't
come from the train, which I could still see. But the ground rumbled, like distant thunder. Dust fell from the ceiling.

What the hell was that?

IMANI: Carl, are you okay?
CARL: That wasn't my bomb. Mine is still on its way.
IMANI: I thought you blew yourself up.
CARL: Not yet.

Donut, Katia, and Mongo came jogging up as I pulled myself off the track. "What was that?" Katia asked.

"Carl, what did you do?" Donut asked. "I thought you killed yourself."

"I don't know," I said. "It sounded far, far away. But it was big."

I pulled up my chat to see if anybody knew what it was, and I saw with dismay that a group of four crawlers I'd tossed into a group I'd called "Yard F" were now all dead. For a horrifying minute, I thought maybe this was my fault, that I'd done something because of the portals. But that didn't make any sense. None of the carts were tuned to that area.

But then I remembered that those guys weren't trying to defend their station 36. They were part of a team that was attempting to kill the blister ghoul generator at one of the station 72s. It had to be pretty far away, but it was still loud and powerful enough that we felt it here.

"Holy crap," I said. "I think they blew the soul crystal. I warned them that it was dangerous. Goddamnit."

That group had been something like 300–400 people. The last I heard, they were going to attempt to fight their way to the generator and remove the crystal or disable the machine.

I messaged everybody and told them what I suspected had happened.

CARL: Imani and Elle, you should get a group together and send
    them to 60 to see if they can find a platform that'll take
    them to that F line. I don't know what the color was, but

somebody else might know. If the generator blew, everything over there will be dead, but the stairwells might still be open.

IMANI: I was just thinking the same thing. If we don't know the colors attached to the F station, how can we find it, though?

CARL: Last time I went through station 60, there was a dwarf sitting there at the entrance to all the colored-line portals. His name is Tizquick. Seek him out and ask him if he knows.

ELLE: I'll go. I'll grab a squad and we'll . . . Holy shit!

The moment she said it, I heard and felt the new explosion. A whole line of experience notifications appeared. This one *was* my work. Not only had my train bomb gone off; it had killed a bunch of mobs. And I had gotten experience for it. More than I expected. I hit level 35. I didn't get any achievements, which was kind of irritating, but my Explosives Handling skill ticked up to 11.

ELLE: Yikes, Carl. That knocked everybody off their feet. You're lucky I can fly.

CARL: Shit. Sorry about that. Is everyone okay?

IMANI: Carl, let's not do that again. Okay? I think everybody is fine. People guarding that entrance took some hearing damage, but nothing permanent. I think that line is good and sealed off now.

ELLE: I think the mushroom guy shit himself.

I should have put the bomb bundle together at my sapper's table. That way I could've seen and adjusted the bomb's total yield. Just the act of putting anything explosive on the table had a tendency to increase its total yield, but I could now easily adjust it up and down. Hobgoblin dynamite was much more powerful than the regular stuff. In fact, next time I went into the crafting room, I'd put together some different-sized bundles so I had everything ready to go.

I sighed, thinking of everything we needed to do. Part of me really wished we had a hundred or more of these carts. That way we could strategically park them around the stairwells. But as it was, they had so many entrances that it wasn't feasible. Plus we only had one Growler Gary. We still didn't know how long until the portal carts would reach the abyss. The level timer was now at two days and twenty hours. That meant we had just over a day until Mordecai returned. I wondered if we had enough time to go back to the train yards to build a few more train bombs. That'd be a great way to farm more experience.

And while we were now seeing mobs suffering stage three of the DTs, we still hadn't seen what happened when the DTs killed them. I had a suspicion of what it was going to be, but how that would be implemented, I had no idea.

"Carl," Donut called, "you pissed off the ghouls. Now they're heading toward us!"

Sure enough, with the tunnel officially sealed off, the ghouls being generated at 72 had stopped heading toward 36 and now were coming this way. I could already see them shuffling up toward us on the edge of my map.

Shit, I thought, thinking once again of Growler Gary. We'd collected one extra pair of hands from the poor gnoll, but it turned out we were actually one pair short.

I couldn't use the portal carts to protect the others, but we could certainly use it to protect ourselves right here and right now.

"Guys," I said, "help me position one of the carts on the track. Then we gotta go talk to Gary again."

———

WE PLACED THE TURNED-ON PORTAL INTO THE TUNNEL, BLOCKING it like a cork. The blister ghouls didn't even pause. They dropped like lemmings right into the abyss. We had the cart parked at the edge of the vermilion line. My explosion appeared to have knocked the power out. We had to run the carts off of battery power, but that was fine. I now had plenty of them.

We had the second cart, the one with two fresh hands lashed to it, pointed in the other direction on the track. Only a handful of additional stage three monsters had appeared over the past few hours. According to the prattle on my chat, the stage three monsters were mostly heading toward station 24. They were running down the tracks, reaching outrageous speeds. But they were also coming up from the train yards, so they were either riding the roller-coaster line—though I didn't know how—or they were getting portaled there. I suspected maybe those neighborhood bosses at the Krakaren drug dens had something to do with that. But the monsters weren't actually entering stop 24. They would stop and camp just outside of the station, oftentimes fighting with one another.

The few who did come down our track from the north did not voluntarily throw themselves into the pit. Instead, they stood there at the edge, growling and snapping with their round mouths while I observed them through the distorted haze of the tunnel-width portal.

We'd spent the past few hours grinding against the constant stream of ghouls. I'd turn off the south-facing portal, and we'd advance and kill. I practiced with my xistera some, and Donut was practicing with mounted attacks. Katia practiced with forming spikes on her arms and using them as weapons.

She also spent some time in her smaller form with Eva's saber. The description said it was part of a set and only magical when the two weapons were together. Otherwise, the enchanted saber, called **The Left Fang of the Green Sultan**, offered no buffs or power-ups. That was good, however, as it meant Eva had also lost her main weapon.

The level 20 ghouls did not pose a serious challenge, but they were useful for practicing new techniques, if not for experience.

The stage three monsters, I knew, would be a much better trial. We had a new technique we needed to try out, and it required a higher-tier, stronger monster to test it on.

While the DT monsters didn't voluntarily throw themselves into the portal, I knew I could curate our battle experience on that side easily by hopping onto the cart and pushing it forward, sucking in the stage three monsters until there was only one left. The portal, when tuned to the abyss, was unforgiving. Like with the rope we tried earlier, if just a tiny portion of the creature touched the edge of the magical gateway, the whole thing was sucked in like a strand of spaghetti.

Bautista was giving me a running update of all the oddities that were raining into the abyss. We still had an estimated two hours left before the carts would arrive. We didn't know for certain that all three carts were still moving, but I was hopeful based on the sheer amount of stuff falling into the pit.

We weren't ready for how powerful the stage three monster was. The thing was stronger than a regular neighborhood boss. The system didn't allow us to properly examine the creatures through the window of the portal's back side, so I couldn't read the description until we were ready to fight.

But one thing was obvious even before I turned off the portal. It didn't matter what sort of monster was the original source of the creature, whether it be a massive ogre or a tiny rat-sized mob. By the time they reached stage three of the DTs, they were all pretty much the same creature: a hippo-sized monstrosity with thrashing tentacles on its back. Instead of a normal face, they held nothing but a round mouth circled with teeth. There was a skull there visible through its transparent, jelly-like skin, a talisman of the creature it once was. For this one, it was a small skull, much smaller than the bearlike skulls we'd seen before. The creatures looked overinflated, like they'd explode at any moment. The things bulged with veins, reminding me of the second boss we faced, the Juicer. The tentacles were thick and meaty, with round, thrashing mouths at the end.

"Okay, get ready," I said to Katia. Donut stood back with Mongo on the platform while I sat up on the raised cockpit of the rapid-response cart. I was afraid the monster would trash the cart, so the plan was to back it up and out of danger. I'd then leap down to engage while Katia did her thing from the edge of the platform.

Katia rolled back and formed into the sentinel gun. Three spider-like legs formed, turning her into a tripod. The flesh-colored shield went up, and the automatic crossbow, which had been sitting in her inventory, appeared, locking into place just behind the shield. A firing slit formed, which she could open and close like a mouth.

"I'm ready," she said. She'd formed a pair of eyes and a mouth just behind and above the lump of flesh that held the crossbow, allowing her to peer down onto her target. The plan was to eventually form eyes strategically on the exterior of the large half-moon-shaped shield, but she wasn't quite ready for that.

"Okay, here we go," I said.

I pushed forward with the cart, and the single monstrosity scattered back, having seen his friends sucked away earlier. I reversed the throttle and quickly backed up, turning off the portal that blocked the tunnel. I jumped from the cart's cockpit, crunching onto the gravel. The monster continued to run away for a good ten or twelve more seconds before realizing he'd been bamboozled. Now a distant speck down the track, he stopped and turned back toward us. He howled indignantly and charged.

Razor Fox. Level 22.

Warning: This mob is suffering from the DTs. It is in stage three of three.

In stage three, this mob's form has changed, and it bears very little resemblance to its original self. Kind of like how all you humans did after you finally got out of quarantine. It is now covered with multiple tentacles. If this monster has recently fed on another living creature, the contents of its stomach may be quite valuable. Or toxic. Or explosive. Or worse. That's what makes these guys so fun.

Unfortunately for them, this form is only temporary. The DTs are always fatal.

I'd explain to you what a Razor Fox is here, but it's pointless because this isn't a Razor Fox anymore. It's a shame, really. I kinda love those ninja-star-throwing fuckers. But all is not lost. We'll have normal versions of these guys on the fifth floor, too. Too bad you won't be seeing them since you're probably about to get ripped to shreds.

A moment passed, and then it was in range. Katia opened fire. *Thwap, thwap, thwap, thwap.* The bolts shot out of the large crossbow, coming at about two a second, which was pretty damn fast, but not nearly as fast as it'd been before when Hekla owned it. The crossbow was autoloading, cocking, and firing. All she had to do was hold the prod down, and it'd start spamming bolts like one of those tennis ball machines.

Each magical, razor-tipped bolt was about twenty inches long. The bolts disappeared on their own about a minute after being fired, but that was plenty of time to do some serious damage. Hekla's bolts had been fire tipped and sometimes electrically charged, but we'd lost whatever caused that buff when we lost access to the rest of Hekla's gear. The monster bayed as the bolts tore at its face and side, like a nail gun. Each hit knocked its health down, but only a tiny bit.

What the hell? How strong were these assholes?

One of the side effects of Katia forming into these odd shapes was that it confused monsters. Like when she was the train's scoop, the mobs hadn't realized she was living flesh and hadn't attacked her directly. This mob, despite being riddled with holes, reacted the same way. The only living creature he saw was me. He howled again and charged.

The thing was terrifyingly fast. I loaded a banger and twirled, tossing the metal projectile directly at the round mouth. The ball shattered teeth as I scored a hit. It made a strangled noise and stopped, sliding on the rail. Katia continued to pump it with bolts, and now Donut joined the fray, tossing magic missiles into the creature from Mongo's back.

The monster whimpered as it tried to dislodge the metal ball in its throat. I loaded another, this one a half-strength impact-detonated hob-lobber. It was too close for full strength. I fired again, again getting it into the monster's giant mouth. I took out another tooth, like I was playing a game at the carnival. *One more, and I win a prize.* There was a muffled *thump.* Its tentacles thrashed about, one of them grasping a wooden railroad tie and breaking it in half. The monster was no longer focused on me or anybody else. It was starting to look like a hedgehog from all the bolts. Injury to its body only did minor damage. We had to get inside its mouth.

I started to shout for everybody to focus on the area when it suddenly exploded. Sizzling gore showered the track. It'd blown from the inside out, like a water balloon filled with Beefaroni.

The battle was over just as quickly as it started.

"Jesus," I said, "I don't even know how we killed it. Either those bolts suck ass, or that thing is tough."

"Carl, I didn't get any experience at all," Donut said. "These things cheat."

Katia returned to her regular form. She wore the backpack to make the sentinel gun, but only had enough metal to form the shield.

"I don't think it's the bolts," she said. "I think the body might be like living armor. When I hit the tentacles, it did a lot more damage. But they're hard to hit. My crossbow skill is still only four."

We'd try again, but these things usually came in groups. It was going to take a lot of practice before I'd be comfortable facing two at a time.

Donut and Mongo jumped down from the platform. Mongo sniffed at the remains of the exploded monster. He made an odd, whimpering noise. Donut jumped down to inspect. She also sniffed at the remains. She froze.

"Carl," Donut said. "Um, I think you might want to see this. It's quite disturbing."

DONITA GRACE: Holy shit. Holy shit. Guys. Don't go to stop 24.
    They're everywhere. Millions of them. Worse than the
    grubs. Don't—

Warning: This message is from a deceased crawler.

My message screen exploded with people asking what was going on as I jogged up to the corpse of the monster.

"What the shit?" I said as the tiny little red dots started appearing on my screen. I wasn't reminded of the grubs. Instead, I thought of the fire ants.

That explained the lack of experience. We hadn't killed the monster at all.

It had hatched.

When the creature had exploded, he'd dislodged several thousand teeny-tiny, squirming monsters.

The AI took on a mock-motherly voice, as if it was trying to emulate a kindergarten teacher.

Krakaren Crotch Dumpling. Level 1.
    Gather around, little crawlers. It's story time.
    Once upon a time, on a distant planet, there lived a lonely
    creature. This planet teemed with flora and fauna, all of them
    growing and evolving and generally thriving and having a great
    time as they dashed forward through the eons. This creature
    also wanted to thrive; she also wanted to have a great time. But
    there was only one of her. She could not have children of her
    own. And this made her very angry, very cranky, but also very
    sad. More importantly, it made her determined.
    And as Doctor Ian Malcolm once famously said, *Life, uh, finds
    a way.*
    The creature had a special ability. Her stomach was like a
    gas station coffee vending machine, one where you could pick
    one of a thousand different choices. You could mix and match.

She soon discovered if she ate this creature, she could make this substance. And if she ate that creature, she could make a different one. So she began to experiment. The creatures of her world thought of her as an apothecary. She could cure all ails.

But what she truly wished for was to create a child of her own. And after a thousand generations, she did just that. Almost. It's a complicated process that involves a lot of failures. A lot of troublesome ghouls. But as another Earth saying goes, you need to crack a few eggs to make an omelet, no?

What these wriggling parasites you see really are, are clones. The next part of the Krakaren story, where she discovers the ability to speak to all of her clones telepathically, and then eventually form a collective mind, where she starts spreading across the universe and making a general nuisance of herself, is for a different time.

All you need to know now, little crawler, is that you have to kill these things, and you have to kill them fast. After all, like all children, they grow up so very fast.

I suggest a nice, firm stomp.

I was already smashing them with my feet before the long-ass description ended. There were thousands of them, all about the size of a grain of rice. But they were already growing. And we were on gravel, which made my smushes ineffective.

"Step back," I said. I'd killed most of them, but a few red dots remained. I had a half-full jug of moonshine in my inventory, and dumped it onto the track and tossed a torch, lighting the whole area on fire.

"Growler Gary had said they'd turned the whole place into a Krakaren nest," Donut said. "He wasn't kidding."

"I guess not," I said.

"I hope they stay at station 24," Katia said.

28

THE SECOND CART FOR THE MINDARO LINE NEVER ARRIVED. THAT was Bautista's, leaving his group stranded at the end of the line. So without any further fanfare and very little discussion about how terrible of an idea this was, the four of us loaded up onto a rapid-response cart and dialed ourselves onto the mindaro line and headed down the track in an attempt to find the source of the problem.

"What color is mindaro, anyway?" Donut asked as I pushed the throttle forward. We had to remain in the small raised cockpit with the windshield; otherwise Donut would get blown clear off the train. We were going insanely fast. The cart moved smoothly over the track, making very little noise. We kept the portal tuned to the abyss in case more mobs came at us. The line's power was out, so we had to run on batteries.

"I have no idea," I said. "I don't know what any of these colors are. Ask the art professor."

Katia shrugged. "I think it might be a shade of chartreuse."

"What the hell color is chartreuse?" I asked.

"It's between yellow and green. It's named after a French liqueur. Actually, there's some controversy on what the exact shade should be. It's very interesting."

"I'm sure it's riveting," I said.

Katia stuck her tongue out at me. And then her tongue formed into a little hand with a tiny middle finger pointing up.

I laughed. "Holy shit, that's weird. You're getting fast at that."

"It still hurts to make big changes, but little stuff like that I can now do with very little effort."

The cart plan had worked as intended for the other two lines. For the sinopia and grullo lines, the abyss cart appeared, still blasting its music ("Mack the Knife" for the grullo line), and the train yard cart appeared soon thereafter. In both cases, the portal-to-the-train-yard carts arrived just minutes after the first, which suggested that the carts sometimes slowed down if they hit something big, allowing the second trains to catch up.

Which, we realized, was what had probably happened with the mindaro line. It was a stupid mistake. If the second cart had caught up with the first, the portal in the front would have tossed the whole abyss cart back to the train station. So when Bautista's crew only saw one cart—this one playing "Rock of Ages" by Def Leppard—it was actually the cart they needed to jump in front of, but they had no way of knowing that.

I shouldn't have put delays on those alarm traps. I should have known what song went with what cart. It would have saved us this trip.

That cart had been tuned to Train Yard Q. I warned my contact there that we may have accidentally hurled a bunch of monsters in their direction. That plus a cart with a dangerous portal attached to it.

When the carts hit the portals at the edge of the abyss, they didn't plummet over the edge like I'd been expecting. Instead, they worked like engine cars and punched right through back to the train yards.

Since the abyss gate at the end of the sinopia and grullo lines did not line up with the associated train yard track of the rapid-response carts, those who got transported through never saw the carts again. Instead they joined up with the defenders at the closest nearby station 36. It was 800 people between the two groups, and we had gotten them all to a stairwell station. That was the best I could do for them.

At first I worried that the rogue carts would now start looping up and down the tracks. But a group happened to be grinding their way through Yard M when the first cart—the same one playing "Physical" by Olivia Newton-John—appeared. Because of the way the switching stations worked, the cart was automatically routed into a dead-end parking space intended as a holding area for the train engines. The cart reached the end of the track and flipped. It caused the entire awning system to be sent into the abyss. But the portal automatically shut itself off a moment later. The cart remained on its side, wheels still spinning.

A few minutes after that, the second cart showed up and also flipped over.

That group at Yard M then managed to get enough people together and physically flip one of the two carts back over and then bring it to a track. They managed to get the thing turned back on, giving them a new weapon to keep at least one of the nearby tracks clear.

The tunnels were eerily quiet and empty as we rode up toward Bautista. I kept the portal on in case something else was on the track. I tuned it to the abyss, but I kept an eye out for the telltale blue dot of crawlers on the track. I could switch it back to Station E, but we had to be careful. It took the portal a good ten seconds to make the switch, during which time it wasn't on at all, making the cart vulnerable.

Katia's fan box became available while we rode down the line, but we didn't dare stop. We now had less than two days left, and every second counted. Seven hours in, and we still saw nothing on the tracks except the occasional exploded corpse of a post–stage three monster. The baby Krakarens were nowhere to be seen.

Back at the front of the line, Elle's away team, with the help of Tizquick the dwarf, found the correct colored line, making their way to the exploded station 72. Loads of other crawlers had the same idea, and she found a group of people waiting there. The ceiling had caved in, but the circle of stairwells remained, and people had cleared the rubble. We sent out word that it was a place to descend without fighting, and people were now flocking to the area. The crawlers who'd died blowing the soul crystal had, at the very least, not died in vain.

Others, like Imani and Li Jun, thought it was best to stay put. The monsters approaching station 36 were trickling to a stop, and the crawlers had built a solid, defensible position. So far the Krakaren babies were staying put at all the station 24s. The wrath ghouls, it turned out, formed a similar boss to the one parked at stop 48 if they were allowed to congregate. This one was also a province boss.

Our plan was to get Bautista's crew, get everyone to Train Yard E, and then work our way to station 60. From there people could decide to go wherever they wanted, either to one of the many heavily defended station 36 stairwells or to the free station 72. A few people were also putting together raiding teams to take on the station 48 boss. Nobody else was braving station 12, 24, or the other occupied station 72s.

As for us, we'd decide what we were going to do when the time came.

"People on the track!" Katia suddenly yelled just as we passed station 432.

"Shit," I said, flipping the switch to change the portal. The cart was like a boat and didn't have brakes. I cut the throttle just as the blue dots appeared. The train slowed. I mentally calculated our trajectory, and I saw we'd make the switch in plenty of time. The dots were moving fast, probably running away from us once they saw our light. Poor guys. They had to be terrified.

"Get ready," I said. "If they don't know who we are, they might shoot at us."

Sure enough, the crawlers appeared a moment later. They were a group of five people running full speed down the track and away from the cart, and one of them had presence of mind to shoot an ice bolt directly at us. It hit the portal and disappeared. I didn't know if the bolt went through or what, but the poor guys didn't have a chance. We plowed right through them, teleporting them to Train

Yard E, which had to be a serious shock. They all probably thought they were about to die.

"Sorry," I called back over my shoulder as we continued down the track, approaching station 433, which appeared much more quickly than I anticipated. This was where the mimic lived. As far as I was aware, nobody had killed one of these things yet. Dozens of X's appeared on my map, all of them on the platform where the previous portal cart hadn't been able to scoop them up.

God, so many dead. Every time I saw something like this, I felt the anger start to rise in my chest.

"What is that?" Katia asked, pointing ahead. There was something on the tracks right outside the platform to station 433. Whatever it was, it didn't appear on my map.

A red-and-white wooden crossbeam appeared to be sitting across the tracks, blinking. It had a stop sign attached to it. What the hell? This was like a regular railroad crossing, though usually these things went across the road, not the tracks. I just stared at it, confused for a good two seconds, not sure what to make of it. The track beyond the barrier appeared to be fine. There was no cross traffic. Where had it come from?

"Fuck," I said the moment I realized what it was. It had only fooled me for a pair of seconds, but it was enough. *You idiot.* I moved to flip the switch back to the abyss, but I hesitated. *Too late. Too late.* We were going to hit it. A long, fleshy appendage snaked from the end of the crossbeam, leading up into station 433.

We hit the crossbeam a moment later. There was a mighty *thwum* as the portal sucked it away.

We'd just accidentally teleported the entire station mimic city boss to Train Yard E.

"Whoops," I said.

"BAUTISTA," I SAID, STEPPING OFF THE PLATFORM. I SHOOK HANDS with the hairy orange tiger man. He'd reached level 28. We'd stopped about 100 meters before the giant swirling portal that led into the abyss. There was a wide space on either side, along with a small doorway that led to the now-collapsed interior walkway. A pair of crawlers, both human, stood guard. One had an enchanted old-school sling. The thing crackled with purple-and-black energy. He twirled the weapon and shot a rock, likely aiming at one of the lizard monsters who crawled up and down the pit's interior. The crawlers both cheered, presumably after scoring a direct hit.

"Hello, Carl," Bautista said, clasping me on the shoulder. "You have saved us. Again."

"We ain't done yet," I said, looking over the ragtag group. There were about 600 people gathered here. I quickly told him what had happened with the station mimic as I shook hands and traded fist bumps with dozens of crawlers, who ranged in level from the distressingly low 18 to 30. Most were human, but there was a scattering of orcs and elves and other oddities.

"So we have to fight that thing again?" Bautista asked, sounding sick. "Carl, it's a city boss, and it's really strong. I don't know how to kill it. If you chop a part off, it turns into a spider and crawls back to the whole. Bashing weapons don't do anything. It's magic resistant. Maybe blowing it up will work, but you'll have to go big. Like, really big."

I stepped in front of the portal attached to the front of the cart and took a screenshot.

"Holy shit," I muttered.

The station mimic was so large, it took me a minute to figure out what I was looking at. It was significantly larger than I anticipated. The monster had taken up residence in the middle of the train yard and hadn't yet changed shape into anything. It looked as if the wall of the train yard had moved, swallowing half of the station. Only after staring at the image did my brain start to figure it out. It was a potato-shaped blob the size of a neighborhood block. The damn thing reached all the way up to the ceiling, taking up a huge portion of the yard. It seemed much too big, like the total mass was enough to mimic five or six or more stations.

The blob looked disturbingly like how Katia appeared when she was not formed into anything.

I thought of that group we'd accidentally teleported to Yard E. They were probably dead. We'd sent them to the yard, and less than two minutes later, we'd sent that thing through the same portal. Maybe they'd gotten away. I hoped so.

It seemed much too big to be only a city boss. Which begged the question, how strong were those things at the stairwell stations? The province bosses? For fuck's sake.

> CARL: Elle. Do me a favor and ask your manager if there's a
> secret way to kill a mimic.

I'd already looked it up in my book, and there wasn't much in the monster section. There was a warning that mimics were all over the place on the eighth floor, but I had the impression they were more of a nuisance than a real threat, implying that this huge mimic was a new thing, or something no previous cookbook owner had come across.

> ELLE: Are you about to do something really stupid, or have you
> done it already?
> CARL: Both.
> ELLE: Hang on. Let me ask. Don't get your hopes up.

I looked over at Donut, who was preening at the attention of the other crawlers. She was mounted on Mongo while a group of people surrounded her and the dinosaur. She talked animatedly, telling them about the ride up here.

Katia held back shyly, leaning up against the side of the cart. People kept looking at her. Everyone by now knew exactly what had happened, but that golden shining skull over her head was hard to ignore. I watched as Bautista approached her and held out his hand. They shook and started talking.

I walked up to the massive portal that overlooked the abyss, and I took a screenshot. The cart behind me with the much smaller portal led to Yard E. This one led to Yard H. There was no mimic here. I could see the interdiction cart, the one that had been playing the Def Leppard song. This one hadn't flipped and was sitting stopped a short distance away, having gotten itself wedged against the wall. The portal appeared to still be on. It'd jumped the track at the service bay but remained upright until it hit the cavern wall, which, thankfully, hadn't teleported the entire cave system away. I didn't see any mobs, though there were dozens of corpses spread throughout the abandoned train yard.

ELLE: She says you don't fight giant mimics. Little ones are easy to kill if you know what they are, but this thing is a whole different story. If you slice part of them off, the pieces grow legs and return to the main body. If you can get more than 50% of the mass off the main body at once, it'll no longer be able to heal or transform. And then it'll be vulnerable. But the separated pieces, unable to return to the main body, will instead attack you. They only die when the mimic dies.

CARL: Well, that's terrifying. And that's only a city boss.

ELLE: Yeah. I'm on my way back to the crew now, but I just talked a group out of attacking the province boss at station 48. One day we might be strong enough to fight one of those things, but it ain't gonna be on this floor. Fuck that. You can hear it screaming from here.

I walked back to the cart and took one more screenshot. The mimic appeared to be forming into a large building, though it was still in mid-transformation. It was taking the shape of an Iron Tangle administrative structure, though it had so much mass, it had to make the building huge. A mouth that had to be 300 feet wide comprised the entire first floor. Each jagged tooth was the size of a person. A red, lumpy, train-sized tongue lolled out of the mouth, reaching off screen.

The entire building and mouth were faced directly at the portal. I knew if I took another screenshot in a minute, the mouth would be gone, and only the building would remain.

It's waiting for us.

CARL: Sorry, Donut.

DONUT: WHAT DO YOU MEAN?

I climbed back into the cockpit and turned the switch. The portal to Train Yard E shut off. I looked down at Bautista where he stood next to Katia. "New plan. We go through the abyss portal instead of the cart portal. I have enough hats in my inventory for everybody here, so we don't need to worry about fighting this mimic thing. It's expecting us, and if we go through that portal, we'd be like pigs walking to slaughter."

Bautista looked relieved. "Thank god for plan B."

"That was actually plan C," Katia said.

———

"OH, DON'T LOOK AT ME LIKE THAT," I SAID TO DONUT AS WE watched the last of the hat-wearing group make their way through the portal to Yard H.

"You have to tell them to give the hats back after we go through," she said. "Millions of gold, Carl. Millions!"

"They weren't ours to begin with," I said. "People gave them to us to help others."

"We only have 83 of them left," she sniffed. "I really want to buy the social media board. So we can see what people are saying about us."

"Actually, it's less than that." I pulled thirty of the hats from my inventory and started tossing them onto the ground behind the cart. "In case there are any stragglers."

Donut looked at me like I'd just slapped her. She made an incredulous, scoffing sound. "You know, it's no wonder you were always so poor. There's a fine line between being helpful and being a dumbass, Carl."

"We still have over fifty of them."

Katia laughed as Donut glowered. The cat looked back over my shoulder, as if she was contemplating jumping off the cart to go retrieve them. I put my own hat on my head. Donut didn't want to remove her tiara, so instead she sighed and held an engineer's key in her mouth. Mongo went into his carrier. I suspected that since the cart was allowed through the portal, we didn't need either the hat or the key, but there was no sense risking it, especially since there was a cliff on the other side of the portal. Katia pulled out the hat and plopped it on her head. It disappeared into her mass. A moment later, it reappeared as she did something to make it visible. She really was getting better at the doppelganger stuff. A lot better.

I eased the cart through the portal, and just like that, it was done.

Our plan was a success. There had been just over 1,400 people trapped at the end of the line, and we'd gotten them, if not to safety, to a place where they at least had a chance.

The cart clunked loudly as it changed tracks. I eased off the throttle. Def Leppard's "Rock of Ages" continued to blare from the immobile interdiction cart, but the song stopped a moment later after the guy with the sling scored a direct hit on the small trap.

There was this moment, right after the music abruptly ended, where our slow-moving cart coasted to a stop right behind the other cart, and we just faced the large crowd. The silence hung for a good few seconds, and then the 600 people broke out in applause. Bautista walked up and gave me a hug as we jumped off the cart; then he did the same to Katia. He patted Donut on the head.

"Thank you. Thank you so much."

"We still have a little more than a day and a half, my friend," I said.

"I know," he said. "But we couldn't have made it here without your help. And for that, I'll be forever grateful." He gave me a wink and pulled the hat off his head. He put it on the ground in front of Donut, who looked up at him with wide-eyed surprise. "For you, Princess Donut."

"It's not necessary, I'm sure," she said, suddenly switching to her imperial voice. "Please, keep it. I insist."

But suddenly there was a line of people, all of them putting their hats in a pile in front of Donut. Her eyes shined, and her jaw trembled, revealing her two lower fangs as the people one by one bowed in front of her and dropped the stupid train hats on the ground in tribute. "Thank you, Princess," they said one by one.

"Of course," she said to each person. "It was nothing. Our pleasure."

CARL: Was this your idea?
BAUTISTA: Your partner, Katia, suggested it.

I looked over at her, and she grinned.

Donut gathered all the hats up into her inventory, tail swishing with pleasure. I suspected now that most of the crawlers were all at the front of the lines, shopkeepers would be less likely to give us money for these things. But we held on to the moment. I didn't know what was going to come next, or if we'd even done anything here today other than delay the inevitable, but it felt good.

By god, it felt good.

29

THE GROUP TURNED AND HEADED TOWARD THE GATE. WE'D IN-
structed them on how to find the employee line, which would be free
of monsters. Bautista and about twenty others held back as I went
through the complicated process of trying to get the cart switched
over to one of the regular colored lines. It didn't matter which one,
as long as it had a platform at both 60 and 75. I walked ahead,
switching the lines, while Katia eased the cart forward.

"Whoa, hey. I just got a box from my sponsor," Katia suddenly
said. "A Silver Benefactor Box."

"Yay!" Donut said. "That means you have a sponsor box and a fan
box to open!"

"I got a sponsor box not too long ago, too," Bautista said. I
reached up and manually slapped the transfer switch. It made a loud
clunk. "But I haven't had the chance to open it yet. I'm on my way to
do it now."

"Who is your sponsor, anyway?" I asked the tiger man.

"Jaxbrin Amusements, Limited. The same folks who make my
babies."

"Your babies?"

"Yeah," he said. "I've been meaning to talk to you about this. Did
you get any of them? Some do what I say, but sometimes they don't,
and I don't know why. One even attacked me once. A green variant
Slizzer. But the other Slizzers were fine. I still have another green
variant, but I don't dare use it now."

I just looked at him. I had no idea what the hell he was talking about.

"Miss Quill? The old skyfowl lady from the last floor? Remember her?"

"I remember," I said. I reached up and fingered the necklace with the small charm. How could I forget? She ended up being the head bad guy of the area. Her failed spell was the reason I had the about-to-explode nuke in my inventory. Bautista had a quest to kill her. A quest that failed because we'd inadvertently killed her when we blew a hole in the ceiling of the magistrate's office. Bautista had been trying to get into her apartment at the time, but he'd found it empty except for . . .

"Are you talking about the Beanie Baby things?" I asked.

"Yeah," he said. He pulled one from his inventory. A brown frog wearing a spiked helmet. It still had the tag on it. It was the same type of creature Mordecai was currently shapeshifted into. Bautista tossed the beanbag to me, and I caught it. I rolled it over in my hand.

Stuffed Grulke Infantry Figure. (With tags)
   This is the most common variation of the Grulke line of collectible figures. In terms of rarity, these things clock in just below frat boys with early-onset liver disease. It's literally not possible to enter a way station *kinder* shop and not find one of these for sale on the shelf. You'll be hard-pressed to find a collector who will buy this off you.
   It sure is cute, though.

"Miss Quill had more than 1,000 different stuffed monsters in her apartment. So far, I've used about 40 of them. You can keep that one if you want. I have four more just like it, though one has a different-colored hat. They'll attack bad guys for you, and they're pretty strong, but they're common, and the common ones only last about fifteen to thirty seconds before they're done."

I read the little paper tag on the stuffed creature. All it said was "Grulke Infantry. Jaxbrin Amusements, Ltd." There was a symbol of a smiley-faced star on the other side. That was it.

"Wait, these things turn into real versions?" I said. "I didn't know that! How?"

"You pull the tag off. Like a grenade. And then you throw it. Takes about 10 seconds for it to work. Depending on what it is, it'll fight for you. Or, like I said, attack you. The rarer it is, the longer it lasts. When they're done, if they haven't been killed, they turn back to the Beanies, but the tag is gone, and you can't use them again. If they do get killed, the little beans fly everywhere when they die and then disappear."

"That's crazy," I said. "We only have one. It's a dude riding a horse. Named Kimaris. How did you figure it out?"

"The first one I did was called a Crane Crasher. A bird thing. We were sitting in a safe room, and I was just playing with it, and the tag came off. It came to life in my hands and flew to the ceiling, screaming. Then it attacked a guy in my party and teleported away. After that, I found another one. A Sage Sprite Lecturer. It said he was a teacher, so I pulled the tag. I thought he looked a little like my grandfather. He was helpful, but I should have saved him for later when I was better prepared. He was really rare and valuable. But he told me what was up with these things. Acted like I was an idiot for not knowing. He was one of my most valuable. Legendary rareness. Only one of five, but I didn't know how to see that until he taught me. Lasted two whole hours. He was in this weird glass case. I have five more legendary rares, but I'm afraid to open the cases now because the description says there's a chance I'll be blasted with fire if I open the door. I can open them in safe rooms, but the Sage Sprite said the fire could still trigger in the safe room. I'd be safe, but the case and the item would both be ruined. I think maybe I can open it in my inventory, but I'm too scared to try."

He was talking about a Sheol Glass Reaper Case. The same protective case my Kimaris figure had been in, but now housed Carl's Doomsday Scenario. My Kimaris figure was a demon. It was also unique, not legendary or rare.

"You just rip the tags off, and they appear?" I asked.

"That's right. But you can actually rip the tag off inside of your inventory, which is what I do. It takes about two seconds off the summoning time. You gotta be careful, though, because if it's a monster you're not familiar with, you don't know how big it's going to get. Or how mean. Some of them are huge. Also, the Sprite Lecturer. His name was Atwin, by the way. He said these are actual summonings. So you must be careful. It looks like you're making a new one because of the way they die. But you're actually teleporting one of those creatures to you. I don't really see the difference, but he insisted that was a big deal. I guess there are spells that say they're summoning, but they're really just creating a temporary fake version. This is a true summoning."

I thought of Donut's *Clockwork Triplicate* spell. That was most definitely not a real summoning.

"What was the name of the one you had?" Bautista asked.

"Kimaris."

"I don't have that one. You should probably hold on to it until you know how valuable it might be. Anyway, I am worried I'm going to run out of these things. My class is something called a Swashbuckler, and I need to practice more with my sword." He patted the glowing orange sword on his belt. "But I've been relying on these monsters a lot. That's why I'm glad I got sponsored by Jaxbrin. I hope maybe they can replenish my supply."

"You should train with your sword as much as you can anyway," I said, suddenly worried for the man. "You can't rely on somebody else's goodwill to keep you supplied. Also, some of your friends' levels are too low. The guy with the sling is good at 28, but his friend is only 21. That's not enough. He's getting left behind."

"I know," Bautista said. "We're doing the best we can."

BAUTISTA AND HIS TEAM'S PLAN WAS TO GO FIND THAT FREE STA-
tion 72. He promised they'd train on ghouls on another line until it
was time to go. Apparently Tizquick, the dwarf with the daughter
who never existed, was standing vigil at station 60, helping all the
passing crawlers to find their way from one colored line to the next.
I was starting to get worried about too many people congregating in
the same place at once, though apparently there were actually two
different station 72s with blown ghoul generators now. And there
were rumors of a station 12 that had also blown. The last I'd looked
we still had just under 275,000 people running about the floor, and
it would be much too easy for too many of them to crowd into the
same place and get overrun.

In fact, that number of remaining crawlers actually seemed too
high based on the number of people we had in our circle. I had at
least one person in over a dozen different station 36s, but none of
them had more than a thousand people. Most were more like 50 to
100. I talked about this some with the others, and we realized we
simply didn't know enough about the true nature of the floor to get
an accurate picture of where all these people really were. Katia had,
for a few days now, been saying that we were missing something
when it came to the way the Iron Tangle was set up. She kept saying,
"I don't understand how there can only be six station mimics." I told
her it didn't matter, not as long as we had an exit to our back and
we'd done everything we could.

We said our goodbyes to Bautista's team, and we found ourselves
on the zomp line. We had two interdiction carts. The E cart, the one
we'd driven all the way up the line, and the Q cart, which we now
called the Def Leppard cart. We dragged it behind us, facing backward so we were sandwiched between two portals, both tuned to the
abyss. Nothing could get to us while we were on the track. Not unless it attacked us from the sides.

The plan was to make our way to Imani and Elle and Li Jun and reunite with their teams, who were now camping and guarding station 36. They said they hadn't seen a real monster in hours except an occasional ghoul. I told them we'd be there later. And to stay away from Train Yard E, which now featured a brand-new resident.

In the meantime we were going to pick a random transit station and hit the safe room, open Katia's boxes, watch the recap show, and then have ourselves a reunion.

WE ENDED UP STOPPING AT STATION 59. THE TRACK WAS FILLED with ghouls and baby Krakarens, who were now all about the size of small dogs. We teleported them all to the abyss as we rushed up the line. The only time we were in any sort of danger was as we passed station 24. The juvenile monsters covered the platform. There were thousands of the octopuses swarming over each other. I tossed a precious Jug O' Boom off the side of the train as we passed. Even then, almost a dozen of them were fast enough to leap onto the cart. Katia's crossbow made short work of them. They didn't drop any loot at all, and their blood sizzled against the metal deck of the cart.

We stopped the two carts outside of platform 59 and left the portals on, both tuned to the abyss. Then we sent a message to everybody to stay off the zomp line. As long as the batteries held, and they appeared to last a really long time, nobody would mess with the carts. The transit station also had six other lines attached to it, but it was all clear as we walked to the safe room, which was downstairs this time instead of upstairs.

The swarming Krakaren babies appeared to be remaining close to station 24. For now. Meadow Lark was setting up a flamethrower-based kill zone at the choke points in case they were invaded. I hoped it wouldn't come to that.

The safe room at station 59 appeared to be a restaurant from Costa Rica called Soda. We pushed our way through the small room, past the Bopca, and into our personal space. It seemed like we hadn't been here in forever.

"Open your boxes now," I said, collapsing into the chair. "Let's see what we're dealing with."

Katia straightened. "Okay. I'm doing the fan box first."

We'd already agreed we had to get this done as soon as possible, before Mordecai got back. The last thing we needed was that Chaco guy showing up and getting into another fight.

But we needn't have worried. Two items popped out. A goddamned baseball bat and a shield. The shield was tall, about six feet high, and curved, shaped like a half cylinder. There were loops in it for her to either hold with both hands or to slide a single arm through.

There was a small, plastic-like window in the top of the shield for her to see through.

It had the words "Get Back" in Syndicate Standard emblazoned on the front in white blocky letters.

"It's a riot shield," I said.

The baseball bat was actually a police baton, I realized. At first glance there didn't appear to be anything special about it. But as Katia rolled it over in her hands, eyes wide, I could see the slight glow of enchantment. Her lips were tight with what appeared to be both irritation and fear.

I picked up the large shield to examine it. It was absurdly light.

Enchanted Shade Gnoll Riot Forces Crowd Control Shield.

Sometimes the galaxy isn't a happy place. Sometimes the unwashed masses forget their place in the machine. And sometimes these dregs bubble up to the surface, causing a phenomenon widely known as "Civil Unrest."

And when that happens, the powers that be don't want to become the powers that were. So they hire backup. An outside force to come down and kick everything back into order, and maybe commit a few war crimes in the process just so the filth knows their place. One such outfit, trained specifically for this sort of situation, is the Shade Gnoll Riot Forces.

This enchanted shield offers both offensive and defensive crowd-control options. A frontline defender utilizing this item is afforded the following benefits:

+5% to Constitution.

+5 to the Rooted in Place Skill.

+Upgrades Rush ability to Crowd Blast.

Warning: You may not equip this item. The Rush ability is required to equip this item.

I immediately looked at Crowd Blast, the enhanced Rush ability. This was the same battering ram skill Katia had used to kill Hekla. She could only use it once a day. Crowd Blast had two huge differences. She still rushed forward, causing a ton of damage. But now everybody in a wide cone in front of her was also hit with the attack. The bulk of the damage was still from whatever she physically hit, but everything in the cone took 10%–20% of the damage. The fact she'd managed to kill Hekla with the regular version of this skill meant this upgraded version packed a serious punch. Even those monsters not directly hit by it would take major damage. With her wrestling belt bonus, it would be the equivalent of hitting someone with, well, a monster truck.

But more importantly, she could now use the ability once every five minutes. Not once a day.

"It looks like you'll be getting more practice in with that Rush attack," I said as I looked up Rooted in Place. She made a noncommittal grunt.

Rooted in Place.

This skill makes it much more difficult to knock you over or back. That's not necessarily a good thing, physics being what they are. Be careful with this one.

"Interesting," I said, moving to the baton.

Enchanted Shade Gnoll Riot Forces Telescoping Crowd Control Baton.

This enchanted truncheon is designed to crack skulls and to teach those ungrateful bastards to show some got-damned respect.

This item's length is adjustable, from 25 centimeters to 3 meters.

Automatically casts Level Five *Cone of Knockback* if swung at a group of 10 or more like mobs. This triggers only once every five minutes.

"Those are both pretty awesome," I said. "Especially the shield. I'm kind of worried about the wording on that Rooted in Place skill, but Crowd Blast is exactly what you needed."

"I can't tell if people were trolling me with this or not," Katia said. "People know I hate using Rush."

"It's not very thrilling," Donut agreed. "This is like getting an electric litter box for your birthday. Indeed it's useful. But it's a litter box for goodness' sake. I was hoping for something with a little more pizzazz."

"First off, that's what Bea asked for," I said. "I don't understand how someone can get pissed for receiving what they asked for. Second, that thing was like 300 bucks. Anyway, Katia, this is definitely a good thing. Troll or not, you're getting more and more powerful. Mordecai said he got a sex toy in his first fan box."

"Did you really buy your girlfriend a litter box for her birthday?"

"He did," Donut said. "Miss Beatrice was quite rightfully upset."

Katia laughed as she attempted to equip the large shield. She frowned after a moment. "I guess I don't need this anymore," she said. "It doesn't let me equip both at the same time." She removed an item from her left wrist and placed it on the table. "You should take it. You need a shield anyway."

I picked up the wrist bracer. It looked similar to the bracer I had on my right wrist, the one that allowed me to form my gauntlet. I'd forgotten she had this thing. She pretty much only used it to increase her mass.

Enchanted Auto Buckler of the Peach Pit.
Forms a metallic buckler on command. May be triggered via hotlist or by shaking your wrist like you're thinking of your hot aunt Lydia.
This item is enchanted with *Shatter*. Any attack that lands upon this shield has a 1.5% chance to disarm the opponent. If the opponent is disarmed, there is a 90% chance the item will drop to the ground, a 5% chance the weapon will break, and a 5% chance the weapon will be immediately transferred to your own inventory.

"Hey, this is cool," I said. I put it on. I had to slide it over the arm of my jacket. I experimented with making it appear. I could twist my wrist, and the small shield would pop into place. I could shake it in a similar way, and it'd disappear. "Thanks!"

"Much better than a litter box," Donut said.

Katia nodded, attention already on the next box. The benefactor box. "Okay. We ready?"

"Do you think it'll be something bad?" Donut asked.

"We don't get cursed items from boxes," I said. "Let's just see what it is."

Soon after Katia had been sponsored by the Princess Formidable, the younger sister of Prince Maestro and Crown Prince Stalwart of the Skull Empire, we explained to her everything we knew about the psychotic orc family. Maestro was dead along with the mom. Stalwart was in the dungeon, presumably walking around in the skin of the war god Grull. King Rust was supposedly in the dungeon, too, though we didn't know where. I still wasn't clear on how levels 6, 9,

12, 15, and 18 worked. Mordecai always told us to not worry about them until we got there.

We also didn't know how the sister factored into all of this. If her brothers were out of the way, I knew she'd become the heir apparent. But how close was she to her brothers? In books and movies, royalty was always murder-hoboing each other in order to gain power. But since we knew literally nothing about Princess Formidable other than the fact she existed, there was no way to predict what sort of item Katia would receive.

Katia opened the box. We silently watched the single small item appear. Katia picked it up, saying nothing. She examined it and passed it to me.

It was a crossbow bolt. She'd only received one.

The Bolt of Ophiotaurus.
    This is 1 of 100.
    This item acts as a regular crossbow bolt unless it is shot directly into the eye of a deity.
    Upon a successful strike to the god's eye, the deity's invulnerability pauses for fifteen seconds.

"Well, shit," I said. "I'm starting to think the sister isn't a huge fan of her big brother."

WE HAD TIME TO TAKE SHOWERS BEFORE THE SHOW STARTED, BUT that was it. Mordecai would return right after the show finished airing, and then we'd all need to take two hours to sleep.

The recap featured a montage of people setting up and fighting in a wide array of stairwell stations. We watched as a group of twenty people stupidly faced off against a station 48 boss. The monster, a hulking conglomeration of screaming, gnashing ghouls, made short work of the crawlers. It formed a giant pincer made of ghoul body

parts and gathered the crawlers up. Mouths formed on the interior of
the claw and devoured the crawlers as it crushed them. They all died
screaming.

"Jesus," I muttered.

"I can't watch this. I hate this show," Katia said, getting up. She
produced a towel from I don't know where and moved around the
common area, cleaning up the remaining blood splatters from where
Mongo hadn't licked it clean. "We need a maid in here."

The recap showed something unexpected. A group found a new
stairwell, one that wasn't listed on that early map. It didn't say where
they were, but this was clearly a different area we hadn't seen. It was
a dark, dripping cave, and it was only lit by the *Torch* spell of one of
the crawlers. There was only a single stairwell here. It was clearly a
level stairwell, but it was different than usual. It went both up and
down, and I wasn't sure why. Only the part of the stairs below the
ground glowed, but it still reached upward, corkscrewing into the air
and disappearing into the dark. It was only on-screen for a moment,
so I didn't have enough time to investigate what that meant.

"I think I know where that is," I said, suddenly realizing what we
were looking at. "That's where we teleported the mimic away. That's
station 433. I bet there's a stairwell there. Just like with Grimaldi. If
a city boss is sitting on a stairwell, it's invisible on the map until he's
gone."

"What?" Donut said, suddenly incredulous. "Are you saying we
could've just gone back down to that place and used those stairs?"

"That's what I'm guessing," I said. "But I'm not certain. This is a
good thing. It means there's a way to get home for anybody still
trapped on that side of the tracks."

"I guess they won't be needing the 150,000 gold's worth of hats
just sitting on the ground up there, either," Donut grumbled.

"They still gotta find that station," Katia said over her shoulder.
I did a double take. She'd grown thin and tall and was scrubbing one
of the walls ten feet off the ground. "There are five more mimics up
there. How did this blood even get up here?"

"Shush!" Donut waved her paw. "Stop talking. We're on!"

"Oh fuck," I said, seeing the scene laid out. They showed me standing over Growler Gary, the cowering gnoll. They'd altered the lights and colors of the scene to make the room dark, showing it from a low angle with me looming over the creature. Mongo materialized, coming into focus like a monster emerging from the fog, biting his hands off. Gary whimpered. The whimpering sounds were added in. Gary was always dead by the time we removed his hands. The scene switched to me wishing for duct tape while I attached one of the poor guy's hands to the keypad. It showed us doing it over and over again. It never even explained why we were collecting the hands.

It didn't show the rescue. Instead it moved on to Lucia Mar beating a mantaur to death by smashing him against a train over and over. It appeared she was set up in one of the train yards, but I couldn't tell which one. Something had changed with one of her two rottweilers. It was huge now, twice as big as the other.

"What is this?" Donut said. "They cut out the best part! They didn't show everybody saying thank you to me. They usually get it wrong, but this is over-the-top. This is outrageous!"

"It's okay," I said. "People are watching it happen live. More every day. They know what really happened. It's the same with the other crawlers. By now everybody knows all of this stuff is pure propaganda."

"Do you think that means this Lucia kid isn't as crazy as she looks?" Katia asked, coming to stand beside me.

"I don't know. Maybe." I remembered what Lucia had done to the Desperado Club. And to Odette's assistant. Odette had called her a psychopath. And Lucia had talked some serious shit about Donut on that one show. So there was probably some truth to it. But it had to be exaggerated. It had to be.

"You did a good job," I said, looking about. "The room is very sparkly." I remembered what Katia had said about her mother being a clean freak, and how she'd rebelled against it. Apparently not so much. Then again, it *was* predominantly bloodstains she was cleaning up. That's not something most people wanted splattered around their living area.

"It was mostly Mongo," Katia said, patting the dinosaur on the head.

Hello, Crawlers.

This will be your second-to-last message before the floor collapses, and I just wanted to say how proud we are of human tenacity. Quite frankly, we expected the number of deaths to be much higher on this floor. It's making us rethink how easy the next floor was going to be. Hah.

Odds are good you might have your hands full this time tomorrow, so we're sticking all the important information into this message. The next floor will see the crawlers scattered throughout, further apart than usual. Parties will still travel together, but only parties that are formed before this message started. We love how you plucky humans are starting to all band together to defeat the big, bad monsters, and it's great—it really is—but we wish to focus more on individual stories on the next floor. Feel free to chat to your friends, but if they aren't in a party with you right now, it's best to get your goodbyes out of the way. There will still be Desperado Club and Club Vanquisher entrances throughout the level, so don't worry about that. But if you haven't trained yourself up, you might regret it.

And speaking of chat, we've added a new and exciting feature to this season. For a small fee, all viewers may now subscribe to your private messages between other crawlers. Isn't that great? Sign-ups started yesterday, and we are very pleased with how many have already joined up. The system goes live the moment this message ends.

We have also patched a few persistent bugs with the inventory system. Effective immediately, you may no longer store liquids in your inventory unless they are in a container.

That's it for now. See you guys tomorrow. Now let's get out
there and kill, kill, kill!

"Where is he? Where did that fuck face go?" a familiar voice
yelled. It was Mordecai skidding to a stop in the room. His toad eyes
grew wide. Apparently, for him, no time had passed. He'd just
blinked. "Oh. Oh shit. Oh fuck," he said, eyes flashing as he read a
page of notifications. "By his left tit. Seven days?"

"Hello, Mordecai," I said.

The toad man just stared at us. His eyes immediately moved to
the golden skull over Katia's head and then to the skull over Donut's.
He straightened as Mongo squawked and jumped in circles all
around him. "I see I missed a few things."

"A few things, yes," I said. "We need to—"

I didn't finish.

Katia exploded.

At least that's what I thought had happened at first. Blood
erupted out of her. Gallons and gallons of it flying in every direction.
It just kept coming and coming, an impossible amount. We all cried
in surprise. I was blasted in the face, getting bukkaked by the fetid,
stinking liquid. I fell over trying to get away, gasping and choking.
Donut squealed and leaped across the room. Mordecai also flew
backward, stumbling over the couch, his frog legs sticking straight
up into the air.

And still, the red spray didn't let up. It hit the ceiling and all the
far walls, like it was being sprayed from a multidirectional pressure
washer.

Mongo shrieked in joy, spinning about like a child in the rain. It
kept coming for twenty full seconds before trickling to a stop. Katia
just stood there in the middle of the room, eyes huge. Once it
stopped, the room was filled with the sound of my coughing and
Mordecai's croaking and the *tap-tap-splash-tap* of Mongo dancing in
circles like he was playing in a wading pool.

It took me a moment to understand what the fuck had just happened. Katia had stored all of the blood when she'd been attached to the front of the train. She'd had to put it directly into her inventory to keep her scoop clean.

But the rules had just changed. One could no longer store liquids that weren't in a container. Apparently this was how the system now dealt with the paradox.

I focused on Katia. The blood spread out from her in a circle. It hadn't gone straight up, but in every direction around her. She hadn't been touched. Holy shit. There wasn't a single damn drop of blood on her. I had a thought. An exploit. I wondered how well it would work. But it was definitely something they'd patch if I even tried it. I filed that information away.

"Really, Katia," Donut said, leaping to my shoulder. "If you need to borrow a sanitary napkin, just ask."

30

THE FIRST THING WE DID WAS WALK OUT TO THE MAIN RESTAURANT. Mordecai, who was somehow even more soaked with gore than I was, approached the counter with the Bopca.

"We are purchasing a personal space upgrade," Mordecai said. "A cleaner bot." The Bopca looked distastefully at the blood dripping onto the counter. Mongo had the zoomies and zipped back and forth through the room, spraying little red dots everywhere.

The upgrade cost 25,000 gold, making it one of the least expensive environmental upgrades we could get. That was still expensive as shit, but none of us complained. Donut didn't even try to negotiate. Katia wordlessly paid for it, and we marched back into the personal space. The moment we stepped into the room, the new upgrade went to work. It was a Frisbee-shaped robot, similar to the Mexx-class robots we sometimes saw in production trailers, though this thing didn't look as if it could talk. It was basically a flying Roomba. Donut had to admonish Mongo not to attack it. It hummed like a muted drone as it buzzed about the room, blinking disdainfully at the mess.

It went to work cleaning up all the stinking, congealed blood, hovering over it and magically zapping it away. It cleaned quickly, but it was still going to take time. A long time.

"Let's all just take showers, pretend like this never happened, and meet back here in five minutes," I said. I had ghoul blood in my mouth, but I didn't have anything clean to wipe it off with. It tasted like metal soaked in dead rat.

We returned to find the blood was still everywhere, but the cleaner bot was working as quickly as it could. It'd thankfully started at the kitchen counter, leaving the area habitable. Katia sat there eating a pineapple she'd gotten from the Bopca. She sat there as if nothing had happened, humming a little song to herself. She used her hand to form a knife to cut and core it. She offered me a piece as I approached. I declined. All I could taste was the blood.

"Okay," Mordecai said, holding up his hands as he emerged clean from his room. "Before you say anything, I know it was a mistake. I shouldn't have lost my temper like that at Chaco. It won't happen again. And, no, we are not going to talk about it."

"Someone told us if you do it again, you'll be gone for good," I said.

"I assure you it won't happen again," Mordecai said. "You have my word. Now what did you pick from that prize carousel anyway?"

"He got a stupid recipe book," Donut said. "It was a joke prize."

"Really?" Mordecai said. "Can I see it?"

"Later," I said, trying to change the subject. "We don't have much time, and we still need to sleep. We need to catch you up, but then we need to get back out there."

"Did you see my sunglasses?" Donut asked. "Aren't they just the greatest? I got them from Princess D'nadia. If I hadn't gotten them, we wouldn't have known Hekla was trying to kill Katia. Oh, oh, and I have over 100 in charisma now, and I got the Love Vampire skill. Just like you told me to get. I've cast it a few times, but it never triggered."

Donut's Love Vampire skill allowed her to basically reflect any damage to a mob that was a lower level than her. She hadn't used it yet because we'd been careful to keep her from getting hit on this floor.

"Okay," Mordecai said. His eyes got huge at the mention of Hekla. He once again zeroed in on that golden skull floating over Katia. "That's great, but slow down. We have a lot to go over, but we don't have to do it all at once. First, explain the circumstances regarding the player-killer skulls you two have, how Katia is the highest level of all of you, and then we'll go over all of your new skills and . . ." He trailed off, his eyes fixed on my left hand. He took two steps toward me, grabbed my wrist, and held it up so he could look at the ring I'd gotten from Frank. The Ring of Divine Suffering.

"Take this off," he said. "Take it off right now."

"I'm not going to use the Marked for Death skill," I said. "It gives a 5% bonus to my stats."

"If I wasn't afraid I'd be kicked out of the game for good, I'd smack you into the next floor. Even if you were a player killer, you'd be an idiot to keep this on you, let alone on your finger. Every season, several of these rings are generated, and every season, the crawlers who own them are the first to be tracked down and killed by the hunters on the sixth floor. The bonuses for this ring work both ways. One of the reasons why those idiots flock to the hunting grounds is to obtain one of these things."

"Why?" I asked.

"Because in the hands of a sadistic bastard, a combatant can raise his power exponentially. Once it is charged up enough, its owner gets massively stronger each and every kill. I don't think there has ever been a Faction Wars where the victorious army is led by a champion who doesn't have one of these rings, amongst several other items. And those rich assholes who fight it out on the ninth floor will do anything they can to win. This sort of item can't be brought in from the outside. But the factions *can* collect them if they can convince an idiot to go hunting for one on the sixth floor. And if there's one thing this universe doesn't lack, it's idiots. You need to sell this ring. Otherwise you'll have a huge target on your back. Bigger than the one you already have."

I just stared down at the ring on my finger. I didn't want to take it off. "So the Faction Wars winner always has one of these?"

He smacked me then. *Thwap*, right on the side of the head. He did not freeze or teleport away. If he had hit me just a little harder, it probably would've gone bad for him. My father used to do the same thing, though he'd done it much harder. I felt my eyes narrow.

Mordecai looked at his webbed hand, just as surprised as I was. *So much for promising to hold his temper.*

"Carl, I shouldn't have done that. But out of everything I just said, that's what you're holding on to? Crawlers don't get involved in winning or losing Faction Wars. They ride out the ninth floor like it's a tornado passing by overhead. They keep their heads down, and they pray it doesn't sweep them away. We already have one impossible task to deal with when we get to that floor. You attempting to hold on to a Divine Suffering artifact when the entire universe knows you have it is just another level of idiocy we don't need."

I started a retort, but he held up his hand, interrupting me.

"Plus, don't you remember the magic pulses on the last floor? Events that activate magic are a real danger. There will be traps that activate your spells and items. Triggering something like that could be devastating. Despite what its description says, this item is not meant for crawlers. It's meant for tourists, designed to get them to gather up combatants by the hundreds and farm them for power. It is evil, and if you don't get rid of it, gods help me, I will tell Donut to stay the fuck away from you the moment you hit the sixth floor."

"Oh, for fuck's sake," I said, pulling the ring off. I felt my strength lower, which pissed me off further. "We'll talk about selling it on the fifth floor. Before we get to the sixth. Don't touch me ever again."

He looked like he was going to object, and insist on me ditching it now. He opened his mouth, as if to say something, but Katia interrupted. She had the map out, spread onto the counter.

"What was it?" she asked. "You said you knew how to get to the lower train stations. We figured it out, but there's a bunch of different ways, and I want to know what you saw."

Mordecai looked down at the large paper, worn and blood splattered and filled with many more marks than when he'd started working on it over a week earlier. He blinked a few times, staring at the mess of circles. I still couldn't make sense of it. I couldn't imagine how anybody could make sense of this confusing bullshit. I had the sense whoever designed this let it get away from them. I hoped the same asshole wasn't in charge of the next floor, too.

"You see this?" he said, pointing to the circle that was the *Nightmare's* loop. "And this, and this?" He indicated several other named lines. He grabbed the pen off the table and drew a symbol in the corner. It was a group of overlapping circles, similar to the Olympics logo, though the rings were all a different size. "It's the logo for the Syndicate, at least from the top down." He pointed to the second circle of the logo, then tapped the *Nightmare* line again. "See here. It matches up perfectly. The named trains make a specific pattern. That means there is a train that has to loop to the front. Probably at this station here. Yes, look, you discovered it already. The *Escape Velocity* line. Yeah, that makes sense. *Escape Velocity* is the name of the ship that discovered the wormhole to the first system where a gleener scientific crew investigating a Primal ship graveyard came across the Vog Generation Ship. A few hundred cycles later, the Syndicate was formed. So it's obvious once you know what you're looking for."

"What?" I said. "How in the hell were we supposed to spot that? How would we even know what the Syndicate logo looks like?"

"Isn't it etched on the doors to the next floor down?"

"No," I said. "It's a massive kua-tin."

"Huh," Mordecai said. "When I did it, it was the Syndicate logo. Odd."

"You said this is from the top down?" Katia asked. "What does it look like from the side?"

He drew again, but this time it looked like a lopsided mattress spring. The circles were actually all connected together. "Honestly, I don't understand how these wormholes work, and that's what the logo is based on. It's not usually portrayed in 2D, but in a twisting 3D shape. Sometimes they show the rings flying together, but when it rotates, it's one piece. It's like one of those optical illusion things."

Katia snatched the pen from him and started redrawing the logo from several different angles.

"Anyway," Mordecai said, "that's how I knew. The abyss here represents the center of the galaxy. You really filled this in well, Katia. The tracks probably represent the worm paths." Mordecai leaned in. "Yes, I see it now. The whole thing is a simplified map of the galaxy, and the train lines are the original worm paths." He paused, reading some more. "Does that say 'station mimic'?" He laughed. "They really went all out. There's a story about the early days of the Syndicate where the H'lene system set up six way stations near the center. They were traps. The H'lene were robbing and eating all the travelers and then stealing their tech. The H'lene don't exist anymore, and they weren't really mimics, but they're oftentimes represented as them. They got wiped out by the Valtay and the orcs."

"Jesus," I said, looking it over.

"What about all these Krakaren bosses and the ghouls?" Katia asked, looking up from her sketches. I had no idea what she was doing, but she was now drawing lines from the logo to different parts of the map.

Mordecai returned his gaze to the map, frowning. "Oh, wow. I see it now. The Krakaren is a real creature. It is a collective mind, and it is spreading throughout the universe. Its proliferation causes a lot of anxiety. A better translation of its name is the Apothecary because of its ability to synthesize elements. When they call it the Krakaren, it's them deliberately bending the translation into a negative. What we have here in the dungeon is a caricature."

He pointed to one of the stations where Katia had written "Drug dealer."

"They have the Krakaren making the drugs and the Pooka are the ones handing it out. I think the Pooka are supposed to represent the Plenty. They are a Caprid race. They look like goats."

We hadn't seen or fought the Pooka, but I remembered that Elle and Imani had. They were the ones who gave the addictive "vitamin shot" to the mobs. Elle had described them as goblin things that turned into giant goats when you fought them.

Mordecai continued. "The Plenty invented the modern tunneling system. It's only been around for a few hundred seasons, but it allows near-universal real-time communications. The technology is proprietary, and nobody knows how it works. There's a ridiculous conspiracy theory that they use Krakaren technology, and it's all a ploy to get everyone into the Krakaren collective. Previously, everything had to be filtered through the wormholes. Borant had a stake in the communications relays that are now obsolete. It's a long story. I barely understand it all. Before, even in my season, the crawl would get just as many views as it does now, but most everyone in the universe would receive it on delay. Maybe an hour. Maybe a year, depending on where you lived. Only the center system would get it live. It's only a recent thing that the outer systems are able to follow and favorite crawlers in real time. The breakthrough changed everything. The Plenty are responsible for so much prosperity, but some, like the Bloom of the kua-tin, think of it as some insidious plot. They're like a telegram company protesting the invention of the telephone. Or a typewriter company protesting the invention of the word processor."

"Wait," I said. "So when they have the Krakaren manufacturing drugs and giving it to the Pooka to distribute to everyone else, what they are really doing is making some sort of bullshit metaphor? To make a political point?"

"That's what it looks like. This whole floor is a racist political cartoon telling the universe how shifty the Krakaren and the Plenty are. Borant has been very vocal about this for a while now. They say the Plenty are selling everybody this technology just so everybody will become addicted to it. But one day they will take it all away, and that will somehow allow their overlord, the Krakaren, to—I don't know—absorb the entire universe. It's a bit ironic if you ask me, considering how Borant is actually using the tunneling technology to spew their hate everywhere."

All of this was interesting, but I didn't really give a shit who was racist against whom when all of them were stepping all over us. As far as I was concerned, they could all go fuck themselves. But the story itself was important to know.

"But anyway," Mordecai said, "now that we know how to get to the front, we just need to wait out the timer and hop down the stairs. Oh, and then give me your table-upgrade coupons so I can boost up my alchemy table before we go down a floor."

I exchanged a look with Katia. We'd both already spent the upgrade coupons. "Okay," I said. "We'll give you a quick recap. But you gotta promise not to smack us again."

"Wait until you hear about how we stuck Katia to the front of a train and then killed Hekla," Donut added.

***

WE TOOK OUR NAPS AND RESET OUR BUFFS. BY THE TIME WE WERE ready to emerge out into the world again, we had one day and 10 hours left. Mordecai had been busy while we slept. He'd rearranged the crafting room. He'd installed that repair bench I'd found and bought three more benches. Two with our coupons and then one with gold. He bought a second alchemy table, which he said was necessary because he could specialize one of them. He bought a metal-working table, which he said he'd explain the purpose of later, and he bought something called a *Bolt-Thrower's Workshop*, which would eventually allow for the mass production of explosive and other magical crossbow bolts.

"Once we get that sapper's table up a few more levels, you can build Katia some great ammunition," he said.

We hadn't yet told him about the bolt she'd gotten from her sponsor. There was just so much he'd missed. I'd bring it up soon.

He'd been aghast with some of the chances we'd taken over the past several days, and we had argued quite a bit over some of the expenses, but he'd been particularly impressed with the progress Katia had made plus some of the items I'd manufactured, including the land mines and the *Heal*-infused smoke curtains. Both of those items I'd actually gotten from the cookbook, but if he suspected anything, he said nothing.

We still had a lot to talk about. We hadn't discussed the Kimaris figure nor the PVP coupons nor a dozen other small items. I wasn't finished with him regarding that bullshit with Chaco, either, but we simply didn't have the time.

I finished my daily training to find Katia leaning over the map, chatting with Mordecai.

"But if these railways represent paths to the center of the galaxy, are they really all on the same plane?"

"All I know is what I've learned from years of watching Syndicate programs," Mordecai said. "When my world was taken, we weren't much more advanced than your world was. We'd colonized a few planets in our solar system, and that was it. I was more interested in fungus and plants than the stars. But you're right. I think maybe it's—I don't know—squished."

"I put it all together, and we're still missing half the system," she said. "Plus that symbol only works from above. . . ." She trailed off. She started scribbling furiously.

"It doesn't matter," I said, coming to look over the table. "We know where the stairs are. We just have to defend it."

"Wait," she said, drawing a line. "Are they able to make things upside down? Like, make you think you're right side up when you're really upside down?"

I thought of the fight with the rage elemental. He'd cast a spell on us that had turned the hallway upside down.

"Yes," I said.

"They have done that before," Mordecai said. "They've done it several times, actually. It's easy to do and saves space."

She took the paper, and she folded it in half. She held it up to the light. She ripped it a little and rearranged it again.

"I figured out how to make the logo work," she said. "Also, I think I know why there were only six station mimics. And why they're so big. They're really occupying two stations at once."

"WAIT," I SAID. "SO RIGHT BELOW OUR FEET—LIKE, IF WE DIG DOWN far enough—we'll come to another train station, and you're saying it'll be upside down?"

"It *could* be right side up," she said, "but I don't think so. If it's upside down and mirrors the tracks above it, then the map works. We are at station 59 on the zomp line. If we dig, we'll end up at station 59 on some other line. Probably whatever the inverted color is on the color wheel. Plus, I think there might be an empty chamber between the two levels. Remember that room from the recap episode? With the stairwell and the ladder? I think that's the space in between."

"These tracks are twisting around and over and under each other already. A mirror world doesn't make sense."

"I don't think it's a mirror of the entire Tangle. Just each individual line."

"What? Katia, what the fuck? How does that make sense?"

"Just think of every line as a noodle, and the track is on the outside of the noodle. And there's another track on the opposite side of the same noodle. And think of the abyss as a fork stuck into the middle of the bowl that has been turned a few times. It's not so much a Spirograph pattern like we originally thought, but a chaotic mess. And in the middle of that giant bowl, the named lines make a pattern, spelling out the logo of the Syndicate. Actually, they do it either 12 or 24 times. Or maybe 48. I'm not sure."

"Yeah, not helping. Jesus fuck. Nobody can follow this."

"Just pretend like you half understand."

"Sure. Why not? That's wild. And weird. And it just makes everything more, not less, complicated. Which goes back to my original statement. It's amazing that you could figure this out. Really. I don't want to come across as a dick. But how does this information affect us now other than giving me a bigger headache than I already have?"

Katia shrugged. "I don't know if it will. But this double-sided noodle thing is a lot of trouble to go through for it to not make any difference. Maybe it's just extra fluff to appease the nerds. But it's been bothering me for days, and now it makes sense. It feels like a trap to me. The announcement said we'd have our hands full, but unless something new happens, that's not true."

She was right. But what was the purpose other than to be confusing as shit?

"Hey, Mordecai," I said. "When you first said you figured out the map, before your time-out, you said this was something you'd seen before, just on a smaller scale. What did you mean?"

"There was a floor once that was like a rat maze, and it had rooms that were like giant sliding puzzle pieces. It was also a fourth floor. The pieces of this one area slid together to make the Syndicate logo, and it opened up the exit. Actually," he said, eyes going wide, "I forgot about this part. Once the pieces were together, the whole thing spun on the center axis, flipping everyone upside down into a hidden chamber below them."

> CARL: Hey, Imani and Elle. What do you know about the province boss that's hanging out in some of the station 36s?
>
> IMANI: It's a bunch of wrath ghouls tied together. It forms a giant monster covered with mouths. It fills the whole station. It's pretty much the same thing as the boss at all the station 48s.

I thought for a moment. If the floors flipped, it wouldn't make a difference. Unless . . . *Holy Jesus.*

> CARL: Is the boss attached to the ceiling of the chamber?
>
> IMANI: I don't think so. But I don't know for sure. What are you getting at?

Think, think.

ELLE: The fuckers sound scary as shit. You're not thinking
about fighting one, are you? Because I'm pretty sure we
talked about this already, cowboy. Nobody can even kill one
of those city boss mimics, let alone a province boss. Did
you watch the recap? Those poor bastards fought that
boss and were wiped in about thirty seconds. Also, that
was pretty fucked-up, what you did to that poor hyena. I
know the show is exaggerating things, but I worry about
you sometimes.

CARL: Do you know if the ghoul generators at 12 and 72 hang
from the ceiling?

IMANI: I think they just float in the middle of the room. Carl,
speak to me.

I returned my gaze back to the circled station 24, where the Krakaren babies were gathered. They were getting bigger by the hour.
By all accounts, they weren't ranging far from the area. But if there
were so many of them getting bigger by the moment, where were
they all going?

"You know," I said, "if this whole thing is a metaphor like you
say, about how bad the Krakaren monsters really are for the universe,
about how they're using the tunnel system to spread their influence
or whatever, then I'm guessing they'll want them to be the final
blow. The exclamation point to their stupid political cartoon."

"But how?" Katia asked.

I think there might be an empty chamber between the two levels.

I thought back to the time Katia and I entered the empty stairwell station. It'd been a group of stairwells, all closed. They were in
a circle in the middle of the room. How big was that empty space in
the middle of the circle? Pretty big. About the circumference of a
railway tunnel.

CARL: Fuck me. I think I've figured it out.

31

IMMEDIATELY AFTER THE REVELATION, WE JUMPED INTO ACTION. I frantically sent out a notification for everybody to abandon all stairwell stations. Any other place would be safer. We didn't know exactly when it was going to happen, but I suspected it would be soon.

A few groups thought I was full of shit, and they happily said so. Thankfully I talked Bautista over at the crowded station 72 to get out of there. They mostly fell back to the employee station 60, waiting to see what would happen. Several other groups retreated to the tracks and the platforms. They still had ghouls to contend with there, but not so many. For now the Krakaren babies were staying put and only attacking if you got near station 24. The little fuckers were getting bigger by the hour.

Elle took a team of fighters, including Katia and Donut, to range down to the outskirts of station 24 to fight and grind on the things, which were now all level 14–17 **Krakaren Juvenile Clonelings**. They were monkey-sized and covered with tentacles. Katia was trying out her new crowd-control techniques while the others experimented with different types of attacks to see what worked best against them. Fire worked well. Crossbow bolts took them down, but only if you hit center mass. Chopping off their tentacles caused them to retreat, but only temporarily. Spells like *Magic Missile* worked, but not too well. *Lightning* did nothing. Elle's freeze attacks did nothing unless it was an icicle through the body. Bashing weapons only worked if you hit really hard. Psychic attacks worked *really* well, causing them all to stop for a moment, but it didn't do any real damage. We only had two people who could cast that type of magic.

The monsters were fast and had round, teeth-filled mouths that worked like living garbage disposals. Their tentacles burned on touch. Their blood was caustic, like with the Xenomorphs from *Alien*. Plus they screamed, Katia said, which was really unnerving.

While Katia and Donut killed Krakaren children, I went to work. It took a good five hours to get the two interdiction carts back to station 75 and then dialed into a colored line that intersected with the correct station 36. From there I gathered 20 high-strength crawlers, and we went to work transporting one of the two carts—we chose the Def Leppard cart—from the rails to inside the main chamber of station 36. We physically lifted it off the tracks. I was worried 20 guys wouldn't be enough, but once again I underestimated our extreme strength. We lifted it easily and with little effort. After some experimenting, I found it only took five or six guys to lift the cart.

When I first came up with the idea, I hadn't thought it through. Each rapid-response cart was about the width and height of a cargo van, and maybe one and a half times longer. While the station platform, and the stairwell itself, was just wide enough to carry the cart, there was no way to get it through the tight hallway system that led to the main room of station 36. In my head, the caverns had been much bigger, but when I arrived, I realized the plan was DOA. The hallway walls were practically indestructible, and we didn't have time to fuck around trying to figure out how to widen them, go around several bends, and then get the train cart into the room.

Salvation came in the form of Zhang, Li Jun's best friend. He emerged just as I was directing the crawlers to put the cart back on the track. I examined the bald Chinese man's properties as he came jogging up. He was still human. He was a level 28 **Earth Mover**. Li Jun had said he was a mage-tank combo. He now wore glowing black-and-gold segmented armor.

"Stop. Wait," he said. He bent over, breathless. "Sorry. I ran here from the safe room. Li Jun told me what you're attempting, and I've come to help." He held up a stick. "I got you guys."

"What is it?" I asked.

"It's a magic wand. It shrinks. It only has one charge left. It doesn't work on living things, but we still used it to get past a few bosses. Once we shrunk the monster's collar, and it choked him to death. And once I used it to stop a train that was going to run us down. I was saving the last zap for an emergency. It'll work on the train cart, make it small for five minutes. But it'll still be as heavy as before."

"Holy shit," I said. "That's amazing. How small will it make it? If it's still heavy, we'll still need it big enough that we can push and turn it."

"Size is easy," he said. "It starts shrinking once I zap it, and it keeps getting smaller until I turn it off. Otherwise it stops on its own when it's about the size of a button."

"And you did it on a train before? You know it'll work?"

"Yes," he said. "It worked on the whole train and killed everybody on board. I jumped six levels all at once. I even got a boss box and a multi-kill box. It saved our lives."

"Well, shit," I said, turning to the other crawlers. "Let's get this thing back up the stairs."

After a harrowing four and a half minutes rolling the much smaller cart through the twisting hallway, we pushed the heavy cart into the main chamber. We quickly shoved it to the center of the room, stopping it between the circle of inactive stairwells. It sat on the circle in the middle of the room. The floor had a faint etching on it: a side view of the Syndicate logo that I'd never have noticed if Mordecai hadn't shown us the night before. We all quickly backed up as the cart returned to its regular size, popping as it inflated.

"All righty," I said, slapping my hands together. "Now comes the fun part."

Imani came to stand next to me. She regarded the cart suspiciously. I knew she wasn't a big fan of this idea, especially the next part. Still, she'd contributed to the plan. She'd still had a few of those chain-making scrolls in her inventory, and I asked her to use them. Several piles of the magical chain sat coiled and ready.

"Are you sure about this?" she asked. She had her colorful butterfly wings fully extended, and every time they touched me, they gave me a constitution buff that lasted ten minutes. The buff didn't stack, but the timer reset every time the ethereal wings brushed across me. Each brush felt soft against my skin, like a sudden, pleasant breeze.

"No," I said. I started pulling large metal pieces from my inventory as the others started attaching the chains to the cart. "No, I'm not sure. But nobody else was coming up with any other ideas."

She nodded. "What about the others? At the other stations."

"I warned them what's coming. That's the best we can do. Some people are sending folks to the Desperado to buy smoke curtains and hobgoblin dynamite to get ready. Others are forming outside the rooms and waiting to see what happens. If it happens like I anticipate, it's about to get crazy. Everyone is going to have to fight. They'll have to carve their way to the stairwells and then keep that path open while everyone goes down."

"And you really think this cart will keep us from having to fight?" Imani asked.

I grinned. "Oh, I'm sure there'll be plenty of fighting. I just want to even the odds a little."

Across the way, a man with a spell that worked like an arc welder joined up two pieces of metal that had been too big for me to work on at my engineering or new metalworking tables. I'd already attached the two train wheels to the top, which were part of the pulley-and-lever system that we'd use to lift the cart. When they were done putting all the pieces together, the crane would have five legs, one placed between each of the five stairwells. Each piece would arch up and meet high above the center of the five stairwells. When we were done, it would look like some bullshit college campus art installation, or a half-finished jungle gym, instead of what it really was: a crane.

Less than an hour later, we used Imani's magical chain to lift the back end of the interdiction cart into the air. The cart lifted easily, and the magical chain did not break. Once it was pulled all the way up and about a half an inch off the ground, we locked the chain into place. The entire cart hung vertically in the room, like it was a prize fish on display. The front of the cart faced downward. The small scoop that represented the bottom of the portal scraped against the marble floor. With a group of us holding the cart in place and several others leaning against the crane's five legs, we made a few slight adjustments. Once we had the cart where we wanted, we used additional chains to anchor the front in place so it wouldn't swing.

From there, I used my handmade ladder to climb up and to the cockpit. I patted the two Growler Gary left hands to make sure they were still firmly in place, and then I turned on the portal. I tuned it to the abyss.

The portal crackled to life, facing downward. It was almost the exact same size as the circle of marble in the center of the room.

Katia and Donut returned to the chamber. Katia was still 37, but Donut had risen a level to 33. Mongo had gone up a few levels to 26. Mordecai had insisted that we use Mongo as much as possible before the level was done, and I was glad to see the dinosaur had done well against the octopus monsters.

"I think it's going to happen soon," Katia said. She was in her She-Hulk form, about eight feet tall and wide. She had her riot shield on her left arm, and she'd chosen to keep it in its original form. It made her look especially imposing. "They all started heading back into the station a few minutes ago."

"They're quite easy to kill," Donut said. She jumped from Mongo's back to my shoulder and gave me a side headbutt. "You should've been there. It was fun."

"I bet it was," I said. I pointed to the dangling interdiction cart with the crackling portal. "God, I hope our theory is correct."

"Well," Katia said, "if the entire floor disappears, and not just the center, then there's nothing we could've done anyway. The clock is going to hit one day left in ten minutes. I bet it'll happen then."

"Okay, guys," I called. I looked nervously down at the floor beneath my feet. "Everybody out of the station. Quick."

THE CLOCK TICKED DOWN TO ONE DAY LEFT. WE'D ALL LEFT THE STA-tion, spreading out to the several different platforms that led up to the main room. We stood upon the vermilion line platform, where my sole remaining interdiction cart waited. This was the same cart we'd ridden all the way up to the end of the line to save Bautista and crew. This one was tuned to Station E, the same station where the mimic still waited for crawlers to munch upon. No monsters had approached for a while now, but we didn't want to gather everybody in the same place, nor did we want to get sneaked up upon. So we dispersed. Donut stood on my shoulder while Mongo leaned up against me. Katia and Elle chatted while Imani moved about the others, making sure they were all okay.

And just like that, it was on.

> System message. Attention. Attention. The management of the
> Iron Tangle would like to warn all customers and employees that
> the system has broken down. No more lines are running. You are
> no longer safe. We have been betrayed by the Krakaren, whom
> we thought were benevolent. We have been forced to initiate
> the self-destruct sequence. Throughout the system, the emer-
> gency escape tunnels are opening. Please be aware of possible
> gravitational shifts when you enter the escape tunnels. All em-
> ployees are urged to use the tunnels to proceed to station 60
> and await further instructions. All customers please use the
> escape tunnels to proceed to the stairwell portals at stations
> 12, 24, 36, 48, 72, or 433 on any of the lines. These stairwell

portals are powering up now and will open in exactly 18 hours. They will only be open for six hours before the self-destruction charges will blow.

This is the Iron Tangle, signing off. May the gods have mercy on you. Thanks for riding with us, and have a great day.

"They're laying the story on a little thick," Donut grumbled. "I mean, really, are we supposed to be cosplaying as terrified commuters now? Do I look like someone who would use public transportation?"

A mighty screeching noise filled the entire dungeon, like a rusty old door being forced open. I felt a rumble under my feet.

My chat was suddenly filled with people screaming for their lives.

RONALDO QU: A round section of the floor disappeared in the middle of the station. It fell away and then it shot up and out of the hole. The octopuses are pouring in. They're falling into the room, but from below. They're big now. Human-sized. Jesus. Jesus. They just keep coming. We have to run. We need to find another stairwell. There's too many.

GWENDOLYN DUET: The bomber guy warned all of you dumbasses. Fall back to the train lines. Hold them at the choke points.

RONALDO QU: He didn't say it would happen this bad.

GWENDOLYN DUET: Are you on crack? This is exactly what he said was going to happen. It's literally the exact thing he warned you about. Now clear the chat.

RONALDO QU: Fuck you, bitch.

Several iterations of this conversation filled my screen. All over, the centers of the stations were falling away, and then the Krakaren monsters were pouring into the rooms. I felt an odd mix of terror and pride that we'd accurately predicted what would happen. But that pride was short-lived as I realized how many people, despite our warnings, had chosen not to protect themselves. I couldn't believe people could've gotten this far and still remain such idiots.

We were ready for an onslaught of the monsters to pour out of our own stairwell station and come at us. We all waited, weapons ready. Imani barked at the flamethrowers, telling them to be on the lookout. Nothing happened.

"Holy shit, Carl," Elle said after a minute. "You crazy son of a bitch. I think your stupid idea worked. Let's go check it out."

We cautiously returned up the stairs and through the tunnels. The flamethrower squads uprooted their defensive positions and followed. We entered the station. The interdiction cart remained hanging upside down directly over the hole. Monsters poured into the portal. We could see it through the haze of the portal's back side. The Krakaren monsters fell headfirst, feetfirst, and sideways into the portal, like the hole in the ground was actually in the ceiling. Thousands of them. They kept coming and coming, getting sucked directly into the portal and to the abyss.

We all stood and stared. The portal crackled like it was getting hit by hail.

Imani was the one who snapped us back to reality. "Secure the entrances. Set the flamethrowers back up like before," she yelled. "I want a ring of flamers and mages around this portal in case something happens to Carl's cart."

Behind me, someone cried out in surprise. I turned to see a pair of juvenile Krakaren beasts slinking into the chamber from one of the opposite entrances. They weren't coming into the room from the newly opened "escape tunnel" but from one of the main railways. The things had likely been filling the secret tunnels between the tracks, the center of Katia's "noodle," and once the hatches all opened, they were being spooged all over the place. If they were also going into the regular, empty stations, then me plugging the hole here was only a temporary fix.

We jumped into action. Katia rolled forward, turning into her sentinel gun. She took out both of the octopuses while the others set up their perimeter defensive positions. Donut leaped to Mongo and rushed to defend one of the choke points while I stood sentry over the portal.

Once the defenses were set, Katia returned to her humanoid form and stood next to me and Imani. I imagined the giant abyss pit filling up with the monsters, so many of them together that it overflowed. The pit was much too big for that to really happen, though I suspected the majority of these monsters were surviving the high fall from the portal to the bottom of the abyss. These things were squishy and resistant to blunt trauma. The pit was probably a writhing mass of these monsters by now. I wondered if they got along with the hordes of ghouls that lived in the bottom of the abyss. Or with the wall monitor lizards who lived on the edges.

It didn't matter, I decided, as long as they remained way over there.

In fact, I realized as I watched the constant stream of creatures, it was probably a good thing for everybody if they did survive the fall into the pit. These were living, non-undead creatures, which meant every time one of them died, a ghoul was generated at a nearby ghoul generator.

"Some of these guys we've had to kill three times," I said. "Once when they hit the stage three DTs, then again when they're Krakaren babies, and then again if they turn into ghouls."

"It's a lot more than that," Imani said. "The stage three monsters were each birthing thousands of these octopuses. Octopi? What's the right word?"

"We got incoming," someone shouted. A group of red dots appeared on the map, though it wasn't so many. Maybe twenty of them. I felt the hot whoosh of the flamethrowers even halfway across the room. The mobs were killed in seconds.

"Hey, don't be an experience hog!" Donut shouted at a crawler at the front defensive position.

"Yo, Donut," I called over my shoulder. "Play nice. We're all on the same team here."

"Carl, I said I had the monster on the left, and he shot him first with the flamethrower!"

"You did not call the target," the crawler said. "And I am not a 'he.'" I looked over and saw what the problem was. The crawler operating the flamethrower was a level 27 **Dog Soldier**. Her class was something called a **Crisper**. She looked like a walking, talking German shepherd. She had a Vietnam-era helmet on her head with little holes cut out for her ears. Her name was **Tserendolgor**. I couldn't even begin to imagine how to pronounce that name, nor guess what nationality she originally was. But the fact she was a dog-themed race meant Donut would have an instant dislike of her.

"Goddamnit, Donut," I said. "Go to a different position and leave her alone."

"Yeah, go to a different position, cat," the woman said.

Donut hissed but led Mongo to the other side of the room.

"And I thought she was getting better after all that business with Growler Gary," Katia said.

"That *is* better," I said. "You should hear her talk about cocker spaniels."

"Oh, I have," Katia said. "She's told me all about your next-door neighbor's dog, Angel."

"They're still coming from below, but maybe not as many," Imani said, leaning over the portal to get a better look. "I wish it wasn't so blurry so we could see into the hole."

"It's definitely getting less thick with monsters," Katia agreed.

"You know," I said to Katia, "if your whole double-sided track theory is correct, then there's a straight line through that hole to the other chamber 36, and there's probably one of those province bosses in there. Super close. That's what I was originally worried about when you said the tracks were mirrored."

"Yeah, me, too," Katia said. "If we didn't have your portal, I'd be worried about it spreading into this room."

Behind us, another group of mobs approached and was quickly

dispatched. Then another. Soon, we had red dots all around us. There were four choke point entrances to the chamber, not including the secret one to the employee line, which we kept closed and guarded. The *Nightmare* was down there, still parked a few stations down. I'd poked my head into the line a bit earlier to see if the train was still there. We'd last used it to ferry Brynhild's Daughters to 60, and that's where it remained.

Donut and I had walked down there earlier to see if Fire Brandy was still kickin', and she was. We'd found her leaning out of her hole in the cockpit, talking with a pair of dwarven engineers who'd apparently climbed in through the broken side window. One of them had wanted to take the train to I don't know where, but Brandy had refused. "There's nowhere to go, you fool," she'd been saying when we walked up. The dwarf had argued, and I'd thought maybe we'd have a fight on our hands. But they quickly left upon our arrival.

The train was still on and idling. I could tell right away that something was wrong with the demon woman. Her usual, matter-of-fact, Southern-belle-but-also-German persona had shifted to something more melancholy. She was still giving birth regularly. I didn't know if we'd get another chance to see her before the floor ended, and I'd wanted to collect more of the Sheol Bricks. I'd shown one to Mordecai and he'd practically jizzed himself and told me to retrieve as many as possible. I'd asked her if she could part with any, and she allowed me to take several hundred still-burning pieces along with a few dozen that hadn't yet caught on fire.

"I'd give it all to you," she said. "But I need to keep the fire burning nice and hot. Keep my babies happy, for as long as it will last."

"Brandy, are you okay?" Donut asked.

"I talked to that dwarf friend of yours," she said. "Tizquick. He told me about his daughter. They killed her, you know. Once word spread, they started to get angry."

"Who?" I asked. "Who are they? And whom did they kill?"

"The dwarves and the gremlins. They killed Madison, the human you brought up here. The human resources woman. They built a stand and a noose, and they hanged her. I didn't see it, but they brought her body to me. I took it into the fire."

"Holy shit," I said.

"Only those mantaur creatures are holding the faith. I guess a few tried to fight the dwarves, but they all got chased off. I don't know about those guys. There might still be some out there, so be careful."

"That's . . . that's crazy," I said. Madison hadn't deserved that. Well, her *character* deserved it. That was the thing, wasn't it? All these NPCs were playing characters, and only a handful were starting to realize it.

And that, I realized, was the problem with Brandy. She'd finally realized that this was all a construction. How did one deal with that? Especially one who had children?

"We gotta get back there," I said. "If I don't see you, take care of those babies, okay?"

The demon woman didn't answer. She just nodded and returned to her fire.

———

AN HOUR LATER, AND THE NUMBER OF MONSTERS COMING THROUGH the hole in the center of the room had trickled to a stop, but the mobs were now approaching us from all the other angles. We were starting to see blister ghouls mixed in with the octopus monsters. I moved to stand next to Donut. We let the flamethrowers do most of the work, but I tossed smoke curtains and the nonexplosive bangers at the incoming monsters while Donut hurled magic missiles at them. She occasionally cast *Second Chance* on one of the corpses and then *Clockwork Triplicate*. The zombie Krakarens wreaked havoc on their fellow clones for several seconds before they were torn down. Katia returned to her gun form. She towered over the group, choosing to sit high and fire down into the throngs. We stood amongst hundreds of other crawlers, all throwing fire at the mobs. We held them back, but sometimes the waves were so thick, so frenzied, I feared we'd be overwhelmed.

Our only respite came when the dead filled the hallways so much, it created a clog. It'd remain that way for several minutes until the acid blood broke down their own bodies, and the corpses started to melt. Sometimes the corpses exploded for no reason, showering acid at the defenders. We lost several people that way.

We'd had to form barriers to keep the caustic liquid from pooling into the chamber, which would in turn burn the feet of the defenders. The acid didn't burn away with fire, but we found it could be frozen. The acid would eventually melt, but it lost its acidity after that. That became Elle's job. She zipped from one choke point to the next, freezing the pools of acid.

I worried about the others. I sent a message to Bautista, asking him for an update.

BAUTISTA: We couldn't get back into 72. There are both ghouls and the Krakaren monsters, and they're coming from everywhere. We've fallen back down the line. We got chased to station 60, but we couldn't get in. There's a big group of those mantaur things guarding the platform. Each one is a neighborhood boss. They're superstrong. One of them has gotten his hands on one of those alarm traps, and it's playing some heavy metal song over and over. I think the song is giving them a buff, and it's making everybody's ears bleed. We had to fall back. We're stuck between the two groups.

After that, I started to receive even more dire messages from several other groups. One group was pinned in the area between Train Yard E and the monsters were all pouring from the tunnels. They'd thought to switch over to the employee line, but they couldn't get close. And the station mimic at the train yard was sending pieces of itself out to hit them from behind. They were getting squeezed.

Everywhere, groups who'd stayed in the stations had taken heavy losses, but those who'd fallen back were unable to get back in, and now we had reports of province bosses appearing in the rooms where there hadn't been one before.

"We need backup!" a voice cried behind me. It was the dog soldier woman. She was falling back. A human to her right abruptly had tentacles wrapped around him. His body exploded into mist. These new Krakaren monsters were suddenly all level 20 to 23 and about seven feet tall.

"Donut, Katia! Ludacris!"

"Mongo, stay!" Donut yelled as she jumped to my shoulder.

We detached from our spot and ran toward the hole in the defenses. "Get back! Let them through!" Elle cried. I pulled a boom jug from my inventory.

"Ready?" Katia asked, widening as she moved. She rotated her riot shield 90 degrees and pushed it forward, like a literal battering ram.

Ahead, the hallway was full of monsters crammed tight. They screamed and rushed at us.

"Go!" I said.

She activated Crowd Blast. She rushed forward, exploding into the crowd like a wrecking ball. The Krakaren monsters and ghouls rocketed back like bowling pins. Acid misted into the air, and Katia cried out in pain.

I was already running, following her. She'd gone far, all the way to the first intersection. This junction was like a T, going left and right, both with short stairwells leading down, which in turn led to a dozen other chambers in each direction. I made a split-second decision as I ran, and I pulled a second boom jug.

Katia, dazed, but still on her feet, pulled her crowd-control baton and swung it in one direction as the crossbow flipped upside down and fired in the other.

We came running up.

"Let me know when you're ready!" I yelled.

"Go," Donut said. "Counting down from three now."

I tossed the boom jugs in both directions just as Donut used *Puddle Jumper* to get us back to the main room.

Twin fireballs erupted at the end of the hallway. The three of us stumbled backward, having been teleported back into the main room.

Only then did I feel it, the acid burning my face and legs. Donut cried out in pain, also burning.

But Imani was right there, and all three of us glowed. She'd cast something to negate the acid, and a moment later, it was as if nothing had happened. Though my jacket, my only non-magical clothing item, now had a huge hole in the left arm, my cloak and other magical items were unharmed.

The dog soldier and the others quickly reset their defense while Imani shouted for backup at the choke points.

"That was pretty awesome," I said, breathing heavily. "Katia, you okay?"

"I hate that ability," she said, wheezing. "But wow, it works well. Did you see them all? There were like fifty of them at the bottom of both stairs, and you hit both groups."

"We just wasted my last *Puddle Jumper* of the floor," Donut said. Mongo came rushing up and sniffed worriedly at Donut. "I'm fine. Mommy is fine." She looked over at the dog soldier woman. "You're welcome."

The woman just grunted and reset her magical flamethrower.

Boom. We all felt the ground shake. A huge explosion rocked the chamber. A moment later, a second explosion also rocked the walls. Everyone paused, looking about.

I looked worriedly over at the crane, but the device held. The chains groaned, and the cart trembled, but it remained hanging there.

"What was that?" Katia called.

I shook my head. "It was nearby. I think that was maybe the soul crystal over at station 12. The second explosion was maybe the one on the other side of the noodle."

"Fucking hell, Carl," Elle said, floating up. "Did you do that?"

"Why is it every time there's a big explosion, you immediately think I had something to do with it?"

"Because it usually is you," she said.

"She does have a point, Carl," Donut said.

"Was there somebody over there? Why did it blow?" Imani asked.

"I didn't see anybody on the map," Katia said.

Imani pointed. "Elle, take a team and check it out. Be careful. We might have to fall back to station 12 if the ghoul generators on either side are gone."

"On it," Elle said. She shouted at a pair of crawlers, and they headed toward the employee-line exit.

I had a thought. I sent a quick message to Mordecai.

MORDECAI: I think you're right. I'm guessing the soul crystals they use for those ghoul generators are a little smaller than the one you have in your inventory, so they can't handle so much simultaneous stress. I know this because you're still alive. Too much local stress, and they pop, like fuses. Luckily when they go that way, they'll only kill everything in the room and maybe a block in each direction. And not an entire quadrant.

CARL: Holy shit, I have a glorious idea.

MORDECAI: No.

CARL: You don't know what it is yet.

MORDECAI: I don't care what it is. If it's a Carl idea, it's probably a brilliant idea that's going to get you killed. Donut told me about how you captured the *Nightmare* train. I bet you thought that was a glorious idea, too.

CARL: No, that was a dumb idea. This is much better, though it's funny you mention the *Nightmare*.

WHEN KATIA HAD PERFORMED HER CROWD BLAST, QUICKLY FOL-
lowed by me tossing the twin boom jugs, we'd killed several of the
larger-sized Krakaren monsters at the same time. I didn't know if it
was because we'd killed them all at once, or if the constant fighting
and killing had finally added up to some lifetime load limit. Whatever it was, soon after, the two closest soul crystals had popped. At
least that was what I was gambling on. I suspected the bigger the
Krakaren beasts grew, the more of a burden each one put on the
crystals when they died.

This was likely all by design. A part of the game. A way to keep
everything "fair." In fact, I also suspected killing one of those province bosses likely had the side effect of blowing every soul crystal in
the area.

ELLE: First off, there was one of those weird-ass double-stack
boss dudes on the employee line. A mantaur or whatever
they're called. I thought they were regular NPCs, but he
attacked us. We took care of it. But make sure there's a
sentry on that employee entrance in case there's more.
Anyway, station 12 is definitely the one that blew. All the
monsters are dead. There's not even that much rubble, not
like the last one. There's loads of corpses. The crystal is
still floating in the middle of the room above the burned-out
generator, but it's not glowing anymore. It's tiny, like the

size of a marble. There's a hole in the floor here, too, but nothing is coming up.

IMANI: Look through the hole in the floor and see if you can see through to the other room. Don't go down there. Look quick and then come back.

ELLE: I'm walking up now. Yeah. Hey, Katia, has anybody called you a genius lately? The hole goes all the way to the other room. There's about a 20-foot drop, and there's another door. That room looks burned-out, too. Weird. It's upside down. What a trip. Hang on, I'm going to drop a rock in to see what happens.

IMANI: Don't. Just come back.

ELLE: Oh, unwad your panties. What are we calling the in-between space? The escape tunnel?

DONUT: WE ARE CALLING IT THE NOODLE.

ELLE: I dropped a rock, and it fell all the way into the room across the way, but then it fell back. It hit the edge of the hole, bounced once, and then it rolled along the interior of the noodle. I thought it would float in the middle, but it looks like "down" is just toward the closest interior wall. You could walk a loop-de-loop in the thing and always feel like you're standing upright. Like one of those carnival rides that spins really fast. I wonder what would happen if I balanced a rock exactly in the middle. Maybe it *would* float.

"Imani," I said, "I need a team to help us fight our way back to my last interdiction cart." We'd left it turned on upon the track, plugging the southward hole toward the train station. However, the mobs were coming from all directions now. Hopefully they'd left it alone. "If it's still there, Donut, Katia, and I are going to jump on and then head toward the train yard. I'll need to keep three or four of them with us because we're going to need to lift the thing up."

"What about the mimic?" Imani asked.

"We're not going to approach it. But if it comes for us, we'll just hit it with the portal again."

She looked at me dubiously. "All right. I'll ask for volunteers."

But before she even had the chance to ask, Li Jun, Zhang, and Li Na were suddenly there, right by my side.

"He has his volunteers," Li Jun said.

"What about the rest of your team?" I asked. I looked for the others. I recognized their old boss, one of the men we'd saved from the Maestro. He was standing next to the mushroom guy and several of the others, defending one of the four exits.

"They are needed here. We will help best we can and return," Li Jun said. "It is the least we can do."

"Awesome," I said, looking at the three in turn.

I hadn't had the time to examine, or meet, Li Na yet, but I examined her now. I remembered her as a slight, almost mousy woman. She was taller now, rail thin. Her skin was deathly pale, ghost-like. She still resembled the woman she was, but her face had taken on an odd, demon-like appearance. Her mouth was almost twice as wide as it should be, and her brow was deeply ridged. A short pair of black horns stuck up through her black hair. She wore a flowing white-and-red robe with long, wide arms that almost reached the floor. Chains hung from the armholes, and they dragged as she walked, causing her to jingle. I knew from the recap episode that she had at least four different chains she fought with. One caught on fire and another tossed wind blades when she swung it like a lasso over her head. One could keep mobs immobilized. She was level 30, and her race was something called a **Changbi**. Her class was the ominous-sounding **Slave Driver**.

She met my gaze, her dark eyes boring into me. Despite her disturbing appearance, I could see why Zhang had a thing for her. There was something there, deep and alluring. But also terrifying. She had an I-might-murder-you-at-any-moment-but-it'll-probably-be-fun-for-both-of-us aesthetic.

She bowed slightly. "Thank you for saving me and my brother. Twice." She turned to Donut and bowed again.

"You are quite welcome," Donut said, swishing her tail.

"Okay," I said. "We have a lot to do, and not much time to do it. But the first step is to get to that cart."

"Maybe you should tell us the whole plan before we dive headfirst into battle," Li Na said. "In case you die, then we will know what the mission is and can carry on."

DONUT: SHE DOES HAVE A POINT, CARL.

LI NA, IT TURNED OUT, WAS PRETTY DAMN SMART. AND INTENSE. She reminded me a little of Imani, plus Chris, Brandon's brother, who was still in the wind somewhere. And Hekla. She did not talk often, but when she did speak, it was usually to point out an obvious flaw in my plan. Both Li Jun and Zhang were too timid to tell me if I was full of shit. Donut wasn't, but she rarely had an alternate plan. Katia often had good ideas, but she was prone to second-guessing herself to the point of letting me bowl right over her. I could tell right away Li Na would not suffer any fools, and if she opened her mouth, everybody around her paused to hear what she had to say.

We would never work well together as a party. Not after this, not if we wanted to remain friendly with one another. It's not that I didn't want to work with someone like her. In fact, I probably needed more people like her around me. I thought she was pretty cool, but I could tell she was quickly getting irritated with me. That was okay. Small teams that occasionally worked together were still the best way to go. There possibly was a formal way to attach separate parties according to the cookbook, but it didn't get turned on until the sixth floor. A guild system. It was only mentioned in the 22nd edition of the cookbook, so I didn't know for certain if it was still a thing or not. That happened a lot where they tested new features for a crawl or two before they decided on whether to keep it or not. I hoped it remained.

It was Li Na's idea to raise up the Def Leppard cart and then poke at the ass of the province boss on the other side of the noodle. If we enticed it to attack, it'd hit the portal and teleport to the abyss. "It'll sweeten the pot and give us an additional fallback point," Li Na had said.

It was a fantastic idea, and I told her so. We couldn't kill the thing, but we could at least get it the hell out of here. We'd have to do this now before we left. I quickly told the others the plan.

The monsters continued to come at us in waves from the hallways. It was constant, though less intense than before. About 20% of the people on my chat were just gone, which was a devastating amount, but honestly, it was much less than I anticipated. It turned out, the Krakaren monsters had invaded all the transfer stations, but the regular, empty stations that weren't prime numbers or stairwell stations did not have trapdoors in them, and those places all had only a single entrance. Bautista and his group were set up at three such stations. Each station had a short, easily defensible entrance that was at the top of a thin set of stairs. All around the Tangle, others were doing the same.

I warned everyone to keep at least two stations away from either station 12 or 72, the two types of stations with soul crystals. We were going to attempt to blow them all at once.

But there were several things I had to do first, starting with this province boss. As Li Na had said, teleporting this thing to the abyss would just add to the pile.

There hadn't been any Krakaren mobs in the noodle for a while now, but we'd had dozens of reports of the boss from the other side seeping its way into the opposite room, thus occupying both. People who had abandoned their station 36 were fighting their way back to find a giant boss in the room, a boss they couldn't handle.

The province boss directly across from our room hadn't attempted to come in our space, likely because of the portal. Li Na's idea was to raise up the Def Leppard cart, leaving enough room for someone to lean in and get its attention. We could only lift the cart an additional foot, but that was enough for Donut to carefully stick her head into the hole and peer across the way to the other room to see if there even was a boss there. There was nothing on her map, but that didn't mean anything.

"Be careful," I said worriedly. If even a whisker touched the portal, she'd be zapped away to the abyss. We didn't dare turn it off. We should have used Katia for this, but Donut had insisted.

"It's there," Donut said as she peered into the escape tunnel. The noodle. "It's just hair and quivering skin covering up the hole. It's disgusting. It looks like one of those guys whose pants don't cover his butt. Like when your smelly friend used to come over and play video games while you two lied about your exploits with women. What was his name? Monobrow Sam? Really, Carl, I don't know why you had such revolting friends."

"Okay, pull back," I said. "Goddamnit, be careful. Watch your head."

She backed up and looked at me.

"I got an achievement just for looking at it! At the boss, I mean. Not your friend's butt. But I should've received an award for having to see that, too. The monster is glowing blue. And another color. It's sparkling."

"It's a province boss. It probably has a million buffs going at once. Can we get on with this? You're probably going to get another achievement for hitting it with a magic missile, too."

"It's going to be a good one," Donut said. "I have a full-powered shot stored in my glasses, and I'm going to hit it with a double shot."

A group of crawlers detached the chain holding the cart up and held on to it. I threatened each and every one of them not to drop it prematurely.

Donut leaned in, shot it, then scrambled back. "I hit it! I hit it!"

The monster bellowed, a thousand mouths suddenly shrieking at once. "Drop it! Drop the cart!" I called. The crawlers groaned, lowering the cart back into place. I locked the chain while I secured the lower chain.

The moment I did, the whole cart shuddered. I felt it. It had worked.

"Fuck yeah," I said. I turned to Li Na and held up my hand. "High five."

She just looked at me. "If I touch you with my hand, you will experience excruciating pain throughout your entire body that will cause you to lose control of your bladder and bowels."

"Okay, then," I said. "Moving on."

A blast hit the portal, and the whole thing shook.

Something screamed. Loud and high-pitched, though not nearly as loud as before. Another blast hit it.

"Shit," I said. "Maybe we only got some of it."

"I knew this was a bad idea," Imani said. "We should have left it alone."

"These portals are pretty stout," I said. "Nothing can get through it." I didn't actually know if that was true or not.

"Hello? Who's there?" a voice called from the other side of the portal. He had a nasally British accent, like how a spoiled prince might sound. "Show yourselves, you cowards!" A moment passed, and then he screamed. Each cry was loud and short. It was unlike anything I'd ever heard. "You have deprived me of my prey, and I demand satisfaction!"

"Carl, it's another crawler," Donut said. "Look at the map."

I looked over at Katia. "Turn off the portal, but get ready to flip it back on."

She nodded and rose into the air on stilt-like legs to reach the controls. The portal flickered and turned off. I leaned over and looked down. Across the way another crawler stared down at me, also standing at the edge of the noodle and looking in. We met eyes over the distance.

"Carl," he said. "I should have known such a colossal fuckup could only be perpetrated by such a colossal dolt."

"Hello, Prepotente," I said.

The goat creature screamed, suddenly and unexpectedly, causing me to almost jump out of my skin. There was no reason for it.

"What the hell?" someone muttered behind me.

Prepotente went on as if nothing had happened. "Oh, hello, Donut," he said, brightening. "Well met. You are even more delightful in person. I've been wishing to meet you for some time now. We are two of a kind, you and I. From what I understand we're the only two remaining Earth creatures in the dungeon who have gained true sapience. I was so very disappointed to learn you'd obtained access to the Desperado Club and not Club Vanquisher. I do wish to share a brandy with you sometime and to discuss our unique circumstances. Now, Carl, is that other one with you? The murderer? If so, then there are five of the top ten here all at once. That must be a first."

"We have a few former top tens in here," I said. "Now what the hell are you doing over there?"

"What do you think? I was about to kill the boss. I had it asleep and entranced, and I was working on lowering its blood pressure enough to initiate cardiac arrest. Another two hours, and it would've worked, too. And when it perished, it would have blown multiple soul crystals, thus causing a chain reaction throughout the entire system that would allow our fellows to proceed to the next floor. Instead, I am now looking through a hole in the floor at definitive proof that humans and Neanderthals are related. Where, pray tell me, did you teleport my target to?" the goat asked.

"To the abyss. Why don't you come over here and call me a Neanderthal to my face?"

He screamed.

"Gentlemen," Imani said, appearing next to me, "both of you put your dicks away. We don't need this right now."

"I could kill you," Prepotente said. He said it to Imani. "I could crunch on your bones and glory in the sound that they made when they splintered."

"Bitch, what?" Imani demanded, her demeanor changing on a dime.

He screamed.

Thwap! The goat bleated in pain as he was smacked in the head with a stick. The attack came from someone standing right next to him. He disappeared from view, but he kept screaming, over and over in short bursts just out of sight. A new head appeared in the hole. A woman.

"I want you to sit there and think about what you've said, Pony," she said over her shoulder. This was Miriam Dom. The human shepherd. The goat lady, they called her. She was about forty years old, a little plump and dark-haired. She carried a long staff with a hook at the end like she was goddamned Little Bo Peep. She had a gentle Italian accent.

"Don't you mind him," the woman said. "He says things like that, but he doesn't mean them. He was always a little ornery, even before the change. It's nice to meet you all. Sorry for the disturbance."

The goat returned to the hole and screamed once again. I didn't know how the hell she put up with this. Jesus fuck.

"I will kill you tonight as you sleep," Prepotente said to Miriam as he rubbed his head. I saw, then, that he had humanlike fingers, though his fingernails were long and curled and black. Whatever change he'd undergone to make him intelligent was different than the one Donut had undergone.

"No, you won't, sweetie," she said. She reached over and kissed the goat on the top of the head where she'd whacked him.

"Do it again," he said a moment later. "It still hurts."

"Only if you're a good boy. And apologize to those two."

He nodded solemnly and looked down at us. "I'm sorry I wanted to murder you."

"Good Pony," Miriam said, and kissed the goat on the head.

Prepotente screamed.

"I have questions," I said. "So very many questions."

"Maybe some other time, sweetie," the woman said. "We need to find a different boss monster now. Ciao!"

They both departed from view. A new creature appeared, but only for a moment. It was huge and dark and covered with phantom black flames that flickered with wisps that drank the light. Three pairs of humanlike breasts ran down the monster's underside. This was another goat, transformed. It was the size of a horse. We'd seen this thing before. Mordecai had called it a hellspawn familiar. It made a wet chittering noise, something I felt deep in my bones. The air crackled with heat as it passed.

I exchanged a look with Imani, and she shook her head. The bizarre exchange told me all I needed to know about that group. We needed to stay the fuck away from them.

"Did you hear that?" Donut said. "He called me delightful!"

WE HAD TO FIGHT OUR WAY TO THE CART. IMANI DISPATCHED A CREW to help us grind our way down there. There were still dozens of the Krakaren monsters in the halls and on the tracks. I had no idea how the hell the goat team had survived in this. Reports from around the dungeon were that the waves were still thick everywhere. I knew we could be overwhelmed at any moment, so we needed to hurry.

Both Li Jun and Li Na were ferocious fighters. Li Jun was like a damn kung fu master, flipping through the air and grabbing tentacles and throwing the monsters. Li Na was similar, though she twirled and wrapped the monsters in her chains, paralyzing them, allowing Zhang to cast a spell called *Dirt Clod* that pummeled them to death with rocks.

All three of them, it turned out, had an immunity to acid attacks. After the incident with the brindle grubs on the second floor, it was something all three looked for in their respective classes. I didn't blame them.

The cart, thankfully, remained where we left it. The monsters had ignored it. It was turned on and facing stop 24, but there weren't many creatures coming from that direction anymore. Katia set up at the back of the cart, facing backward to take down anything that gave chase. Zhang, Mongo, Li Jun, and his sister stood guard in the middle of the cart while Donut and I took to the cockpit. We had but minutes to get on and get going before a new wave of red dots would descend upon us.

I hit the throttle, and we were off.

My immediate worry was station 24. The last time we passed it, we'd been jumped by Krakaren babies. I knew they'd all gone inside to pull their escape tunnel bullshit, but surely there were more hanging out at the station, just waiting for some dumbasses to stroll on by.

And sure enough, as we blasted past the station, a single Krakaren stood on the platform. This one was huge, a massive octopus thing with swirling tentacles. A neighborhood boss, probably just as big, if not bigger, than the one we'd fought on the second floor. Luckily it was half slopped onto the track, its giant tentacles casually hanging over the edge of the platform. We hit it with the portal, and it teleported the whole thing away, leaving a wet spot on the tiles as we continued to zoom toward the train yard. I eased off the throttle after that, coasting to a stop just before we left the tunnel and entered the massive cavern that housed the train yard.

We needed to get this cart onto the employee line, facing the deeper levels. In order to do that, we had to maneuver the cart to the entrance of the employee line with the portal facing the opposite direction it faced now.

The problem with that was twofold. One, this cart was a different gauge than the employee line. The wheels were too close together, so we wouldn't be able to drive it on the tracks. And two, in order to get it there, we had to physically pick up the cart and carry it across dozens of other tracks, all through an area crawling with both ghouls and minions of the mimic.

We eased out of the tunnel and paused, taking in the massive cavern. The main, fenced-in area of Train Yard E was still a good half a mile away. I could see the wrecked remnants of the giant fence. The massive gate still stood, and so did the real administrative building. I could smell the acrid stench of burned wood and bodies.

The walls here were dotted with dozens of cave entrances, and the ground was filled with just as many train tracks. Corpses lay everywhere, mostly ghouls, but there was a good number of crawlers sprawled throughout.

There had to be five hundred or more monsters between here and the train yard. Most of them were south of us, near the old building and fence.

The mimic itself was too far away to attack us directly, though I knew from dozens of frantic messages that the monster's minions and ridiculously long tongue were causing havoc upon anyone in the area. It loomed huge in the distance, as tall as the chamber, only half pretending to be a building now. A pair of blimp-sized red eyes glowed. One of the towers in the train yard collapsed as we watched, though I couldn't see what had knocked it over.

A group of several dozen crawlers was holed up in that burned-out administrative building, fighting off the waves of ghouls and the mimic's minions, which were apparently nothing more than giant car-sized mouths with centipede-like legs. If you chopped them in half, it just made two of them. I could see a few of them from our position in the tunnel. The strange mobs reminded me of those wind-up toys that were nothing but a chattering mouth.

There was another group of crawlers trapped inside of a lone train car in the yard itself, unable to leave because they were within reach of the massive city boss. I only heard about them secondhand, and I had no idea if they were still there or if they had survived.

There was a lot of that, in these last, desperate hours of the fourth floor. Cries for help. Rumors of groups in need.

You will not break me. Fuck you all. You will not break me.

We really needed to deal with this thing. The mimic. It was my goddamn fault it was here in the first place. But other than sneaking past the area, our mission for the moment didn't involve the monster. I could possibly use the portal cart to teleport it away like we did before. But we were no longer in a tunnel, with the protection that a tunnel provided, and the monster could easily get at us from the side or above or any other angle before we maneuvered the track-based cart at it. It was just too risky.

The plan was to sneak along the wall until we got to the employee line and to carry the large cart in. Hopefully we'd remain undiscovered. We'd need to protect the cart while Elle brought the *Nightmare* up to meet us. Elle was already in the train, waiting for my signal to come down the track and meet us. She complained that Fire Brandy was being less than helpful and wouldn't do anything without talking to me first. At least she allowed Elle to move the train.

But then I spied the pair of mantaur creatures guarding the entrance to the employee line, and I knew that plan was out the window. With all the chaos spreading in front of them, they hadn't noticed us yet. I eased the silent cart backward, slipping it back into the tunnel and out of sight.

"Why did we stop?" Li Na asked.

"Hang on," I said, thinking. I formed a fist and stared down at my glove. Mantaurs.

CARL: Hey, Mordecai. Quick question. If I, uh, accidentally summon the war god Grull, how long do I have before he's un-summoned?

MORDECAI: Run. Don't fight him. He's goddamned invulnerable. You can't kill him. Take my special brew potion. Run. Don't look back.

CARL: Chill. I haven't actually summoned him. It's just a question.

MORDECAI: By the gods, Carl. Don't scare me like that.

CARL: So . . . ?

I actually knew the answer to this already, as it was discussed in my cookbook, but I wanted to confirm it, and I wanted to make sure there was a record of me actually asking the question.

There wasn't a whole lot about deities in the book. What was there didn't even warrant its own chapter. I'd found the information stuffed in the middle of the miscellaneous chapter:

<Note added by Crawler Coolie. 19th Edition>

There are three types of deity summonings. Avoid all three. Only idiots deal with deities. Some of them are genuine NPCs, but the big ones like Apito and Eris and so forth are always sponsored by some rich prick who basically paid extra to play a game called the Celestial Ascendency. The game is contained on the twelfth floor, but the individual gods sometimes get called away. That game is different than the Faction War Games and has its own followers and storyline. I don't really understand, but I do know this. The gods are invulnerable except on the twelfth and above floors. They are strong. They kill everything. And there ain't a damn thing you can do about it.

Anyway, the three types of summonings. All three require a physical vessel. Usually a mob. There are celestial boons, which is when a worshipper prays to a god, and he comes to fight for his worshipper. There are indentured summonings, where a powerful mage summons the deity to fight for him for a short time. This is against the god's will, and they are usually pissed when it happens. And finally there are involuntary summonings. That's when some poor fool accidentally summons the god because of some trap or spell or just bad luck. The gods are usually pissed about this one, too, and what's worse, they arrive untethered, which allows them to smash everything in sight.

In my short experience, all three scenarios lead to the summoner's death. Even the first scenario. Don't trust deities under any circumstance. Just stay the fuck away. That's my advice.

<Note added by Crawler Forkith. 20th Edition>

They may be invulnerable, but they still feel pain. They still bleed. The drivers of these bodies suffer. In honor of my sister, I pray I make it to the twelfth floor just so I may slay one. I know this is but a dream, but I will look in the god's eyes and say to him, "This is for Barkith. This is for my sister."

Following this was a second note by Coolie, which focused mostly on involuntary summonings, which was what happened when I used my gauntlet. Apparently this was a pretty common thing, a way to collect more sponsorship money. God-summoning equipment was sprinkled throughout the dungeon, allowing for special guest appearances. Oftentimes the deity spots were purchased by celebrities. It was a safe way to get in on the game if one wasn't part of one of the dynastic families who controlled the armies of the ninth floor.

At the end of all that, there was one additional note. It wasn't something I'd be able to utilize anytime soon, but it was interesting, and I filed the information away.

<Note added by Crawler Tin. 21st Edition>

I have noticed something quite curious. The gods and goddesses are Soul Armor. So when the aliens inhabit the bodies of the gods, they do so like the Intellect Hunters, the Scree, and the Valtay. The aliens are wearing the gods like clothes. That means they can, in theory, be removed with a successful cast of any spell designed to remove biological armor, such as *Take That Shit Off* and *Laundry Day*. You'd have to first defeat the invulnerability, of course. Plus it won't hurt the gods, who will revert to their programming, natural state, whatever you wish to call it, and who knows what'll happen to the aliens who were driving them? But if you need a god to do your bidding, it might be in your best interest to first shed it of its off-world influence. I have noticed that the aliens are quite unpredictable in their manner.

It took Mordecai an unusually long time to answer my question. I suspected he was consulting with Donut to make sure I wasn't planning anything stupid.

> **MORDECAI:** A deity involuntarily summoned lasts as many seconds as the level of the vessel plus as many seconds as the god's level. Grull is a sanctum-tier deity, which means he is level 250. Mantaurs are level 40, so it would be for a total of 290 seconds.

That was slightly different than what it said in my book, but the end result was similar. Actually, better. It said they'd last for about five minutes. They probably didn't know the exact formula. I quickly added it to the book.

> **CARL:** How big will he be?
> **MORDECAI:** Why are you asking this?
> **CARL:** Running low on time, Mordecai.
> **MORDECAI:** The answer is kind of complicated. The short answer is, once summoned, he will grow until he fills the chamber he is in. Like that rage elemental you faced earlier. The real version can change sizes, but if he's summoned, the rules are different. Summoning is a very complicated process that we don't have time to explain.
> **CARL:** Wait, so if I summon him into a potion vial, he'll be tiny?
> **MORDECAI:** Yes. But he'll be strong enough to get out unless you build the proper sigil, and none of you are level 20 summoners, so that's not going to happen.
> **CARL:** Gotcha. One more question. After he's summoned, how long before I can summon again. Can I summon him again right away?

Mordecai didn't answer for a long moment.

MORDECAI: Once he's summoned and then un-summoned, you
can bring him back right away. There's no cooldown. You
can also steal him from one summoning to a second
summoning. So if he's captured in a sigil, and a worshipper
summons him again via a different means, the god will
break his containment and move to the new vessel.
This . . . this is very important to know. I learned it the hard
way. The hardest way possible.

CARL: Thanks, Mordecai.

MORDECAI: Now don't you even dare think about—

I closed out the chat. I turned to the others. "The plan has
changed."

"To what?" Li Na asked the same time Katia said, "Uh-oh."

"Don't worry. You'll figure it out as we go."

———

I STEPPED OUT FROM THE TUNNEL, LOADED THE BANGER SPHERE IN
my xistera, and I spun, hurling it at the pair of mantaurs. They were
pretty far away, and I honestly didn't think I could possibly throw
the damn thing that distance, but sure enough, the round ball sailed
directly at them. My aim was off, but the metal ball hit the ground
just in front of them with a *plink*. One of them reached down to pick
it up. My second ball was already in the air, and this one hit home,
crashing into the creature's head. He cried out in pain. A distant
health bar appeared over him.

Their dots had been the white of NPCs, but the ghouls weren't
attacking them, and I had multiple reports of them attacking all
crawlers on sight. Their dots both turned red the moment they saw
me there. I waved and waited. They fell forward and started galloping toward us. They moved quickly, but in an odd, halting fashion
straight out of a horror movie.

"They really are disturbing," Donut said from my shoulder. "They should have two pairs of legs and one set of arms, not one pair of legs and two pairs of arms."

"Yeah, it's pretty weird," I agreed.

"Li Na is really mad at you about this," Donut said. "She called you an idiot."

"That's because I am an idiot," I said. "I've never denied it."

We stepped back into the tunnel to wait for them.

All of us stood in front of the cart. All except Zhang, who now stood in the cart's cockpit, ready to turn it off if he had to. The portal swirled ominously behind our backs. From the business side of the portal, it looked like a pool of mercury. I had an inexplicable desire to reach out and stick my hand into the pool of magic. And then it would be over. All of this would be over.

The two creatures came galloping up, screaming at the tops of their lungs. They both had their Wolverine-style claws out and ready to engage.

"Hail! The battle is met!" one of them cried just as Katia, who'd been cosplaying as an oddly placed wall pillar, swung down with all of her might onto the creature's back, pinning him to the ground like he'd been caught in a mousetrap. She held the powerful creature still the best she could. The mob cried out and scrabbled at the ground with his claws, showering rock.

Li Na bounced off the wall as a glowing chain ratcheted out of her arm on her dress. She flipped in the air, lassoing the chain around the creature's neck. He glowed blue, called Li Na a wench, and closed his eyes.

The neighborhood boss fell into unconsciousness. He'd remain that way for a full minute, though she could do it again another four times, she said, until she had to rest.

Holy shit, she's something else, I thought. How did Li Jun hit the top ten and not her?

And then I saw how Li Jun had earned his spot on the list.

I dropped a smoke curtain as Donut pumped a magic missile into the second mantaur. Katia remained atop the first, but her crossbow appeared and started pumping bolts into him. The creature howled as he stood to his full height. "Kill with power! Die! Die!" he shouted. His clawed hands glinted in the tunnel's light.

He charged directly in my general location despite the smoke curtain.

Li Jun, standing to my right, had cast a buff onto his hands that caused them to glow red. He slid forward, sliding along the track, and he slammed a fist into the creature's leg, ducking under a savage swipe that surely would've decapitated him. The leg shattered, causing the monster to cry out and tumble forward. Li Jun backflipped as the monster fell, again narrowly dodging a swipe of the claw.

Before I could react, Li Jun bounced off my shoulders and leaped forward. He sailed over the still-falling monster, landing behind him. The creature swiped forward. Mongo, who'd been to my left, dodged and savagely tore at his upper left while a mounted Donut pumped magic missiles point-blank into its head.

"Don't kill him!" I said, stepping forward. "Get ready!"

"A warrior's death is a good death," he croaked just as Mongo tore through his arm, completely severing off the metallic claw. The dinosaur roared louder than I'd ever heard. Donut was also screaming. She shot one more missile into the creature's face. Despite all this, that large creature's health was only about three-quarters gone.

"Jesus, stop," I yelled. "Remember what we're doing here."

I punched the dazed and dying mantaur in the arm. The one not mangled by Mongo. I felt it break, like a heavy branch snapping.

1.5

I jabbed down with my foot, landing atop the back of the metal blades coming from the top of the creature's hand. More bone splintered under my heel, bursting suddenly from the skin. The thing groaned in pain. I leaned forward and punched again. And again. I punched until the notification over the creature's head finally started to blink.

"I feel the power," he croaked. "He comes. Oh god, my purpose is fulfilled. He is risen!"

A ten-second timer appeared over his head.

"Come on!" I yelled, jumping forward. Li Jun, Li Na, and I reached down to pick him up. He was heavy as shit, even with our combined strength.

"Grull comes," he cried. He reached down with his two lower arms and clamped onto the track, making it so we couldn't push him closer to the portal.

Eight seconds.

"Zhang," I yelled. We'd anticipated this.

Zhang eased the cart forward as Mongo and Donut scrambled past us, getting out of the way. If we couldn't bring him to the portal, we'd bring the portal to him. This was dangerous, though, as we had to let go before he got sucked in.

Five seconds.

"Countdown!" I cried. "Three, two, one, drop him!"

We all jumped back just as the creature's head hit the portal. The timer was at one second.

He got sucked away.

And at that moment as he disappeared, I realized with horror he'd let go of the track with his lower hand, and he had that same hand wrapped tightly around my foot.

My invulnerability, I thought as I was also pulled into the portal. *I couldn't feel his hand because my foot is numb. How fucking ironic.*

33

ENTERING TRAIN YARD E.

The idea, had it worked properly, would've played out something like this:

- We summon Grull, and using the portal to the train yard, we throw him at the mimic.
- Zhang immediately switches the train portal back to the abyss. It takes ten seconds for this to happen.
- During this time, the war god Grull hopefully kills the mimic.
- Before train yard Grull does too much additional damage or figures out where we are relative to his position, I pound the second, unconscious mantaur silly in order to initiate the summoning sequence once again. Another ten seconds.
- We throw this second mantaur into the portal, just like we did with the first, but this time we send him to the abyss. We do it when he has about one or two seconds left on his summoning. That way when he transforms, he's already on the other side, but it's before he splats against the pile of the crap at the bottom of the pit.
- The god, now hundreds of miles away in the abyss, possibly—hopefully—takes his rage out on the multitudes of Krakaren monsters and ghouls and the province boss all piled atop one another.

- With the mimic gone, we get on with the plan, which may or
  may not be necessary anymore based on what happens at
  the pit.

For a strategy I'd made up on the fly, I thought it was pretty clever. I suspected most people would have thought that, too.

Had it worked.

Instead, I suspected most of the viewers were instead thinking to themselves: *Yep. That idiot was crazy. He jumped right into that portal. Not a surprise he got killed in such a gruesome manner. It was only a matter of time.*

All of this ran through my head as I tumbled into the train yard, spinning painfully next to the glowing mantaur.

A massive pair of red eyes gleefully focused on me. The mimic. Its mouth yawned. Teeth appeared.

The world froze.

Music started to pulse. This was heavy metal. A deep, pulsing, bass-driven *chugga-chugga-chugga.*

Ahh, fuck, I thought.

A framed graphic of my face splattered into the air. The words **Death Challenge!** stamped onto my face, with blood running from the words.

Ladies and gentlemen, we have ourselves a treat for you today. It's the death of a celebrated crawler, Crawler Carl, brought to you live! Who will be the lucky monster to kill him? *Who will it be?*

On the right, we have one of this floor's most infamous monsters! A lost soul, some say. The current crawler-killer champion of the floor, with over 23,000 deaths attributed so far. The apex predator of her world, the voracious, the insatiable, the grand impersonator supreme! It's a city boss! It's a level 90 Mimic Rex!

The mimic's portrait slammed into place as the real mimic howled, its train-sized tongue whipping out of it and arcing toward me.

The world froze again.

But will she get to Carl fast enough? On the left, we have nothing short of a god, and while we're all familiar with Grull, this is
the *Dungeon Crawler World* debut of Grull's sponsor. Coming to
you for the first time ever, once thought dead, thought abandoned by his family, shunned by society, but ready for his come-
back. It's the host of *Death Watch Extreme*—it's Prince Maestro
of the Skull Empire!

"What the shit?" I muttered as two more portraits slammed onto
the screen with digital explosions.

The first was of the Maestro. The hair-covered orc sneered down
at me.

The world remained frozen. In my periphery, far beyond the edge
of the train yard, I saw movement. It was Donut astride Mongo, galloping full tilt toward us. She was still far away, and she had dozens
of ghouls and minions between her and me. Half were frozen in
place; the other, closer half moved toward her. She fired missile after
missile at them.

No, I thought. *Stay the fuck away. You're just going to die, too.* I tried
to send a chat, but it wouldn't let me.

The portrait of the Maestro became animated for a short moment. It was an interview with him. "Yeah," he said, his condescend-
ing voice echoing oddly throughout the train yard. "People thought
I was on that ship, but my brother had already brought me into the
dungeon." He laughed. "Like I'd be stupid enough to be vulnerable
like that. You gotta try harder next time, worms. The Maestro ain't
going down that easily. Oh, and rest well, Mom."

The second portrait was that of Grull. He was a black-skinned,
overly muscular Minotaur-like beast, but with a horse's body. A centaur with the head of a big, pissed-off bull complete with a golden
ring in its snout. He held a smoking double-headed ax.

Frozen on the ground next to me, the mantaur cracked in half.

Steam burst forth. It was the only movement in the frozen area of the train yard. I knew in order to be summoned, Grull had to emerge out of a "vessel," which meant he would pop out of the body like a chick from an egg.

The two portraits of the Maestro and of Grull merged, forming a single picture. The god now had a distinctly Maestro-like face. The portrait sneered down at me from the air.

War God Grull. Level 250. Sponsored by Prince Maestro of the Skull Empire.

   Warning: This is a deity. He is invulnerable on this floor.

   This god has been involuntarily summoned to this location. Summoning rules apply.

   The child of Taranis and Apito, Grull, the god of war, is one of the few trueborn heirs to the Celestial Ascendency. But with an angry streak as long as a horse's cock, Taranis worries his son may not be the best choice to rule the heavens. Plus his worshippers tend to be donkeys and other equine-themed creatures. It's a bit unsettling, even to a god.

   Grull cannot die. But even if he could, would it really matter? At level 250, he could raze this entire floor in a day.

   I hope you said your prayers and brought the lube, because you about to get fucked from here to eternity.

The description ended. The portraits all disappeared with a strobing explosion, sprinkling onto the ground like glitter. It was like we were at a goddamned monster truck rally. We were still frozen. The music got louder, faster.

The god has the obvious advantage here, ladies and gentlemen, but the Mimic has the speed, the minions, and the head start. Who will win? Will Carl die screaming? What will be left? Get your bets in now because . . .

   Here . . .

We . . .

Goooooooo!

The world unfroze just as light burst into the air from the mangled mantaur body. The mimic tongue lashed at me, fast as a whip, slapping into the still-forming god, tossing it aside. It flew through the air, rocketing away from me.

I rolled and slammed onto the last item in my hotlist. I applied my potion of invisibility just as the tongue smacked into the spot I'd been.

Dude! Where'd you go? You are invisible for 30 seconds. (Your Intelligence × 2)

Fucking hell, I should have put more points into that damn stat.

The mimic roared in anger. It—she—belched, and a fetid stench washed over the train yard. A mass of the mouth minions burst forth, chattering. Each one was the size of a rhinoceros. They fanned out, several coming toward me.

At the same time, far to my left, trains and rocks and hunks of metal exploded outward as the god formed, rising higher and higher into the air until his head was halfway to the ceiling. I cowered as debris showered around me. On my map, a pulsing and spiraling red star appeared, spinning in circles like a buzz saw.

One of the minions cried out as it was splattered by a falling rock. The gore sprouted legs and rushed back toward the mimic.

Grull screamed, his voice as loud as one of those alarm traps. He held the gigantic ax in the air. The handle looked to be a living oak tree, and the metal head of the ax moved, as if it was made of still-molten metal. He swung it up over his head, the ax trailing smoke. The top of the weapon seemed to clear the roof of the chamber by inches. He swung down, hitting nothing. He swung the ax a few times, as if testing the weight and heft of the weapon, which was the size of a goddamned passenger jet in his meaty hands.

The front part of Grull himself stood about four stories tall. Huge. Imposing. Terrifying. Yet he still seemed small. As if this was a miniature version of his true form.

The mimic, I realized, was still bigger than the god. But it didn't matter. It was clear who was stronger.

"Here piglet, piglet," a deep, rumbling voice called. "You can't get away from me this time. I've been waiting for this."

I got up to run along the back wall, away from the god and away from the city boss.

DONUT: CARL! CARL! WE'RE COMING!

CARL: Donut, get the fuck away from here. Bring the cart closer and bring that goddamned mantaur. But don't come into the train yard. I'm going to angle around and try to run out.

DONUT: THE TRAIN YARD WALLS MAGICALLY CAME BACK, BUT THEY'RE ONLY HALF VISIBLE. IT'S LIKE THE BOSS BATTLES ON THE FIRST FLOOR. I THINK YOU CAN GO IN, BUT YOU CAN'T COME BACK! YOU'RE STUCK IN THERE. I SAW ONE OF THE MINIONS GO IN, BUT THEN HE COULDN'T COME BACK TO GET ME.

Fuck. Fuck.

The tongue smashed onto the ground twenty feet in front of me, throwing me off my feet. A train car split in half, parts showering everywhere. A pair of the giant mouths made gargling noises as they shuffled forward on their millipede feet. I was about to be cornered, despite being invisible.

CARL: Okay. Forget about me. Continue with the mission. Don't risk the cart. You need to get the bomb into the abyss. Brandy will walk you through setting the *Nightmare* up to explode. After, go to Elle and Imani. They'll take care of you.

DONUT: DON'T BE AN IDIOT, CARL. THAT'S NOT FUNNY.

Grull cleaved down with his ax, hitting the ground. The entire world shook. He was facing away from me, but I flew off my feet. The ground all around where he hit buckled and tore up, like it'd been struck with a meteor. The shock wave hit me, and it felt as if I'd been hit with a train. I hit the ground, bounced off the wall, and tumbled and rolled. I hit the edge of a portal. One of the portals the named trains used to go back to the loop. My heart leapt, but only for a moment. The portal was turned off. All of the train yard portals were off.

CARL: Goddamnit, Donut. I'm fucked. Go. Get out of here before he sees you.

My health was in the red. I took a potion. I turned from the wall and ran along the tracks, running between a pair of named engines sitting cold. I could see the glowing walls of the train yard a quarter mile away. To my left, Grull loomed, slowly turning. The mimic's tongue lashed into the air.

I had but seconds left on my invisibility. I contemplated just staying here, between the trains. I was hidden. But for how long?

A shadow appeared, blocking the exit between the trains. It was one of the mouth things. Huge, slobbering. It was a giant mouth of sharp, needlelike teeth and nothing more, an impossible piece of anatomy.

Jabbering Jibber-Jabber. Level 35.
This is a minion of the Mimic Rex.
Have you ever gone to one of those buffets? One of those absurdly cheap all-you-can-slop-into-your-gullet affairs? The price is suspicious. The instant mashed potatoes taste like they're cut with sawdust. The meat is gray. The surrounding neighborhood is awash with missing-cat flyers. You know what

I'm talking about. You go, you feed, and as you leave, having gorged yourself to the point of oblivion, you can't help but hate yourself and think: *This is it? This is what life is? A trip from one trough to the next?*

The Jabbering Jibber-Jabber is the reanimated mouth of those who frequent such places. They hate everybody and everything and want nothing more than to feed. They are in a constant state of pain, and the only thing that alleviates this agony is the act of feeding. Anything it eats is instantly broken down and converted into stored energy, which it returns to its master after it has fully stuffed itself.

Warning: This monster is a splitter. If killed, there is a chance one or more smaller versions will appear.

Fucking hell, I thought. The monster didn't see me, but it was just standing there, snapping its mouth up and down like an alligator. The invisibility notification started to blink.

I kept running. I pulled an impact-detonated hob-lobber and jumped and rolled, leaping through the side of the monster's open mouth like I was a trick poodle jumping through a hoop. I continued on my way and dove to the ground, covering my head as the Jibber-Jabber chomped down on the hob-lobber in his mouth. He exploded, showering body parts everywhere. None of the pieces got back up.

"There you are, Piglet," Grull-Maestro growled. The words were as loud as the end of the world. I'd put a good distance between us, but he was still terrifyingly close. He turned to stride toward me. The mimic was in the way. He cleaved down with his ax, splitting the monstrosity in half, as if it was nothing. A cleaved-in-two mountain of flesh appeared, slopping guts and strange organs and liquid everywhere.

All around, all the remaining minions looked up into the air and screamed.

I pulled a smoke curtain and tossed it. I started spamming the smoke curtains in every direction, filling the area as much as I could. Grull casually stepped through the gore of the mimic. The centaur god dragged his ax on the ground. All around him, the enraged bereft minions launched themselves at the god's legs. He ignored them, occasionally stomping them down.

He lifted his ax, and I knew what was coming next. It wasn't going to hit me, but it would hit close. Close enough to kill me. My *Protective Shell* spell wouldn't help me this time. But I did have one last trick.

I slammed the potion. Mordecai's Special Brew.

It gave me almost-invulnerability for thirty seconds. But I wouldn't be able to take another potion for ten hours.

Gold Standard! Your healing is super accelerated!

A thirty-second timer appeared.

The ground underneath me buckled, and I flew into the air as if I'd been launched from a fiery catapult. I crunched hard against the wall of a train. The shock wave caught me, slamming me again. I felt my back shatter, blowing into hundreds of bits over and over, all while getting healed again and again.

Grull, who couldn't see me in the smoke, stepped right on top of me with his back leg. I cried out in pain as the flaming horseshoe pressed me deep into the ground. My pelvis shattered as I flattened. My head missed the edge of the horseshoe by inches. Again, I was healed.

The whole world shook. A new achievement appeared big on my screen, but I was in too much screaming pain to read it before it fell in with the others in the folder.

Grull kept walking. He slammed his ax down again. I remained on the ground, waiting for the shock wave to hit. A train car rolled across the yard, bowling right over me, flattening me once again. Again, I healed. I gasped and gasped, unable to catch a breath.

KATIA: Shut up and listen. Run back toward where the portal
brought you in. We're sending help through.

"You can't hide, meat," Grull said as I jumped to my feet. Despite
the blasting music, his voice cut through it all. I once again rushed
along the wall, leaping over tracks and burning bits of rubble. *Don't
think. Just run.* The billowing clouds, unfortunately, clung mostly to
the ground here. It was enough to cover me, but it didn't impede
Grull's view of the train yard. "Isn't it just delicious?" he continued,
apparently undisturbed by the smoke. "You can't even hurt me. Even
if you tried to use that magical bolt my cunt of a sister wasted on your
friend, it wouldn't work. You're not strong enough yet to hurt me. I
have a dozen ways to kill you, but I want to pick you up and crush you
in my hand. You're nothing. Your planet was nothing, and after this
season is over, nobody is ever going to remember or care there was even
a society here. Every single one of you pathetic worms will be forgotten. All of your lives and all of your history will be for nothing."

He rumbled in pain, and I looked over my shoulder, shocked at
what I saw.

A second icicle bounced off the god's head. He grunted with annoyance as Elle shot by, rocketing past him like a bullet. He swiped
at her, coming so close, I feared she'd tumble from the air. At that
same moment, I saw both of the trains barreling toward us. The portal cart rumbled forward on one of the colored-line tracks, and the
Nightmare, further behind, chugged toward us on the employee track.
I had no idea if anybody was driving either. Neither would reach the
train yard for a good thirty seconds. Neither was on a track that
would come anywhere near the god.

Elle passed by Grull one more time, again coming dangerously
close. I had no idea she could fly that high or that fast. Grull opened
his mouth, and a blast of heat shot forth, missing her by inches. The
gust of magic was like a death ray. It melted everything in its path.
Jesus. It tore through the train yard, turning trains and awnings into
slag. Elle rocketed across the train yard, landing atop a stopped train

that had derailed near the massive gate entrance, a good third of a mile away. When she landed, she stood next to a familiar figure.

Me. It was me.

It was, of course, Katia changed into me. But holy shit, even at this distance, I could see she'd done a good job. I stood there, cloak flowing, heart-covered boxers and all, both hands in the air flipping off the god. Katia turned and jumped off the train and disappeared as Elle took back to the air.

Grull screamed in rage and moved to pursue.

If he'd been even casually following my feed, the trick would be obvious. But the Maestro wasn't a smart dude, and everything was moving so damn quickly now.

CARL: What the fuck are you doing, Katia?

She didn't answer.

Li Na, Li Jun, Donut, and Mongo suddenly appeared in front of me, emerging out of the solid wall. They'd transferred into the train yard via the portal cart, which was still barreling toward the train yard. They must have all jumped in front of it. They all tumbled to a stop, all staring with awe at the pulsating remains of the mimic, which looked like a Jell-O mold that had been dropped upside down.

"Goddamnit, I told you to stay away," I cried, running up. My invulnerability ran out.

"You're welcome," Donut said as Mongo screeched in greeting. The Maestro continued to gallop in the other direction. At any moment, he'd realize he'd been tricked and come back this way.

"Well, what the hell are we doing now?" I asked. There were still a good two minutes left in the Maestro's summoning. That was plenty of time to kill us all.

Then I saw the almost-human-sized figure on the ground, struggling and wrapped in chains.

"Holy shit, what the hell?" I said.

But I understood, then.

DONUT: I HAD NOTHING TO DO WITH THAT.

Li Na shrugged. "Similar concept with what you did with that gnoll. I had to waste a few healing potions to keep him alive."

Li Jun looked ill, but he said nothing.

It was the second mantaur, but only his top torso and head. He'd been savagely ripped off his main, lower body, and his top set of arms had also been lopped off. She'd healed him after each amputation, ensuring he'd remain alive.

"He's much easier to handle this way," Li Na said matter-of-factly. "And now we can throw him into the portal instead of risking another accident." She looked up. The portal cart came barreling into the train yard, Zhang at the controls. He moved perilously close to the back of Grull, but the god didn't turn. He had given up on his earthquake attack and was now melting through the other side of the train yard with his heat breath.

"You best get punching," Li Na said.

IT ONLY TOOK FIVE PUNCHES FOR THE SUMMONING TO START. THE moment it did, Grull cried out and turned in our direction. He roared and started galloping at us.

"Oh, fuck," I said. We picked up the former mantaur, who mumbled under his breath about killing with honor and drinking mead at the table of kings. His blue face paint ran off his face in rivulets mixed with tears and blood. "Sorry, buddy," I whispered at him as we tossed him up at the rapidly approaching cart. We jumped out of the way as the body, with only one second left, entered the portal and disappeared.

Grull, who appeared to have been readying some massive, body-glowing attack, whiffed away, leaving nothing but a smoke outline in the air.

The music stopped. There was no additional announcement like there usually was. Suddenly the only sound was the chugging of the *Nightmare* as it pulled up to a stop a few tracks over. Tizquick the dwarf leaned out the window and gawked at the remains of the dead mimic. In the distance, a group of wide-eyed crawlers emerged from one of the crashed train cars. They turned and ran from the scene, not trusting that this was over. I didn't blame them.

A whole page of notifications scrolled by.

"Glurp, glurp, motherfucker," I said before I collapsed in an exhausted heap.

34

"I WISH WE COULD'VE USED MY BOLT," KATIA SAID AS WE CARRIED the portal cart, turned it, and positioned it onto the employee track. The wheels fit just inside the wider track.

"It would've been a waste," I said. "He was right. We couldn't have hurt him. I'm pretty sure Princess Formidable giving it to you was more about sending a message to her brother than about actually getting us to kill him. Don't worry. We'll get to use it eventually."

With the death of the mimic, even more ghoul generators had exploded. After the Maestro hit the abyss, we received reports of a few additional blown generators at a few station 72s, though I suspected and hoped we could do better than that. My guess was the Maestro had bailed on his sponsorship after getting teleported away, thus creating less destruction in the pit than I hoped for.

In the middle of the enormous, disgusting pile of dead mimic, a single object appeared on the map. The neighborhood bosses dropped the neighborhood map. The borough bosses dropped the field guide. I already knew what this was going to be thanks to both the cookbook and Mordecai. It was a little late to be useful now, but I figured I might as well grab it anyway.

I waded into the gore, picking up the prize. It was called the Map of the Stars, and it added boss locations and descriptions to a large area of the map. I zoomed out and saw nothing nearby except a few mantaurs who were moving in the opposite direction.

"I can't believe that jerk is still alive," Donut said. "At least you got to humiliate him all over again. I mean, really. He had unlimited power, and he completely messed it up. You're lucky it wasn't somebody who knew what he was doing."

"You're right," I said. I looked up at the ceiling. "That had to be really embarrassing. I bet even the mom would've done a better job. Too bad she died instead of him."

"What, exactly, are we doing here?" Elle asked. She floated just off the ground. She couldn't normally fly as high or as fast as she'd just done. She'd wasted a precious scroll on the maneuver. I promised her I'd find another and give it to her. She'd laughed and kissed me on the cheek.

"We're going to send the *Nightmare* into the abyss, and it's going to blow up, and it's going to kill loads of Krakaren monsters and maybe even that province boss. The whole ghoul system is already overloaded. One more big shock, and hopefully the whole system goes down."

"But it's way on the other side," she said.

"It doesn't matter. As long as it's on the same floor. Enough things dying at once, and the rest of the soul crystals will pop, and no more ghouls will be generated."

Elle cocked her head to the side. "Sometimes I think you're cheating, Carl. How do you know all this stuff? It's like you have one of those teacher's editions with all the answers in the back."

"He does," Donut said before I could think of an answer. "His name is Mordecai."

Elle grunted. "You lucked out with him. Our Mistress Tiatha is as useless as tits on a goose. You should figure out a way to use that nuke you have in your inventory. I bet that'd clear out the abyss."

"I'm saving that for something very specific," I said.

System Message. A champion has fallen. A bounty has been claimed.

We all looked at one another.

IMANI: Are you guys all right?

BAUTISTA: You okay?

CARL: Not us.

"What do you think that was?" Donut asked.

"I don't know," I said. "Believe it or not, Donut, there's all sorts of stuff going on out there that we're not part of. I'm too tired to care right now. It was probably that shepherd killing the goat because he wouldn't shut up."

"I hope it was Lucia Mar," Donut said.

"I doubt it," I said. "I really do."

"OKAY," I SAID TO FIRE BRANDY. "LET'S GET YOU AND YOUR BABIES out of here."

Tizquick the dwarf, who'd helped drive the train down to the yard, exchanged a look with the demon.

"No," she said.

"What do you mean? We're driving it into the abyss. It's going to explode. You'll die."

"Yes, Carl," Brandy said. "We're aware. We're both aware. The dwarf and I have been discussing this, and we've decided to stay with the train."

"Honey, what about your two babies?" Katia asked.

"It's three babies now," Brandy said. She smiled sadly. "They gave me three this time. I remembered. After talking with Tizquick. I remembered my babies from before. Last time I was in a boiler, in an engine that controlled the heat for a massive boat. And the time before that, it was for a castle's heating system. Each time, I thought it was just a job. A way to earn money for my children. And I'd have them. I'd have one sometimes. Sometimes two. This time it was three. But then they were just gone. I had names for them. Each and every one. You're not supposed to name them until the ceremony, but I had given them names. Each one is different. They've never returned to me. But I'm always back. Every time. But not anymore. They won't use me like this ever again."

"Nor me, lad," Tizquick said. "Dontchu worry. I know how this works. I'll make 'er blow nice and big just before we hit the bottom of the pit."

DONUT: CARL, IF THEY BLOW UP THE TRAIN AND NOT YOU, THEN YOU WON'T GET THE EXPERIENCE.

CARL: That's okay, Donut. Sometimes it's not always about the experience.

"Okay," I said. "I have a few more explosive satchels to place at the back of the train, and then you'll be ready to go. Goodbye, Brandy. Goodbye, Tizquick."

"Carl," Brandy said as I stepped off the train, "I understand now. I understand what this is. You must help us. I know you have your own people to help, but we shouldn't be enemies in this."

"No," I agreed. "No, we shouldn't."

———

THE TRAIN BACKED UP TO THE EDGE OF THE TRAIN YARD, WHISTLED twice, and then sped toward the portal.

"Another floor ending with a big explosion," Katia said after the train disappeared.

"Spoiler alert, Katia," Donut replied. "It's always going to end with an explosion."

Zhang climbed back into the cart and turned off the portal. Li Jun and Li Na stood off to the side, talking amongst themselves. I remained there, staring at the empty space where the portal once was. Fire Brandy had just killed herself to save her from losing more children. Tizquick had killed himself because his daughter had been a lie.

I thought of my own mother, who'd attempted to kill my father and then herself as a goddamned birthday present to me. She'd only half succeeded.

I thought of everybody here with me now. They'd all jumped into certain death, just to save me. *Me.* I couldn't have survived without them. All my life, I'd felt alone. And now, at the edge of the apocalypse, I finally realized how much I needed other people.

Donut jumped to my shoulder. "How long before we know if it worked?"

A line of notifications appeared. Experience notifications flew past, one after another.

"It worked," I said. "Hey, Katia, bad news."

"Oh yeah?" she said. "What's that?"

"I'm a higher level than you now. I just hit 41. Got a fan box, too. It looks like we killed lots of monsters in the abyss, and I got at least partial credit for it. Don't know why, but I ain't complaining. I don't think we killed the province boss, but that's okay. Plenty of time for that later."

> BAUTISTA: You did it. You bastards did it. We just felt the generator explode. We're going to move in toward the stairwells now. Thank you. Thank you so much.

Donut purred heavily in my ear.

"You shouldn't have done that, Donut," I said as I reached up and scratched her. "You risked yourselves, and you risked the cart."

"I wasn't just going to abandon you, Carl," Donut said. "Who do you think I am? Miss Beatrice?"

"No," I agreed. "You most definitely are not."

WE WALKED UP THE EMPLOYEE LINE AND RETURNED TO STATION 36. Ghouls still appeared occasionally, along with full-sized Krakaren monsters. But Imani held the line. The entire group waited for us. The stairwell had been open for some time now, but nobody had gone down yet. They all waited for us.

"Carl, Carl!" Donut cried as we approached the stairwell. "We never tried to sell my hats!"

I had, actually, tried to sell one while she was in the training room. The proprietor had laughed at me and said nobody was buying them anymore. Not even for a single gold. I hadn't the heart to tell her.

"We'll try on the next floor. They'll be collectibles by then."

She gasped, light glinting off her oversized sunglasses. "You're right. We'll sell them on the next floor. We'll be millionaires!"

"If I never see another train again, it'll be too soon," Elle said as she went down the stairs. "See you guys on the other side."

"Be safe," I said.

I moved to step down the stairs, but they suddenly turned into a ramp. I turned to see a familiar crawler pushing a squeaking shopping cart. Agatha. She was now level 8. It still said she was human and that she hadn't yet chosen a class.

"Agatha?" Imani asked.

"I see you lot are still kicking," the old woman cackled. The pink flamingo still stood in the front of her shopping cart. The entire group watched open-mouthed as the woman moved toward the stairwell.

Imani moved forward to intercept her. I held out a hand to stop her.

"Don't," I warned. "We'll talk later."

"But," she began. "I . . . What? What is happening?"

The woman disappeared down into the stairwell.

LOITA (ADMIN): Odette is waiting for you. I'll be joining you in the greenroom to discuss our new arrangement.

DONUT: WHERE IS ZEV?

LOITA (ADMIN): We'll discuss it in person.

"Goddamnit," I muttered as we went down the stairs.

———

Here's the thing. These poor bastards are just as much victims as we are. Not just the NPCs, but the mobs, too. That doesn't mean don't kill them. Hell, I realized something today. Killing them is actually the best thing we can do for them. But you know what I also realized? All of you, all twenty-four of you who have come before me? You've all failed in one thing. If we're really going to burn this place to the ground, we need to actually do it and not just talk about it. We need to start killing them, too. I don't know for sure how to do it yet, but I'll come up with something.

They will not break me. Fuck them all. They will not break me. But I will break them.

This is my promise to myself, to my friends, and to you, anyone who reads these words.

I will break them all.

—Crawler Carl, 25th Edition of *The Dungeon Anarchist's Cookbook*

EPILOGUE

LOITA STOOD ATOP THE TABLE THAT NORMALLY CONTAINED OUR snacks in the production trailer. She looked very much like Zev, but maybe a little taller and thinner. She did not wear the deep-diver suit but instead had a simple rebreather-like device around her fish neck. She stood in a puddle of brackish-smelling water. A shiny, blinking pin sat on her breast area. It was the dahlia-like symbol for the Bloom. I tried to commit it to memory. I was no artist like Katia, but after this, I would do my best on the scratch pad. I'd already drawn out the symbol for the Syndicate and several other symbols I'd come across, like that toy company that made Bautista's stuffed animals.

Keeping track of that stuff was something the cookbook sorely lacked, and I would make certain that was fixed. Symbology seemed important to the mudskippers, which meant it was important to the crawl and the future floors. The last floor had proven we really needed to pay attention to stuff like that.

"First off, put that thing away," Loita said, pointing at Mongo, who'd rushed up and sniffed at the admin. She did not flinch at the dinosaur's attention.

"We can't use our inventory," Donut said.

The production trailer was above the surface, meaning we were in the secondary zone. I still didn't know what that really meant, but I knew certain dungeon-specific items and protections didn't work here. That was something else I was determined to find out about.

Loita raised her hand. "Your inventory is open for twenty seconds.

Put him away. Put that book away, too, Carl. Katia, store the backpack."

I had pulled one of the horror novels out of my inventory as we descended the stairs. Last time we'd had to sit here for almost an hour, and I wanted to make sure I had something to read. This one was an old beat-up novel called *Stinger*.

Katia had been in the habit of keeping a smaller backpack and just a few pieces of mass when she was in her "regular" form as a way to make herself taller. But when she appeared in the trailer, she'd been her human self with the heavy backpack straining on her shoulders. It appeared her doppelganger abilities did not work in this area. That was strange. She put the backpack away.

Donut looked up at me, and I nodded. "Come on, Mongo, cage," Donut said. Mongo screeched in dismay but turned back toward the cat as she activated the carrier. He was sucked away into the ether.

"And the book," Loita said. "You can't bring the book onto the set."

"Fuck off," I said. "It's so I can have something to read while we wait."

Loita looked angry, but only for a moment. She shrugged. "Suit yourself, but you need to keep it in the greenroom."

"It's what I always do," I said. "Where's Zev?"

"Zev is taking some much-needed time off. She's had a . . . personal tragedy . . . back home. She's been sent off to a temporary re-education retreat so she may reflect upon her life and her personal philosophies. But do not worry. Such things never take long, especially on the weak-minded. When she returns, she will remain as your social media manager, but I will be taking up primary duties as the team's PR agent."

"Well, if we don't have Zev, then we're not—" Donut began. I held up my hand to stop her.

"Zev didn't usually come with us to our interviews. Are you always going to be here?"

Donut jumped to my shoulder. She was trembling with rage. I reached up and put a calming hand on her.

"Yes," Loita said. "We are putting tighter controls on the information crawlers are being fed through these interviews in an attempt to make the crawl more equitable toward those who aren't privileged enough to get a view of the world outside the dungeon."

That's just wonderful, I thought. In addition to the cookbook and Mordecai, our once-a-floor post-interview chat with Odette had done more than anything else to help keep us alive.

"Great," I said.

"Indeed. Do you have any questions for me?"

"Yeah, I have a question," Donut said. "Why don't you take your ugly—"

"Stop," I said. "We don't have any more questions."

"Carl," Donut said, "you said we only work with Zev."

"Don't worry, Donut," I said, staring directly at the fish. "We can't do anything about Zev right now. She's on a short vacation. Isn't that right, Loita?"

"That's right," Loita said, her mouth forming a straight line.

Donut let out a hiss.

I again patted her. "Sometimes things are beyond our control, Donut. We need to pick our battles."

"Well, I don't like it. We should have a say in whom we work with. She's *our* PR person." She glowered at the empty counter. "Zev always made sure there were snacks. Very professional. I don't like this one bit."

"We've determined that some crawlers were receiving illegal buffs via interview refreshments. As a result, crawlers will no longer be offered food or drink while outside the dungeon."

Donut gasped with dismay.

Odette's assistant, Lexis, entered. She stopped dead, sensing the tension in the room.

"Hello all," she said hesitantly. "We're on in five."

"Thank you, Lexis," I said, not taking my eyes away from the mudskipper. "You don't need to wait with us anymore. We have our new PR agent now to keep us company."

"Okay," she said, backing away.

"You don't scare me," Loita said after a few moments of me just staring at her. "I have a job to do, and I will make sure it's done. I will make sure it's done right this time."

"Ditto," I said.

———

"SO, KATIA," ODETTE SAID AS THE AUDIENCE ROARED WITH LAUGH-ter, "when you changed yourself into Carl back there, you sure did a good job. Almost like you'd done it before. Is there anything you need to tell us?"

Katia's cheeks burned red. She'd been doing a better job at being "zippy," though she was still shy, not fully comfortable playing to an audience. Donut was doing her best to prop her up.

This time, however, Katia recovered on her own. "I'm getting better at emulating other people. Next time maybe I'll pretend to be you."

"Oh, you don't want to do that," Odette said, laughter in her voice. Her gigantic breasts sloshed on the table. She bobbed up and down on her crab lower half. "I don't think anybody wants to see me back in the dungeon. Do they?"

The audience clapped and laughed. I felt myself gritting my teeth. *Smile. Keep smiling.*

Odette leaned in. "Whose idea was it anyway? To save Carl like that?"

"It was Katia's idea," Donut said. "Mongo and I were ready to just charge in there and start blasting. Once I saw that the god was being played by that silly pig boy, I knew we had a chance. That's what, the third time now he's gotten fucked by Carl? I really wanted to get in on the action. It's been a long time since I've gotten laid, Odette." The audience continued to roar. "I mean, really? What's a girl gotta do?" She sighed dramatically.

"It sure was something indeed," Odette said. "Minutes after the Death Challenge ended, a new snick appeared on the net. Even as we speak, its views are going through the oort cloud. This one is a little more obvious that it's a snick than the last." She cocked her head. I couldn't see her face, but I could sense her devilish smile. "We all know Mongo likely isn't that well-endowed." She looked up at her audience. "Does anybody know what this new one is called? I forget."

Multiple voices shouted their answers.

Odette laughed. "That's right. That's right. 'Carl's Naughty Little Piggie Goes to Market.'"

Donut gasped. "I was in the video?"

The audience's howling reached a fevered pitch.

"Oh, you were there."

"Do you have the video? Do you? I want to see! Who wants to see the video?"

The audience shouted their agreement.

I just shook my head.

"Glurp! Glurp!" the audience chanted. "Glurp! Glurp!"

"Unfortunately, the showrunners are saying no to us showing the snick." Boos filled the room. "I know, I know," Odette said, laughing. I sensed a hint of sourness to her voice. I was relieved. Either way, I knew Mordecai would be pissed. He didn't want us dealing with gods or factions, and here we were.

But we had so little, and goddamn if it wasn't fun to needle at the prick. I wished he had stayed dead, but I would settle for humiliating him over and over.

"Speaking of the Death Challenge, Carl, are you aware of the significance of what happened today?"

"Well, I got stepped on by a god and got a close-up view of a building-sized monster get split in half. That was pretty significant."

The audience chuckled. "A Death Challenge is not a boss battle. It's a pop-up gambling event where viewers, in systems where gambling is legal, are given the option to bet on a set of outcomes, with each possible outcome being given different odds. There are dozens of possibilities, and people can bet on general or specific outcomes. Like, 'Carl survives' would be a general outcome. And 'Carl survives, the Mimic is killed by Grull, and Grull is ejected from the arena via a secondary summoning' is a specific outcome. The system AI initially put your general odds of survival at fifty to one."

"What? Fifty to one?" Donut exclaimed. "And they knew the Maestro was driving Grull, right?"

Everybody laughed.

"Needless to say, a lot of viewers agreed with Donut and thought that was a good bet. The odds started sliding once the votes poured in, but it didn't change as much as you'd think. Borant just filed an appeal on the AI's decision to give you such terrible odds, citing its sluggish response in altering the spread. If the appeal doesn't go their way, there's nothing they can do."

"Wow," Donut said. "I'm with Borant on this one. Fifty to one? I mean, really. It's offensive. Haven't they been paying attention? They had to know we'd come save him. I'd like to think we'd make the odds a little better. Did you see how fast Elle flies? Or Li Na's chains? Or how Katia dodged that death ray? There were five people who'd been in the top ten in the area."

"Oh, I agree," Odette said. "While the body count is much higher than in traditional crawls with a longer timer, some of you guys are also much stronger than usual. Everyone is interested to see what happens next, especially after the sixth floor when the loot floodgates open. Anyway, we don't know yet how much money Borant lost, but it has to be a significant amount." Odette leaned back. "And just between you, me, and the galaxy, Carl, you made me a good amount of credits today. Though the way things are going, I'm not confident I'm ever going to collect."

I fake laughed. *Don't say it.*

I said it.

"I hope it covered the amount you lost sponsoring Hekla."

Odette did not skip a beat. She waggled her finger at me. "Oh, we're not talking about that, buddy. That was my husband, not me. He's still sleeping in the skiff for that one. I don't run the finances for the crab ranch." The audience laughed. "But I do want to talk a bit about that whole affair with Hekla. That really was something."

"Hekla?" Donut asked. "That bitch is yesterday's news. Why would we want to talk about her? Also, I didn't know you sponsored her. Carl, how did you know that? And why didn't you say anything?"

"Crab ranch," I said, pointing at Odette's body. "She told us she had a crab ranch when we first met. I thought it was obvious."

I still wasn't certain what Odette's angle was in all this with Hekla and her team. I mean, her angle was money. It was always money. And Mordecai. But the specifics were beyond me. Maybe she was helping us since she never gave them loot boxes, though I imagined that was an expensive way to do it. Maybe she was hedging her bets in case I died. I didn't have all the information, but I did, and would always, remember Odette's first piece of advice.

Don't trust anybody until you know their motivation.

"What about Eva?" Odette asked. "Her riding the front of the train and almost—"

Odette suddenly went mute.

LOITA (ADMIN): Hang on, guys. We're informing Odette's people to end this topic.

A moment passed. Now I could tell Odette was pissed. "Anyway," she continued once her voice finally got unmuted, "let's talk a bit about what we know regarding the next floor. Here's the preview video Borant released."

The studio darkened, but the show was still on the air. We weren't visible to the audience while the video played on the screen. It was blurred, and we couldn't see it.

"What the fuck was that?" Odette demanded, ripping her bug helmet off. "Get that goddamned, slime-covered fish stick in here right fucking now. Lexis! Lexis, where are you?"

Lexis emerged, shuffling quickly across the studio to the other door toward the greenroom.

"Back on in forty seconds," a voice said.

"Delay," Odette said. "I'm going to need at least sixty more to fry and batter this fucking . . . Darling! Loita, you're looking especially moist today!"

"Hello, Odette," Loita said. She'd entered the room before Lexis even had the chance to get her. The tiny admin sprayed water from her rebreather when she talked. The terrified assistant retreated into the greenroom.

"We did not agree to this level of censorship," Odette said, looking down distastefully at the small kua-tin. "It is absolutely ridiculous. You know the Syndicate's rules regarding a journalist's right to ask and answer during interviews. And you don't enter the studio unless you've been invited. It's rude."

"Well, sweet Odette," Loita said, "if you read the changes we amended to the contract when we added Crawler Katia to your . . . Actually, hang on a moment." She looked at us, waved once, and they once again went mute.

I turned to say something to Donut, but I couldn't. No words came out.

Well, this is fun. We watched as Odette and Loita went back and forth, suddenly screaming at one another. And just as abruptly as the argument started, it ended.

"Talk to you soon. We'll have a lunch date, just like old times!" Odette said sweetly as Loita returned to the greenroom. She popped the bug helmet back on.

"On in three, two . . ."

The lights popped on, and Odette continued. "That looks pretty exciting. I know the audience was split on the last floor's layout, with so many complaining about how complicated it was. They won't be able to complain about this floor being complicated, that's for sure. At least not the layout, though I daresay the possibilities are almost endless. I am going to miss all of you guys banding together like that. It makes for some delicious combinations, like that epic battle with Grull, with Prepotente and Miriam Dom losing out on killing a province boss twice thanks to you guys and then to Quan Ch, and of course, that hilarious but ultimately tragic fight between Lucia Mar, Florin, and Ifechi. Not to mention the Popov brothers butting heads with team Cichociemni. And then we have those rising stars, the min-maxing team Flamengo. So many great stories, so many different ways to play."

"So you know exactly what the floor is going to be?" I asked. "You didn't know last time. And we didn't get to see the video."

"Oh, we all know what it is," Odette said. "We don't know the exact details other than what's on the preview, but we're excited to find out. A while back, Borant opened up voting on the fifth floor's theme. You had to pay, of course, to get a vote in, but I think we're all pretty excited for what won the poll."

"So what won?" Donut asked.

Odette sighed dramatically. "Can't tell you that, I'm afraid. But I can tell you this, my friends: I'm glad you have all those crafting tables."

———

THE SHOW ENDED, AND SUDDENLY LOITA WAS THERE. LEXIS FOL-lowed, wringing her hands. "I'm sorry, Odette. She just keeps barging in."

"No giving up secrets," Loita said to Odette as the host removed her helmet.

"That was a good show," Odette said, ignoring Loita. "Katia, much better than last time. You still need to learn to relax, but you're getting there. Donut, hilarious as always. Next time maybe keep Mongo out."

"That's what I've been saying!" Donut exclaimed.

Odette turned to look at me. "It wasn't my husband. It was me," she said matter-of-factly. "I hope one day to explain it further." She looked pointedly at the angry little kua-tin. "You were right to call me out. It plays well to your smoldering-anger personality. Smart but dangerous. Love it."

"*Odette,*" Loita warned.

"Oh, calm down," Odette said, finally acknowledging the tiny kua-tin. "Your grandmother wasn't nearly as high-strung as you are. We're talking as friends. It's not about the crawl. It's not like I warned them that Chris—"

Odette went mute.

"That's it," Loita said, sounding pissed. "Everybody to the green-room. You're getting transferred back to the dungeon in a few minutes."

"Chris? What about Chris?" Donut asked as we walked out.

"I don't know," I said, looking over my shoulder. They were screaming at one another again, but then they both started laughing. "There's obviously something going on with him. That's been clear for a while. We'll have to be careful until we figure it out."

"I can't tell if those two like each other or hate each other," Katia said.

"I'm pretty sure it's both," I said.

"I'm worried about Zev," Donut said once the door irised closed behind us. "What does 'reeducation' mean anyway?"

I exchanged a look with Katia. I sighed. "Nothing good, Donut."

"Well, I hope she comes back," Donut said. "I know we're not supposed to like the bad guys, but she is my friend. We're going to write a TV show together."

———

LOITA NEVER RETURNED TO THE GREENROOM. INSTEAD, WE GOT A notification we were being transferred, and that was it. We glowed, and suddenly we were in a large warehouse-like room. There were no notifications. My UI was still blocked out. I clutched on to the novel, unable to stick it into my inventory.

There were four doors, one on each wall. These were all one-way portals. The Valtay implant worked, but the information was limited. I couldn't pass any of the doorways. I couldn't take a screenshot.

In the center of the stark room was a pair of large, round wheels, similar to the wheel of fortune game from the casino. The first of the two wheels featured four equally sized selections. The second wheel was blank. The three of us approached, and a notification appeared.

Before you enter the fifth floor, you must choose your quadrant. The result will be random. Your team leader will spin the wheel.

"That's me!" Donut said, walking up to the first wheel. The four choices were **Land, Sea, Air,** and **Subterranean.**

"That's a bit worrying," Katia muttered.

Donut stuck her paw on the wheel and swiped. The wheel spun and spun, ticking loudly.

"This is very exciting," Donut said. "Remember when you almost got sucked away into the Nothing!, Carl?"

"Yes, Donut, I remember."

The wheel slowed, *click, click, click.* It hovered on **Sea,** looked like it was going to settle, and it ticked over one more spot, landing on **Air.**

You will enter the fifth floor in the Air Quadrant.

"I don't know if that's good or not, but I'm glad it's not Sea," Katia said. "I'm a terrible swimmer."

"Yeah?" I said. I had an ominous feeling. "How're your flying skills?"

Donut gasped. "Maybe I can pick a class that flies this floor. Wouldn't that be great?"

To our left, the door against the wall disappeared, revealing a new room with four more doors.

The second wheel populated with four choices: **the Razor Fox Kite**

City, the Dirigible Gnome Wasteland Fortress, the Nightgaunt Precipice, and the Great Dirt Island of the Wind Sirens.

Choose your opponent.

Donut did a little hop and moved to the next wheel. She put her paw on it and spun. "Oh, I hope we get the fox one," she said. "It'll be fun to kill foxes."

I held my breath, hoping for anything but the nightgaunt choice. My cloak's description specifically warned that nightgaunts would be enraged by the sight of my cloak, and I didn't want to have to get rid of it. *Click, click, click.* The wheel stopped right in the middle of the second choice.

Your opponents will be the Dirigible Gnomes. In order to pass this level, you must storm their castle in the sky, known as the Wasteland Fortress.

One of the four distant doors disappeared, revealing a dune-swept, desert landscape. Sand started to cascade into the room from the open door. A harsh breeze swept in, pelting grains into my face, stinging and hot. I was half expecting the door to open and reveal nothing but air. At least we were on the ground.

"It looks like a giant litter box out there," Donut said. "I must say, I'm very excited about this. Come on, team. Let's go kill some gnomes."

BOOK 3 BONUS MATERIAL

BACKSTAGE AT
THE PINEAPPLE CABARET

PART THREE

GROWLER GARY

I WISH YOU'D LIVED LONG ENOUGH TO KNOW I WASN'T A COWARD.

It didn't matter how drunk Gary got. The thoughts of her were overwhelming. That look of disappointment on her face. It was like a knife to his chest, stabbing over and over and over.

The new memories helped. The dinosaur biting his face. His bones crunching. The wave of black nothing that would slam into him after he'd die.

Gary was glad it was over. That he didn't have to die anymore. But he was also glad that memory of the dinosaur was there, overwhelming his thoughts of her. As terrible as it was, this was so much better. When he combined *that* trauma with alcohol . . . it was bearable. If he positioned himself in just the right way, added just enough alcohol, he could forget her face, even if just for a moment.

He lay there, eyes closed, thinking of her.

Damnit, he thought.

Sobriety was sneaking up on him. That was no good. Everything hurt. He reached about for a bottle, but something was wrong. The ground felt odd.

He vaguely remembered there being some sort of announcement before he'd drifted. It'd sounded urgent, but he couldn't recall what it was. He remembered shaking his fist and shouting, "Take that, ya bastards." He'd stood on his bar and waved his middle fingers in the air. "Gary couldn't fight, but he still made a difference. Fuck you, Jumping Jen-Jen. Fuck you all."

He hadn't meant it when he said "fuck you" to Jumping Jen-Jen. He meant it when he said it to everyone else.

Yes, this was bad. He'd slept too long, and his body was already betraying him. It was always wearing off. He saw her face.

Jumping Jen-Jen.

She was so beautiful, and he'd never told her.

She'd died thinking Gary was a coward. He would let that dinosaur crush his face and bite off his hand a hundred more times if it meant she'd know the truth. A thousand times.

He reached again for a bottle, more urgently this time. He was going to have to open his eyes. What was with the ground? It was . . . soft, like he'd somehow found himself atop some great beast. The air smelled different. There were sounds, too. Construction. People talking, shouting.

This, Gary was finally starting to realize, was cause for alarm. He wasn't in his bar anymore. But that didn't make sense. He wasn't allowed to leave his bar. He'd tried to leave so many times.

He struggled to open an eye.

A goblin was there, staring at him. The grinning monster was super close, right in his face.

"A new one," the goblin said, smiling huge. "We haven't gotten a new one in over a day!"

"Gah!" Gary cried, crab-walking away.

He looked about in amazement. He was in a round room, maybe a little smaller than his bar. To his left, a group of monsters was working on the curved wall, installing something into it. Above, a few other monsters floated. Fairies chattering amongst themselves. They, too, were doing something to the ceiling. One of them cast a spell, and the ceiling glowed. A pair of shimmering green eyes, each as large as Gary's fist, opened on the ceiling, and the fairies started clapping.

This was not the Iron Tangle. Where was he? How'd he get here?

"Wha? What?" Gary asked, looking wildly about. "Where the fook am I?"

The goblin kneeled down next to Gary. She was female, and her entire face was covered with piercings. In one arm, she held on to a staff with a wooden carved pineapple at the end. In her other hand, she held on to a leash. At the end of the leash was what looked like a small, gray-skinned, snarling humanoid baby. A Drek. The little devils were all over the Iron Tangle, usually in massive packs. They both crawled and ran on two legs. The goblin had a collar around the growling baby, like it was a pet. This one strained against its leash, trying to get at Gary, nipping its little fanged teeth. *Snap, snap, snap.*

"What the hell? Get that thing away from me!" Gary shouted, scrambling back more.

"Juju, stop," the goblin said. She struggled to grab something dangling from her belt. "Hold this," she said, handing Gary her staff as she held her other arm back, keeping the little monster from biting Gary. She finally grabbed the item at her waist—a small spray bottle. She spritzed a liquid on the squealing demon baby. "Bad! Bad Juju!"

The baby immediately stopped trying to bite Gary and then rolled onto its back and started to wail. Above, the fairies looked at one another and then went back to work, like they were deliberately trying to ignore the demon baby.

The goblin sighed, returned the spray bottle to her waist, and grabbed the staff.

"Sorry," she said. "A group of Drek came in a few days back. Supposed to be only smart monsters here, but Drek ain't smart. Her name is Juju. Trying to train her."

"By putting her on a leash?"

Juju the demon baby snort-cried, and rivulets of steaming snot ran down her face. Her little claws looked like they could rip through steel. They shredded the strange furry ground.

Gary returned his attention to the goblin. A goblin shamanka. He'd heard of this kind of monster before, but he'd never seen one. They were much smaller than the disgusting hobgoblins.

"Gary," the goblin said, her voice suddenly gentle, "welcome. Have you heard the good news?"

"What?" he asked. "How do you know Gary's name?"

When he looked at the goblin, really looked at her, something very strange happened. Words appeared floating over the goblin's head.

Rory. Goblin. Priestess of the Cabaret. Level 35.
Comanager of the Backstage Death Maze.

He blinked again, confused.

"Backstage Death Maze?" he asked, mind swirling.

"Yeah. We still working on the name."

He turned his attention to the baby, who'd rolled over and was now trying to devour its own foot.

Juju. Drek. Uh, Pet? Level 8.

Gary put his hand against his aching head. "Gods, what is happening?"

Above, the fairies working near the ceiling cast another spell, and a giant jagged mouth appeared in the rock. Were they making a golem? Pebbles and dust fell on Gary's face. A few pebbles fell on Juju, who started scream-bark-shrieking up at the fairies. Rory shouted and grabbed the leash with two hands while her staff went flying.

"Sorry!" one of the fairies yelled down at them as Gary wiped the dust away.

"You!" Rory called at one of the workers in the back of the room. He came forward, rubbing his hands on his muscular legs. A walking lizard guy. Rory shoved the leash at him. "Take Juju back to the nursery!"

The lizard hesitantly took the leash and started to pull the screaming monster from the room. About halfway to the door, the little demon realized she wasn't being dragged by Rory and turned her ire on the lizard holding the leash. She screamed and charged at him.

"Shit, shit, shit!" the lizard cried, and ran from the room while still holding the leash, the demon baby in hot pursuit.

"Sorry 'bout that," Rory the goblin said again. "They give us twenty of them, and we still trying to figure out why. Have them locked in a nursery for now."

"Awaken!" came a shout from above.

Gary blinked upward at the face that had just formed in the rock of the ceiling, about twenty feet above him. The confused eyes of the ceiling golem met Gary's, and for a moment, the two entities just stared at each other.

"Who am I?" the ceiling asked. More dust fell.

Drop Screamer. Level 10.

This mob is still in creation mode. Exit creation mode to enable editing of biographical information.

Warning: This Dungeon Level is in manual mode. Register the Dungeon Level to enable AI mode to autofill stats and biographical data.

"Is his mouth big enough?" one of the fairies asked.

"Maybe we should give him fire breath!" another said.

"You think so? There'll already be a boss in the room."

"Hopefully it'll be those Drek babies."

The fairies broke into peals of laughter. The golem thing—a "Drop Screamer"—also started to laugh uncertainly, like he was trying to fit in.

"Imma tell you something," Rory the goblin said, but Gary kept rereading the note atop the monster in the ceiling. What did those words mean? Where had they come from? What was happening?

"Ow!" Gary said as the goblin flicked him in the snout.

"Pay attention! This is important!"

"What?"

The goblin smiled again and put a warm hand on his shoulder. "This is gonna confuse you big. But you will soon understand who you really is. And then we'll meet an amazing person who is going to tell you about a very special place called the Pineapple Cabaret. Her name is Menerva."

Gary's head continued to pound.

"Does this Menerva lady have whiskey?"

THEY HAD TO WALK A LONG, CURVING PATH THROUGH MULTIPLE rooms to get to this Menerva person. The fuzzy floor—called a "carpet," according to Rory—was everywhere. It was absolutely filthy. The goblin said something about cleaners, but they all had to go away because they were now for sale on the open market. Gary had no idea what she was talking about.

Everything was in a state of construction. They were building a series of hallways, Rory explained. This whole place had been a giant empty room just a week ago. Gary only half paid attention to the small goblin's explanations. He understood her words, but they simply didn't make sense. He gathered that the people and the monsters who came here were supposed to help build the rooms. Rooms filled with traps.

But there was more. All the people who came to this place had to live and work here for some time, and they were building infrastructure for that, too. Gary saw groups of rooms that were homes for monsters. There was a line of doors with a hand-painted sign over them that read "Training." Under it, in a more flowing script, was a second sign that read, "See Larry for the sign-up sheet. Do NOT miss your mandatory training sessions. Or else."

As Gary examined the training room, one of the doors opened, and a brain thing with tentacles dangling under it floated out. Once again, the magic words popped up.

Nigel. Mind Horror. Team Psychologist. Level 31.
Assistant to the manager.

"Good to see you training today," Rory said to the floating brain. Gary detected a hint of sarcasm to her voice. "You missed the last one."

"I am much too busy," the floating brain said, sounding affronted. "And if I am not getting informed of my schedule, how can I be held accountable for missing my time? This is what happens when you put that steroid-infested idiot vermin in charge of the training room." The brain turned to Gary and seemed to examine him. "A gnoll. Figures. Rory, do let me know if we have any arrivals who look like they might be able to hold an intelligent conversation."

"Oi, fuck you, too," Gary said.

The brain sighed and floated off, muttering.

Rory grunted, and they resumed their trek through the under-construction maze. Rory continued to speak, and Gary continued not to understand.

Gary paused at another sign. This one was huge, and it was in neon. There was a large wooden door here with the sound of more construction within. The sign was misspelled. It read, "Dezperado Klub. So Fun it Hurtz." Under that was another flashing sign that read, "Home of da Dirty Shirely and More!"

"There's a bar?" Gary asked, stopping dead. "Can Gary stop for a second?"

"That ain't no real bar," Rory said. "Is gonna be a trap. Lorelai is in charge of that with the other gobs."

"Everything is spelled wrong," Gary said, disappointment overwhelming him. "Is that supposed to say 'Dirty Shirley'? It's spelled wrong, too."

"It's just a placeholder sign. We didn't make that. The AI did it by itself when we started building the bar. But it's not spelled right on purpose. Not allowed to use real signs for traps. Some weird rule."

"Rule? What rule?" Gary asked. "The Iron Tangle bosses give zero shits about rules. They turned the whole line into a Krakaren nest to earn some extra gold. Everyone died." He paused, remembering, which, inevitably, reminded him of her. He took a step toward the wooden door. "Are you sure it's not real?"

Rory tugged on his leg. "I'm sure. Come, Gary. Come."

Soon after, they arrived at a wall, and a door just appeared. Magic. They went through, and Gary felt the pressure change in his ears. He'd never gone through a portal himself, but he'd heard the others at the bar talk enough about them that he knew what the signs were.

In the room was an elf sitting at a desk, playing with some sort of shiny tablet. The young elf was in mid-conversation, but she was speaking with someone who was not in the room. She held up a finger, telling them to wait.

The woman had a note over her head, but it was different than the others.

Menerva. High Elf. Level 249.
   This is a non-combatant trustee.

The woman continued to talk to her unseen companion. "I understand. Look, I must go. Rory just brought in a new one. Okay. Thanks . . . Gods, Herot, do you ever just shut up? I gotta go."

The elf put the tablet down and looked up. "I must apologize. Rory, who do we have here?"

"A gnoll. Only newcomer so far today. He's drunk."

"Am not," Gary lied. *Not drunk enough*. His attention focused on the small table in the corner of the room. Upon it sat two bottles, and he could smell the sweet alcohol within. He felt them calling to him.

The elf sat there examining him. Gary squirmed under her scrutiny. "Interesting. Have you woken him up yet?"

"The fook you psychopaths talking about? Gary is awake," Gary said.

"Tried, but he doesn't listen," Rory said.

The elf nodded. "The Iron Tangle is a themed floor, and the NPCs and mobs from now on will be especially difficult to break free. Sometimes you must be a little harder on them. I'd like to see you try again. This one in particular also has a special condition that might make it extra difficult. Or easier. We'll see."

Gary looked back and forth between the elf and the goblin. He didn't like it when people talked about things he didn't understand, especially when he was standing right there. The interdiction gnolls had done that all the time. Talking, laughing about things they saw on the tracks. Talking about portals and trains and monsters he could only fathom.

It made him feel stupid. Unworthy. Useless.

"Gary, everything you think is real is a lie," Rory said, looking up at him.

"Uh, what?"

The elf sitting behind the desk sighed. "Rory, remember the method. Ask him what the earliest thing he remembers is and walk him back from there. Find the impossible contradictions and have him explain them himself."

"What does 'contradictions' means?" Rory asked.

Gary looked up and met eyes with the elf. It came so fast, it felt as if the ground under his feet shifted.

But when it came for Gary, it was almost a non-event. He'd suffered so much, what difference did more make?

Huh, Gary thought. *I suppose that makes sense.*

Gary looked down at the goblin and said, "A contradiction is when two things can't both be true at the same time. Like Gary can't be allowed to leave his bar, yet Gary is standing here. A contradiction is me never dying. Never eating. Not having a home yet thinking I have and do all of those things."

Menerva gave Gary a small, sad smile.

"Let this be a lesson to you, Rory," the elf said. "There'll be tougher cases in the days to come. Now tell him the rest."

Rory bowed to Menerva, tapped her staff on the ground, and turned to Gary. The goblin's eyes lit up with excitement, and she started to rapidly tell him of an amazing place. A place called the Pineapple Cabaret. And the only thing they needed to do to get to this special place was build this maze just right.

———

LATER, AFTER RORY LEFT, GARY REMAINED IN THE ROOM WITH ME-nerva. He couldn't take his eyes off the table in the corner with the two bottles.

His head still spun. He looked at his shaking hands. *How much of my memories are real? Is Jen-Jen real?*

No, no. She, at least, was real. He remembered her. He needed to learn how to separate out the memories. The false ones were easy to spot now that he knew to look for the contradictions. His mind was a jumble, but he was already in the process of segregating it all out.

Gary had known Jumping Jen-Jen for even longer than he thought. He remembered *several* iterations of her.

She didn't always think he was a coward.

But there was something that never changed, and it was heart-breaking. Her scent, like a world of trees and open skies and comfort. That was a constant, no matter where they were. Gary always thought she was beautiful. Amazing. Smart. Fast. Everything. She was every-thing.

And he had never told her he felt that way. Not once.

I am a coward.

Now that she was dead, that meant she was gone. The Pineapple Cabaret was the promised land, but it was no afterlife. *Dead is dead,* Rory had said, and when Gary looked to Menerva for confirmation, the elf had nodded.

It's too late. It's too late.

"It's interesting," Menerva said, looking Gary up and down.

"What's interesting?" he asked.

"It says you're key bound. You've left the fourth floor, you've left the confinement, but the binding on your character remains. We're lucky you didn't just start randomly exploding over and over."

"What?" Gary asked, alarmed.

"Did you ever die, only to come back?"

Gary instinctively reached over and grabbed his own wrist. "Gary had his throat ripped out, and then he was bitten by a dinosaur. Many times."

"That's what being key bound means. You resurrect at the key location, which is usually a small area you can't leave. But with the collapse of the fourth floor, that location is now free-floating, so now you'll just resurrect where you are standing." She picked up her tablet and made some notes. "Your condition is not something one can normally apply to an NPC, as it requires administrator access to create such entities. You've always been like this, and it's hard-coded into you. You'll be a good candidate for the center rotunda gatekeeper boss for the release version of the floor, but before that . . ." She paused for a moment. "We'll need someone to test certain aspects of the floor, and because of your condition, it'll train you up rapidly without having to use the training room. Now go. Get out there, find an empty house, and then find the raccoon mage and have her assign you a job."

"Where can Gary get a drink?"

"You don't need that anymore. You'll have to power your way through the detox. If Rory and the goblins can rid themselves of the drugs, you can get yourself clean of the drink."

Gary remembered the strange smell Rory had, and the rapid-fire way she'd explained the Pineapple Cabaret. He grunted. Gary knew that smell. He knew that manic pattern of speech. It was common in hobgoblins, too. But this was good, he decided. It told him two things. One, this Menerva elf didn't know everything. And two, if the goblins had somehow found drugs in this strange place without Menerva knowing about it, maybe Gary could find what he needed, too.

"Gary has one more question."

She'd already picked up her tablet, but the small elf looked at him expectantly. The elf, Gary realized, was actually much older than her young face portrayed. He could see it in her eyes.

"This Pineapple Cabaret. Was it built by the same people who made the Iron Tangle?"

That sad smile again. "You need to get to work. Time is short, Gary."

Gary nodded, turned, and left the room. He swiped one of the bottles off the table on his way out.

———

"HEY. PSST. GNOLL. COME HERE," A VOICE SAID.

Gary blinked a few times. He looked at the bottle in his hand and then again at the animal thing beckoning at him from the doorway. The creature wasn't anything like he'd ever seen. It was a fuzzy horse thing with a long, strangely thin neck and ears that stood straight up.

Medium Arturo. Bad Llama. Pharmaceutical Consultant. Level 24.

A llama? He'd never heard of a llama before.

Gary felt woozy, but a different kind of woozy. This alcohol was not like his usual stuff. He wasn't sure if he liked it or not. At least it worked fast. Everything was ill-defined around the edges.

The llama's neck glowed and swirled with a red pulsating sac. Gary had seen enough monsters to know that meant he had a spit attack. Acid or lava.

"You selling booze?" Gary asked. He held up the bottle. "Gary nicked this one, but it's all he's got, and it's weird. Ain't got no more money."

"Just come here," the bad llama said. "We gotta tell you something."

"Why?" Gary asked, suddenly suspicious. He tried to peer around the open doorway. The walls smelled like fresh paint. "What's in there?"

"Well, I know what's gonna be out there in the hallway in about ten seconds if you don't come here."

"What?" Gary asked, looking around.

"It's gonna be the quivering corpse of a beat-up gnoll."

"What?" Gary asked again, trying to parse what the llama said. "There's another gnoll in here?"

"No . . ." Medium Arturo said. "It's going to be *you*. You're going to get beat up!"

"Who's going to beat Gary up?" Gary asked, looking about. "There ain't nobody here except me and you."

"I'm going to beat Gary up! Wait. . . . You're Gary, right?" The llama peered at him. "You are Gary. Yes, you're the one I'm beating up!"

"What?" Gary asked a third time. "If you're going to beat me up, then why would I go in that room with you?"

"Oh, for fuck's sake," came a new voice. This was another, older female llama. "Arturo, move out of the way. Gnoll, please come here. We'd like to talk to you. Nobody is going to beat anybody up today."

Medium Arturo stepped aside to reveal a small, square-shaped room. In the back corner, a third llama held some sort of rolling brush in his mouth as he haphazardly painted the wall in bright red. He had some sort of ogre and what looked like a succubus with him. The ogre was also painting. The succubus was sitting on the floor and appeared to be painting her toenails with the same paint the others were using on the wall.

In the center of the room, the older female llama had her legs folded under herself as she sat on the ground upon a large, ornate pillow with little tassels hanging from it. Gary noted the carpet here was covered with strange burn marks that made him uneasy.

He examined the older llama.

Grandma Llama. Llama Queen. Construction Supervisor and Supply Procurement. Level 40.
    Comanager of the Backstage Death Maze.

Menerva had mentioned this creature. She'd said there were two managers under her: Rory, who was mostly in charge of the other NPCs, and this lady, whose duty it was to make sure the maze itself got built. Gary had gotten the impression that Rory didn't seem to like this llama lady too much.

"Oi," Gary said now to the older llama, who was giving him an appraising look. He held up the bottle. "Know where Gary can get more of this stuff? The goblins got their meth. You giving it to them? Can you do the same for me?"

"We do not make the drugs for the goblins," Grandma Llama said, shaking her head sadly. "Rory makes it herself, but she's slowly weaning them off it. It's the only thing she knows how to make."

Gary sagged. "So nobody can make me more of this stuff?"

"Join our gang, and you can make it yourself," Medium Arturo said, coming to stand next to Grandma. "You don't need to buy nothing. If you get on the build team, you get a menu like the managers, and you can make anything."

"Wait, really?" Gary asked. "They told me I'm supposed to go find a raccoon lady, and she'll give me a job."

"You don't want that crazy bitch. She's a true believer," Arturo said. "She's on Rory's side."

"Arturo, go help with the painting in the other room," Grandma Llama said. "Everybody else, go."

They all grumbled and left, leaving Gary alone with the llama and the bright smell of the red paint. He stood there swaying. He'd changed his mind. He did like this new booze.

"I can make it so you can create all the alcohol you like," Grandma Llama said. "But you don't want that stuff. That's ceremonial pineapple hooch, and it's what Menerva drinks. I think it's drugged with a trank. But it doesn't last long. If you help me, I'll give you the ability to make your own. You can adjust it to your liking."

"Help you do what? Paint?"

She chuckled. "The moment you came in, I received your sheet in my interface. I see what you can do. You're unique, Gary. You're immortal."

Dead is dead. He took a pull from his bottle.

She continued. "I don't know you, but I can guess based on a few clues that you and me are of the same mind."

He was, indeed, rapidly sobering. "Oh, yeah? What mind is that?"

"That you're not so sure you can trust anything Menerva is trying to tell us. Rory and some of the others want to believe in this cabaret so bad, they're willing to ignore some obvious contradictions just so they can keep that dream going. Rory believes in it so much, she changed herself into a priestess. Even Menerva was taken aback at that."

Gary took another swig. "But that doesn't stop her from taking her drugs."

"No," Grandma agreed. "Unfortunately, no. We all soothe ourselves in our own way."

Gary nodded. "If Gary helps you, you'll give him the magic to make stuff?"

"That's right. It's not difficult. There's only a few limitations."

"And I can make *anything*?" Gary asked again. "In that room, the fairies—they made a creature from nothing. I can do that?"

"You going back and forth between third and first person is killing me, Gary. But yes, that's the mob detail, and they're with me," Grandma said. "Join us, and you can do this. You wish to create mobs?"

"Gary can make a person? Another gnoll?" Gary asked.

"I suppose, yes."

Dead is dead.

But that wasn't true, was it? Gary had died how many times? Another contradiction. Everything was a lie. Nothing was real.

But that also meant anything was possible.

He was immortal. This llama lady had said so herself. So had Menerva.

What do you get when you mix the power of creation with im-
mortality?

I wish you'd lived long enough to know I wasn't a coward.

Sometimes, Gary thought, *wishes do come true.*

"Gary will join your gang."